Tanya A Guinness was born in Sydney, Australia, in the late sixties. In the mid-seventies, she moved with her family to the Mid-North Coast of NSW, growing up on a farm until she finished her schooling. After having two children, she – wanting more opportunities for herself and them – moved back to Sydney. Tanya's children have since grown up, now living with three grandchildren whom she adores. Writing has always been a passion of hers as is musical theatre which Tanya has been involved with for over thirty years.

For Jessica and Thomas, never give up.

Tanya A Guinness

Brett: 'Love of My Life'

AUSTIN MACAULEY PUBLISHERS™

LONDON * CAMBRIDGE * NEW YORK * SHARJAH

Copyright © Tanya A Guinness 2022

The right of Tanya A Guinness to be identified as author of this work has been asserted by the author in accordance with sections 77 and 78 of the Copyright, Designs and Patents Act 1988.

All rights reserved. No part of this publication may be reproduced, stored in a retrieval system, or transmitted in any form or by any means, electronic, mechanical, photocopying, recording, or otherwise, without the prior permission of the publishers.

Any person who commits any unauthorised act in relation to this publication may be liable to criminal prosecution and civil claims for damages.

A CIP catalogue record for this title is available from the British Library.

ISBN 9781398416512 (Paperback)
ISBN 9781398416529 (Hardback)
ISBN 9781398416536 (ePub e-book)

www.austinmacauley.com

First Published 2022
Austin Macauley Publishers Ltd®
1 Canada Square
Canary Wharf
London
E14 5AA

Thank you for all your support and encouragement with my first novel: Carolyn Fieldus, Lisa Mifsud, Serafina Pollari, Michelle Sutton, Karina Tudor and Amber Hatch.

Part 1

Chapter 1

"Just close your eyes and think of somewhere nice and then it will be all over." The earliest I can remember was when my sister was holding me in bed telling me this; I was about ten years old. I didn't know what she was talking about.

My stepdad, we called him Max, he was the only one to get up in the night if any of us kids needed anything. Mum just kept sleeping; she worked long hours at the hospital as a cleaner.

Max was so gentle and kind to me when I was little, but later things changed, especially when he was drunk, which was often. One night, I was sick with a cold, coughing. It was late, and everyone was asleep. He came into my room with a jar of Vicks to rub on my chest to help stop the coughing. Max pulled up my pyjamas and rubbed his hands over my body; it was nice and warm but stunk like a strong minty smell. He kept rubbing his hand over me. It felt strange; I started to feel uneasy. He was sitting on my bed, making heavy breathing noises. I couldn't see, only shadows.

"What are you doing?" I innocently asked, still coughing.

He stopped. "Go to sleep," he said and left my room.

When I was about eleven, Max told me that when I grew up, boys would want to kiss me, because I'm pretty. But to make them love you, he said, you need to let them touch you, but you must tell them you like it and how good it feels. Max told me that he would teach me how. I didn't like being touched. He told me to close my eyes and everything would be okay; it was our secret. I was so scared, but Max kept telling me it was okay. I didn't want to, but he told me I had to learn to like it; otherwise, boys wouldn't like me. I just closed my eyes and disappeared.

I started to learn which nights Max would come to my room, usually Friday nights. That's when he would come home drunk, and Mum would fall asleep drinking in front of the TV. Max had a bad back, so he wasn't working at the moment. Instead of going to the pub, he would drink at home. I used to play at my friend's house as late as I could, so I didn't have to be alone with him.

When I was thirteen, I took my mother's sleeping pills from the medicine cupboard in the kitchen, and I hid them under my pillow. That Friday night, I took about six tablets. I thought I would sleep, and I wouldn't hear Max come in. After some time, I woke up feeling sick. I sat up and threw up all over my bed. I felt awful; Max came in. He thought I must have caught a bug; he left me alone that night. I changed my bed and put the dirty covers in the laundry and slept with a blanket from the hall cupboard.

My sister, Stacey, was two and a half years older than me. When she was sixteen, she got a boyfriend; his name was Robert. He was very kind to me. He and my sister went out every weekend. Robert had a car, so he used to take her to the drive-in movies every Saturday night. On Friday nights, I was allowed to go with them roller skating. I loved skating. I used to skate so fast, and the music was so loud; it was my escape.

When it was the school holidays, we used to have parties at home. Everyone loved Mum and Max as they had the best parties. Max loved Robert. He used to come over with a carton of beer and a cask of wine for Mum. Robert used to invite his mates over as well. Everyone would be so drunk; this made it very easy for me to sneak some wine. I would get so drunk and dance around, and I loved dancing to the music. Robert's mates were kind to me. One of his friends was Phillip; he was twenty-four, and I liked him. I thought if he loved me, he could marry me, and I could move out away from this place. He would protect me from Max.

One night, Phillip and I were sitting in the kitchen just talking and drinking. Everyone was in the lounge room; the music was blasting, and it was late. Mum had gone to bed.

Phillip was telling me how grown up I was.

"How old are you?" he asked.

"Fourteen," I said, wanting to be older. Phillip started to kiss me, his hand going up my shirt, touching me.

"You've got little boobs," he told me. Oh, no! He thought my boobs were too small. He wouldn't want me. I went all quiet, not sure what to do. He kissed me again.

Just then, Max came in to get another beer. Phillip pulled his hand out from my shirt. Max was drunk, and he didn't even notice.

"I hope she's looking after you Phillip, do you need another beer?" Max asked.

"No, I'm doing good thanks." Philip held up his beer. Nothing else happened that night. I knew it was because my boobs were too small; I wished they would grow.

After my fifteenth birthday, I was in year nine at high school. I hated school. The teachers called me dumb. I couldn't spell or read very well, and my letters would get back to front all the time. I tried to tell a teacher once, but she said I just wasn't smart.

I suppose my low confidence started at a very young age when I was in primary school; I went to a small school. I was always a happy kid and had plenty of friends. We played together at lunchtime. That was my favourite time. I had always struggled with my schoolwork; my reading and spelling were so hard for me. I found myself at the bottom of the class. It was the seventies. I still have some terrible memories of a teacher who treated me like I was stupid.

It wasn't just me; the whole class was scared of Mrs McGee; she had a long ruler and used to whack it over your knuckles if you weren't listening.

One particular day, we had a spelling test. I was always getting my spelling words wrong, back to front and mixed up, no matter how hard I studied. This day, Mrs McGee was having one of her torture days. She grabbed me by the ponytail and dragged me to the junior class. In front of the whole class, she announced that I was so dumb and that everyone in the class was brighter than me because I couldn't spell. I didn't cry; I think that's where I learnt how to bottle things up. It was the only way to survive.

When I got home that day, my sister found out what had happened and couldn't wait to tell Mum. Mum just shook it off.

"Don't worry about it," Mum said. "You can't help being dumb. Plenty of people are dumb." Mum's idea of a pep talk.

High school was a whole new chapter in my life. That's where I started to learn about boys. In year seven, boys only liked you if you let them touch you. In art class up the back of the room, the teacher couldn't see a thing. Wayne was a spunk; he asked me to sit up there with him next lesson. I was so excited!

Kathy was always sitting up the back with Donald. He was a surfer and loved drawing pictures of the surf. Kathy told me what to do.

"Spread your legs and keep working so the teacher won't come down the back."

I so wanted Wayne to like me. About ten minutes into class, I was working on some stupid art drawing. I could feel Wayne's hand touching my leg. Oh, my God, it was happening. I had to be cool.

"Spread your legs," he whispered to me. I opened my legs wider; his hand got into my knickers, I could feel his fingers making their way inside me. He pushed his finger right in deep then he pulled it out, smiling at me like I was some sort of trophy; this went on every art lesson, usually not with me though.

He dumped me a week later, but I had a few other boyfriends in year seven, some were nice. I didn't love any of them. I thought boys were just for show; if you had a boyfriend, you weren't a dork.

In year eight, Peter was my boyfriend. He was a lot nicer. The best times were when we had to watch a film. We had this room at school called the darkroom. Lights would get turned off as we watched the film clip, and it would be so dark the teacher would doze off. As long as we were quiet, the teacher didn't notice us kissing up the back for most of the lesson. Peter was a good kisser. High school went on like that pretty much to year nine. That's when things changed; boys wanted a lot more than a kiss in a quiet corner, and the pressure was on for sex.

I was so brainwashed by my parents. They said no one would ever want me, as I was too stupid and not pretty. I was going to end up working in a factory in a dead-end job. My sister was the pretty one who was going to land a great husband because she had the brains as well. Well, with all that encouragement, I was a rebel. Whatever my sister did, I wasn't going to do.

When my sister was seventeen, she had a boyfriend and was making her debutante ball. It was so old-fashioned. Mum bought her this long white dress and high heels. Everyone in the family was so excited, saying how beautiful she was. They even had a photographer to take photos. I couldn't believe it.

That became the Christmas present for everyone in the family that year. What joy! Her picture was everywhere.

High school was my escape. I didn't like school that much, but I got to see my friends. Peter and I broke up. I dumped him as he was putting the pressure on me to have sex, but I was too scared of getting pregnant. STDs or AIDS wasn't around then, or if they were, we didn't know about them. I was only fifteen.

Then I met Michael. He was my sister's boyfriend's friend's brother. He was eighteen and had long blonde hair and worked at the Timber Mill. Michael was a great boyfriend. All we ever did was kiss; he was quiet and shy. He didn't have a car, so we had to get lifts with his brother to go to the drive-in movies.

He was perfect! I had a boyfriend that was eighteen and not at school, so all the boys left me alone at school. I think they were scared that my boyfriend would bash them if they came near me. All my friends assumed I had to be having sex, dating an older guy. I told them I wasn't, but they chose to ignore me. I didn't mind. They thought I was so lucky to have a boyfriend that worked at the mill.

Max left me alone now that I had a boyfriend. Michael would come over to my house nearly every night. We would sit in the lounge room and watch TV. We would hold hands and kiss when no one was looking. On weekends, we would go roller skating then he would walk me home. Max would drink beer with him, which annoyed me. I used to go to bed and leave them to it. I think it bugged me that Michael liked Max. He thought he was great. If he only knew.

Chapter 2

I would spend a lot of time in my bedroom drawing pictures of houses, dreaming of one day moving out and having a great husband who loved me and I would have six kids, like the *Brady Bunch* on TV. Dreaming my life away and my music was my escape from the world.

I would sometimes get so depressed thinking about my life; I always felt like there was no one to talk to or no one that would listen. As my sister was older, I always felt left behind. I think she learnt to escape by having boyfriends. That got her out of the house.

At a young age, I learnt to bottle my feelings up and escape into my dreams of great things. I think that's what gave me hope, my thoughts and dreams. The belief that my life would get better. Sometimes I couldn't wait for bedtime, so I could go into a dreamland, where everything was perfect, and I was far away from here.

I was always falling in love. I think my first crush was our neighbour Steve. He was so hot, but he was married with two kids. I used to babysit on Friday nights for Steve and his family every now and then.

I loved going over there; they treated me like an adult. When I was sixteen, they gave me a scotch and dry when they came home. It was so cool! I use to dream of his wife leaving and then he would marry me. I could look after his kids; they loved me. But nothing ever happened. It was just a fantasy.

Year nine at school, now that was a troubled year. My friends were doing crazy things like sniffing whiteout or glue. They would sit in class, stoned off their faces. I was sure they would get brain damage. I wasn't going to do that. However, I did take up smoking. That was a cool thing to do in year nine.

Michael and I broke up. He lost his job and moved up to Queensland, which was fine as I was getting bored with him anyway. Sixteen was a big year for me! It was 1981, and I started to go to the underage disco. I so loved to dance! It was an excellent time in my life. I lived for my Friday nights! I would dress up in my skin-tight jeans and high heels, makeup, hair frizzed, ready to go.

That's what the eighties were all about, disco. I didn't have a boyfriend at that time, but I was crazy in love with Darren. He was this spunk at school, but he didn't know I existed. I told my best friend that I liked him. She had such a big mouth; she told his best friend and he told Darren. I could have just died! But nothing happened; he still didn't know I existed.

A couple of weeks later, I was at Disco Galactica, our underage disco. I spotted Darren there. Oh my god! I was so excited, but I had to be cool. So I got up to dance with Katrina. *We're the kids of America* by Kim Wilde was playing. I loved that song. We always changed the lyrics to *We're the Kids of Galactica*, which we used to scream out while we were dancing. Darren disappeared. My eyes searched all over the place, but he was gone.

My friend Vicky came running over to tell me.

"Darren was here, but they've all gone over to the park, in the back lane. Do you want to go?"

I checked my watch. It was 9.30. We were getting picked up at 10 pm by Katrina's mum.

"Yes, of course, I do."

Vicky and Katrina came with me; they were my best friends from school. We walked out of the disco through the arcade, down the lane, a block to the city park. There were about ten people there and hardly any streetlights so I couldn't see who they were until we were almost next to them.

The kids were sitting around a picnic table, smoking a bong. I recognised some of them from school. They were from the brainy class. I couldn't believe it, what were they doing? They could do anything with their life, and there they were, smoking a bong, killing off their brain cells. But I would never say that out loud.

I couldn't see Darren anywhere. Vicky's friend Dianne was there; they were neighbours. Dianne was very smart; her dad was a doctor. I'm sure he would have freaked if he had known half the stuff Dianne got up to. Dianne told us Darren had left with his older brother.

By the time I got home, I was so excited about seeing Darren that I couldn't sleep. Maybe he would be there next week!

Sundays were always dull, so I usually walked over to Vicky's house. She lived about two blocks away. It was pouring with rain, so I took an umbrella and headed off. As I walked along the path and across a small bridge, a car came flying along and hit a puddle, which splashed up and soaked me to the skin.

"Shit!" I yelled. The driver kept driving. I cut across a park to get to Vicky's place. Vicky had a large family, five sisters and one brother. She was the youngest girl; her brother was still in primary. Her sisters had all left school and had jobs. Vicky often said she couldn't wait to finish school. She was always getting into trouble at school; she hated it!

She had a boyfriend, Ricky. He had left school last year and got a job as an apprentice mechanic. They had been going steady for nearly two years. Vicky and I went out to the front yard and sat under the carport, so we could talk without her sisters listening in. We mainly talked about the guys we had seen last night. I told her I wished Darren hadn't left early. She thought he was a drip. He only used girls because he was so hot looking. I didn't care; I still loved him.

"Have you ever smoked a bong?" Vicky asked me.

"No way, Mum would kill me," I lied – Mum wouldn't care. "Have you?"

Vicky hadn't but her sisters had. She told me how her sister Karen went to a party once and came home stoned; her dad beat the crap out of her, and she was grounded, for a month. But Karen was now twenty-one and had a full-time job at Woolworth's on the checkout. She had a flat she rented with her boyfriend. How lucky was she?

Vicky and I talked about leaving school all the time. We couldn't wait to get a job and move out, but at the moment, we had no money.

Vicky's dad drove in the driveway, and he walked past us with his paper in his hand. "Did you get a bit wet, Steph?" he said grinning from ear to ear.

"Was that you? Your dad splashed me with his car when I was walking over," Steph said.

"Sorry," he said, heading in the front door still grinning.

I babysat my neighbour's kids, little Josh and Danny, who lived across the road, and Tim and Peta who lived next door. Nearly every second week, I minded Josh and Danny, but Tim and Peta only once a month or so. I spent most of my money on clothes, and I was saving up to buy my roller skates. I almost had enough.

Going roller skating was so much fun! On Friday nights, they had disco skating. We went nearly every other week when we weren't going to Disco Galactica. We usually walked down as it was only about a ten-minute walk to get there. Katrina was my skating buddy. I would meet her there; her mum would drop her off, as she lived across town. We went there so often we were regulars, so everyone knew us.

Mr Watt, and his wife, were the owners of the place. Mrs Watt worked at the ticket box and the shop. Mr Watt looked after all the skate hire and repairs; they were often faulty. That's why I couldn't wait to get my own skates. I would always be there when the doors opened and grab our favourite spot, right next to the DJ box. Dave was the DJ. He lived in the street behind where I lived. We were always asking Dave for requests for our favourite songs. He was okay; he rode a motorbike and was a lot older than us.

I finally got my skates off layby; they were so fabulous – black with a bright orange stripe on the side. I couldn't wait to get on the rink and skate around to my favourite songs. I used to go so fast. They always had two guys working on the floor to slow us down, but I was pretty good. I never fell over, well, hardly ever.

They would play games; one of my favourite games was cards. The rink was in four sections: diamonds, hearts, clubs and spades. When the music stopped, you had to stay where you were. They would pick a card, and that section would leave the floor until there was only one person left, and they would win a free ticket for next time. I had won three times; Katrina won only once.

My favourite thing was speed skating. All the slow ones had to leave the floor. There were usually only about eight or ten people; we went so fast it was awesome! Katrina wouldn't go in speed skating; she wasn't as good as me.

We would always check out if there were any cute guys. Sometimes they would ask us to skate with them, so we would hold hands and skate around when the disco lights were on; it was a little darker, and a bit more romantic.

None of the cool guys from school would ever go skating. I suppose skating wasn't cool enough for them. They loved to surf. But I didn't care; I loved skating; it was my escape. I could disappear into the music, my own, little world where no one would hurt you. The music kept your mind safe; that's how I could switch off from everyone.

Chapter 3

Saturday nights were the drive-in movie nights. Vicky was my drive-in buddy. Her sister would drive us. She would drop us off at the gate, and we would walk in. They had a room for people to sit who didn't have a car, but we would usually find someone that we knew who had a car. They would sit on their bonnet or the back of their Ute, or they would reverse park and have a mattress in the back and blankets.

This night, we couldn't see anyone we knew. I spotted a guy who looked like he was from out of town. I smiled at him, so he came over.

"Do I know you?" he said.

"I don't think so."

Before long, we were chatting; his name was Cooper and his mate was Dave. They were from up the coast. They came down for the weekend. They weren't that good looking, but they seemed nice. They had an old Holden; it was a bit of a wreck, but it was a car.

Vicky's boyfriend was out with his mates drinking, so she was pissed with him and flirting with Cooper. Before long, they were in the back seat. Dave and I sat in the front seat watching the movie *Cannonball Run*, which had Burt Reynolds in it. He was so good.

Dave tried to hold my hand, but it was very awkward. Vicky and Cooper were making out in the back; I don't think they saw much of the movie. At the interval, Vicky and I went to the toilets, as that's where everyone went to talk about things we didn't want the guys to hear.

It's always crowded in the toilets. We sat on the wash counter and lit up a smoke. "What are you doing with Cooper? What if Ricky finds out?" I asked Vicky.

"He won't. Cooper is not even from here. What do you think of Dave?" she asked me.

"He's a bit boring. He tried to hold my hand. He hasn't even tried to kiss me," I said, a little disappointed. "But no one else is here tonight; it was a bit of a drag."

They offered to drive us home, but Vicky's sister was picking us up. So we told them we would meet them down the beach tomorrow.

The next day, Vicky rang me to tell me she couldn't go. She and Ricky had made up. I rang Katrina to see if she would like to go to the beach. Katrina was having visitors and wasn't allowed out. So I spent another Sunday bored at home dreaming of moving out.

I lay on my bed with my music playing, drawing houses. I planned the bedrooms, living room and kitchen, what colours they would be. All I ever wanted was to have my very own house, which I would have when I left home.

Mum yelled at me to clean up my room. Then she yelled at my sister because she came home too late last night. My sister was a bitch to Mum; she would swear at Mum telling her to fuck off. Max was out the back doing his gardening. I think that was his escape from the screaming fights of Mum and my sister.

If he heard my sister swearing at Mum, she would cop a belting. Although the last time Max tried to give her a belting, she told him she would report him to the cops. So he kept his distance with her now. I overheard him and Mum talking one night; she said that we were getting too old to hit. The neighbours might call the police. Yeah, they wouldn't want that, I thought.

My sister's eighteenth birthday was coming up. Mum and Max were planning a party for her; I think they were sucking up. Stacey was the one who was going to do great things. She had just dropped out of school and got a job at the Big W department store; she had been working there for two months.

Mum bought her a car so she could drive herself to work. I thought it would be great; she could drive me around, but no, she was a bitch, and she wouldn't drive me anywhere.

Her party was the next Saturday night, and Mum hired an old scout hall. Mum had been cooking all week putting cakes and stuff in the freezer. They had been buying beer and wine casks over the last few weeks, stocking up for the party.

The day of the party, we went down to the hall to put up decorations. It was my job to blow all the balloons up; Stacey's boyfriend, Robert, helped as well. Mum had so much food. They were doing a barbeque, so all the meat had to be packed into the fridge in the kitchen.

My nan and aunty turned up to help. They were all hovering in the kitchen, fighting about what to do first. I think that's why we hardly saw our family. All they did was argue. I just kept out of the way.

Stacey was getting her hair done at the hairdresser, so we had to do all the work. Robert was stuffing around with the balloons, blowing them up and letting them go, they would fly around the room. Sometimes, Robert was fun!

Robert's mates turned up to help, Phil and Keith. They rode motorbikes. Keith had a black leather jacket, which he hung over the back of a chair, as they sat at the end of the hall. I was still blowing up balloons; we already had about 20 of them. I sat down for a rest next to his jacket, so I tried it on. It was kind of heavy. I paraded around in it.

"Hey, Keith, can you take me for a ride?"

Robert spoke up before Keith answered, "No way, your mum will kill you; get that jacket off."

I just pulled a face and took it off. I couldn't wait to move out; even Robert bossed me around. They didn't stay long; they said they would come back later.

With the last of the decorations up and the tables set up, everything was ready, so we headed home so we could get ready.

I had a brand new outfit Mum had bought me. Black knickerbockers which were like short trousers just below the knee with elastic gathered around my legs and a white top with tiny black spots with frills from my shoulders down to my waist. I pulled on the new long black boots I had talked Mum into buying for me. I looked pretty good.

We had to get back to the hall quickly as the band Mum had hired needed to get in and set up. Stacey was still in the bathroom, putting on her makeup. We were all finally ready, so we piled into the cars. Robert had his car too, so Stacey went with him.

The hall looked pretty good. The band was setting up, with drums, guitars and other stuff. They were kind of old looking. Mum hired them because they were cheap. She said she had heard them down at the bowling club a few months ago and thought they were pretty good; they played old rock n roll.

People started arriving. Mum had invited everyone she knew, I think. All our relatives, even the ones we hated, neighbours old and new. Everybody was drinking and having a great time.

I snuck a beer and went outside the back kitchen door with my friend Vicky. I was allowed to invite one friend. While we were hiding out the back one of

Stacey's friends appeared with some guy; they both went into the men's toilets, Vicky and I just laughed. We snuck around the side of the toilet block and banged on the wall and took off, laughing our heads off.

We saw them come back about twenty minutes later.

"They must have had sex," Vicky whispered to me.

The band was pretty good. Everyone was up dancing, even the old relatives. My mum's cousin Ray was very drunk, dancing so crazy. He was all sweaty. It was a pretty good party. There were so much food and plenty to drink. Towards the end of the night, a few of Robert's biker friends turned up. I heard the motorbikes from inside. Vicky and I went out to see who it was.

There were three of them: Keith and two others who I didn't know. They took off their helmets. One had a big bushy beard; his name was Bubbles, not sure why he looked scary. But the other one was Split Pin. What a spunk. He was so hot looking. I just had to say hello.

"Come on, Vicky. Let's say hi to Keith."

We walked over to where they were standing next to their bikes.

"Hi, Keith," I said, trying to look cool. Keith just nodded and looked past me. Robert was following behind me.

"You two should go back inside," Robert said firmly.

Vicky and I sat over on the front fence at the side of the hall.

We could still hear a little. The guys were talking about one of their friends; he was in the hospital; he'd had a motorbike accident. Robert was going to see him tomorrow. I found out later his name was Kent. There were two bikes involved. The other guy was okay, but Kent might have brain damage.

When the party ended, we had to clean the hall. Everything got put into garbage bags and dumped in the big bins out the back. Max was so drunk he could hardly walk. Mum was drunk too but not as bad as Max, so she drove home.

Chapter 4

The next day, our house was full of bodies everywhere. I had to step over two of Stacey's friends that were asleep on my bedroom floor. I made it to the bathroom before anyone else was up; otherwise, there was always someone in there, and we only had one bathroom. I made my way through the lounge room, stepping over people everywhere. Got to the kitchen for a drink – I was so thirsty. Vicky had gone home last night. I grabbed a quick bit of toast and headed over to her place.

She was still in bed when I got there. Her mum let me in. Vicky was still half-asleep. I tried to get her to come down the beach to the Milk Bar. There was this Milk Bar called Checkers on the beach strip, which was very popular with the kids from school. Vicky said she was meeting up with Ricky for lunch, so I gave up and went home. As I walked in, nearly everyone was awake and having coffee; they were so hung over. I could hear someone in the bathroom throwing up. Gross. I just wanted to get out of this place.

Katrina would come to the beach, I thought, *I'll give her a call*. It was Sunday, which was so dull as nothing was on TV until six o'clock. Then it was Countdown on the ABC. I never missed it.

Finally, Katrina answered.

"Do you want to go to the beach?" I asked.

"Yes, that would be great." She was bored as well, she said.

We made arrangements to meet up at the beach. Katrina's sister was going to drop her off. I got myself ready and headed off.

I walked everywhere; we didn't live far from the beach or the shops, so getting around was easy. As soon as I got to the corner, I lit up a smoke; I didn't want Mum or Max to see me. By the time I got to the beach, I had my second smoke. I sat in the park waiting for Katrina. I was sweltering even though it was only spring.

I didn't have to wait long. I saw Katrina's sister pull up to drop her off. Katrina's sister was a lot nicer than mine; she would always drop her off at places. Katrina was a bit of a tomboy. She played hockey on Saturdays and always had bruises. I couldn't wait to tell Katrina about the biker I had met last night and the spunky one called Split Pin. I had found out he worked at the Holden dealer south of town, in the spare parts section. We walked over to Checkers to get a coke and to see who was hanging out there.

To our disappointment, no one was there. So we put 20 cents in the Space Invader game and played a couple of games. It didn't take long before two guys came in. They didn't look like boys from school. They set up the pool table in the back for a game. They were kind of cute. But they looked a bit young. So we finished our coke and headed down to the pier. We liked sitting down there, watching the waves roll in. We would talk about what we wanted to do when we finished school. Katrina's mum was making her finish year twelve. What a bummer. I was leaving at the end of this year, so I could get a job and move out.

I wanted to be an actor and make movies. One day, I hope to win an Academy Award. Well, that was one of my dreams. The other was to meet the perfect guy and marry him, have some kids and a great house. Katrina wanted to be a nurse. Her sister was going off to nursing college next year. She was in the same year as my sister, but they weren't friends.

We lay back on the pier, talking about the biker.

"Mum and Dad would kill me if I even looked at a biker," Katrina said.

Her dad was a biker, but he didn't ride with them anymore.

"I would so love to go for a ride," I said as we lay there looking up at the clouds in the bluest sky.

"Vicky will probably marry Ricky; they've been together forever," said Katrina.

"I don't want to get married until I find the perfect guy. I want him to have a motorbike and a good job," I said, still gazing at the clouds drifting by.

"I don't think I want to get married," Katrina said. She probably said that because she had never had a boyfriend.

We walked along the beach most of the day. We talked about what we might do next weekend.

"There's a new disco called 'Fonzie's' that has just opened up. I would love to go some time," I told Katrina.

"But its next door to a nightclub, Mum will never let me go," she said.

I had to get home by four o'clock, and Katrina's sister was going to pick her up back at Checkers, so we headed back towards the Milk Bar. When we got close, I noticed two motorbikes parked out the front. I recognised one of them. It was Bubbles who I met last night.

I walked straight over to them.

"Hi, remember me from last night at Stacey's party? You're Keith's friend," I said, feeling very confident.

"Oh, yeah, you're Robert's girlfriend's little sister."

"That's right, Steph," I said, trying to sound grown-up. Bubbles was a very large hairy, biker. But he wasn't scary after all; he was a decent guy. Well, he was friends with Keith, and Keith had been friends with Robert for years. The other guy was Phil, but he didn't say much. He wasn't so friendly.

"This is my friend, Katrina." Just then, a car tooted. It was Katrina's sister.

"Oh, shit, I have to go. Bye." Katrina ran across the road jumped into her sister's car. I hoped she wouldn't get in trouble for talking to biker.

"I suppose I better get home or I'm going to be late," I said to Bubbles.

"Do you want a lift?" he asked.

Oh, hell, yeah, but Mum would kill me. "No, I better not," I said reluctantly.

"See you around then," Bubbles said as he started up his motorbike. I so loved the sound of his bike. It was a Harley Davidson.

Nearly every weekend, I ran into Bubbles, and that's how I first met Brett. He was so different from any of the other guys I knew. He rode a Triumph black and silver motorbike. Brett looked like the kid on the wrong side of town. He had rugged light brown hair, the bluest eyes and tattoos on his upper arms and across his fingers saying 'Love' on one hand, and 'Hate' on the other. There was something about him I just loved.

I had seen Brett around different places. He used to hang out at Checkers, as it was one of the few places open after 8 pm, so everyone used to go there after the drive-in movies. It became our regular hang out. They made the best hamburgers, so I heard. I didn't spend much money there, as I didn't have a job and only got five dollars a week from Mum and my babysitting money. That money went on 'Space Invader' games and the drive-in on Saturday nights, where I still crouched down in the back seat and pretended I was twelve. If I went in a car, it was only a dollar if you were under twelve. As for smokes, I had to bludge them off whoever I could.

Chapter 5

Going to school was shit lately; a girl in my class had committed suicide. The teachers told all of us in English class. Then they wanted us to talk to the school counsellor. What shit. Her name was Lisa, and she wasn't one of my friends. I don't think I ever spoke to her. She was always a bit weird. In year seven, she used to cut herself. She had scars on the top of her legs. When we played sport, you could see them; she always tried to cover them up. Rumour had it that some guy had dumped her, so she killed herself.

All the shit I had to put up with, but I wouldn't kill myself. I thought the best payback was to be a success; I'm going to show them all, one day.

That day at lunch, I sat in the middle of the oval with my group of friends. Vicky lit a smoke, took a drag and passed it around. We would keep it low and shaking it hid the smoke. We had a good view, so if any teachers were coming, we would see them. We didn't talk that much. I think Lisa dying made us think about what we wanted in life. We were sure as shit didn't want to stay at school. Vicky and I decided to wag last period, but no one else was game.

When the bell rang, we met near the toilets and then took off, down to the beach. Vicky handed me a smoke. She always had smokes as she pinched them from her dad. We went down under the pier and sat there, smoking.

"You know, I bashed Lisa when she was in year eight," Vicky said.

"Really? Why, what did she do?" I asked.

"She tried to take Ricky from me." Vicky was upset but more angry than upset.

"I'm glad she died," Vicky said, taking another drag of her smoke. I don't think she meant it; it was bizarre. We just sat there smoking.

The next day at school, we were in music class. Vicky and I sat up the back; we didn't like music that much, more of a bludge subject. Vicky was still in a weird mood. She started ripping up her music book.

"Shit, Vicky," I whispered. Just then, our teacher Mr Munro screamed at Vicky and sent her to the principal.

I had decided to leave school. Vicky got expelled for ripping a music book. So I went, in protest, well, that's what everyone thought. Mum had already agreed. I wasn't doing much at school; I might as well get a job she said.

I had just turned sixteen, so I went to the dole office. They set me up with a job interview at the Ampol Road House Service Station. It was on the south side of town; Mum dropped me off; I walked into the café. It was about two in the afternoon, so it was quiet. There was a lady behind the counter. Feeling very confident, I introduced myself.

"I'm Stephanie; I'm here for the job interview."

She told me that's next door at the service station. I'm sure my mouth must have dropped. I turned around and headed out the door. What the hell? I couldn't work in a dirty servo.

However, I went into the service station. It was small and dirty and full of car stuff. An older man was filling up the cigarettes. This time, not feeling so confident, I met Rod. He was the owner of the roadhouse, and his wife Judy ran the café. He told me I would be filling up cars with petrol, checking the oil, water and washing the car windscreens for all the customers. I tried to look excited.

I got the job. After getting over the shock of working in a service station, I was quite excited to have my first job. I start on Monday – 8.30 till 4 and Saturday for half a day. Fantastic! I would finally have some money. Rod had to teach me how to put petrol in the cars, check the dipstick for oil levels and wash as many windscreens as possible. Customer service was essential; he kept telling me.

Every Saturday, I had to wash Rod's car; it was a reddish Saab. I learnt a lot about cars; I couldn't even drive yet.

My first weeks' pay went to my layby, a pair of red, skin-tight jeans. They were ninety-two dollars. I only earned seventy-six dollars a week, but when I tried them on, they looked too good. I just had to have them. They were on layby for three weeks when I finally got them out. They looked so good with my black low cut top and black stilettos, which made me look much taller.

I was going to the drive-in with Vicky, her sister and her boyfriend. They parked up the back row in their panel van. Vicky and I went up to the shop to see who was there. I spotted the motorbikes straight away parked along the front. There were three bikes. I quickly scanned around to see who they were. I spotted Bubbles, Keith and Brett. My heart missed a beat.

I went straight up to them.

"Hi, guys!"

I was falling crazy in love with Brett. Vicky went back to her sister's car. Brett and I talked for ages. He didn't even try to make out with me, but I was sure he liked me. I told him where I was working, and he said he would come by for some fuel for his bike. He even bought me a can of coke. We sat on the brick wall next to where his motorcycle was parked. We talked about music; he told me he played the guitar. I told him I wanted to be an actress. He didn't laugh. We just got on so well; he told me he had a flat down near the jetty. I didn't want the night to end.

That night, I went to bed dreaming of Brett and riding on the back of his motorbike. He had a Triumph. It was a classic, not that I knew much about bikes.

Work was excellent. I got the hang of things pretty quick, filling up cars, washing their windscreens. Now and then, I would hear a motorbike; it would take my breath away for a second, but it wasn't Brett.

Saturday came around. It was nearly knock-off time, and I was filling up the smokes when I heard motorbikes coming in. I looked up. Oh my god, it was Brett and Keith. They pulled in to the fuel pumps, to fill up their bikes.

"Hi, guys," I said, trying to be so cool. "I was wondering when I would see you two." Brett asked if I was doing anything tonight.

"Not much," I replied.

He invited me to a party. "Do you want to go?" he asked.

"Yeah, that sounds great," I said, trying not to sound too desperate. Brett paid fifty cents for the fuel. Just before they drove off, I yelled out, "What time will you pick me up?"

"7.30. See you then."

They rode off. I had a date with Brett. I couldn't wait till knock off time to go home to get ready.

Chapter 6

By the time I got home, it was nearly six. Mum had dinner on the table. I was starving, but I wanted to get ready, so I gulped down my dinner. Then I raided my cupboard. Oh, no! My new jeans weren't there!

"Mum," I screamed. I raced out to the laundry. "Where are my new jeans?"

"In the ironing basket," she said. I raided through the basket until I found them. They were so crushed, but that was okay, they were skin-tight so they would iron out on me. I quickly had a shower after my sister finally got out. She was always in the bathroom.

Stacey was going nightclubbing with her new boyfriend, Danny. Robert and Stacey had a huge fight, and they broke up a week after her eighteenth birthday. She spent two weeks sulking about it.

My jeans were so tight; they looked so good with my black sleeveless top, my chain necklace and stiletto shoes on. I better wear my boots, I suddenly thought. I sat on the edge of my bed so I could get my boots on. My jeans nearly cut me in half; I could hardly breathe. Finally, I stood up and looked in the mirror.

Makeup. I borrowed my sister's mascara and eyeliner. She had already gone out. Otherwise, she would never have let me.

I applied the eyeliner, making my eyes catlike to the sides and a bit of mascara, perfect. Now, what bag should I take? I was finally ready. I checked my watch; they should be here any minute.

They came in Brett's car. I found out later it was his brother's car. Keith was with him. Mum insisted on meeting him, so they came to the door. They already knew Keith, that's why they let me go out with them. They said hi, and we left. I jumped in the back seat as Keith was in the front. The party was just out of town on a property at 'Neal's place'. He had bought it with the money he received from an accident that wasn't his fault. Neal was married to Lisa, and they had a baby girl named 'Hope'. Rumour had it she tricked him by getting pregnant so he would marry her; she was a real bitch.

They had a big bonfire in the side paddock. Next to the house, they had a keg of beer and a lamb on a spit cooking. There were people everywhere. I suddenly felt a bit nervous. Brett got me a beer, which I drank rather quickly. It went straight to my head. I got talking to this guy, 'Jonesy'. He was a younger brother of 'Levi' who was a well-respected biker. If Levi was your friend, everyone was your friend. As we got talking, I discovered Jonesy lived up the road from me. After my third beer, I was feeling a bit drunk. That's when I noticed Brett had gone. I started to panic. I saw Keith over near the spit, chatting to some other guy.

"Where's Brett?" I asked Jonesy.

"He's gone to pick up Sharon," he said as if I knew.

"Who's Sharon?" I asked.

"His girlfriend," Jonesy replied. I swear my heart just smashed to a million bits. I wanted to cry, but I couldn't, so I had another drink.

I got so drunk I started to flirt with this guy that I didn't know, Mitch. He was cute and rode a Ducati. I was falling all over him when this girl came over and shoved me, pushing me to the ground. Jonesy caught me and tried to calm the girl down. She was about to deck me.

"She's with me; she's drunk," Jonesy said.

He walked me over to the fire away from her and sat me down on the log.

"No more grog for you," he said. "That was Mitch's girlfriend. You don't want to mess with her." Keith came over to check on me. I just wanted to crawl into a hole and die.

"Brett should be back soon. If he isn't, Jonesy can drive you home, Steph?" But I was mad at Brett. I didn't know he had a girlfriend. He only just met her a couple of weeks ago apparently.

Brett never turned up. By eleven, Jonesy decided to drive me home. I went back to Jonesy's place first. He made me a coffee. I didn't drink coffee, but this time, I drank it. Jonesy was like a big brother. He walked me home. I had to sneak in as it was past twelve, hoping Mum wouldn't hear me. But I tripped over something in the hallway. "You just getting in?" I heard from my mum.

"We had a flat tyre!" I yelled back and went to my room, crying myself to sleep. My heart was broken; I felt like a fool.

A week had passed. It was Friday again. Keith called in at work to fill his bike up. "How are you doing?" he asked.

"All right," I replied, not wanting Keith to know how pissed I was with Brett and still feeling a little embarrassed from last week.

"What time do you knock off?" he asked.

I looked at my watch. "In 20 minutes."

"Can I pick you up at your place in about an hour?"

I perked up a bit. "Yeah, where are we going?" I asked.

"I'm taking you out!" He smiled and rode off.

By the time I got home, I only had 30 minutes to get ready, which wasn't a problem as I could always get ready fast. I had the quickest shower. I put my black stretch jeans on with my black low cut T-shirt, my black ankle boots and to top it off my new black jacket with gold sparkles on the shoulders. It was a skirt and jacket set, but I couldn't wear a skirt on a motorbike.

Just in time, I could hear a motorbike pulling up out the front.

"Bye!" I yelled as I headed out the door. Mum was watching TV and Max wasn't even home yet. It was Friday; he always went to the pub after work on Fridays and always come home late. Then he would start fighting with Mum. Best to go out.

"So where are we going?" I asked as I put Keith's helmet on and he went without one.

"Brett's place," he said.

I got on the bike feeling pissed off again. I still loved Brett, but how could I deal with his girlfriend? I couldn't even remember her name.

I so loved being on the back of a motorbike, the smell of leather, the cold air on my face. My arms around Keith's waist. I just wished it was Brett that I had my arms around. Keith was more like an older brother. He was my protector and always looked out for me.

It didn't take long to get to Brett's place as living in a small town nothing was far away. As we rode in and pulled up outside his single-storey flat, the music was playing. There was Brett, leaning up against his bike, talking to a guy I didn't know. No sign of his girlfriend. We got off the bike. Keith shook hands with Brett and introduced Rod, Brett's brother from Melbourne. He was different from Brett; they didn't look like brothers. Rod had short black hair, neatly dressed. He looked like he worked in an office for a living.

We walked inside, I noticed an old sofa and an armchair, years old by the look of them. There was a small TV, but it wasn't on. A stereo was playing with huge speakers; the music was so loud. I didn't recognise the music at first. I had a look at the cover; it was a *Queen* record playing. I knew some of *Queen*'s songs, but I didn't know the songs on this album.

"This is *Queen*'s first album from the seventies. They're one of my favourite bands. They're English," Brett told me. He had a poster of them on the wall. They had the hottest drummer.

"I'd love to see them live," I said.

"Maybe I'll take you some time if they come to Australia," said Brett.

"I'll hold you to that," I said.

Brett gave me a beer. I sat down, going through his records. He had a lot of heavy metal stuff and most I had never heard before. Brett also had a guitar leaning against the wall in the corner. It was electric. He had a massive amplifier with empty bottles of Jim Beam sitting on top.

They were talking about getting pizza for dinner. Rod took Keith with him to pick up some pizzas.

For the first time, I was alone with Brett. I knew I only had about 20 minutes. Brett picked up his guitar strumming along to the music. I was flirting with him trying to get him to look at me.

"Sorry for leaving you last week," he said. "I had to go pick up Sharon from work."

I was not impressed with the conversation so far.

"I like you as a friend." I think my heart just exploded. He put his arm around me. "Do you think we can be friends?" he asked.

"Of course," I said looking into those beautiful blue eyes, as he leant over and gave me the sweetest kiss. He started to play his guitar. I so loved him. Friends! I could wait.

They were back with the pizzas before we knew it. We sat on the sofa, eating pizza and drinking more beer. I started to wonder what the hell I was doing here. Then Neal pulled up out the front and walked in with Jacky. Great, I thought, finally someone to talk to. Jacky had a bottle of Vodka and a bottle of orange juice with her. Fantastic! We went to the kitchen, which was in the same room as the lounge room. It was a small flat. Jacky and I could whisper at the sink without the others hearing us.

"What the hell are you doing here with Neal?" I asked. I knew Jacky from school. She was a year older than me. Jacky told me she had just met him at the pub down the road.

"I think Neal's hot, don't you?" she asked.

"No! But he's married to Lisa and has a baby," I told her. She was crazy. Lisa would kill her if she caught her.

"What are you doing here?" Jacky asked.

"Keith and Brett are my friends; I've known Keith for years," I said, trying to deflect that I was really after Brett, but I wasn't telling Jacky that as she had a big mouth.

Neal told Jacky that he was leaving Lisa and that their marriage was over. I still didn't think it was right. We made our drinks up and started to dance to the music. Jacky was all over Neal. She ended up on his lap, pashing him off. Jacky had always said that she was a virgin. I hoped she knew what she was doing. The two of them disappeared into the back bedroom.

I just sat on the floor listening to *Queen*. I so loved this band. The music was so loud. Jacky finally came out from the bedroom, indicating for me to follow her outside. Neal had fallen asleep on the bed.

"Steph, what does it mean when he asks, 'Have I come yet'?" Oh my God, how should I know I wanted to say, but everyone from school thought I'd had sex.

"You know when he's finished," I told her. I was too embarrassed to admit I had no idea. "Did you do it then?" I asked. I already knew the answer.

Chapter 7

A week later, I finally got to meet Sharon, Brett's girlfriend. She was beautiful with long dark brown hair, and she was tall. I already hated her. I hadn't met her before as she lived about an hour from town. Her family were wealthy, and they had a large property. Sharon had a job uptown at the Pizza Hut. She worked almost every weekend. But she had just moved in with Brett. I was so jealous!

I got along with Sharon, okay, but I didn't like her. I thought she was stuck up. She seemed to think she was better than everyone else. I couldn't see what Brett saw in her, besides being beautiful. I think he was impressed she came from a well-to-do family. Not like us, our very dysfunctional families. Well, we all became friends even though I secretly hoped they would break up.

Things at home were worse than ever, my sister was doing drugs. I overheard Mum talking to Max one night. Stupid Bitch. Max was drinking more than ever. Mum and Max had a massive fight last week, and he gave Mum a black eye. She tried to hide it with makeup. I'd had enough of living at home. Lately, I was always at Brett's place. We got together every weekend. Sharon worked at night, which meant I had Brett to myself most of the time. I asked Brett if I could move in, and he said yes. So I decided to move out. I had a good job. If we split the rent three ways, or four if Jacky moved in, it was only fifteen dollars a week.

After work on Friday, I went home to see what to pack. I only had one suitcase. I packed my clothes, only the ones I liked. I left the rest. I wanted to take my records, but I knew Brett wouldn't like most of my albums. I loved them, though, *Grease*, *ABBA*, and *The Partridge Family*. My mum bought these for me when I was fourteen. I loved my records, but I didn't want them to get wrecked, so I left them behind.

I told Mum I was moving out. She threatened me, saying I was a slut like my sister, and if I left, I wouldn't be allowed back. Max wasn't home, so I took what I could carry and left. I didn't care if I never saw them again. Brett picked me up with Keith's dad's car, and I was free. I was scared but excited at the same time.

It was Friday afternoon; Sharon had to work. Great, just me and Brett at home. I had a shower and got out of my work uniform and put my jeans on. Brett was working on his bike out the front door. The music was going as always, loud, for Brett to hear outside, as well as the rest of the street. It was *Queen* again – *Doing All Right*. I loved that song. How appropriate. It was as if the words were for Brett and me. I so wanted Brett; he could have me anytime, but Sharon…*Some Day, One Day* maybe, Brett would be mine. I loved that song too.

Brett and I became such good friends. We talked a lot, and he would tell me how he wanted to be in a band; he was pretty good on the guitar. I told him he should follow his dreams. I would have loved to see Brett in a group. Everyone would be chasing him. He was already so hot and playing in a band would make him even better.

I told him about my crazy family and my stupid sister.

"I think my stepdad screwed her up. She's on drugs now." I told Brett about my drunken parents. I was never going to get married unless I truly loved someone. Brett had the same thoughts. He had a stepdad as well, and he hated him too. I think we were both a bit damaged, that's why we got on so well.

Brett dropped out of school after year nine as well. He only stayed at home to protect his mum, he said, but one night when he was out, Brett came home, and his mum was dead. His stepdad had killed her. They took him away to prison.

"I wanted to kill him," Brett told me. We held each other that night, and I calmed him down. He was still hurting, and I could see his pain in his eyes. Life was shit. We had almost a full bottle of scotch that night.

Brett and I told each other everything. He told me he loved Sharon because she was from a decent family that had money and respect. I think that's what Brett wanted. I suppose my family were too much like his.

We ended up getting pizza for dinner; that was all we seemed to live on those days. I would have to start cooking one day. I used to cook at home. Mum would work late, so if you wanted to eat, you had to cook.

We were talking about what we wanted to do with our lives. I said how I would love to move to the city and be an actor in a musical. I loved to sing and dance. Only last week we went to the drive-in-movies and saw *Grease 2* even though everyone said it wasn't as good as the first Grease movie. I loved it; I so wanted to be like Michelle Pfeiffer; she was my favourite. Although I had never had lessons, we could never afford it. Mum always said it was a waste of money.

"When I move to the city, I'm going to change my name to 'Stephanie Zinone'," I said so proudly.

"Like the character from *Grease 2*," Brett said, giving it some thought. "I like it. It would suit you. Stephanie Zinone."

One night when it was just Brett and me, we were playing *Queen*. Brett told me this was *Queens II* album, their second record, and it was one of his favourites; his brother sent it to him. Brett would play his guitar, and I would sing. We were a great team and had the best nights.

Brett would listen to me, and he never laughed. He used to say, "Don't forget me when you're a megastar." He made me laugh; I would always remember those nights. He was my first true friend. He believed in me when nobody had ever before. He got me. He was my soulmate.

Brett told me we're going riding tomorrow. Keith was coming over with one of his mates. He wanted to go up the coast where this great camping place was, called Middle Creek, and he wanted to check it out. It sounded like a nice ride. I didn't have to work; I only worked every second Saturday. Brett had a spare helmet. Sharon had brought her own now, so he gave me his spare one. Sharon didn't think Brett should give it to me, but it wasn't her choice, it was Brett's, and he knew I had no money.

Brett gave me a beer as we sat on the sofa watching TV; we never had the sound up as the music was always going. Sharon was due home about eleven. We just mucked around. I pinched his smokes, and he tried to get them back. As we were wrestling on the sofa, he pinned me down playfully and looked in my eyes. I so wanted to kiss him, but I didn't. That night, I couldn't help dreaming about Brett. I know he felt something. I saw it in his eyes.

The next day, we all got up early. Keith and his friend Shane turned up on their bikes. Shane seemed nice, not bad looking. I was going on Keith's bike. It looked like it was going to be a sunny day. Great for riding.

I had to climb on Keith's bike. He had a backpack on the back of his bike, and I couldn't get my leg over. They were all laughing at me. I was finally on and off we all rode. Even though I had no romantic feelings for Keith, it was so lovely hanging on to his leather jacket. I just loved the feel of it and the smell; it was almost intoxicating.

We rode for about half an hour. Then we all pulled over into a roadhouse for a drink and a smoke. I could hardly walk when I got off to have a stretch. Sharon and I went to the bathroom. While we were fixing our hair we talked.

"What do you know about Shane?" I asked.

"He's got a girlfriend. She's away in Sydney for the weekend; otherwise, she would have come. Why? Do you like him?" Sharon said, smiling, the bitch.

"No, I was just wondering." I wanted to say, 'I'm waiting until Brett dumps you,' but I didn't.

We got back on our bikes, and we should be at Middle Creek in about twenty minutes. We turned off the highway onto a dirt road, and it was long and straight. There was nothing but bush everywhere. We were heading towards the ocean. Finally, we found an open area like a camping ground, but there was only one tent next to a Ute up the end. No one was in sight. There were a few wood fire barbeques around. So we parked away from the Ute up the other end. There was even a picnic table there. We could see some tracks heading into the bush.

"There's supposed to be large sand dunes, down one of the tracks," Brett told us.

"Do you think our stuff will be safe here?" Sharon asked.

"Yeah, there's no one here," Keith said, stating the obvious.

We unpacked our gear, and everything got dumped on the table. It was warming up. We took our jackets off. There was a sign that said, 'To the Beach'; we headed down that track. We hadn't walked far before we came to a small creek. It was evident that we would get our boots wet. We all stopped to take our shoes and socks off. We made our way across the creek. It wasn't that deep, but I was glad I had rolled my jeans up.

Once we crossed the creek, the view opened up, nothing but sand, massive dunes. I couldn't see the beach anywhere. We started walking up the dunes. Oh my God, it was so steep. I was racing Brett and Shane up to the top; Keith and Sharon just complained about how hard it was. By the time we got to the top, they were only halfway.

"Wow, what a view!" I yelled back at Keith and Sharon. "We can see the ocean." We were so high. Shane found an old cardboard box, which he flattened out.

"Watch this," he said, as he sat on the box like a bobsled. He pushed himself over the edge, down he went so fast. Oh my God, that looked incredibly fun.

"I want a go next," I yelled. Shane still beat Sharon to the top for the second time. Shane told me to hold on to the front of the box if I wanted to go fast. So I hung on. Down I went, screaming all the way. It was fantastic! I wanted another go, so I dragged the box to the top. Brett had a go next, then Sharon and this went on for about an hour. We were all getting sunburnt, so we decided to head back to camp. Shane and Brett tried to roll down the dune; they got covered in the sand, but it was a funny sight. By the time we got back, I was so thirsty.

The guys had a beer, but Sharon and I had a coke. Beer makes me sleepy, and I didn't want to fall off the back of the bike going home. The guys didn't drink much as they had to ride. Brett and Shane got the fire going so we could cook our sausages and onions. Sharon also had potato salad and bread rolls.

Before lunch, Sharon and I went looking for the toilets. They were in the bush at the other end of the camping ground. There was a timber fence around it. We walked around the back to the opening and looked in, and it stunk. There was no toilet, only a hole in the ground.

"Gross. I'm not using that," Sharon said. But I was busting. It was so hard to use. I pulled my jeans down and crouched over the hole. There wasn't even any paper, I shook myself and pulled my pants up, that was all I could do. I couldn't wait to get home for a shower.

We ate our well-cooked snags and potato salad. Brett and Sharon headed home early because Sharon wanted to go to the loo. So we were left to put the fire out and clean up.

By the time we got home, it was five o'clock. Sharon had already had a shower and was sitting on the sofa, as it was her night off. Brett was cleaning his bike. Shane went straight home. Keith dropped me off and said he might come back later after dinner. I went in to have a shower. I was so tired. As I stripped, I noticed how sunburnt I was. My shoulders were so red. After my shower, I rubbed some moisturiser cream into my shoulders. I couldn't put my PJs on yet as we always had people dropping in pretty much every night.

I was starting to feel the effects of not much sleep. We never got to bed before eleven mid-week, and on weekends, it was two or three in the morning. By the time I came out of the bathroom, Neal and Jonesy had arrived with a carton of beer and a bottle of bourbon. So they were here for the night. It wasn't long before Jacky walked in; Neal just ignored her. What a bastard!

Sharon made up some spaghetti Bolognese; we all helped ourselves and sat down at the table. All the guys were hogging the sofa. Brett wasn't impressed with the spaghetti, so he was covering it with tomato sauce. That pissed Sharon off. Ha, I was a better cook then she was. Brett loved the Bolognese that I had cooked the other day.

Sharon was so pissed off she said she was tired and went to bed early. She shut the door. Didn't stop the party though, the music just got louder.

Even though I was tired by the time Keith came back, I was on my second beer and in a party mood. Jacky was into the bourbon and coke and was getting seriously drunk. I didn't like bourbon.

"You better slow down," I tried to tell her, but she was shitty with Neal. Surprise, surprise, he hadn't left his wife. He was only using her.

Two other guys turned up on Harleys. The windows shook when they pulled up. They were friends of Keith's. They were older, at least twenty-five. Dave and Chook. Chook was tall and skinny, but Dave was big all over and covered in tats. Everybody was drinking and having a great time. Sharon never came out, not even once that night.

Brett was getting drunk, and he was very flirty when he became intoxicated. He put his arms around me.

"We had a great day today," Brett said, nearly falling over. "I think I'm a bit drunk."

"Maybe you need to sit down before you fall down," I told him while I tried to hold him up. I couldn't help but laugh at him; he was so funny and cute, looking at me with those beautiful blue eyes.

"Can I sleep in your bed tonight," he asked so nicely. "I think Shaza is pissed with me." He was smiling so innocently.

"I don't think Sharon would like that so much," I replied. If Sharon hadn't been asleep in the next room, I might have been tempted, even though she can be a bitch, I couldn't do that to her, or could I?

I helped Brett to the sofa, which he fell into and passed out, out of trouble. While I was distracted with Brett Jacky had disappeared. I looked around. She wasn't in my bedroom or out the front. Where the hell was she?

"Anyone know where Jacky went?" I yelled out. Chook was missing as well. No one seemed to care. Jacky was so drunk and upset; I was worried she was likely to do anything.

I went outside and walked out to the road to see if I could spot them. It was all quiet except for the dull rumble of our place. I started to walk back when I thought I saw something behind the shrubs at the side of our flat. As I walked closer, I couldn't make out who it was. It was Chook. I kept walking. Oh, my God! He was having sex with Jacky. I didn't know where to look or what to do. I think I froze for a second before I went back inside.

I poured myself a drink. There was a little bit of vodka left in a bottle from last week, no orange juice, so I had Coca-Cola with it. It tasted like crap, but I drank it anyway. Brett was still asleep on the sofa. Keith was trying to play Brett's guitar, and he sounded okay. Dave was watching the TV with no sound, and he didn't seem to notice; the music was so loud.

I didn't like the music that much. I went over to have a look at what was playing on the stereo, good, it was almost finished. I flipped through the records to find something I liked. I didn't know most of the bands. *Black Sabbath, Led Zeppelin* and *Queen*. I loved *Queen*; Freddie Mercury was so outrageous. I loved his voice and his costumes, but I loved Roger Taylor; he was hot. I had a thing for drummers. The guys loved Brian May, only because they all wanted to play the guitar like him. I still secretly loved *ABBA*, but these guys would have given me a hard time about that. That's why I left my *ABBA* records at home. They would use them as Frisbees.

Just as I changed the record, Chook came in, grabbed a beer and sat in the armchair. I waited a few minutes then discreetly went out to see if Jacky was okay. She was sitting up, not looking too good. Jacky stunk. Oh God, she had been throwing up. Jacky saw me and started crying. I helped Jacky up, took her to the bathroom and made her have a shower. I put her clothes in the washer and lent her something to wear, then put her in my room to bed. I had two beds in my room. I closed the door and came out.

Chook was lying on the floor behind the sofa, and Brett had gone to bed. Keith was still playing the guitar, *Stairway to Heaven*. I only recognised it because Brett was always playing it. I decided to go to bed. I told Keith, thinking he would go home, but he just nodded and turned the music down a bit. So I went to bed.

Chapter 8

It had been two weeks since the party and Jacky stopped coming over. I was going to visit her, but I didn't. I figured she was embarrassed about what she had done. It was Friday morning. I was ready for work munching on a piece of toast and vegemite. Brett came out of his bedroom half-dressed, his jeans undone and pulling his Tee shirt over his head. He looked so hot. I watched as I ate my toast, then Brett lit a smoke taking a drag. He sat on the sofa to put his boots on.

"What time are we going?" he asked me, with his smoke hanging from his mouth. He was dropping me off at work.

"I should be leaving now; I just have to clean my teeth," I said, heading to the bathroom.

By the time I came out of the bathroom, Brett had his leather jacket on and putting his helmet on. I grabbed my helmet and followed him out the door. Brett had been taking me to work ever since I moved in, and Keith drove me home in the afternoons. Keith was a truck mechanic and worked across the road from my work, but he started too early, so Brett drove me in the mornings.

My favourite part of the day was riding on the back of Brett's motorbike, my arms wrapped around his waist, for a short moment, my heart was on fire. I just wished I worked further away, as it only took 20 minutes to get there. When I got to work, I stepped off the bike, took off my helmet, pulled my skirt down, fixed myself up, tidied my hair and watched Brett ride off as I headed into work. That was pretty much my routine from Monday to Friday. I liked my job, but I just loved my weekends more. I was working in the café for three days and the servo on the other days. I was very good at my job. I could run it on my own now, which I did when it was quiet.

A few weeks later, we all got invited to Neal's. He was throwing himself a party. It was an 'I-hope-I-don't-go-to-jail' party. About three months ago, he got busted with a load of marijuana and drunk driving. His excuse was he was out of beer, so he went out to buy some. What an idiot!

When we got to Neal's place, the first thing I saw was a bong loaded and ready to go sitting on his coffee table. They already looked stoned off their faces. Neal had to go to court on Monday. I just headed out the back. Outside there was a drumfire going and a few familiar faces. I spotted Bubbles. I hadn't seen him in ages. I went over to say hello. He told me he'd been travelling up North, and he made it to Cairns in Queensland. That's almost the top of Australia. I wanted to travel, but at that moment, I couldn't even afford a bottle of scotch.

We chatted for a while. Bubbles gave me a beer; he didn't have any scotch he said with a smile.

"Why haven't you got any money? You still working?" he asked.

"Yeah, but I moved out. I'm living with Brett and Sharon. It costs more than I thought. I might have to move back home; I don't know yet." The party wasn't that great; they all just sat around and got stoned, drunk or both.

I was even thinking of going home when this guy Pete turned up with a motorised type of go-cart / beach buggy, on the back of his trailer. This looks like fun! They unloaded and tried to get it started. Pete had built it himself. It took him about ten minutes to get it going. When it did start, smoke poured out the exhaust pipe, but it kept going, made a hell of a noise. Just as well, Neal didn't have any neighbours too close by.

Pete had a go first. He took off down the driveway, which was a dirt road, and the dust made him disappear. There were no streetlights out there and only one spotlight on the front of the buggy. We could hear him though. I so wanted a go.

We could hear him coming up the hill as he suddenly appeared through the dust.

"Can I have a go?" I pleaded, looking very hopeful.

"Not on your own," Keith piped up from nowhere. "I'll go with you," he said.

"Okay, but can I drive?" I said. There was only one seat, but there was a rack on the back behind the chair, so Keith kneeled on the frame leaning over me to make sure I knew what I was doing.

I got in, fastened my seatbelt, put my foot on the accelerator, and we took off. We were flying down the road so fast. It was the most exhilarating feeling, and I didn't want to stop. Keith started screaming at me, "Slow Down!" It was like the adrenalin took over. I felt like I could fly. Keith grabbed the wheel, pulling it hard left as I hit the brakes and we slid sideways.

"Holy shit, that was unreal!" I screamed.

"You got a death wish?" Keith yelled at me. He was pissed off. He had the shits with me after that and insisted on driving back up the hill. I didn't care. He just panicked, that's all. At least the party had improved.

Chapter 9

Unfortunately, I had to move back home. But only to save some money. My sister had moved out with her druggy friends. I got the room to myself, but it didn't last long. Max tried to tell me that I couldn't go out on Friday night. I told him, "You can't tell me what to do." He got nasty and smashed me into the glass cupboard. Shards went everywhere, and I had cuts to my arms.

Mum came in from the bedroom and screamed at me, saying it was my fault. I tried to explain what happened, but she took Max's side. So I stormed out of there, with just my handbag and headed back to Brett's.

I went back a few days later to get my stuff, and Brett came with me. I knew no one would be home. I took all my stuff, this time, even my records. I was never going back, I told myself.

About a week later, I got a message from my aunty. She called in at work telling me my sister had died from drugs and my mum needed me. But I refused to see her. I hadn't seen my sister in months anyway.

Brett said I should go to her funeral, but I couldn't. A day later, Brett drove me to the cemetery to put a flower on her grave. No one was there except us. That's when I broke down and told Brett about Max and how he used to abuse us.

"She told me to close my eyes, and everything would be okay…but it wasn't. Max killed her. Now he's trying to kill me." Tears were running down my face. I put the flower on her grave, and Brett put his arm around me, not saying anything.

"Now you're free," I said, thinking of the shit life we'd had. Now my sister was free.

We didn't go straight home. Brett drove me down to the beach. We walked along the headland and sat on the grass looking out to sea.

"There has to be something better than this," I said as I laid back on the grass looking at the sky. The sun was starting to go down. Brett lay back on the grass next to me.

"You need to follow your dream," he told me. "I'm stuck here, but that's okay. I'm happy here. You know I love you, but you need to love yourself." He leaned over and kissed me on the lips. "I just hope I get to see your success because I know you can do it; you don't need me holding you back."

"But I do." Brett was the only good thing in my life.

"No, you don't. I'm damaged goods. You have to put this life behind you. I know you can make it out of here," he told me. We laid on the headland looking at the first stars coming out in the clear night sky.

"Starlight, star bright, first star I see tonight, wish I may wish I might make my wish come true tonight," I said, pointing to the first star.

"I hope your wish comes true, every time I see that first star, I will think of you," Brett said as he held my hand.

I had wished for him.

My boss sold the business to people from Sydney: Mike and Wayne. Wayne was married to Sue. Mike was single and looked a bit like Tom Selleck from Magnum P I. I think he was Tom Selleck.

On the first Saturday morning, Mike came into the shop from the house where they lived, which was out the back, with this bimbo he had picked up the night before. Oh my God, he was trying to impress her by cooking breakfast. It was sickening to watch.

I taught them everything, as they had no idea. Then I was told my hours had been cut. That gave me the shits, how was I going to live? So I went out to look for another job.

There was a job at a bookshop. I could do that I thought. I was very confident in the interview until the boss asked me who my favourite author was. *Shit,* I thought, I couldn't think of any. Then she asked me what book I read last. I hadn't read a book since school. Well, I didn't get that job. A few days later, I had another interview for a gift shop, quite classy. *I can be classy,* I thought. I dressed up for the interview. Brett parked around the corner so the boss wouldn't see me get off a motorbike. I straightened my dress.

"Good luck!" he yelled. I looked back to see him lighting a smoke, smiling at me.

I got the job. It would start on Monday, and it was only about fifteen minutes walking distance from home. I didn't tell Brett that, because getting a lift with Brett was my favourite part of the day.

After the second week, I realised it was such a tedious job. All I did was dust. I would start at one end, make my way through the shop, and by the end of the week, it was time to start again. I hated dressing up as well. But the pay was excellent, and I needed the money. So I stuck it out.

Our flat was so small, we all decided to look for a house to rent. It didn't take us long. We found this fabulous big house with three bedrooms and a built-in back veranda. So we moved in. I didn't have much, only a bed, which I got cheap. Moneybags Sharon had bought a great big corner sofa lounge, and it was so soft. Another friend Yowie moved in as well, which made the rent cheaper. Yowie had a car, which helped with moving stuff in.

The house was on a corner block. Yowie was a friend of Keith's. He wasn't a biker, but he needed somewhere to live. He was a nice guy, and he had a job so he could pay rent. He was so funny! He came to our flat for a party before we moved. He liked to drink, didn't do drugs and wanted to party, so he was going to fit in well.

He worked in a packing yard; I wasn't quite sure what Yowie did, but Keith vouched for him. We were all getting on quite well. We all had day jobs except Sharon who worked night shifts at Pizza Hut. So she slept in every day and cleaned the house when she got up. As we arrived home, Sharon would be heading out to work. Then we would party. Yowie was so tall and had muscles like a wrestler, but there was not a mean bone in his body.

His real name was Kevin, but everyone called him Yowie. Yowie loved his Southern Comfort. He always had a bottle. Brett still loved beer, but occasionally, he would buy scotch. I would help him drink it. He knew I had no money, and he didn't have much either.

Brett was an excellent motorbike mechanic. But he only worked when he needed extra money; otherwise, he would take his guitar downtown and busk. Some days, Brett would make a hundred dollars for a few hours' work. I loved how money didn't mean anything to him. He only made what he needed.

We managed to pick up some furniture on the side of the road. People threw out good stuff sometimes. We picked up a table and four chairs, just a couple of blocks away. Brett and Yowie brought them back in shopping trolleys. Yowie's bedroom was off the back veranda. The veranda was built-in like a room, and that's where Brett set up his guitar and amplifier. Yowie had a set of drums, he didn't play; he got them from a mate who owed him money, but he would have a bash. He wasn't that good.

Since moving in, we started going out to a nightclub called 'Night Moves'. It was uptown, and we became regulars every Friday night.

I made friends with the manager, Gary. He was so hot, and he used to wear black leather pants with a black leather vest and no shirt. Well, sometimes, he would. He was gay. That didn't stop me from flirting with him. I suppose he was my first gay friend.

The guys continually reminded me he was gay. I think they were a little afraid of him being gay. I didn't care; he was a nice guy, and it was 1982. Get over it, I would say to them.

He was a great dancer. When he wasn't behind the bar, I would get him up for a dance. I think he was about thirty. I'm sure he thought I was eighteen because I never got asked for ID. I so loved to dance. The DJ was fantastic; he played great dance songs; he even played *ABBA's Dancing Queen*, and the floor would be so packed.

Brett never danced. Sharon would turn up after work, as the club didn't get going until ten o'clock. We would party on till three in the morning when it closed.

We had so much fun! I never drank more than three drinks. That was all I could afford. I would drink ice water in between each scotch. It was a good thing, as I didn't get a hangover then. I danced almost nonstop, so I got pretty thirsty. Sometimes, Gary would give me a free drink. He was a lovely guy.

Sharon would turn up after work. We were becoming good friends, but I never told her I was in love with Brett. She just thought I was on the prowl as I was always checking out any new bods that came in.

On that Friday night, Gary was talking to me at the end of the bar. He asked if I would like to go to a private party on Sunday night. It was a public holiday long weekend. The club was only open by invitation.

"That sounds like fun; what time does it start?" I asked.

"Ten o'clock. It's fancy dress, 'Punk Rock'."

"Can I bring some friends?"

He said I could bring three friends. Brett, Sharon, and maybe Keith, I thought or Yowie.

Sunday came. I was getting dressed. I had my black, shiny tights on, my new blacktop I had bought last week. I pulled my hair up high, styling it forward and spraying it with coloured hair spray, red and gold. I had a studded armband on one arm and my black stilettos.

I came out to show the others. Yowie couldn't stop laughing, but Brett said I looked fantastic. Brett had some clean chains he lent me; I put one around my waist, the other with a padlock around my neck. I did look fabulous.

Brett just went as himself his ripped jeans, stud belt, black Tee shirt and his leather jacket. He was so hot. The others just dressed in their regular gear, which was so dull.

Yowie ended up coming with us. It was a good thing as he had a car. His car was a bright green Mazda. We all piled in, and I sat in the back with Sharon as Brett sat in the front seat. When we got there, they had security on the door, checking IDs. Sharon was already eighteen. But I was only weeks from turning seventeen.

I tried to bluff my way in the door.

"I come here all the time. I left my ID at home. Gary invited me, ask him?"

They looked at everyone else's ID. In the end, they let me in. Thank God, my heart was starting to race. The club was filling up fast. We grabbed our usual table.

I went up to the bar. Gary was busy. He had hired an extra barman for the night so that he could enjoy the party. He looked amazing. Gary had his black leather pants on with a chain-studded belt and a ripped black shirt exposing his gorgeous body, and to top it off, a black leather cap.

"You look great, Steph," he told me.

"So do you," I shouted back, as the music was so loud.

"Dance later?" he asked.

"Sure, later," I said. Gary gave me a free drink, scotch and coke; he knows what I like to drink.

I went back to the table, and just then, the song *Eye of the Tiger* started to play.

"I love this song, come on, Sharon." I grabbed her by the arm to drag her onto the dance floor. It was packed. We danced all night. Gary came over to dance with us when *Queen's Crazy Little Thing Called Love* was playing. He was so close to me I could smell his sweet sweat. Oh, I was so getting turned on. We danced for two more songs. Then Tina Turner's *Nut Bush City Limits* came on. Gary shook his head and indicated he had to get back to the bar. He's so hot. Maybe he's not gay! I looked over at the bar watching him work. He was too hot to be straight.

Everyone on the dance floor was dancing to the *Nut Bush*. I needed a drink, so I went back to the group. Brett was getting drunk again. Yowie was driving so he was on plain coke. So Brett and Yowie just sat there smoking. Brett refused to dance so Sharon was trying to get Yowie up, tugging on his arm. After finishing my scotch and coke, I went to the bathroom. I opened the door and found two girls smoking pot. They tried to hide it, but I could smell it. I quickly went to the nearest cubicle and got the hell out of there as fast as I could. I didn't want to get stoned, well, not tonight anyway.

When I got back to the table, Brett was on his own. I looked up at the dance floor; Sharon had Yowie up dancing. So I sat across from Brett looking into his glassy blue eyes. "You look like you're having fun," he said to me.

"Yep, I am." I smiled back at him.

"Do you want another drink?" Brett offered. "Yeah, scotch and coke, thanks."

Brett walked over to the bar. Just then, it was one of my favourite songs from *Queen*, *Another One Bites The Dust*. I just had to dance.

I raced up to the dance floor. I had never felt more alive. I danced on my own and didn't care. I was right into the music, nothing in the world mattered; the music made me move; I just disappeared into my safe little world.

I felt someone behind me holding my waist; I turned around, and it was Gary. We danced close, moving our bodies to the music. I put my arms around his neck. It was the best night. I knew he was gay, but he made me feel good; he was such fun.

The party was supposed to finish at three, but it was still going at 3:30 when they announced the last song – *ABBA's Dancing Queen*. Everybody was up dancing. You could hardly move on the dance floor. At the end of the song, Gary kissed me on the cheek.

"Thanks for coming," he told me. Definitely gay, I thought, with a smile.

Chapter 10

One Saturday afternoon, we were all sitting around the house. Yowie was lying on the sofa, trying to sleep. I was sitting nearby, watching TV. Sharon had gone to visit her parents and Brett was outside working on his bike. It was a dreary day and so hot. I went out to the kitchen to get a drink. Nothing but beer, but it was too early for beer. I just got some water.

While drinking I noticed water balloons on top of the fridge. Cool, we could have a water fight. That would liven things up around here. I started to fill some balloons up with water. I just filled the fourth one when Yowie came in.

"What are you up to?" he asked.

"I'm going to chuck them at Brett." Yowie wanted to join in. We made two more and headed outside.

We crept down the front steps. Brett had his back to us still working on his bike. We started throwing the balloons. Splat, mine landed right on his back. Yowie's water-bomb landed nearby. Brett jumped up.

"You bastards!" he yelled at us, ducking for cover as we threw two more.

We ran inside to grab the last two and then headed back outside.

"Where did he go?" I said as we looked around. The next minute, Brett came running out from beside the house with the garden hose. I screamed and threw the last balloon, running up the stairs and inside for cover, but he kept chasing us through the house with the garden hose. I screamed again laughing so much, and water was everywhere. We were soaked; Yowie and I couldn't stop laughing. Brett took the hose back outside. Oh my God, I laughed at the watery mess. Shaza is going to kill us, but we kept laughing. The carpet was soaked all down the hall.

By the time Sharon came home, we had soaked up most of the water with the towels. Hoping she wouldn't notice. She didn't. We were all sitting down watching the telly, looking very guilty. It was almost like Mum had come home, and we didn't want to get in trouble.

Sharon came into the lounge room and looked at us. She knew something was going on but wasn't sure what. She went to the bathroom a few minutes later; she came back.

"Why are all the towels in the wash?" Everyone froze, so I spoke up.

"Yowie accidentally left the plug in the washtub, and the washing machine overflowed, so we had to mop it up." Everyone was still frozen.

"You idiot," Sharon said to him as she went back to the bathroom. We all burst out laughing again.

"Why did you blame me for?" Yowie said, still laughing.

"Because she won't get mad at you," I replied.

I had noticed Sharon flirting with Yowie, but I wasn't quite sure why. Yowie was a great guy but very rough around the edges. He was just so enormous, and he didn't ride a motorbike.

It was just little things I'd noticed lately. Like one day, Yowie came home saying his back was killing him. He was always complaining about his bad back. He did a lot of lifting with his job. Anyway, Yowie was lying on the sofa, and Sharon went over and climbed onto his back to give him a massage. Brett wasn't home at the time. A bit over the top for a housemate. But I liked Yowie, and he was a lot of fun. I just wasn't attracted to him.

Last week, Keith had been drinking all day with Brett. He was helping him with his bike. Something was wrong with the engine, some mechanical thing. Mid-afternoon, Keith wanted to sleep it off, so he ended up crashing out on my bed. I didn't notice until Brett came inside to wash up he had grease all over himself. As he walked to the bathroom, he saw Keith asleep on my bed, face down. Brett backtracked to the lounge room where Yowie and I were watching TV.

"Hey, Steph, you know Keith's passed out on your bed." I jumped up, ran towards my room, ready to yell at Keith to get off my bed when Yowie beat me to it. He threw himself on to my bed, bouncing Keith off and into the wall, leaving a rather large hole.

Brett came out of the bathroom in a towel, as it made a hell of a noise.

"Holy shit," Brett said, standing in the doorway with his towel barely covering him. Keith was still on the floor, wondering what had just happened.

"Holy shit is right," I said. "How the hell are we going to fix that?" I asked, looking at the large hole in my wall.

We all couldn't stop laughing. I then noticed Keith was having trouble getting up. "Shit, are you okay?" We helped him up, looking for any damage, but he seemed okay.

"My fuckin' ass hurts," he said, rubbing it.

"That's why the hole is so big, you smashed it with your ass," Yowie added still laughing.

We couldn't help but laugh. Brett went back to his shower and Keith went to the kitchen for a beer. Yowie and I stood there thinking, how do we fix this? Sharon's going to chuck a fit. She keeps going on about the bond, which she paid and how she will never get any money back.

"Hey, I know what we can do," Yowie said, sounding very positive. "Let's cover the hole with the wardrobe."

"Great idea." We had floorboards in the bedroom, which made it easier to push furniture. Yowie had plenty of muscles. So he pushed the wardrobe, and I guided the front. Perfect! No one would ever know, and Sharon never did.

It was my birthday. I was seventeen, but I didn't tell anyone; it was a Saturday so that meant we would be having a party most likely.

That night, we stayed home and had an awesome party. Neal and a few of his friends turned up with a couple of cartons of beer and a bottle of rum. The music was blasting. I didn't know where all the people came from, but the word must have spread. Everyone was having a great time. Brett built a barbeque out of some bricks he had found up the road last week. He had brought them back and found a hot plate. Now we had a barbeque.

Neal turned up with a bag of sausages. He knew a guy who worked as a butcher, and he got them for free. Sharon and I were making up some salads in the kitchen. She was making some weird thing with walnuts, and I was sticking with potato salad. Everyone likes that.

The party was going well as far as our parties went. The music was pretty loud. There was a bong on the coffee table in the lounge room, which Neal seemed to be hogging. Out the front, Brett had the BBQ cooking with his cheer squad standing around watching. Another motorbike had pulled up. It was Bubbles with some girl on the back. That was different. He never had a girl.

The snags were cooked and ready to eat. So we sat the salads on the outside table, which we had made from an old door we found. We put some plastic plates out and knives and forks. Everybody started to help themselves. I grabbed a plate, a snag, some potato salad and sat on the front steps next to Jonesy. I hadn't seen

Jonesy since I'd left home. We talked for a while; he was telling me about his mate Terry. Terry had got knocked off his bike by a truck and was in a bad way in the hospital. Jonesy had just been up there to visit him. He was in a coma for five days, with a broken back and might not walk again. They were moving him to a Sydney hospital on Monday. He might need an operation, but they had to wait until he was stable before they could transfer him. How awful, the poor guy. He had just had his twenty-first a month ago.

Talking to Jonesy was making me depressed. I needed a drink. After eating, I headed for the kitchen. Sharon was in there making a cocktail, her latest fad – inventing drinks. It was green. Yuck, I decided to stick with a beer.

There was the sound of Brett's guitar coming from the back room, and someone was playing the drums. I went to investigate. It was Neal's mate, Steve on Brett's guitar, and Pete was playing the drums. They were pretty good. I just had to sit and watch. It was familiar like one of Brett's records. I couldn't pick the song, one of those heavy metal bands I think maybe *Led Zeppelin*. I couldn't walk away, so I just sat there, drinking my beer and listening.

After a while, Brett came and sat next to me.

"I think I'm in love with your guitar, either that or I'm very drunk," I said.

Brett put his arm around me and kissed me on the side of my head.

"Don't get too pissed," he said, then he walked off. I stayed there just listening to Steve and Pete play *Smoke on the water*. I knew that one from Deep Purple.

There were a few nice looking guys here, but none of them did anything for me. None of them was Brett. Even watching Steve play the guitar, all I could think of was Brett. Time had passed, and my beer was empty; I should get another drink.

I went into the kitchen where Brett was giving Keith a tattoo. Brett had 'Love' and 'Hate' tattooed across his knuckles. He was putting a knife blade tattoo on Keith's lower arm. It was looking good. I wanted a tattoo but only where no one could see it but not a knife.

The music had started up again, so I grabbed another beer. This time it was music I knew, *Liar* by *Queen*. I went to the lounge room, but it was very smoky. Jonesy was making out with some girl on the sofa. It was the same one that came with Bubbles. At least he would leave me alone. I looked out the front. The barbeque had died down, a few people had left, and it was nearly 2 am. Sharon had gotten so drunk she'd gone to bed.

I went back to the kitchen, where Brett had just finished Keith's tattoo. Wow, it looked good.

"Can you do a small tattoo on my hand as my birthday present?" I pointed to my palm.

"Yeah, are you sure?" he asked. I would let him do anything to me, I thought. So I sat there looking in those beautiful eyes for about twenty minutes.

I didn't feel the needle at all. Brett was so gentle, or maybe I was a bit too drunk. I so wanted him.

"I don't think movie stars have tattoos," he said with a smile. When he had finished, he said, "Now you will remember me for life."

I looked at my hand. I had a star in the centre of my palm.

"A star," I said questioning Brett.

"One day you will be a star," he told me and kissed my hand. "So don't let me down. Happy birthday!" He smiled.

Everyone had left pretty much, and I could hear Brett on the guitar. I headed out to the back veranda. Brett was strumming *Love of my life* by *Queen* on his guitar. I sat down to listen and then I started to sing, *Love of my life* don't leave me… it was a special moment, the way he looked at me. I knew he loved me.

Chapter 11

By 3 am, everyone who was leaving had left, and everyone else had found a spot to sleep. There were bodies everywhere. I was having a shower when I heard the door open. There was no lock. I froze, then the shower curtain opened and there, naked, was Neal's mate Steve. Oh my God, I jumped out of the shower, grabbed my towel and got the hell out of there.

Brett was outside the door just coming out of the loo.

"Are you okay?" he asked as I nearly ran into him. I told him what happened.

"I'll knock his lights out," Brett said, slightly staggering with that scary look in his eyes, I had seen that look before. He was a bit wasted, and Steve was twice as big as Brett.

"No, Brett." I had to pull him back. He was going to kill him. I managed to pull him away from the bathroom door. I pushed Brett into my room and shut the door, just realising I only had a towel around me. Brett only had his undies on as he was going to bed.

He was so close to me; he had his arms around me, pulling me closer. I felt like I had stopped breathing as his lips came onto mine. I had never felt so much passion as we made our way onto my bed. I dropped my towel to the floor, my arms around his neck, our naked bodies melting into one. I could feel him inside of me, my whole body came under his spell of pure lust, evolving into love, and this was what love was. I never wanted to let go.

We laid in each other's arms, catching our breath. I wanted to say, 'I love you Brett, and would never let you go', but we just lay there not saying anything. Then Brett got up, found his undies on the floor, put them on and left my room.

The next day, Brett seemed to avoid me. He stayed in his room sleeping, so Sharon said. My heart was breaking. I wanted to talk to him and tell the world about our beautiful night together. But I kept quiet. Things went a bit strange after that night. I thought it was me, but later that week, I felt sick at work, so my boss drove me home early. It was unusual for me to come home early. I didn't expect anyone to be home, so I was surprised to see Yowie's car out the front.

I walked in, expecting to see Yowie on the sofa, but he was nowhere to be seen. He must be in bed, I thought, the lazy bugger. I dumped my bag in my room, then headed towards Yowie's bedroom. His door was shut, so I pushed his door open. Oh, my God! Yowie and Sharon were having sex! I think I stood there for a second with my mouth open until I quickly shut the door.

Oh my God, Sharon is cheating on Brett, with Yowie. I went back to my room to get out of my work clothes. Then I laid on my bed, as I didn't feel well. I had a rotten headache. I lay there thinking of what I had just witnessed. Suddenly, I felt for poor Brett. He loved Sharon. He would be so devastated if he found out.

Sharon finally knocked on my door. She had the nerve to ask me not to tell Brett. Sharon said that she was going to talk to him that night. If she only knew about what Brett and I had done. So I agreed not to say anything. I went and got myself something to eat from the kitchen. Brett was due home soon. I went to bed after taking some Panadol.

A few hours had passed, and it was now dark. I must have dozed off. I woke to the sound of fighting and crashing sounds. I sat up, wondering if I should go out, listening, trying to hear what was going on. My curiosity got the better of me, so I got up, opened my door and walked out. Yowie was sitting at the kitchen table; Sharon was crying, things were lying on the floor that once sat on the table. I noticed Yowie had a bleeding lip and a black eye. Then I heard Brett's bike start up. I ran to the front door, but all I could see was his tail light going down the road. I so wanted to run after him. I felt his pain, and my heart ached for him.

I came back inside. That's when I noticed the massive hole in the wall, obviously where Yowie's head must have gone through.

"So you told him," I said to Sharon, quite cross that she could hurt him like that.

Brett never came back that night.

The next morning, I walked to work. I had to leave early. When I left, no one else was up. In the afternoon, when I came home, Yowie was sitting on the sofa watching TV, as if nothing had changed. Sharon had gone to work, I assumed. I asked Yowie if Brett had been back.

"Nope." He seemed a bit down, and he should be. I was worried about Brett, and his heart must be breaking. I wanted to hurt Sharon. I could tell her about

Brett and me, but I could never betray Brett. I would never hurt Brett as Sharon has. I'm glad they got found out.

I wanted to cheer up Yowie, so I made some hamburgers for dinner.

"You hungry?" I asked as I walked in the lounge room, carrying two plates with my homemade burgers on top. He perked up on seeing food. Yowie was always hungry.

We sat there quietly eating and watching one of our favourite shows. *The Young Ones* was so funny and yet stupid. When the show had finished, Yowie picked up our empty plates and headed to the kitchen.

"Can I get you a drink?" he asked.

"Yeah, a coke, thanks," I said, lying on the sofa.

When Yowie came back, he started to open up, talking about how upset he was about hurting Brett. Sharon had spate the dummy with Yowie, and she went back to her mum and dad's. She said she needed some space.

Good riddance, I thought, I hoped she wouldn't come back.

She told Yowie she thought she still loved Brett.

Oh my God, what a bitch. I was starting to feel sorry for Yowie as well as Brett.

By Friday, Sharon had come back, and she and Yowie were together. Brett had been staying at Neal's place. He came over in the morning and packed up his things and he and Yowie made up and shook on it. So Yowie told me.

Brett. Oh, my heart is so breaking right now. I have to see you. I need to tell Brett how I feel.

I got myself a drink and went to the back veranda. Brett's guitar was gone, and the drums sat in the corner on their own; it looked so sad.

Keith came over later. I asked him if he had seen Brett. I wanted to make sure he was okay.

Keith said, "He's gone."

"No, he can't be," I said out loud.

"Brett told me to give you this." It was his *Queen* album. His favourite one. "He said to tell you he's sorry; there's a letter inside."

Brett was the love of my life. He was the only one who believed in me. He couldn't be gone. How could I go on without him? I went to my room, shut the door, laid on my bed and opened my letter.

Dear Steph,

    I'm sorry I can't do this in person, but I had to get away. I do love you. The other night was truly amazing. But I'm no good for you. You have such grand dreams, and I know you can make them come true. I will only hold you back.

    I'm sure we will see each other again one day when all your dreams have come true.

    You are such a beautiful person; don't ever doubt yourself.

    Love to my beautiful Star.

Yours always,
Brett xx

Chapter 12

It had been two months since Brett left. I had been just miserable. I had been going to bed early, lying there listening to the *Queen* record Brett had left for me, crying myself to sleep. I had no way of reaching Brett. I had heard that he was travelling down to Melbourne to stay with his brother. Nobody knew what I was feeling. I loved Brett. They thought I was getting a cold or flu or something. Great friends, they had no idea about me. No one knew me as Brett did.

We still had our parties, but it was like I was in a fog. I couldn't get out of it. It was at one of our parties that Shane turned up. I hadn't seen Shane since that bike ride out to Middle Creek, but that was months ago. We had never really spoken much, but we got talking that night. He had a new motorbike, a rather large road bike. He offered to take me for a ride the next day. He seemed nice, so I agreed. I hadn't been on a motorcycle since Brett left.

Shane arrived to pick me up at ten in the morning. He let me wear his leather jacket. It was rather heavy, and the arms were a bit long, but I didn't care, the smell of leather reminded me of Brett. Ooh, I breathed it in. I climbed on behind Shane and off we went.

We had a lovely day, as we rode down the coast for about an hour; it was so nice to getaway. We stopped at this small beach town where there was a burger shop across from the beach area. We parked near a picnic table, where we sat our helmets on top. The view was so pretty, and the water calm. If it had been summer, it would have been so lovely to swim there. There was hardly anyone around; it was so peaceful. For the first time since Brett had left, I felt kind of happy. Maybe I could fall for Shane, he wasn't bad looking, and he rode a motorbike, but he wasn't Brett. We had hamburgers for lunch. The ride back was just what I needed. Shane was an excellent rider, and I felt safe with him.

A week later, Keith came over. Keith was a good friend. I think he was worried about me. He was the only one that noticed how depressed I was. We used to talk a lot about stuff. I told him about going out with Shane, how we had a great day out together.

Keith dropped a bombshell; Shane had a girlfriend. That's why Shane hasn't been around all week.

What a bastard! You couldn't trust any guy, and I was starting to like Shane. What a bastard!

Keith had brought over a bottle of scotch, what a guy – my favourite drink. We drank and partied on to the wee hours of the morning. Yowie had moved into Sharon's room the day after Brett left. We had been trying to find someone to rent Yowie's bedroom, as I couldn't afford the extra rent. I told Sharon she had to pay Brett's share since she was the reason he left. We had no luck finding anyone, so it stayed empty, except on the weekends when Keith was too drunk to drive home.

We hadn't been to Night Moves for ages. I missed going and seeing Gary. Next week, we should go, I suggested. Sharon was the only one who seemed a bit interested. This group was starting to get so boring. I missed Brett.

The next day, Shane came over for a visit. Keith and I were having a coffee, sitting on the front steps when he rode his bike into our driveway. I just played it cool like I didn't give a shit about Shane, he was talking to Keith anyway. So I got up and took my empty mug inside. I went to my room, shut the door and laid on my bed. I put my cassette player on. I had *Air Supply* playing. They only seemed to play sad love songs, but that was my mood, feeling sorry for myself.

It wasn't long before there was a knock at the door.

"What?" I yelled out. It was Shane.

"Can I come in? Is everything all right?" he asked.

"Yeah, I'm fine. How's your girlfriend?" I blurted out. Then Shane explained that he'd had a girlfriend, but she broke it off two weeks ago, then she wanted to get back together. So Shane decided to end it for good. That put me in a better mood. But I still didn't trust him.

Shane and I started dating. The following week, we all went to Night Moves. We went in Yowie's car with Sharon, Shane and myself. It was just like old times. Seeing Gary helped cheer me up. Shane wasn't quite sure about Gary. I had to explain that Gary was my gay boyfriend. I don't know why straight guys feel threatened by gay guys. I only had one dance with Gary, who whispered to me, "I think your boyfriend is getting jealous." Shane was sitting there staring at

Gary…if looks could kill. When the song finished, he kissed me on the cheek and went back to the bar.

I went back to our table where my drink was waiting. The music was so loud it was hard to have a conversation. So we just drank. Shane kept buying me drinks all night; he seemed to have endless money. I don't know if he was trying to impress me or get me drunk.

He did have a full-time job as a mechanic, as he had finished his apprenticeship. He was 24, seven years older than me. That didn't bother me, as I always liked older guys. By the time we were heading home, I was pretty drunk. I had to hang on to Shane while we walked to the car. I didn't usually drink that much, not on my budget.

Shane came into my room when we got home.

"Do you mind if I stay the night? I've had too much to drink," he said.

I didn't care. I just stripped off, put on my large Darkwood rally Tee shirt that Brett had given me ages ago and flopped into bed. Not sure how long I was asleep for, but I woke with Shane on top of me. Oh my God, I didn't remember saying yes to this. When he had finished, he rolled over and went to sleep.

I didn't know how I should feel. It didn't feel like love.

The next morning, I pretended I was feeling sick and stayed in bed. Shane kissed me as if everything was great. Then he left, he said he had to help a friend with his car. I was glad he had gone. I felt like I had betrayed Brett, even though I might never see him again. I laid there looking at the tattoo on my hand. Brett would always be in my heart, as a tear rolled down my cheek. Why did he leave me?

Shane came back later that day with a bunch of flowers. He said he hoped I was feeling better. Maybe Shane was a nice guy, and perhaps it was just me. I was so drunk; perhaps I asked for it and don't remember. I stayed in bed all day. Shane didn't stay long.

After he left, I went out to the lounge room. Sharon and Yowie were watching TV. Sharon was full of questions.

"Did Shane bring you flowers? He's such a nice guy, so are you two dating now?"

I didn't know where to start, so I just went with it.

"Yep, we're dating." I suddenly felt better. Maybe I was making more out of this than I should be. He's a nice guy and has a good job. "He's coming over on Friday, and we might go to the drive-in movies."

A few weeks later, Shane and I had been out every weekend, and the drive-in movies were becoming our Friday night routine. We hadn't been to 'Night Moves' since that first night. I don't think Shane trusted Gary.

I was starting to like Shane, but I still wasn't sure if I could love him. We had sex every weekend, but it wasn't love. Shane thought I was a virgin and that he was the only guy that I had ever been with. I could never tell him the truth that Brett was the only one who had my heart.

A few days later, I was looking in my diary when I realised I was late for my period. Five days late, I was never late! But we had used a condom every time. Oh, no! I suddenly thought, the first time we did it, I couldn't remember if he did or not. Oh, God, could I be pregnant?

By the time Friday came, my periods had still not arrived. Should I tell Shane? It was the longest day. After work, I got ready to go out. Shane would be here soon. He had his car tonight, which was handy for the drive-in movies. I hardly said a word on the way there.

Shane asked, "Is everything all right?"

"Yeah, I'm just a bit tired."

We went to the shop after we parked. Shane bought some Maltesers and some drinks. We went back to the car. I could tell Shane was starting to wonder what was going on. I knew I should say something. The movie was starting. I'll wait, I thought.

"I think I'm pregnant," I blurted out as if I couldn't stop myself.

Well, that ruined the night. I don't even remember what movie it was. Shane assured me that I might just be late. I should go to the doctor to be sure.

"But what if I am?" Shane was so kind.

"Don't worry. If you are, I'll take care of you."

That night, Shane didn't stay over. He had to have an early start in the morning. So I went to bed alone. I was feeling much better now since Shane had said he would take care of me. If I'm pregnant, he would surely marry me and look after me and the baby. I was almost eighteen. I hadn't thought this was how my life was going to end up.

Tuesday afternoon, I finally had an appointment with the doctor. I was so stressed and anxious. I called in sick for work because it was making me sick just thinking about it. I had been going to this doctor forever, and he was as old as the hills. I felt like I was in trouble when he said, "What can I do for you,

Stephanie?" In his headmaster tone of voice. I told him, and he looked over the top of his glasses.

"How old are you?"

He ordered a blood test and sent me out to the nurse. She took some blood and told me I could ring for the results on Friday. I couldn't get out of there quick enough. I walked home. It wasn't far, and I needed the air. It just hit me that I had to wait until Friday. I had to take my mind off things.

I had to work the next day, and I probably wouldn't see Shane until Friday. By the time I got home, Yowie's car was in the drive. He was in his usual seat on the sofa. I went and dumped my things in my room and joined him. I wished I could talk to him about my problem, but I couldn't. So I just tried to forget it, for now.

Yowie was telling me that he and Sharon wanted to get a place on their own. Oh shit. Where the hell would I live? I couldn't afford rent on my own. Yowie thought I might move in with Shane.

I hadn't thought about it until now, that could work. Shane had a good job. We could rent a house to raise our baby. Oh my God, what was I thinking? *Please, God, make me not pregnant.* I shook my head, trying to get it out of my head. I was only seventeen. I had so much I wanted to do before I settled down. I wasn't sure what I was going to do, but I hoped it would be something great and not stuck in this small nowhere town.

Friday finally came. It was the longest day ever at work. I finished work and headed home, stopping off at the post office to ring my doctor. They put me on hold, and my heart was racing. It felt like hours.

Then my doctor spoke, "Hello, Stephanie, I have the results. They are positive."

I don't remember what happened after that. I think my brain had shut down. I don't remember getting home. I went to my room, put on my music and cried. I had never felt more alone in my life.

Chapter 13

I must have laid in my room for over an hour. It was getting dark. I got up and went to wash my face. My eyes were all bloodshot. I took a breath, told myself everything would be all right. Shane would be here soon. He said he would look after me.

Yowie and Sharon went out for dinner to some restaurant. It was good they were gone by the time Shane got here. I was sitting on the sofa when Shane came in. I tried to keep it together, but I just burst into tears. Shane guessed that it was positive. I was pregnant.

He sat down next to me and told me he had found out there was a place just over the border that would do abortions. I couldn't believe what I was hearing.

"What if I don't want an abortion?"

Suddenly, Shane sat up to face me, really serious. "If you have this baby, I don't want any part of it." He didn't want a baby yet. "But if you get rid of it, we can move in together."

I went numb, trying to take it all in. I sat there in silence for a while.

Everything was going through my mind. If I had the baby, I would be out on the street, or worse, I would have to go home to Mum. No way! I couldn't do that, and I had no choice. I had to agree.

Shane had found a flat for us to rent, but we still had two weeks before we could move in. That cheered me up a little; at least he meant what he said. I had an appointment for next Friday at the clinic. It was a five-hour drive, so we took the motorbike. At least, I didn't have to look at his face.

Part of me hated him for what he was making me do. When we got there, they took me in and told Shane to come back in four hours.

"You're not taking her home on a motorbike, are you?" the rather large nurse said. She knew we had a long drive home. I was just like a zombie in a fog. "You had better get a train ticket for her to get home," she added, before taking me through the doors.

After changing into a gown, I had to climb up on this cold table and put my feet in stirrups. I lay there with tears running down my face. The nurse was very kind.

"Are you okay? Is it hurting?"

"No." I shook my head. I couldn't feel anything except my heart breaking. I hated Shane for making me do this.

When it was all over, Shane picked me up, showing the nurse the train ticket he had bought. It was a short ride to the station. I never said a word as I walked onto the train alone. I sat there looking out the window. I cried all the way home. Just before I arrived home, I took a breath, told myself I was going to forget this ever happened. I had a doctor's note for the next five days off, and then I was never going to think about this week ever again.

A week later, Shane and I moved into our new flat. It wasn't huge, but it had two bedrooms and a carport. We picked up some furniture from the second-hand shops. Shane had a TV and a bed. So we had everything we needed. Our flat wasn't far from work, which was good. I could walk there. After we moved, we never saw much of Yowie and Sharon. I hardly saw any of my old friends. Shane didn't seem to get along with them.

We made friends with our new neighbours, John and Molly. They had a motorbike as well, so we made a lot of road trips together. Almost every weekend we had plans to go somewhere. I had a leather jacket now; Shane bought it for me for my eighteenth birthday and leather gloves. We would get up early on a Sunday morning and ride up to the mountains. It would be so cold, parts of the road would be foggy. I enjoyed riding up the hills, going so fast around the bending, winding roads. It was like nothing else mattered.

We would have a picnic lunch in the National Park. Molly and I would talk. John and Molly were from Queanbeyan. She told me John had been in a lot of trouble with the law down there, so they had moved to the country to start again. I told Molly how I hoped to move out of this town and would love to live in the city, but Shane hated the city. Shane got on well with John, so we pretty much did everything together. We had a lot of fun.

Shane bought a dirt bike for us. He wanted me to learn how to ride, so I went down to the RTA to get my learner's permit. I still couldn't drive a car yet.

One weekend, we went out in the bush. Shane was going to teach me how to ride. He sat on the back and gave me instructions about what to do. I was sitting on my DT 175 Yamaha Dirt bike – no fear at all – off we went. The track was reasonably level. A few dips and rocks, but I think I did okay. Shane was getting bored, so we swapped over, and Shane drove. Shane went a lot faster than I did; I just hung on.

I wasn't that good I heard Shane tell John when we got home. Shane was always putting me down. I wanted to get my car licence, so I nagged Shane to teach me. We had an old brown Ford, and it was kind of cool. Shane took me on the back streets. I was picking up a bit of speed, and then I slowed a little for a bend. Shane screamed at me and hit me right across the face. I slammed on the brakes and stopped.

"Why did you hit me?" I yelled at him.

"Because you're an idiot. You would have smashed into that car," he said, pointing at a parked car.

"That car is miles away," I yelled back.

"Don't fuckin' argue with me, or I won't teach you," he screamed back. I shut up and kept driving. I had to get my licence I told myself.

He didn't hit me anymore, and a few weeks later, I went to the police station to do my driving test. I was so nervous. The policeman got in the passenger side, and I started the car. He told me to go straight down the main street, turn right at the roundabout and come back. The policeman didn't even look up, and he spent the whole time writing on his clipboard. We got back to the police station, and I angle parked perfectly. He signed the paper. "Congratulations."

I had passed! I was so excited. Shane was waiting for me when I came out of the police station with my red 'P' plates.

Shane just shrugged. "I knew you would pass; they pass anyone," he said, trying to take my joy away. He never thought I was good at anything.

When I got home, I ran next door to show John and Molly. They were happy for me.

"We should celebrate," Molly said. "Let's go to the pub. There is a good band on tonight." The pub was only a short walk down the road so we could have a few drinks.

"That sounds like a great idea." Shane wasn't that keen but agreed to go.

I loved live bands. I hadn't been out to the pub or nightclub in ages. So I was quite excited to get dressed up in my black jeans and my sparkly blacktop. By the time we got to the pub, it was pretty packed. It cost five dollars for the cover charge to get in. Shane complained about that. I didn't care. I wanted in.

Once in, we pushed our way into the bar to buy drinks. We could hear the band; they sounded pretty good. There were no tables available, standing room only. I just wanted to dance. We all headed in carrying our drinks. The place was packed, and my glass was getting bumped. Screw this. I sculled my drink, dumped the empty glass on a table and got to the dance floor. The band were great. The two of us just danced all night. I hadn't seen Shane for ages, but I didn't care. I was having a great time with Molly.

There was a cute drummer I was flirting with; when the band stopped for a break, he came over to say hello. He offered to buy me a drink. I wanted to say yes, but if Shane saw me, I'd be in the shit. So I told him I already had one. He asked my name. His name was JT, which was short for John Taylor. Maybe I should have run off with him that night, as he was from Sydney. I didn't know why I stayed with Shane. He treated me terribly. I think I couldn't see past that, and I had nothing else in my life.

The band were playing again when John came over looking for me. I was dancing right in front of the band. John yelled in my ear, "We have to go, Shane's been kicked out."

Great, I thought. "What has he done now?"

I pushed myself through the crowd, following John. Molly was already outside with Shane. Shane had blood all over his shirt; he had been fighting.

"Are you okay?" I asked, concerned. He was in a foul mood.

"I'm fine. Let's just get the fuck home," he grumbled at me. We walked home, not saying anything much. That night, Shane went to bed not talking; I stayed right over on my side of the bed. I lay there wondering how the hell I had ended up here.

Chapter 14

A few weeks had passed. Shane and I hadn't been talking much. Even John and Molly had been avoiding us. On Friday, Shane came home in a good mood for a change.

"I put in for some holidays. I'm taking two weeks off," Shane announced. "I want you to put in for holidays too," he told me. I'd never had a holiday, so I started to get a bit excited.

"Where are we going?" I asked.

"Surfer's Paradise," he said. "I went there years ago with my mum and dad before he died. I think I was about five or six. We had some relatives up there. I don't remember too much."

John and Molly decided to come with us. We booked a cheap motel right near the beach. The day finally came. We had to plan what to take as space was minimal on bikes. We headed off early to beat the traffic, stopping a couple of times, to stretch our legs and relieve our bladders. I didn't smoke anymore, but Shane, John and Molly did, so our stops were a smoke break for them. I think I quit because I couldn't afford to buy any and Shane used to complain if I asked him for one.

It was a perfect day, and the sky was so blue. Maybe this was like a new start for Shane and me I thought, as we rode along the highway.

We just needed a holiday away from all the troubles. I still thought about Brett. I wondered what he might be doing. Brett was always my first love. I so missed our conversations, his beautiful blue eyes and his wonderful laugh. I would still have Brett in the palm of my hand. I looked at my star tattoo before I put my glove on. We got back on our bikes. We only had about an hour to go.

We eventually made it. We all climbed off our bikes. I ached all over.

Our motel had a spa and swimming pool, which I couldn't wait to use. We were upstairs. Luckily, there was a lift as we were on the sixth floor. Wow, this place is massive compared to our flat at home! It had two bedrooms, a kitchen and a lounge room, with a round table at one end. I opened the curtains. We had a balcony with a view of the ocean! It was the best view. Yes, this was my new life. It could only get better now. I was so sure a holiday was going to fix any problems Shane and I were dealing with:

The guys were exhausted! All they wanted to do was watch telly and drink beer, as John walked in with a carton over his shoulder. There was a bottle shop across the road, which he had noticed when we first arrived.

Molly and I changed and headed down to the spa. When we got down there, it was so great; no one else was there. The spa was sitting there waiting for us. We pushed the button to start the Spa and climbed in, and it was nice and warm. We were aching all over, and it felt so good!

"The boys don't know what they're missing."

We must have been there for over an hour. We talked about what things we might do tomorrow and the rest of the week. 'Dream World' was a theme park nearby. It had only opened a few years ago, and I had always wanted to go. I remembered friends at school had been there. They said it was awesome! Mum and Max never went anywhere or took us anywhere.

"Are you getting hungry?" Molly asked.

"Yeah, I'm starving actually." We got out, wrapped our towels around ourselves and headed upstairs.

The boys were still drinking beer getting drunk, watching some comedy show, laughing.

"What are we going to do for dinner?" we asked.

"We could go out?" I suggested.

John sounded drunk. "I don't think I could walk anywhere." He laughed.

Molly and I were not amused and decided to go out and get takeaway. We got changed out of our wet swimmers and headed out the door.

We were close to a lot of shops and restaurants and didn't have to walk far. There was a Chinese restaurant that looked okay. We ordered our food, ten minutes they said so we decided to go for a walk. A couple of blocks and we came across this restaurant called Olivia's; it looked American. All the waitresses were on roller skates. How cool, I thought.

"We should go there one night," I told Molly.

I looked at my watch. "Our dinner should be ready."

We picked up our Chinese food and headed back to the motel. After we ate, Molly pulled out the cards.

"Who wants to play?" she asked. We sat up at the table to play cards. I had picked up a bottle of scotch and some coke to have with it. We played a few hands of poker. Shane was getting the shits because I was beating him. Molly was stirring him up, which only made him worse. In the end, Shane threw the cards and headed for the sofa.

"Sore loser," Molly added. "Steph, you're good at cards!"

"Thanks, Molly."

Shane looked right in my face. "It's the only thing you're good at." He said it with such hatred, my smile didn't last.

The next day, everything was forgiven. We decided to go to 'Dream World'. We had an early breakfast, got on our bikes and headed off to 'Dream World'. We had heard that it was the best theme park ever.

We finally got there. It was further away than I thought it would be. Walking in the gates was so magical; we picked up a map. I wanted to see everything, and John wanted to go on the Thunderbolt Rollercoaster. So we ran in that direction. There was already a queue, but it wasn't that long, so we lined up. I had never been on a roller coaster before, it looked terrifying, but I wasn't going to be left behind. We all climbed on, Shane and I were in the first car. Molly and John were just behind us. The padded bar came over our heads and locked us in. It started to move, no turning back now. My heart started racing as we slowly climbed the steep track. Finally got to the top and off we went. I was so scared; I shut my eyes and was too terrified to scream. When it was finally over, I opened my eyes, relieved to be pulling up to stop. Shane was screaming, "That was awesome!" So were Molly and John. They wanted to go again. But the queue had doubled. Thank God.

What else could we do?

Next was a car ride. They were like old-fashioned cars on tracks. Very slow, which was a nice change. It was a great day. We got wet on the log ride, which floated on water tracks, like a timber mill.

It was the best day I thought, and we headed back exhausted and happy. Too tired to go out. We ordered pizza for dinner.

The five days went by really fast. It was our last day, so we went up to Olivia's for lunch. It was an American café like *Happy Days* on TV. The waitresses were all on roller skates, and it had sixties' music playing. They sold mainly hamburgers and fries. John wanted to trip the waitress, but Molly threatened to kill him if he did.

The last day! We headed off for our five-hour trip home. I had to go to work the following day, as I couldn't get any more time off.

The next morning, I got to work to be hit with a bombshell. The business where I worked had just been sold. That wasn't the worst of it. The new owners wanted me to work part-time, Saturdays and Thursday nights only so they could have those days off. Stuff that. I was going to get another job.

Chapter 15

I couldn't quit until I had found another job. So I started looking through the paper. Not much out there. A florist shop. No, I don't think so – not for me. A job was going in the new plaza that had just opened at a coffee shop. I could do that. I rang up and got an interview. It was a lovely coffee shop owned by two sisters, Jan and Irene. They seemed friendly, and they liked me, so I got the job. It was my last day at the gift shop. I hated working there; anyway, I had been there long enough.

I started my new job, and I caught on real quick. We mainly sold sandwiches and coffee. I worked with Karen. She was a little older than me, but we got on well. It didn't take long for us to become friends. It was nice to have a friend that didn't know Shane.

Shane and I had been living together for ten months now. Sometimes, he would be romantic. Shane would show up at work with flowers for me after we had had a huge fight the night before. I think it was all a show, so everyone thought he was the best.

He always knew how to hurt me, so no one ever knew. The mental abuse was terrible. He had me believing that it was always my fault and that I wasn't good at anything. I never told anybody how terrible things were. Everyone at work thought he was the nicest guy. Jan kept asking if I was going to marry him. "You don't want to let this one get away," she would say. "He's a keeper." What would she know?

But these comments made me think about it. We hadn't talked about getting married. I was always going to do big things with my life, but I was never going to earn enough money to move to Sydney. I guess this was as good as it would ever be.

One night, we had just gone to bed, and I asked Shane, "What do you want to do with your life?" I didn't want to put pressure on him.

"What do you mean?" he asked.

"Well, do you want to stay in this town forever?"

"Yeah, why not?" he said as he rolled over to sleep not much for talking.

A few weeks later, Shane and I were watching TV, when he asked, "Do you want to get married?"

Wow! How romantic I thought, how could I refuse? He wasn't even looking at me. Before I had a chance to say anything, he continued, "You won't get anyone better than me."

For a second, I thought he was having a joke with me. I nearly laughed. Until I realised he was serious. I tried to make it into a joke by saying, "Well, there are plenty of other guys out there!"

"Yeah" – he half-laughed – "but you wouldn't get anyone as good as me." Maybe he was right. "So how about it?" he asked.

"Yeah, okay," I replied. Shane continued watching the TV. I guess I was getting married.

I don't know why I said yes. I suppose I couldn't see anything else in my future. No one was going to offer me anything better.

"I'm getting married." Molly was so excited. More excited than I was. Everyone I told seemed more excited about me getting married than I was. I tried to get enthused, but it wasn't like how I thought it would be. I felt myself slowly disappear like I had no control over anything anymore.

Molly took me shopping. I tried on wedding dresses, not feeling anything.

"What if I don't love him?" Molly tried to brush my comment aside as pre-wedding jitters. She organised the whole wedding. I was like a puppet being pushed and pulled, going along with whatever was happening. My life was no longer my life. I went to work, and I came home. I cooked dinner. Nothing had changed. I think I just kept telling myself once we're married things will be better.

My wedding day came, and Molly dressed me. She did my makeup. It was like it was her wedding, but I was playing the part.

As I walked to the door of the church, I went to step inside, and my shoe became stuck in the mat at the door. It was like a 'greater force' was trying to stop me, but it came loose, and I walked down the aisle. We only had a few people there. My friends from work, a couple of Shane's workmates; John was best man, and Molly was my maid of honour.

I never told my family. I hadn't spoken to them since I left. I think Shane liked it that way.

I was married. I couldn't remember getting married; it was all a bit of a blur. Everyone was so happy for me, telling me how lucky I was to have Shane. That night we went back home. Shane didn't want to waste money on a motel. We left the next morning for the Sunshine Coast, on the other side of Brisbane. It took us two days to get there. We slept in the car on the edge of the road the first night, and the next afternoon, we got there.

We hadn't booked anywhere, so we drove around to find somewhere to stay. We stopped at what looked like a nice motel with a pool.

"This looks all right," I said as we walked into the office.

Shane whispered to me, "If it's over fifty dollars, forget it."

It was sixty-five a night, so we walked out of there. I was getting the shits; this was supposed to be our honeymoon! It was getting late. At the next motel, I suggested I should run in and check the price. Shane agreed and waited in the car, and I went in; it was sixty dollars a night.

"I'll take it." I paid with my money. I told Shane it was fifty a night. I was tired and sick of driving. I just wanted to change and have a swim.

I was a bit quiet because I was shitty with myself for having to lie. I went for a swim. I dived into the pool. It was beautiful and cold, and it made me feel a little better. There was a young couple in the pool swimming. They looked like newlyweds I thought as I wiped the water from my face and looked at the star on my hand. I felt sadness aching in my heart for Brett, wondering if he ever thought of me. The couple left so I just slowly swam laps.

After a while, Shane came down to see if I was hungry; he thought we could get takeaway.

Later that night, Shane wanted sex. He finally noticed we hadn't had sex since we got married. I wasn't in the mood. I needed a few scotches in me. Having sex with Shane was like such a chore. I had to fake it every time and was glad when it was over.

After a few days like this, I was so bored. I wanted to go home. I missed my friends. Shane must have sensed this, so he booked us on a boat ride for dolphin watching. Finally, something I could put into a photo album. I was looking forward to this. Shane kept reminding me how much it cost as he was paying. I was supposed to be very grateful.

In the end, it was a great day; we went on this large vessel. There were about twenty other people on board, and the weather was lovely. We headed out quite a distance, and then suddenly, there they were about eight dolphins swimming along next to our boat. Scooting along, some were jumping out of the water and showing off. They were beautiful and free, and I so wanted to join them.

It was a perfect day. We ordered some takeaway to take back to our motel, then we both went swimming; it was lovely. I didn't know if I had forgiven Shane for being a scrooge with the money or if I was just pleased to be heading home. Either way, it was a good day.

Chapter 16

A few months passed, and things were pretty much back to normal. Shane went to his work, and I went to work at the coffee shop. On Saturday nights, we started going to this new club called the 'Hairy Grape'. It was more like a wine and cocktail bar. There was music but no dance floor, so you just sat around and got pissed. John and Molly told us about it.

One Saturday night, we went there, and Yowie and Sharon turned up. Sharon and I caught up. I told her I was married. She told me Brett was back in town. I swear my heart missed a beat. She said he was staying with Neal. I hadn't seen Neal for over a year. Last I had heard, he was in jail, but that was a while ago.

Just when I had stopped thinking of Brett, now I couldn't stop thinking about him. I just kept drinking Harvey Wallbangers all night. I got pretty wasted. I would have Brett back in a second if he wanted me. I sat there looking at my tattoo, wondering what Brett would think. I was married! Oh God, how had I ended up here? The rest of the night was a blur.

A week went by. I thought I would have run into Brett, as it's not a big town. Just when I had given up, I looked over the counter at work and there he was. His beautiful blue eyes were smiling at me.

"Oh my God, how are you?"

I asked my boss if I could have a break now.

"Who's the biker?" she asked.

"Just an old friend," I said, not wanting to tell any of them about Brett.

I met Brett in the food court. He gave me a hug that felt so good.

"I hear you got married," he said. My heart sank. We sat down, and Brett bought me a coffee. All my feelings came flooding back. He said he would love to meet Shane one day. God, no. I didn't want them to be friends.

We talked about the old days and laughed. We had had such good times back then. He said he was glad I was happy. *But I'm not*, I wanted to tell him. I'd had my chance and stuffed it up. On the inside, I was falling apart. *I love you, Brett, take me away with you; I will make you happy, take me.* But I couldn't say it. I was an idiot for marrying someone I didn't love. It just hit me. I didn't love Shane, and I never had. But I said nothing. I felt like the weight of the world was on me with no escape. Inside I was screaming, trapped like a caged animal, not knowing what to do. I felt like I was dying with no way out.

We said goodbye, and he gave me the tightest hug. I didn't want to let go. Brett told me he was going up to Queensland to live. He would send me his address when he got settled. I had to hold back my tears as I watched him walk away.

What the hell had I done? I had married the wrong guy.

That night, I hit the scotch pretty hard. I hated myself and felt like my life was falling apart. I had no control over anything. I wanted to crawl into a hole and never come out.

My life had become an automatic robotic life of routine. I got up, went to work, came home, cooked dinner, went to bed, over and over. I was drowning, drinking every night. As soon as I came back from work, I hit the scotch. I was feeling so sorry for myself. I used to be so full of life with lots of thoughts about the future. Now I felt nothing. I never saw Brett again.

I started going out to the local pub with Karen from work. She had been trying to get me to go out for ages. So I finally said yes. Her boyfriend was in a band. Shane never wanted to go anywhere. John and Molly had moved back to Queanbeyan. We said we were going to stay in touch but never did.

I'm sure Shane knew I didn't love him. He used to complain about the flat being messy, and that I was a lousy housewife, only good for one thing he would always tell me. So I would go out without him. I couldn't get too dressed up, or Shane would accuse me of trying to pick up guys. So I just dressed low key; I didn't care; I just wanted to go out.

Going out with Karen now and then to listen to her boyfriend's band was the only bit of fun I had in my life. I didn't even check out any guys, and I didn't care anymore. I mainly stayed home watching videos that I rented from the shop down the road. Shane took up shooting and joined a gun club. It was a good distraction. It kept him busy.

He also started to nag me about having a baby. I wasn't sure I wanted one, maybe I wouldn't be able to fall pregnant since my abortion.

Work was not going very well; Jan and Irene sold the business. I thought it must be me. Every time I get a job, they end up selling the business. The new bosses were taking over on Monday. A husband and wife. The husband was an ex-policeman. That's when I found out I was pregnant. I couldn't be; I was on the pill. But I knew I was because I had been drinking so much. I used to forget my tablet sometimes. At least, I could quit work for a while.

I stopped drinking and started taking better care of myself. I was a little worried I might have already done damage to my baby. I was nineteen now. It took me a while to feel anything for my baby. What if it's just like Shane? After I went for a scan and saw pictures of the baby, that's when I started to realise that this was going to be my baby, and I began to get excited. It was real, a part of me.

Shane changed a bit for the better. He started treating me a little better. We saved a lot of money since I stopped going out drinking and partying. We had enough for a deposit on a house.

I was six months pregnant when we moved into our very own little house. It was my first real home. I started to feel happy. I was decorating the nursery, I didn't know what I was having but was secretly hoping for a girl. Of course, Shane wanted a boy.

Shane still wasn't home much. On the weekends, he would go to the gun club, which was fine by me as I liked being on my own. Every few weeks, he would go away with his new friends on shooting trips. I didn't mind. I spent my time reading books on raising a healthy baby and what to expect during my pregnancy. I would sing songs to my baby. I wanted her to know my voice and that I would always be there for her.

On Thursday night, we were watching the TV when the phone rang. It was the hospital. My mum had had a heart attack and was in an emergency ward. She had me down as next of kin. I didn't know why, because I hadn't spoken to her since I had left home over two years ago. They told me she was stable; I should go up and see her, I thought to myself, but I didn't feel anything for my mother. Shane said he would take me up in the morning. By morning, Mum was dead. I didn't know how to feel, and I didn't even cry. My aunty organised the funeral. I went and sat up the back where no one would see me. I was the black sheep of the family, the outcast. I slipped away without talking to anybody, still not a tear.

Shane didn't even go. He said he had a lot of work to do. I didn't care. He had never met her anyway. Driving home after the funeral, I decided I was going to be a good mother to my child and never let anyone hurt my baby.

Weeks passed. My aunt dropped off a box of my mother's belongings. She thought I should have them. She was so cold to me. I think she thought I was to blame for my mother's problems because I didn't go home when my sister died.

I started going through my mother's items when I found her diaries. I didn't know Mum had kept diaries. I found myself sitting on the floor in the nursery, reading them. It was dated the day of my wedding, the diary read, "Today, my daughter got married to a wonderful man who I know will look after her. I know I was a terrible mother to my daughters. I tried my best." I started crying. The tears were running down my face. I kept reading. "I always hoped my daughter would marry someday, that would make me so happy. I couldn't be more proud." I was sobbing. I hadn't realised my mother even knew I was married. There were a few pieces of jewellery, nothing valuable, my mum didn't have that much, and a picture of my dad, my real dad. It was old and a bit crumpled. I had never had a picture of my dad. Maybe things would have been better if he hadn't died.

After that day, I decided to try harder to be a better housewife. I kept the house tidy. I tried to keep everything as perfect as I could. I was trying to please Shane, wanting him to be pleased with me. I cooked his favourite foods. He still found faults in the things I did. The food was too dry, and the chips were cold. I didn't think I could ever please him. I was sitting at the table writing out my shopping list, and he was looking over my shoulder, telling me what we should and shouldn't buy.

Shane controlled our money, and I wasn't allowed to overspend on groceries. He checked the dockets when he got home from work, making sure I didn't.

Once, I bought a new dress I liked. It was on sale. We fought over the price. I told him I needed it as I had outgrown all my clothes. I didn't have anything except Tee shirts and tights to wear. He let me keep the dress, but every time I wore it, he reminded me about wasting money and would comment, "It just makes you look fat anyway."

"I'm pregnant!" I would fight back.

"You better fit back into your old clothes when the baby's born," he would say to me. "I don't want a fat wife." Then he would try and tell me he was joking. I knew he wasn't.

The day came; I was in labour all day. Shane just left me there. He said he was busy at work, and the nurse told him it could take all day. He made it back in time for our daughter to be born. Elizabeth, I called her. Shane didn't care what name I chose, because it wasn't a boy. I had disappointed him again.

I loved my baby. She was beautiful. Blonde, blue eyes, perfect. She was my reason to live. I had to look after her. I wasn't going to let anyone ever harm her, my beautiful Elizabeth.

Shane was the perfect dad in front of his friends. Making out he changed her nappies and fed her bottles, with his beer in the other hand. His friends would say how lucky I was to have such a good husband. I never told anyone about the mental and physical abuse I had to live with, and I had no confidence; he had drained it all from me. He was making me paranoid about everything I did. I felt worthless.

He never hit me much, but he would grab me by the arm so hard when he was trying to make me listen to him, which left me with bruises. If I went out, I would usually wear long sleeves, so no one noticed.

I loved the long weekends. Shane would go away for four days. I loved having that time to myself, and I could play my music. I had my old records, all my favourites. *Bohemian Rhapsody* by *Queen* on my *A Night at the Opera* album. I would sing at the top of my voice. I never sang when Shane was around. He would tell me, "Shut up, you sound like a sick dog."

Elizabeth loved me singing. She would lie there, smiling at me.

"I have to get out of here…" I would sing so loud with real meaning behind those words. Elizabeth knew all my dreams. I told her. One day, we would get out of here. I had to for Elizabeth.

Chapter 17

Elizabeth was growing fast. She was nearly one. I thought about getting a job. I had to get out of the house. I was going stir crazy. I needed to have some grown-up company. I never saw any of my old friends. I don't think any of them knew where I lived.

I saw a job in the local paper at a steak house part-time, working nights. That would work well. Shane could watch Elizabeth. She slept well so we wouldn't need a sitter. The extra money would be nice. I could buy myself some new clothes. Shane never let me buy anything; he said we couldn't afford it.

I cooked a special meal, roast chicken dinner with gravy, Shane's favourite. I got Elizabeth to bed early, so I could get the dinner ready on time. At ten past six, I heard the bike pull in the driveway. It was the same every night. He would come in and complain about what a crap day he'd had. I had a cold beer waiting for him.

"Dinner's ready," I told him, handing him a beer.

"Good, I'm starved," he replied. "Roast chicken. Great, my favourite." He sat down to eat.

"Shane, I was wondering about getting a part-time job."

"You can't. You have to mind Elizabeth," he snapped back.

"Yeah, I know, but if I only worked a couple of nights a week, the extra money would come in handy, and you could watch Elizabeth. She would sleep anyway."

He said nothing for a while, just ate his dinner. Finally, he spoke. "Maybe one night a week. But you'll never find a job anyway. Who'd hire you?"

The next day, I rang up about the job at the Steak House. I had an interview on Monday. I asked my neighbour Mary if she would mind Elizabeth. She was a nice old lady who spoke to me often over the fence and loved Elizabeth. She said she was happy to look after her. I hardly saw any of my old friends anymore, so I had no help at all; I was very much a loner. I hadn't been on a motorbike since being pregnant. I missed our bike rides. Shane still went on long trips, every now and then, but I stayed home. I had the car there, but that was for shopping.

Monday came, and I went for the job interview. I didn't tell Shane just in case I didn't get it. He would just put me down. I had a lot of experience making hamburgers from working at the Ampol, and I'm sure I could handle steaks. The interview went well, and I think I had a good chance. They said they would call by Friday.

I did my shopping on Thursday, as I wanted to wait by the phone in case they called. I still hadn't told Shane.

I waited at home all day. It was nearly four o'clock, and I was starting to think I didn't get the job. Finally, the phone rang. My heart was racing. It was Jerry from the steak house, and I got the job! He wanted me to start on Saturday night, from 6 pm till 10.30 every week. Fantastic, I thought.

"Mummy's got a job!" I shouted as I picked up Elizabeth from her play mat. She was giving me the best smiles.

Shane was not impressed when I told him. He just wanted to know how much they were paying me and told me I better not neglect the house or Elizabeth or I would have to quit. God, he can be a bastard when he wants. But I was not going to let him get to me, because I was so excited.

Saturday came. I put Elizabeth to bed at 5.30 pm. I hoped she would sleep well, or I would hear about it when I returned home.

I arrived at work. Jerry was my boss, his wife Margaret worked there too. They hired me so Margaret could have a night off. Troy, their son, also worked there. He was a bit up himself, but he was okay. We served steaks with baked potatoes and lots of different toppings. We provided takeaway as well as sit-down service. This place was trendy. We were flat out busy, and I thought I kept up okay. I had to follow Troy around until I learnt the ropes. Troy was only 18. I wasn't used to getting told what to do by someone younger than me. The time flew so fast, and it was 10.30 pm before I knew it. They seemed happy with me.

I had been working for Jerry for three months. I was practically running the steak house on my own. Sometimes I worked Friday nights as well. Shane didn't mind, and I think he liked having his personal space.

Until one night, when I came home, Shane was so pissed off. Elizabeth had been sick, and she had thrown up all over her cot. I went in to check on her. Her bed had been stripped, and she was lying on the bare mattress in her cot, wearing only a nappy. She was asleep, but I could tell she had been crying. She must have cried herself to sleep; I picked her up and cuddled her. I put her on my bed, still asleep. I made her cot up and dressed her in her pyjamas and tucked her in. I didn't bother arguing with Shane, as I was tired. I had a shower and went to bed.

After that night, I was thinking about what was best for Elizabeth. Did I want her to grow up in this place? I'd made a big mistake marrying Shane. I used to think that Elizabeth needed her father, but after that night, I wasn't so sure. Elizabeth shouldn't have to live with my mistakes.

I used to have such dreams of making it big, getting out of this town. Maybe I could do it. I could head down to Sydney, get myself a good job and maybe do a course. I didn't know what but anything had to be better than living here.

The following week, I received a call from work. It was Margaret. She told me Jerry was sick and they had to go to Sydney for his treatment; he had leukaemia. They needed me to help Troy run the restaurant.

Oh, my God. I hope Jerry will be okay.

"Yes, of course, I'll help, but I'll have to bring Elizabeth with me." So I packed the fold-up cot and a few toys and set it up in the corner of the shop. I had left a note for Shane before heading off to work. I went in every day to work for two weeks. I didn't get paid for all that time. They couldn't afford it while Jerry was having treatment. After two weeks, they came home. Jerry looked awful, and he was so thin. They came back for a break. He still had to have a blood test every day.

Jerry had woken up with a burst blood vessel in his eye. That's how it started. He went to the doctor and had a blood test. Bang! He had leukaemia, just like that.

Jerry wasn't home long, only five days before he got rushed back to Sydney. The treatment wasn't working. Troy's sister turned up. She was at uni in Adelaide. It wasn't looking good for Jerry.

A week later, Jerry died. It was a Thursday. They decided to close the doors of the steak house for a week so that the family could organise the funeral. It was so sad. One minute you're okay, the next you're dead.

After the funeral, Troy told me they were going to sell the business. I kept working two nights a week until the steak house had sold. It took eight weeks.

Having Jerry die like that made me so angry and more determined to get the hell out of this town and away from Shane. Jerry was such a nice bloke, always having a joke, making us laugh. Why did he have to die? There are so many people out there that should be dead, but they keep on living. Life sucks.

Chapter 18

New people bought the restaurant. They were okay, but it wasn't the same. I decided to quit and do a TAFE course at college. I went to enrolment day to see what I could do. I didn't have any computer skills. Computers were just about everywhere now, so I decided to do a computer course for beginners.

I wasn't feeling very confident. I hadn't been very good at school, and my spelling was terrible. I would get my letters back to front and mixed up. My teachers used to think I was so dumb. We only had a few computers at school, which I never got to use. If I were going to have any chance of making it in Sydney, I would have to learn how to use one, so I could get a good job.

I started a course in 'Computer application for the office'. It was supposed to be an excellent starting course. There were about fifteen women in the class. I made friends with a few of them. One, in particular, was Caroline. We hit it off straight away. Caroline was so much fun. She would always say exactly what was on her mind and didn't care if she offended anyone. She would say, "If you can't handle the truth, don't sit with me." I loved that about her. She was brilliant. She was always helping me with the computer as she was only doing the course as a refresher. She could already type, really fast; I was so slow. I had to work on my typing to get my speed up.

My teacher noticed my typing mistakes. She asked me if I was dyslexic. I had no idea, and I didn't even know what that was. She was so lovely and gave me some information on it. She said her brother had dyslexia. After reading all about it, I realised that maybe I was dyslexic. That meant I wasn't dumb at all. She said her brother started reading every day and had improved. Perhaps I could do this course and get the hell out of this town.

I went to TAFE for two days a week. Mary next door looked after Elizabeth for me. She was so lovely. I think she felt sorry for me. I'm sure she must have heard Shane screaming at me, but she never said anything.

Caroline and I became good friends. She was married too. She had two sons, but they were both at school. She would visit me during the day when Shane was at work. Caroline came from Sydney, as her husband got a transfer with his work. He was a technician. I'd never met him, but Caroline said he was her second husband, her first husband used to beat the crap out of her.

"How did you leave him?" I asked. She told me that one night he had bashed her so severely the neighbours called the police, and he was arrested. Child Services put her and her sons in emergency accommodation, and she hadn't seen him since. I thought about it for a minute. Shane would kill me if I did that. He always said while cleaning his guns, "If anyone came in to take his family away, he would shoot them without a second thought." I would have to come up with a better plan than the police.

Some days, Shane was quite good. He would play with Elizabeth. Sometimes, he would get a bit rough, and she would cry, but then he would make her laugh. I don't think Shane knew how to love, and I think it frustrated him. He was so hot and cold. I think his father must have beaten him or something. He never talked about his family; he had a sister, but I'd never met her. I was not even sure where she lived. Part of me felt sorry for him. The other part of me wished he would disappear.

My course only went for six months, which seemed to go quickly. Caroline had a good job working as a secretary for a law firm. She was so lucky, as she already knew what she was good at; I didn't want to be a secretary sitting at a desk all day; I knew I'd go nuts. I only just passed the course. Caroline helped me get through it, but I still didn't know what I wanted to do. I always loved movies and wanted to be a movie star or a director of films. That would never happen by staying here. I needed to get out of this town. But how?

Chapter 19

I got another job at a coffee shop, this time it was a rather large café and very busy. I worked with seven other girls. I didn't like them much as it was a very bitchy group. There was only one person I got along with at work, Melissa. She was a lot older than me, in her thirties. I was twenty now. We had our breaks at the same time. I told her about wanting to get out of this town and move to the city. One day, she noticed a large bruise on my arm.

"Did your husband do that?" she asked, I didn't say a word, but she knew.

She told me about her sister, who lived in Sydney. She worked at a club in Kings Cross as a stripper, and she made a lot of money. She had already bought herself a house in the city.

"I don't think I could be a stripper," I told her.

She laughed. "No, I mean she has a spare room she might rent to you if you need a place to stay."

Oh, wow, that would be great, I thought. I finally had a tiny light of hope. I told her about Brett and how I was hoping he would come back someday; he was my best friend. But if I moved, he wouldn't know where I was, and he'd never find me. If I left Shane, I couldn't stay in town. He would track me down, but it gave me something to think about anyway.

A few months had passed when I ran into Keith at the shops. I hadn't seen him for the longest time. We had coffee.

"How have you been?" I asked, quite excited to catch up with him. He asked about Shane and Elizabeth.

"They're both fine. Elizabeth is with my neighbour."

I don't know how he knew, but he knew I wasn't happy.

"If he's not treating you well, you should get out," he told me.

I told him it's not so bad. I asked him if he ever heard from Brett.

"I thought you knew."

"Knew what?" I asked.

"Brett was killed in an accident."

I couldn't believe what I was hearing. I think Keith was a little shocked at my reaction. No one knew what Brett and I had together. Our friendship was pure. My eyes just overflowed with tears.

My grief was unbearable. I had to pull myself together, and I had to get out of this town. That was my goal now. Nothing was keeping me here.

I worked hard and saved money on the side. It was hard to hide the money from Shane, so I went without a lot. My goal was three hundred dollars. I figured that would get me by, at least for four weeks to give me time to find a job. I was going to do this.

It took me nearly three months to save enough money. Shane was planning a shooting trip away for a few days. That might be the perfect time to take off to Sydney, no chance of him getting suspicious. I set the date I was to leave in two weeks on Saturday morning. Shane was going away on Friday after work. That gave me Friday night to pack. I booked a train ticket to Sydney for Saturday morning. Shane wouldn't be back until Sunday night. I would be already in Sydney by the time he got back.

I spoke to Melissa about my plan. She gave me her sister's address and phone number. Melissa talked to her sister about me, and she was happy to put me up for a while. I gave notice at work.

The day had come. I hadn't packed anything as I didn't want Shane to have any inkling of what I was about to do. I came home from my last day at work. They gave me a box of chocolates for my farewell, which was kind of them. They didn't know I was moving to Sydney. I didn't tell them in case Shane came looking for me. I told them I couldn't work because of Elizabeth. Melissa kept my secret. She was such a good friend, and I would miss her. She said she would come down one day for a visit.

When I got home, I gave Mary my neighbour the chocolates for minding Elizabeth. I couldn't keep them; Shane would think I was having an affair or something. There would be too many questions.

I came home, fed Elizabeth and got her ready for bed just like usual. Shane came in, eager to get out the door. I could have had my bags packed. He never looked twice at me.

As soon as he left, I grabbed my suitcase. I wasn't going to be able to take everything. I had to take Elizabeth's things, as well. She'd outgrown a lot of her clothes. I just grabbed the clothes that fit her, and I couldn't take many toys. The rocking horse she got for Christmas would have to be left behind. I packed a few photos, not that I had many. I couldn't fit my coat in so I decided to wear it. I packed only one record, *Queen* that Brett had given me. I had to leave the rest, and I'll rebuy them one day, I thought to myself. I sat on my case so I could zip it up. I also packed a sizeable nappy bag with baby bottles and snacks for the trip and a few books for Elizabeth to read. She loved her books.

The train was leaving at 7.58 am. I would have to get up early so I wouldn't miss the train. I set my alarm for 6.30 am. Elizabeth usually woke up at about 7 am.

I went to bed early so I would wake up on time, but I couldn't sleep. I tossed and turned all night, looking at the clock every hour. When my alarm went off, I awoke feeling awful. I was feeling sick to my stomach. I got up and had a shower. I thought that might make me feel better. It did slightly.

I ate some breakfast, then went and threw up in the toilet. I had to get myself right, so I poured myself some lemonade. It seemed to help a little. I booked a cab for 7.15. It was getting late, so I better get Elizabeth up. She was still asleep.

I gently woke her. She rolled over having a stretch. She probably would have slept another hour at least. I picked her up, laid her on the changing table to change her nappy and get her dressed. I gave her a bottle. I would give her some breakfast on the train. I sat Elizabeth on the floor with some toys while I moved our suitcase out the front. The cab would be here any minute. I also had the pram, which would come in handy when we got there. Elizabeth was nearly one and a half and very heavy. I saw the cab pull up, and the driver got out to help me load the car. I went back in to get Elizabeth; she was already running towards the front door, so I picked her up and the nappy bag and locked the door.

I booked my suitcase and pram through with the luggage. I only had the nappy bag and Elizabeth to carry. By the time I found my seat and sat down, I thought I was going to collapse. It was so good to sit down. We now had an eight-hour trip to Sydney. I didn't realise I was trembling. It suddenly hit me as the train moved off that I was free; I caught my breath. I had done it!

Chapter 20

Elizabeth was pretty good. She slept for about two hours after breakfast. I just kept feeding her, trying to distract her. She started to get whingey for the last few hours. I gave her another bottle, so she slept for another hour and then woke with twenty minutes until we reached Sydney. A nice lady was sitting across the aisle, and she offered me some fruit. I was feeling a bit hungry, so I took an apple and said thanks. She asked where I was heading. I told her I was going to our new home.

I read Elizabeth her three books I had brought with us at least ten times. As the train made its way into Sydney, I was so excited. I had never been to Sydney before. Looking at the buildings, I thought I might see the Harbour Bridge, but I didn't. We stopped at Strathfield for a short time. The next stop was Central, that's where we get off. I packed up all our stuff, making sure nothing was left behind. There weren't many people left on the train. Central was the last stop; everyone was getting off.

I picked up Elizabeth and carried the nappy bag with my other hand. As the doors opened, we stepped onto the platform. I looked around, trying to see where to get my luggage. I spotted a sign and headed up to get my bag and pram. The attendant helped me open the pram up so I could put Elizabeth in. That was a relief – she was so heavy. I thanked him.

We had arrived. I had Elizabeth in her pram, with the nappy bag on top so I could carry my suitcase. I started pushing Elizabeth down the platform at Central. This woman was waving, heading straight for me.

"Stephanie!" she yelled. It was Melissa's sister, Rachel. She looked just like Melissa, except a lot younger.

She was so lovely, helping me carry my bag. She talked nonstop as we walked.

"Melissa said you had a beautiful daughter. She wasn't wrong. She is just gorgeous."

"Thanks," I managed to get a word in. "I thought you lived in Kings Cross?"

I noticed a sign to Kings Cross, but we were heading in the other direction as we walked up the road.

"No, I work at Kings Cross, but I live in Redfern. It's cheaper."

It was quite a walk up the hill, and I was starting to feel it in my legs. Rachel must be fit, as she didn't seem to notice the steep hill at all.

We finally got there. It was a two-storey terrace house. Rachel's place was at the end of a row of them. We walked through the gate and three steps in the front door, down a long hallway, which was quite dark. The light at the end was the kitchen.

"Come straight through," Rachel said as she led the way. It was a very narrow house, but there was plenty of room. Rachel showed me around. I picked Elizabeth up out of the pram and followed her back towards the front door. On the right was going to be my room, which I would share with Elizabeth. It was quite large with a double bed and a cot. Rachel told me she picked the furniture up on the street side for free as someone was throwing it out. Great, I thought, it looked like new. Opposite my bedroom was a small lounge room with one armchair, a sofa, a coffee table and a small TV in front of the window.

Rachel pointed up the stairs. "My room is upstairs. I have my bathroom and a study that is full of junk. Back through the kitchen and down the other end is another bathroom for you and Elizabeth," she said as we walked through the kitchen. The bathroom was near the back door. Out the back, she opened the door, a rather small courtyard and a shed, which was the laundry, a clothesline and a small garden full of weeds.

This place was amazing! I put my bags in my room and changed Elizabeth, and her nappy was so wet. Rachel had made some lasagne for dinner. She had to go to work, so she gave me a key. Rachel showed me where everything was in the kitchen. Then she left. She said she wouldn't be home till after 2 am.

I fed Elizabeth and put her to bed, heated some lasagne for myself then sat at the small table. I was so tired. I had a hot shower then I lay down and fell asleep. It was only 7.30 pm.

I didn't hear Rachel come in.

I tried not to make too much noise in the morning, as Rachel would be tired. She would need a good night of sleep after working so late. I did some washing, as we didn't have many clothes. So I washed what we wore yesterday and hung them on the line. I put the kettle on to make a cup of tea, and Elizabeth went down for a morning nap. I then sat at the table to drink my tea. Rachel didn't show herself until near lunchtime.

We sat and talked. I told Rachel I needed to get a job. She was so accommodating. She told me about this coffee shop only a short walk away.

"They might be hiring," she said. Rachel was twenty-five. She had been living in Sydney since she was eighteen. She didn't have a boyfriend. "It was hard to keep a boyfriend when you're a stripper. They can't handle it," she said.

But she told me she loved her job. She made a lot of money, and nobody controlled her, and that was the way she liked it. She said she didn't want to settle down until at least thirty-five so she had plenty of time. She said men were no good until they were forty. They never knew what they wanted. She seemed to have them all worked out.

After lunch, Rachel, Elizabeth and I went for a walk. We pushed the pram down the road and turned the corner. Wow, there were so many shops lining the streets. Restaurants, a book shop, clothing shops, takeaway food shops, minimarket and coffee shops. Everything you could ever want right around the corner. I was starting to feel like I had made the right decision.

Rachel watched the pram while I went into the coffee shop to ask if there might be any work going. The first coffee shop said no, but took Rachel's phone number in case anything came up. The next coffee shop sounded more promising. They said they might be able to offer me three days a week. The boss wasn't there at the moment, but they told me to call back in an hour.

I took Elizabeth home for a nap. Rachel watched her while I walked back to the coffee shop. I spoke to the boss, and I told him I was very experienced at working in coffee shops. He said I could start tomorrow at 10 am till 4 pm. Fantastic! I felt so relieved I had a job. Rachel said she wouldn't mind looking after Elizabeth, as I would get home before Rachel went to work. I hadn't felt this happy in such a long time. I couldn't stop smiling.

Chapter 21

Living in the city was so fabulous. My job was going well. My boss was lovely. His name was Colin, and his wife was Daniella. She didn't work there, but she popped in every day to do the banking. Last week, Rachel brought Elizabeth up to meet everyone. After I had been working there for two weeks, I felt like part of the family.

I wasn't earning much, so money was tight. It was a good thing I had saved before moving to Sydney. I had to spend money to buy some linen for myself and Elizabeth as I couldn't keep using Rachel's. She was already so kind and generous to us. She only took a small amount of rent, and she said not to worry about the electricity or phone, but I didn't know anyone to ring anyway.

Colin had two sons. They went to high school and usually stopped into the shop after school to have a feed. Sarah was the other lady who worked there. She only worked for two hours over the busy time at lunch. I worked Wednesday, Thursday and Friday. They offered me work on Saturday, but Rachel worked late on Friday and Saturdays and slept until midday so she wouldn't be able to mind Elizabeth. But it was okay. I earned enough to get by. Rachel and I split the food bill, and we took turns cooking. I still managed to save a little.

I had been living in Sydney for three weeks and hadn't been down to the harbour. So I took Elizabeth, and we caught the bus down to Circular Quay. Oh, wow! It was beautiful. The Harbour Bridge was spectacular, and we walked around to the Opera House. It was amazing. Far better than any pictures I had seen. I walked my legs off. We went around past the Opera House, through the Botanical Gardens, and we stopped to have a picnic lunch that I had made. Elizabeth was chasing the seagulls, having a lovely time. It was the best day. I truly fell in love with Sydney that day.

That night, I slept well, feeling very safe. I hadn't felt this happy in the longest time. I felt good about my decision to move to Sydney, and I knew Elizabeth was going to be happy here too; this was our new home.

Nothing much changed until I met this fantastic guy, Adrien. He was gay and such a fun guy. Adrien started to become a regular customer. We used to chat when I had my break. We just got on so well becoming good friends. Adrien worked in the city and had just moved a couple of blocks away from where I worked. I invited him over to my place for lunch on Saturday; he said he would love to come. I told him all about Elizabeth, and he couldn't wait to meet her.

Saturday came. I got up reasonably early to tidy up, not being too noisy as Rachel was still sleeping. Elizabeth was now twenty-one months old and was running around everywhere. I had made her a sandpit in the backyard, which she loved. She would spend most of her day out there.

Adrien was a vegetarian, so I made a veggie lasagne and put it in the oven. It would be ready in time for lunch. That's when I noticed Elizabeth covered in sand coming in the back door. I took one step towards her when there was a knock at the front door.

"Oh, Adrien must be early." I went to open the door. "Adrien, Hi!"

He kissed me on the cheek. "Hello, darling." He called everyone darling.

He came in with a bag full of stuff. We walked through to the kitchen, and he set his bag on the table and started to unpack.

"Wine for us." He handed me two bottles of red wine. "Water crackers and dip for later and a cute ragdoll for Elizabeth." He looked around "Where is she?" he asked.

"She's still out the back. She's been playing in the sandpit, so she's a bit grubby."

I followed Adrien out the back. Elizabeth was in her sandpit, digging up all the sand and dumping the sand all over the path and making a mess.

Adrien and Elizabeth got on famously, and she loved him. He was just a big kid himself. We had a lovely lunch, and Rachel came down and joined us. It was such a great afternoon.

Adrien was telling me all about this theatre group which he belonged to and wanted me to join. It was an Amateur Theatre Musical Company, and they needed extra people all the time. They met twice a week for rehearsals. I was so tempted, I wanted to, but Elizabeth was still only a baby.

"No excuse," Adrien said. He didn't leave till after eight o'clock. He was going out clubbing with his gay friends. Nothing happened until after eight.

That night, all I could think of was joining the theatre group. It was what I had always wanted to do. Well, I wanted to make movies, but the theatre was kind of the same.

A few weeks had passed when Adrien dropped in at work to tell me there was an audition on tonight for *Godspell* the musical.

"You're coming, and I'll pick you up at 7.30."

Before I had a chance to argue, Adrien had gone. I looked over at Colin.

"I guess you're going to audition tonight," he said, handing me someone's order. I took the coffees to a table.

I was feeling slightly nervous. I didn't think I could audition; it terrified me.

It was a Wednesday; Rachel said she would mind Elizabeth for me. I had Elizabeth in bed sound asleep. Adrien was picking me up; he had a little Mitsubishi Hatch. It was only a short drive to the theatre; it was called 'Blue Line Theatre'. We went inside and everybody knew Adrien. There was a lady named Sue in the foyer. She had two forms to fill out. One was to become a member and the other one was what part I wanted to audition for; I suddenly got nervous again. I can't audition. I started to panic; Adrien noticed the panicked look on my face.

"It's okay, just put down chorus. You don't have to audition for the chorus," Adrien said.

"Oh, thank God!" I was about to run and hot tail out of there.

It was open auditions, so we got to sit in the theatre and watch everyone audition. It was quite good. The director's name was Bill. He played the piano for some of the auditions. Some had their music on a cassette tape. In the end, everyone went out to the foyer for tea or coffee and a chat so the director, choreographer and casting committee could talk. I met a few people of all ages. There were young teens about eighteen and some as old as seventy and everywhere in between. Everyone was friendly, a great atmosphere.

After about 20 minutes, they opened the theatre doors, and we all went back in and took a seat. They announced who had been selected for the various parts. Adrien and this guy Stephen had got the two leads. Stephen was Jesus, and Adrien was playing John. They were so good; Adrien had a beautiful voice. The part of Mary went to this girl called Cassie. Adrien said she always got the lead, but she was excellent.

They told us all rehearsals would start next week – two nights a week, Monday and Wednesday from 8 pm till 10.30 pm. The show would be on in 14 weeks. Rachel was able to mind Elizabeth on rehearsal nights, which worked out well. I was so pleased. Otherwise, it would be too hard if I had to take Elizabeth all the time.

Wow! I was in the chorus. The first night we were given sheet music to learn. The songs were great – very upbeat. We just all sat there learning the songs. I couldn't read music, so I just winged it, following everyone else. I met a few people. Gabriella was on the committee, and she was so lovely we hit it off straight away. She was just a little older than me. David, he was so funny; he was a retiree and had an Irish accent, but he had been in Australia for over thirty years. He was such a great character and very friendly. He always came out with funny jokes, usually Irish.

After a few weeks, we were starting to sound pretty good. The leads came an hour early, to practise one-to-one with Bill. That night, Sue and Andrew came to measure us for costumes. They asked us if we had anything that would be suitable, of course, I didn't, but I offered to help by looking in op shops. They told me what to look for; they wanted seventies' style clothing with bright colours.

On my day off, I took Elizabeth for a walk in the pram to visit the op shops. There were a few in walking distance. I found a fantastic rainbow vest for $1.50. Great. I also found hot pink Saturn pants, they looked terrific, and they were only a dollar. I bought them both. I also picked up some clothes for Elizabeth. They were practically new, and she was growing so fast that nothing was fitting her. I also got myself a pair of boots. I tried them on, they were perfect, and they still had plenty of wear left in them. Only two dollars a bargain. Going to the op shop became my Monday outing with Elizabeth. I picked up some great clothes, so cheap.

At the next rehearsal, I took the clothes that I had bought in to show Sue and Andrew. They loved them. Not for me, though. Sue said they had found this mini skirt and long black boots for me. I wasn't so sure about the boots; they were way too high. Thank goodness, they were too small.

Rehearsals were going well, and the show was starting to take shape. Everyone was learning their lines. We all got on really great. No bitching except on the way home Adrien might have had a little bitch about someone; he was such a drama queen.

Gabriella was the secretary of the company, so she used to make sure we had plenty of tea and coffee for rehearsals. She always turned up with her arms full of milk and biscuits. We were becoming good friends. Gabriella had been with the company for two years; she said it was her little hobby.

Chapter 22

The show was taking shape. We had learnt a few dances and making progress having such a great time. We opened in three weeks. The 'move-in date' for the set building is next week. Everyone was supposed to help with the set build or costumes. I was looking forward to it. I couldn't sew, but I could paint and hammer a nail. Gabriella laughed.

"There will be plenty to do," she said.

Our set designer was Mitch. He had just started to turn up at rehearsals, and he also set up the lights for the shows. He was an electrician, not bad looking; he had a girlfriend called Tracy, and she seemed nice too. Gabriella was good friends with them and introduced us. Gabriella helped backstage as part of the stage crew. I was so impressed. I wished I could do that, although I would have preferred to direct. I wanted to learn everything about making a show. I felt like I was finally where I was supposed to be.

I paid attention to everything. I watched Bill, how he directed, how he had his vision of what he was creating. I wanted to learn it all.

When the set building started, I had to take Elizabeth with me. She was nearly twenty-two months. She had a ball, and everyone loved her. She just wandered around the theatre. I kept her off the stage as there were too many things going on, like power saws. They were building this large scaffold, which was going right along the back of the stage. It was to be climbed on for most of the scenes in the show. The scaffold was the only part that wasn't to be moved, so it had to be stable.

Old Bill was our carpenter, and he did most of the building. He picked up some scraps and made Elizabeth a wooden truck with wheels. She thought it was great. She played with it all over the theatre.

It was getting close to the morning tea break, so I went to help in the kitchen. Gabriella had been shopping and had bought some cakes, bread and fillings for lunch. I helped make tea and coffee for everyone. Old Bill was the president of the company. He was such a friendly guy, probably in his sixties; he was very old-fashioned and didn't take any crap from anybody.

Everyone stopped for morning tea. We had cans of drink for the ones who didn't like tea or coffee, which was mainly the younger ones.

Elizabeth was whingeing. She was overdue for her nap. I changed her, put her in her pram with a bottle and rocked her until she fell asleep. Everyone was back working by then. I went to help Gabriella clean up. The kitchen was a bit of a mess, coffee cups everywhere. Gabriella and I were still getting to know each other. She was married and had a daughter who was eight, called Becca, and her husband ran his own business. He was an accountant. She said her husband didn't like the theatre much. But he was happy for her to be involved. He sounded like a nice guy. Shane would never have let me join a theatre company.

Gabriella said she just enjoyed the people and this was her social life, gave her a break from home. She was quite happy, but she needed her own space, and the theatre gave her that. I knew what she meant.

Almost everyone involved in the show had regular day jobs, so we only really had the weekends to set build. We couldn't work during rehearsal because it was too noisy. Sometimes old Bill would try hammering something during rehearsals only to be told to shut up by Bill, our director. Old Bill would grumble under his breath then pack up and head home.

Adrien was such a drama queen. One week, he picked me up for rehearsal with blue hair. He had dyed it for the show and said it made him look more dashing. It was so crazy. He said I should dye mine.

"No way," I was quick to answer. I had plans to plait my whole head with tiny braids. Rachel said she would help me.

We finally made it, dress rehearsal, and that's where I met Chris. He was running the lights for the show. The lighting box was at the back of the theatre. Mitch had a few extra people working as stage crew: Karen, Pete and Tracy. They all worked together during the last show and made a good team.

I only had one costume. I ended up wearing rainbow pants with a bright yellow T-shirt. I didn't have to wear any shoes, which made the dance I had to do a lot easier. Bill, the director, had an electric piano, which he set up on the side of the stage. We also had an electric guitar that belonged to Wayne. He played pretty well. We had two dress rehearsals, which was a good thing as the first rehearsal was terrible. There was a problem with the sound and the microphone wasn't working. Everyone was getting very stressed. We were glad when it was time to go home.

The next day, Rachel had to plait my hair. We sat in the lounge room watching a video of *Grease*. Rachel loved it, and so did I. It took most of the movie to do my whole head. I had forty-seven plaits. She put a coloured bead on the end of each braid. It looked fantastic when she had finished. I got up to look in the bathroom mirror. Wow, I loved it. All ready for final dress rehearsal tonight.

The last dress rehearsal was much better, but Stephen kept forgetting his lines. Everyone was worried. The chorus and the rest of us were pretty good. Opening night was the next night. It was all so exciting, and tickets were selling well. There were still some seats left, but they were hoping to sell them at the door.

After rehearsals had finished, a few of us helped finish the set build. Mitch, Trace, Karen, Pete and Chris all stayed back. There was still a lot of things that needed to be finished, just fiddly stuff, like tying back cords that were hanging or taping them up if they could trip people, a little touch up of paint here and there. Gabriella was still there as well. She was filling up the fridge in the kitchen for the canteen in preparation for the show. She had a lot of boxes from the can drinks that she had unloaded into the refrigerator. I helped flatten the empty boxes so they could fit in the rubbish bin. Chris walked in at the right time to help carry them to the dumpster out the back.

Opening night finally came after all of our hard work. I knew we had a good show, as long as Stephen remembered his lines.

Well, he did, and we had a full house. It was fabulous. We got a standing ovation, and it was magic! I had never experienced anything like it. I loved being in the show. Everyone had friends or family attending. They all ran up into the foyer to see them. I didn't have anyone to come and see me, but that was okay. I was doing this for me. For the first time, I was starting to feel good about myself. I was beginning to get confidence.

After the show, we had the best opening night party. Adrien got so drunk that I didn't know how he would perform the next night. Gabriella, Trace and I bought some scotch, which we shared between us. I didn't drink too much as I had to drive Adrien home.

We had the music playing, *INXS, Queen* and *ABBA*, which I loved. Some of us got up on the stage to dance. We partied into the early hours of the morning.

At about 3 am, Gabriella and I went down to the green room to check everything was locked up. As we walked through, we saw Cassie making out with Stephen. Oh my god, bare bums everywhere.

We ran back upstairs, cracking up laughing. Mitch, Trace and Chris were virtually the only ones left as well as Adrien who had passed out on the lounge in the foyer. Chris was packing his car. Cassie and Stephen came up with their bags and stuff, pretending that nothing had happened. Gabriella couldn't stop laughing. She ran to the toilets to hide, but we could still hear her from the foyer now that the music was off.

"See ya!" Cassie said as she left and so did Stephen. They were both married to different people, so Gabriella told me. I went into the toilets and Gabriella was still laughing.

"They've gone, you can stop laughing now," I told her. Gabriella was so drunk.

"How are you getting home?" I asked as we walked out to the foyer.

"Trace is driving me," she slurred out, but Tracy was drunk too. Mitch said he was driving as he'd only had a couple of drinks.

Chapter 23

Every night was just as fantastic as the first night, except it was always the same people staying back after each show, Tracy, Mitch, Chris, Karen, Pete, Adrien, Gabriella and me. Sometimes one or two of the others would stay back if they didn't have work the next day.

We were all becoming terrific friends. Karen was a nurse at St Vincent's Hospital. Karen's husband, Pete, worked night shifts, so he wasn't at every show. Pete worked at the same hospital, but he wasn't a nurse. I wasn't sure what he did. But he made sure he was coming to the final show. Chris was married too, but we never met his wife. Chris was an electrician as well as Mitch; they didn't work at the same place though, and Tracy worked for a ladies fashion shop somewhere near Broadway.

Adrien had been chasing after Mark since rehearsals started. Mark was in the chorus. But Mark said he wasn't gay. Adrien thought he just hadn't come out of the closet yet, so he was still hopeful.

We were having a half-way-through-the-show party at old Bill's place on Sunday for lunch. Everyone involved with the show had been invited. He had a pool, so he told us to bring our swimmers. I didn't own a swimsuit, but I thought it was too cold for swimming anyway. It was only August.

Everyone took a plate of something. Adrien and I brought our homemade bean dip with cob bread, and Adrien had two bottles of champagne. He told me I was driving. I didn't mind, as I could still have fun. Elizabeth came too, so I had to keep her away from the pool. A couple of people went swimming, the younger ones. They were jumping in saying how cold it was. Tina was in the chorus, and she was wearing the smallest bikini I'd ever seen. All the guys couldn't take their eyes off her. She was only eighteen and loving the attention.

I got talking to Chris. He was a nice guy, about forty maybe, he didn't look it. He was quite good looking. He had been with the company for two years as well, like Gabriella.

Adrien got on the piano playing some old musical favourites, and before long, everyone was singing along. We had a great day. Adrien didn't get that drunk, but I drove us home. Elizabeth was asleep in the car. We got back around five, so I put Elizabeth straight to bed. I think the week had caught up with her.

We sat in the lounge room watching the telly. We had no shows until Wednesday night. Rachel was heading out to work. We just sat there watching Countdown on the ABC, exhausted but happy.

"I've been watching Countdown since it started," Adrien said.

"Well, I'm not that old," I said, trying to get a bite from Adrien.

"You're older than me!" he yelled.

I laughed. "Only about a month."

"We should have a huge party next year when we both turn twenty-one," Adrien said.

"You can. I've never worried about my birthday."

Adrien just sat there looking at me for a moment. "Well, twenty-first is a good time to start," he said.

"We could have one party half-way between both our birthdays," Adrien suggested. Nothing more was said about birthdays that night. We just drank our tea.

We were planning a tremendous end-of-show party, and the theme was *Grease*. The movie was released a few years ago. It was an excellent movie, and it had Olivia Newton-John and John Travolta in it. I would love to do that musical someday. I had already picked out what to wear to the party, black tights, a black off-the-shoulder top I had found last week in my favourite op shop, my stilettos and Adrien had a wig he said I could borrow that looked just like Sandy from *Grease*.

We had such a good run of shows. Almost a full house each night and two matinees, which were already sold out. How great was that? I so enjoyed the theatre, but I knew I wanted to direct a show rather than be in it.

I tried talking to Karen about directing, but she laughed it off, saying I needed a lot more years working in shows before I could consider directing a musical.

"Maybe you could be my assistant for the next show," she said before walking off.

"Yes, I would love to!" I said, without thinking twice.

It was our last night. I went shopping to buy some food to take in. We were going to have such a fabulous party. I bought a bottle of scotch, which was going to make me broke, but I wanted to have a good night. After the show finished, I probably wouldn't go out for ages, well, I wouldn't be able to afford it anyway. I paid my rent and had enough food until next payday. I was well over-due for some fun. Rachel was coming to the final show and was bringing Elizabeth. I hoped she would be okay. I thought that Elizabeth was a bit young to sit through a musical, but Rachel had convinced me that she would love it. She said she would take her home after the show so I could stay and party. What a great friend.

Chapter 24

The show went fabulously. Everyone was so full of energy and the backstage crew were all in a real party mood. They were all wearing long hippy wigs with their usual black attire. They looked like part of the show. We had a full house, and they even put a few chairs from the foyer in the aisles because we had people at the door wanting tickets after announcing we had sold out. Mitch was saying that it was illegal and a fire hazard but they did it anyway. The final number was incredible, a standing ovation. So we did an extra encore, they loved us. Everyone was on such a high!

After the final curtain closed, we all ran down to the green room. Some of the cast were already opening bottles of champagne. I quickly got changed and ran up to the foyer to see if Rachel and Elizabeth had enjoyed the show. It was very crowded. Rachel was holding on to Elizabeth, and she was sound asleep. I offered to drive them home. Rachel insisted she was okay; she had already rung for a cab; it would be there any minute. I walked out with her, carrying Elizabeth's bag. Rachel said she had stayed awake for most of it.

"It was brilliant, and you were amazing," she told me. Nobody had ever said that about me before. I was feeling fantastic.

After they left, I went back in for the party. I ran back down to the green room to get my stuff. There was stuff everywhere, clothes, costumes and a foul smell of B.O. Ooh, I had to get out of there! I grabbed all my stuff and put on the wig that Adrien had lent me. I had a quick look in the mirror. I looked great, like sandy from the last scene in *Grease*. I headed upstairs.

The last of the audience were getting ushered out through the exit doors, and they were locked. We could now start our closing night party! The music was on and turned up, and almost everyone had dressed up. Adrien had a fake leather jacket on and had greased his hair. The blue had faded a little, but he looked great. Cassie had a pink wig like Frenchie from *Grease*; she looked so good.

I helped put the food out. Everyone had brought a plate of something, dips, chips, cakes, sausage rolls and meatballs. There was plenty for everyone.

Now all I needed was a drink. Gabriella handed me a glass of bubbly, which I happily drank. I sculled my drink when I heard *Queen's We are the Champions*.

"Let's dance!" I yelled as I ran up on the stage to dance. I loved this song. Everyone started singing. I began to have fun as I used to with Brett. He would have come to see me if he was alive, I thought. I drank so much that night, and I was having a ball.

We partied all night and by about 3 am most had left. Mitch had taken his guitar out, and Adrien was on the piano. Gabriella, Tracy, Karen, Pete, Stephen, Cassie and a couple of others were sitting around singing along to old show songs from Oklahoma and South Pacific to name a few. We kept singing until the sun came up. Adrien was sober by the time we were heading home. So he drove me home. We only had a few hours' sleep as we had to come back at 10 am to pull the set down. It was all over, which was kind of sad.

I went home and crashed into bed. It was 6.10 am. I set my alarm to wake at 9.30 am.

By the time we got back to the theatre, there were only a handful of helpers that turned up, all the usual ones. We were all so tired, but we worked hard. Pulling down a set is a lot faster than building one. We all said our goodbyes and 'see you at the next show', for some. Some people we never saw again; they moved on.

Chapter 25

After the show ended, life went back to normal. I went to work, and Elizabeth was getting older. She was turning two now and up to more mischief like pulling out all Rachel's records. Oh my God, I quickly put them all back before she could notice.

"You mustn't touch," I tried to teach her.

My life wasn't that exciting, being a single mum. I knew my priority was Elizabeth. I wanted her to have everything I didn't have growing up, like a loving home.

Her second birthday was kind of low-key. I didn't know any other kids to invite over for playdates. I decided to throw her a birthday party. I could invite Gabriella and her daughter Becca. Adrien and his boyfriend Peter, I hadn't met him yet, but Adrien was raving about him. I would have loved to invite Tracy and Mitch as well, but I didn't know how to get in touch with them. Gabriella would know. I could give her a call later.

Firstly, I needed to work out if I could afford the birthday party or not. I was sitting at the table with a pen and notepad working out what items would cost. I had overspent during the show, so I was paying for it now. Pretty broke, I thought. I had borrowed money from Rachel, and I had only just finished paying her back. I only got paid on Thursday every fortnight.

If I told everyone to bring their own drinks that would save me some money. I could handle the food – we could have a sausage sizzle with bread rolls. I could make a vegetarian lasagne, as Adrien wouldn't eat meat. Yes, I thought it would be okay.

I rang Gabriella. She said she would love to come and would bring Becca with her. She gave me Tracy's phone number so I could ring her. Gabriella said she would bring some dip and chips as well as a salad.

"It's a good idea for everyone to bring their drinks. It's too expensive, and people don't mind," she said.

That made me feel a little better. I rang Trace, and she said they would love to come. I saw Adrien every Friday after work. He walked me home so that he could have a bitch about everyone at his workplace. Lately, he had been dropping in a few times a week. Adrien was like my best friend.

I had been cooking all day. It was Saturday. Elizabeth's birthday was actually on Wednesday, 14 August, but she wouldn't know. It was more convenient to have a party on a Saturday. I was hoping the weather would warm up a bit, but it was still freezing. We would have to stay inside.

Adrien said he would cook the sausages on the Weber out the back and then bring them in. I told him not to be late. He promised he wouldn't be.

I had everything ready. I put Elizabeth to bed to have an afternoon nap so that she would be awake for her birthday party. I then went to get changed. Rachel said she had the night off so she could help, which was great if Rachel was home. Rachel had been dating this guy from work, Marc. I thought Marc was a sleaze bag, but she liked him. Anyway, they went to pick up some drinks two hours earlier and hadn't come back. Elizabeth was stirring so I quickly got changed when I heard a knock at the door.

It was Adrien by himself.

"Where's Peter?" I asked.

"Don't ask," he said as he walked inside through to the kitchen. I shut the door and followed him through.

"I plan on getting shit-faced tonight. Men are shit," he announced and poured himself a glass of wine. "Where's Elizabeth?" he asked.

"I was just about to get her up." Adrien went to put some music on. I went to get Elizabeth ready.

It wasn't long before everyone had arrived; even Rachel and Marc had finally turned up. Marc was so far up himself; I didn't know what Rachel saw in him.

Mitch ended up cooking the snags as Adrien was too busy getting pissed. I still didn't know what had happened to Peter, but I was sure I would hear about it later. We were all having a great time – the food was excellent. It was getting late, so I got Elizabeth's birthday cake ready. It was in the shape of a rocking horse like the one we had to leave behind. I was always second-guessing myself, whether I had done the right thing. It was Elizabeth's birthday, and no time to think about bad memories, I told myself.

I had hidden the cake on top of the washing machine. I carried it in as everyone sang happy birthday. I placed it on the table in front of Elizabeth. It had two candles, and I had to help her blow them out. Elizabeth was getting tired, but she still ate her cake with most of it all over her face.

Adrien was quite drunk by the time I was putting Elizabeth to bed. Rachel suggested putting her upstairs in her bed, as she would sleep better with less noise. Rachel was going to sleep at Marc's place. They were going out to some nightclub later. Gabriella's husband came by to pick Becca up, as she had netball on tomorrow. What a great guy! So Gabriella could stay and party with us.

After I tidied the kitchen, we all moved to the lounge room where I put some *Queen* music on and sat down with a nice scotch.

Adrien complained, "Not *Queen* again!"

"I love *Queen*," I said quickly.

"We know!" everyone said at once. Mitch dug out a *Led Zeppelin* album.

Before I knew it, *Stairway to Heaven* was on. I suddenly felt depressed. My heart was aching. I looked down at my hand, at my star from Brett. He had always played *Led Zeppelin*; I shot down my scotch. I hadn't told anyone about Brett. He was buried deep in my heart, and I still missed him all the time.

Mitch got his guitar out to play along with the record. Tracey, Gabriella and I decided to play cards for shots. The loser had a shot of scotch. Mitch sat in the corner on the beanbag, strumming his guitar. Adrien was asleep on the sofa. Rachel and Marc had left so we girls sat on the floor around the coffee table playing poker. I was pretty good at poker.

After a few games, I was getting quite pissed myself. I thought I should slow down or I was going to be ill. Tracy was hopeless, even when I let her win, she didn't. Gabriella was getting wasted as she was also drinking champagne. After a while, I was suddenly craving some pot. I knew Adrien would have some; he always had some. I hadn't had any dope since before I'd had Elizabeth. Well, I'd only had it twice before. I couldn't stop thinking about Brett.

"Adrien," I tried to wake him.

"What?" he whined. When I mentioned I wanted a joint, he woke up, a bit surprised. "Really?" he looked at me. I never let him smoke joints in the house usually. I grabbed his bag and gave it to him; he opened up the side pocket and pulled out a joint, lit it and took a drag and then passed it to me. We all had some as we shared it around. After *Led Zeppelin* finished, I put *Queen* on, and we all started to sing, except Trace who ran off to the bathroom.

We all just sat there singing along to all the *Queen* songs. So nobody realised Trace had been in the bathroom for so long. It wasn't until the record needed changing that we noticed Tracey didn't come back.

I went out to the kitchen looking for her, and then I checked the bathroom. I opened the door, and there was Trace lying on the floor. She had been throwing up.

"Are you okay?" I asked. She looked awful, but then Mitch appeared at the door.

"I think I should take her home," he said with a sigh.

Gabriella decided to sleep on the sofa, so I gave her a blanket. Adrien put himself in my bed. I locked up and climbed into bed next to Adrien. Adrien cuddled up to me. He was still upset about Peter and their break up. I was feeling emotional and a little stoned. Before I knew it, we were making out. I think Adrien needed someone, and I needed someone. We were both drunk enough and stoned enough. We gave each other exactly what we needed, sex, nothing complicated. In the end, we just held each other, and he told me about Peter breaking his heart. I told him about Brett and how I had lost him forever. We were both in tears.

To lighten the mood, I said, "Are you sure you're gay?" as we lay there holding each other.

"Fucked if I know, darling." We both fell asleep.

Chapter 26

Nothing changed between Adrien and me. We loved each other, but we never had sex again, and we stayed the best of friends. We were just there for each other when we needed to be.

It wasn't long before Adrien had a new guy that he was crazy about.

We had a peaceful Christmas and an even quieter New Year as Rachel and Adrien went home to visit family. Elizabeth was my only family. It was so tranquil.

It was a new year. I was another year older. I was glad Adrien was away for my birthday. I just ordered some takeaway and played my records. Every birthday, which was 8 January, I played my *Queen* record that Brett left me, which I kept safe in my room. I had a cry and a drink to myself. I was twenty-one now.

We were about to start a new show, 'Anything Goes'. Adrien decided to perform in the show. But I wanted to learn to direct, so I became the assistant director to Karen. I could learn a lot from Karen as she had been doing shows for over 20 years.

I sat on the casting committee and so did Adrien. He was helping with the choreography as well. Julie was the choreographer, but she couldn't be at the auditions. So there were just the three of us. We had a few new people audition that we didn't know, which was great really. Fresh blood, Adrien called them.

Lauren had just moved to the area. She was terrific and had the most beautiful singing voice.

Adrien whispered to me, "That's the ugliest woman I've ever seen, with a voice to kill for."

I couldn't believe he had said that. "That's not very nice."

The auditions went well. We had a great turn up, which made casting easy but also hard, as we had too many choices.

It was a long day. Rachel dropped Elizabeth off at the theatre, as she had to go to work. We had finished by then, but we were still talking and arguing about the lead. Adrien and I thought Lauren was perfect for the role, but Karen was used to working with Cassie. Adrien disagreed. Cassie had been the lead in the last four shows, and it's time we had some new blood.

"Let Cassie do the part of 'Hope', and Lauren can do 'Reno'," Adrien argued with Karen once again. Karen finally agreed but wanted to talk to Cassie first. I think she was worried Cassie might not want that part.

It was getting dark. I wanted to get Elizabeth home. She was running up and down the aisles, driving me crazy. Finally, Karen came back.

"Okay, it's settled, Cassie will be Hope." Hope's part was more for a dancer and Cassie could dance, so I thought it was the best choice.

Everybody had been told their parts and given their scripts and rehearsal times, so we packed up and went home.

I was going to be at every rehearsal this time, being the assistant director.

I was practically living at the theatre. Gabriella was amazing. She was on the committee as secretary of the 'Musical Comedy Company'. She organised tea and coffee, sometimes she even made dinner and heated it for us.

This show was going to be on at the end of summer, so rehearsals went through January and February. The summer flu was going around. Cassie was sick, so she had to take a week off. I had to fill in for her so that rehearsals could continue. It was kind of fun, knowing I was only filling in took the pressure off. So I just mucked around, but I knew all her lines. Karen joked that I was the understudy.

I laughed. "Yeah, right." I hoped she was joking.

A week passed, and Cassie was back good as new.

Two weeks before we opened, we had started the set build. It was to look like a cruise ship with two funnels and two staircases going up each side to the centre. It was going to be a huge set. Karen had her vision of what she wanted, and Bill had to build it.

We had been having quite a few late nights working on the set. We didn't complain; we all enjoyed it; otherwise, we wouldn't do it. Gabriella, Trace and I did most of the painting. We worked well together. One particular night, Chris had joined us. Chris was doing the lights for the show, so he was continually climbing ladders. Mitch was working on the lights helping Chris. Elizabeth was sound asleep. I had made her a bed on some of the seats with a doona, so she was very comfy.

Chris was kind of good looking. A little older, probably in his early forties. The nicest guy. I think I had a crush on him. I needed a cuppa.

"Anyone want a cuppa?" Orders came from everywhere.

"White with two," Mitch yelled.

"White with three," Chris yelled from the top of the ladder.

Bill just said, "Usual, thanks."

We all knew that meant five sugars. Bill had a sweet tooth. Once Gabriella put ten sugars in to see if he noticed, he didn't. He drank it, saying it was a good cup. We all sat down for a break drinking our tea or coffee and eating biscuits.

Not saying that much as we were all exhausted.

"Do you think we'll finish this set by Friday?" Gabriella asked.

"Yeah, no worries," Bill replied, he was always the optimist.

It was getting close to ten o'clock.

"I'm heading home," Bill said. Bill was in his seventies, so Gabriella told me. I hadn't realised he was that old, and he had been here since four o'clock, so Mitch said.

After Bill left, Gabriella, Trace and I decided to start cleaning up, washing our paintbrushes. We had finished most of the painting and were tired. I had borrowed Adrien's car as he said he didn't need it for a few days. So I started to pack the car with my stuff and Elizabeth's endless stuff. She was still asleep, so Chris offered to carry her to the car. That was so nice of him. Such a nice guy, I thought as I drove off home.

The dress rehearsal was chaos. The stage hadn't even been finished yet, and we were opening the next night. We were going to have to stay back late. It was just fiddly things, but they still needed to be done. At least the rehearsal had gone okay, and everyone seemed to remember their lines. Chris was taping down cables on the stage areas so nobody tripped on them. Mitch had been working on all the mics making sure the sound was up and running. We had an electric piano, which was rather loud but sounded great.

Rehearsal had finished, so pretty much everyone was heading home. Everybody needed to rest as it had run late; it was after eleven. Rehearsals were going longer because we had to stop and start a few times for all the sound checks. Adrien took Elizabeth home for me. He said he would stay the night, which he was doing a lot lately so that I could stay later. He got a lift home with Karen and left me the car.

I must have looked stressed as Chris came up behind me to give me a shoulder massage. Oh, it felt so good he gave me goosebumps. I wanted to turn around and rip his clothes off and have him right there on the theatre floor. I couldn't believe I was having such thoughts. I suddenly felt embarrassed. Then he stopped.

"Better get back to work," he said. He walked off to the lighting box to do light checks. I didn't realise how much I was craving his touch. I felt like I had just had the wind kicked out of me. I went out to the kitchen to get a drink of water. I was breathing deeply, almost light-headed.

Gabriella spotted me. "Are you okay?" she asked.

"Yeah, I'm just a little tired," I lied. I was just a bit hot and frustrated, wanting Chris. What was wrong with me?

We headed back into the theatre to look at Mitch's list to see what we still needed to finish. Tracy was walking around with a paintbrush touching up here and there. We had a massive pile of rubbish in front of the stage, so Gabriella and I started carrying the offcuts of timber out to the skip, which we had out the side door. The skip was getting emptied in the morning.

Mitch was about to call it a night. He said there were only a couple of things left to do, which he would do tomorrow. Chris was still playing around with the lights. Gabriella left.

"See you all tomorrow," she yelled, walking out the door.

Mitch and Trace said good night. Chris had to lock up. I walked up to the lighting box. "Hey, Chris, you nearly finished?" Just then, music came over the sound system, and it was *Queen, Somebody to Love*. We both looked down at the stage. No one was there.

"Mitch must have put it on as he was leaving. He knows I love *Queen*."

Chris looked in my eyes, and I looked at him; I suddenly felt my heart racing. We didn't talk; we just came together. Our lips, our arms and our bodies, I so wanted him, and he wanted me. He pulled his shirt off. What a bod! He looked so good. I wanted him in the worst way, so we stripped off our clothes like we were under a spell; we couldn't control ourselves. It happened so fast. Before I knew it, we were on the floor in the lighting box having each other in sweaty, orgasmic lovemaking of sheer bliss. We both came together with such passion. It wasn't planned; it just happened.

Afterwards, we lay there, trying to get our breath back. Lying flat on our backs gazing at the ceiling, we turned to look at each other. *Another One Bites the Dust* came over the sound system, and we both started to laugh.

As we cooled down, I realised how dirty the floor was, and I was getting cold. It was late. We got dressed and locked up. Chris walked me to my car and gave me a very passionate good night kiss. I didn't want to leave, but it was after one, and I would see Chris tonight.

I couldn't sleep that night. I couldn't stop thinking about Chris.

Chapter 27

I had to bring Elizabeth with me to opening night, so I set her up in the wings backstage. I was helping out backstage so I could keep an eye on her. The show started at 8 pm on the dot. We all had headsets on; this was our first show to use them. It was pretty cool. We could listen to Mitch's instructions for in-between set changes, and Gabriella would say something funny. Usually, funny comments about what was happening on the stage. Everything seemed to be running well for opening night.

Elizabeth fell asleep before the interval, which was good. She was terrific – she could sleep anywhere.

At the interval, we had a set change to get the stage ready for the second half. Chris came backstage with his coffee. We only had ten minutes left of interval. We all sat backstage, drinking our coffees. Gabriella had made a chocolate slice, which she shared around. Chris sat next to me, gently touching my leg. I wasn't sure how to respond. Nobody except Mitch knows about us, even though he didn't really know.

"Time! Trace, can you turn on the foyer bell? Let's get this show on the road," Mitch said, putting his cup in the basket for us to wash later. We all got up.

Chris finished his cup, touching me on my arm. "See you after the show," he said. I just smiled at him. His touch made my heart ache for him. Mitch noticed; he just smiled at me. I said nothing and went to the green room to give the cast a five-minute call.

The show went well. It was another standing ovation, and everyone was on a high. When the curtain came down, the stage crew set the stage for the next day's matinee. We had an 11 am and an 8 pm show.

That didn't stop Gabriella breaking out the bubbly. The audience had left, so we all sat on the edge of the stage drinking our champagne, Trace, Mitch, Gabriella and me. Chris came down from the lighting box. He took a beer and gave one to Mitch and then he came over to me. My legs hanging over the front of the stage and he put his arm around me, so I leant over and kissed him.

The look on everyone's face! What the hell, when did that happen? They must have been thinking. The last of the cast were still heading out the door. Gabriella spoke up first, "When did you two become an item?" Mitch said nothing. He just grinned as he had another swig of his beer.

"You never told me," Trace said.

Karen came over to us. "Thanks guys, a great night. See you tomorrow."

Karen didn't even look twice at Chris and me. Maybe she's just tired, I thought. Then she turned back.

"Don't do anything I wouldn't do," she said, looking at Chris and me with raised eyebrows. Everyone laughed.

We didn't have a late night, and I tried to have a sleep-in the next morning, but Elizabeth was wide-awake by 7 am. I had to get her breakfast. Rachel was going to mind Elizabeth today, so I let her have a sleep-in. She would have only got home at about 3 am.

I was so tired. I got up and made breakfast for Elizabeth. She liked porridge these days and so did I. It was unusual weather; it was so cold.

After breakfast, I had a shower. I had to wash my hair. I put Elizabeth in the bath so I could have a shower in peace. She loved playing in the tub, and I could keep an eye on her. By the time I had got dressed and dressed Elizabeth, it was ten o'clock. I might have to wake Rachel if she didn't get up soon.

I got my bag packed with scotch, cheese and bickies for tonight's show. Our group were all going out for a late lunch / early dinner between shows. There's a pub two blocks down from the theatre and the food there was pretty good. Just then, Rachel came downstairs yawning her head off.

"Shouldn't you be leaving?" she said mid-yawn.

I said goodbye to Elizabeth and Rachel. I put my coat on and headed out the door. Adrien just pulled up out the front to pick me up.

"Perfect timing," I said, jumping in the car.

"Spill the beans," Adrien demanded as we drove off. "What the fuck is going on with you and Chris?" Adrien said with a big grin on his face.

"Who told you?" I asked.

"It's only all over the theatre, darling. I know Chris is like, really hot, in a straight way, but he's like, twenty years older than you, what the fuck?"

"I like him; he's so sweet and sexy and nice," I said with the biggest smile on my face.

"So it's just sex? You know he's married?" Adrien said.

"I'm just having some fun," I said trying to defend my actions. "It's been a long time." Adrien said nothing.

"I don't want him to leave his wife or anything," I said.

"So you're not falling for him?" he asked.

"No," I said, starting to doubt myself.

After the matinee, we set the stage up for the evening show and then we all walked down the road to the pub: Tracy, Mitch, Gabriella, Karen, Adrien, Chris and me. I walked ahead of Chris with Gabriella. I think I was still thinking about what Adrien had said to me. Maybe I was falling for Chris. It was starting to freak me out. I can't fall in love with him, as he would break my heart. Don't be stupid. He wouldn't fall in love with me anyway. I just had to make sure I didn't fall in love with him.

When we got to the pub, I went straight to the bar and ordered a scotch and coke. I needed it to stop me from freaking out. I think Chris was sensing something was up. I drank my drink, trying to chill. We all sat in the beer garden. Chris climbed in next to me. I suddenly felt awkward, and I could feel my face getting heated. I drank some more. Gabriella passed around the menus.

"Hey, Steph, do you want to share oysters again?" Gabriella asked me. We loved oysters. I didn't have that much money to spare. If I had oysters, I wouldn't be able to have a main meal. What the hell.

"Yes, that sounds great." I could always eat later. So Gabriella ordered two dozen oysters a la natural with lemon.

Chris had his hand on my leg under the table. I started to relax a little as I had already finished my drink. Chris got up and headed for the bar and bought me another scotch.

"Oh, thanks," I said, a little taken aback. I wasn't used to guys being kind to me; it almost felt wrong.

Why would he want me? All my self-doubt came rushing back. I was drinking too fast, and everyone was talking and laughing. Nobody seemed to notice how uncomfortable I was feeling. Chris seemed oblivious to it as well. I felt invisible and almost panicked, then Chris grabbed my hand under the table. I looked at him, and he smiled. I started to relax as he leaned over and whispered in my ear.

"Are you okay?"

"I'm fine," I lied again. It was becoming a habit.

Just then, Gabriella, who was sitting opposite me, announced, "Our oysters are coming."

The waitress put a rather large plate in front of Gabriella and me. Two dozen oysters. Wow, they looked good. Everybody's meals started arriving. Chris ordered steak and chips.

It didn't take Gabriella and me too long to get through our oysters; they were so good. We all had quite a few drinks, and I was feeling a little pissed. I realised as I stood to walk to the loo that I better not have any more; we had to do another show in an hour.

When we had all finished, we started to head back up the road to the theatre. This time, Chris had me by the hand. I think he thought I needed help, as I was a little wobbly on my feet. Shit, I drank too much. When we got back to the theatre, I made myself a cup of black tea. I was trying to sober up, so I could help with the show.

Mitch noticed how pissed I was.

"Steph, I want you to help Chris with the spotlight."

"Why, where's Ben? He was supposed to help."

"Can you do it, please? I thought you would jump at the chance," Mitch said with a quick smile. I headed up to the lighting box. Chris gave me a quick lesson, as it was pretty basic. On/off switch, point to the stage on the right person when Chris told me to.

By the time interval came, I think Chris was feeling nervous. I gave him a very passionate kiss, and I was feeling a little turned on. I think he was worried I wanted to jump him right here and now.

"I need a coffee," he said. As he got off his seat and headed down to the stage door, I followed. Gabriella had some cheese and crackers that we shared around. The show was going well. We were all yawning – the late nights were starting to catch up with us.

After the show finished, the cast was in a party mood. Most of them stayed back and shared some bubbly and a light supper that the company supplied. I opened my scotch. I only had one drink, as I wasn't feeling the best. We just sat in the theatre too exhausted to dance. Mitch had music playing, and some of the cast were up dancing on the stage.

Chris was having a beer. I didn't know how he always drove home. He never seemed to get drunk, though. I was feeling quite sick. Adrien came over.

"You want to go home? You look like shit."

I just nodded; he helped me to my feet, and we headed out the door. I didn't even say bye to Chris, but I think he was in the loo.

Adrien drove me home and put me to bed; he laid down beside me, and we both fell asleep.

Chapter 28

The next morning, I was woken up by Elizabeth climbing all over me. Adrien was already up and standing in the doorway.

"Wake up, Mummy," said Adrien holding a cup of coffee. I was still wearing my clothes from last night, and I felt like crap. I pulled the covers over my head.

"Come on, Elizabeth, your mum needs her rest." Adrien took Elizabeth out and closed the door.

An hour later, I got up, got out of my jeans and put on my trackie daks. I found Adrien and Elizabeth watching cartoons, sitting on the floor in the lounge room with building blocks. I kissed Elizabeth and laid down on the sofa. I made eye contact with Adrien and mouthed, 'Thank you'. Elizabeth was happily playing with her blocks on the floor, so was Adrien; she loved Adrien. He was just a big kid himself. We were like a family now.

"Do you want a cup of tea?" he asked; I nodded. Adrien knew me so well. We had a lazy day at home.

It was about four in the afternoon. Adrien had gone home, and there was a knock at the door. I went to see who was there. With the door opened, my heart missed a beat. It was Chris standing there. He was holding a lovely bunch of flowers. I suddenly felt very awkward.

"Hi," I said, standing in the doorway.

"Can I come in?" Chris asked.

"Yeah, come in, sorry, you just surprised me."

"I was worried about you," he said, handing me the flowers.

"Oh, they're beautiful, come on through." I walked to the kitchen, feeling very uncomfortable. Shane was the only one who had given me flowers before, and that was after we fought and always in front of witnesses.

"I didn't know you knew where I lived," I said.

"Mitch told me; it's okay, isn't it?" he asked, noticing my weird behaviour.

"Yeah, that's fine," I said. I didn't sound very convincing. "Sorry, I'm not feeling the best." I was trying to cover my real feelings, but I didn't know 'what' my feelings were? I was so confused. "I was just about to have a shower and an early night." Elizabeth had brought her blocks to the kitchen, giving them to me. I picked her up. "It's nearly your bedtime, isn't it, Elizabeth?"

Chris got up to leave. "I better go; I just wanted to check you're okay and you are, so I'll head off."

I felt awful as he leaned over and gave me a quick kiss on the lips.

"Thanks for the flowers. I'll see you on Wednesday?" He headed to the door, gave a slight wave and was gone.

That night I couldn't sleep. I tossed and turned, thinking about what an idiot I was. Chris bringing me flowers scared the hell out of me. I couldn't fall for him. He was married; I would ruin his life. He couldn't care for me, as I would break his heart. Elizabeth had to come first. And what if Chris asked me about my past? If Shane ever found me, I would have to run again.

I couldn't have anyone in my life until I knew it was safe, and Elizabeth had grown up. I couldn't trust anyone. That's why Adrien was my dearest friend. He was gay, so I knew he would never fall in love with me. Even though we had sex once, that was just friendship, not love. I felt safe with Adrien knowing I couldn't fall in love with him. But I did love him, and he was my best friend. He was around more than Rachel lately. Rachel worked late nights, so I only saw her on Sundays and Mondays. Rachel told me that she was going to be moving in with her boyfriend, but she wouldn't leave me in the lurch. That was on my mind too.

Wednesday came, and I decided I should talk to Chris. I didn't quite know what I would say, but I had to end it. I headed backstage, fixed up an area for Elizabeth with her toys and doona. Gabriella came in behind me. "How are you piss pot?" She laughed.

I hadn't seen Chris yet. He was running late, so Mitch said. The audience was starting to arrive. The show was to begin in twenty minutes.

We were all ready to start, and finally, Chris arrived. He went straight to the lighting box after picking up a coffee from the canteen on his way through. Ben was already up there to do the spotlight. Thank goodness. I didn't want to do the spot tonight.

By the time interval came, I was feeling a bit nervous, but Chris didn't come backstage for his coffee. I started to feel upset with myself for being such an idiot. I would have to talk to Chris after the show. I would apologise and tell him that I was just not ready for a relationship.

The show went well. Now I needed to talk to Chris.

But I never got the chance. The show had finished. By the time we had set the stage for Friday night's show, he had gone. We all met in the theatre as we did after every show, to talk and have a drink, but everyone was tired.

"Where's Chris?" said Tracy.

"He's gone home," said Mitch. "He's got an early start for work tomorrow."

So we all had an early night.

Adrien's birthday was next week, so I decided to get him a birthday cake for Saturday night. I told Gabriella it was his 21st, and I wanted to surprise him with a party after the show. She thought it was a great idea and said she would take care of the cake, as she knew a great bakery. That worked out fine for me as I had work Thursday and Friday and time was going to be tight.

By the time Friday came around, Chris was acting like nothing was going on between us. We were suddenly just friends again. Part of me was relieved, but part of me was heartbroken and guilty because I realised I did care for him. I just couldn't let anyone into my heart. I didn't need anybody. I could never depend on anyone except myself. I would never let anyone control me ever again; that's how it had to be to stay safe.

The final show was here. I tried to get there early, but Adrien was picking me up, and Elizabeth was slowing me down; she pulled everything out of my bag that I had just packed. I wasn't planning on drinking too much as I would be driving home. Adrien finally arrived to pick us up. We put all our stuff in the car and headed off to the theatre.

When we got to the theatre, I set up Elizabeth's space backstage. She had her drink, snacks and some books to read and colour. Gabriella was already there, as was Mitch and Trace.

"Did you get the cake?"

"It's in the upstairs fridge," said Gabriella.

After the show, we would surprise Adrien. I loved Adrien; he meant so much to me. I was quite excited, as he always wanted a party, he had told me several times. Gabriella asked me to distract Adrien after the show by keeping him in the green room so that they could set everything up.

"No problem," I said. "Adrien said he would do my hair for the party. So I'll get him to fix my hair after the show in the green room, good plan."

The show went well. Elizabeth fell asleep. Everyone was fantastic, and another successful show had ended. I went down to the green room.

"Adrien, you promised to do my hair!"

He was very good at hair as well. We sat in the dressing room while he worked on my hair, and he was pretty fast at braiding. I hoped Gabriella had enough time to get things ready. Just then, Trace came in.

"I wondered where you two were!" Trace said. That was my cue. We headed upstairs. It was very quiet as we walked down the corridor from the backstage into the foyer.

"Surprise!" everyone yelled. There was a huge banner hanging in the foyer that said, 'Happy 21st Steph and Adrien!' I looked at Adrien slightly puzzled, as he looked at me thrilled we could celebrate together.

Gabriella told me later Adrien had wanted to surprise me and then I asked to surprise Adrien. So Gabrielle decided to surprise both of us.

It was a fantastic party! We had a massive cake with our names on top with twenty-one candles for each of us to blow out. It was a birthday I wanted to remember for a long time.

Chapter 29

After the show had finished, I decided I wanted to try a drama company for something different. Adrien told me I should try this theatre group that did play readings in a church hall, a little further away but not too far. Adrien wanted to give them a go as well, so I went with him.

They were a very different group, an older group. We were the youngest there, but the people were very friendly and welcoming; Elizabeth was welcome as well.

We were put into groups and handed a short play. Mine was called 'Bus Stop'. We were both given our parts, and I was a passenger waiting for the bus talking to another passenger. Adrien thought it was shit, but I read my role. He didn't want to do it, but we stayed. At the end of the night, they told us they were having auditions for the pantomime 'Pinocchio' the following week. Now that sounded interesting! Once a year, they did a children's show, which made them some money so they could put their plays on. Plays weren't as popular as musicals or pantomimes.

As Adrien drove us home, I talked to him about auditioning, but Adrien wasn't as keen as me. I looked at the roles.

"I could play the wicked gypsy?"

He just laughed at my enthusiasm.

"Can't you help me prepare for the audition?" I pleaded with him.

"Okay, I'll help you," he finally agreed. But he didn't want to go in it.

Adrien came over every night that week. I agreed to cook dinner if he helped me rehearse. So after dinner, I put Elizabeth to bed, and we practised. I had to learn the lines by heart because I shook so much when I was nervous that I couldn't read the lines on the script.

Finally, I went to the audition. Adrien had given me some confidence. I suffered such anxiety that I almost made myself sick. The auditions were so laid back. I started to relax a little; it was just like the play reading. They made me feel so comfortable. At the end of the night, they told me I had got the part. I couldn't believe it! I was so pleased with myself.

Rehearsals started the next week on Tuesday and Thursday nights. Adrien said he would drive me, or he would mind Elizabeth and sleep over so that I could drive myself.

He had decided to move in as Rachel was moving out. I was so excited but also sad Rachel was leaving.

I met up with Tracy and Gabriella for lunch on Saturday and told them all about Pinocchio and my part. They were so happy for me.

Rehearsals were going well; the cast was very different from the Musical Comedy Company. They took everything so serious. Acting is art said the director. He would say things like, "I want you to think about how you would feel if you hated everybody and everybody hated you. Close your eyes." I would close my eyes, thinking this is shit. Some people would start crying – really sobbing. I just opened my eyes, feeling no different. Actually, I felt like an idiot, but I went along with it.

I started to get to know some of the cast. Sue was the Blue Fairy. She was beautiful but a bit too goodie-two-shoes. Dominique was the mum of Mandy and Luke; they were two of the kids in the show. Dominique was crazy but in a good way. I liked her. She was divorced. She had three kids, Luke was ten, Mandy six and Max was nearly five, and her mum was Dot.

I loved Dot; she was so with it and the coolest grandmother to her grandkids. Max and Elizabeth would chase each other all over the hall. But I did take Adrien up on his offer and left Elizabeth home with him most of the time. I liked having Adrien at home to come back to. He took my old room, and I moved upstairs. Elizabeth had the study for her room. Rachel always had it full of junk, so we cleaned it out. It was great to have my own bedroom again.

The production was coming together really well. It was a smaller company with little money, so we made our own costumes, which was fine. I wasn't much of a sewer; it was a good thing Adrien was. He was a great costume designer, so he made my outfit. It was a long black dress with a swishy skirt. Well, he altered a dress he found at Vinnie's second-hand shop. It fitted me perfectly. I wore my black boots with it.

I had to practise cracking a long whip; it was six metres long. They let me take it home so I could practise. I had to hold the rod with one hand and wind the whip a certain way so when I raised the rod to flick it, the strap would unwind to flick out and hopefully crack. It was quite hard. I had to practise in the street as there wasn't enough room in our courtyard. Rehearsals were going well; there weren't too many lines, which was good.

Opening night was getting close. We had built a simple set. We had three different backdrops and a table, that was pretty much it. As this was a pantomime, all our shows were early as our average audience was eight-year-olds. So we had three shows on Saturday and Sunday, 10 am and 2 pm and 6 pm. Tickets were selling quite well. Dominique wanted to take me out after the show to her favourite nightclub in the city. She said she went there all the time, 'The rainbow house'. I wasn't so sure.

I asked Adrien what he thought. Adrien didn't like her; he called her a fag hag. He reckoned she was always trying to get into his pants. I didn't think so. She was just very loud and a bit full on.

So I decided to go out with her. She said she would meet me at my place. Dot was going to drop her off after our 6 pm show. This company didn't have parties and I kind of wanted to party. I said I had to go home first to check on Elizabeth. Adrien said he would stay home, as he was in-between boyfriends at the moment.

We had a great day of performances. We had a sausage sizzle in-between the 2 pm and 6 pm show. After the last show, it was nearly 8 pm. My whip only cracked once. It was tough trying not to hit anyone and crack it at the same time. The audience seemed to enjoy the pantomime, which was the main thing, but I enjoyed it too.

After the show, I drove Adrien's car home to get ready to go out. Elizabeth was all ready for bed, so I said goodnight and tucked her in. Adrien had rented some movies to watch. I was a bit tired, and part of me wanted to stay home.

But Dominique was knocking on the door; I was still getting dressed.

Adrien stuck his head up the stairs. "Don't take long. I don't want to entertain Dominique for too long," he said, screwing his face up.

I didn't take long. Dominique was already drinking Adrien's Vodka.

"I'm ready," I announced. We called a cab. We were only five blocks away, but I had high heels on and didn't want to walk that far.

When we got there, Dominique and I headed straight to the bar. The club was already quite busy, and it was almost nine o'clock. They all knew her.

"Hey, Barney, can we have some shots?" Dominique asked. She seemed to be planning on getting very drunk. We shot them down. "Is Dave there?" Dominique asked.

"Out the back," Barney replied.

"Come on." Dominique grabbed me by the arm and led me to this back room. It was very dark.

Oh, shit. It was a drug room, and people were snorting up what I assumed was cocaine. Fuck! What the hell had I got myself in to now? Dominique gave Dave some money; she sat down at a table, and he gave her a glass tray with white powder on it.

"Come on, Steph, sit down, have some," Dominique said as if she was ordering me a milkshake.

"No, thanks, Dominique. I have to go." I hot-tailed out of there, never looking back.

Once I was back on the street, I realised I had no way home. There were no cabs, so I started to walk…It was only five blocks. As I was heading back home, my mind was racing. I was so angry with Dominique. How could she do drugs? She had kids. What was she thinking? What if she died? What would happen to her kids? I was so mad that I didn't notice this gang of punks heading towards me; I just hung on to my coat and kept walking. I must have looked scary. No one would be game to mess with me. They tried to block my path.

"Fuck off!" I screamed at them, and I just pushed my way through. I wasn't going to look back for fear they might be following me, so I just kept walking until I saw my place. Only then, I turned back, and no one was there.

I didn't realise how much I was shaking until I tried to put the key in the lock. Once inside, I shut the door and locked it. I could hear the TV. I walked in to find Adrien laying on the sofa with a drink in his hand. I noticed the Scotch on the coffee table.

"I need a drink," was all I could say.

"What happened? Why are you home so early?" Adrien sat up as I was all flushed and in such a state. I poured myself a drink and shot it down.

After telling Adrien everything, he put his arms around me, so I felt safe. "You should have called me. I would have picked you up."

I went to get changed. I put on my warm PJs and curled up on the sofa in Adrien's arms and watched *Smokey and the Bandit* with Burt Reynolds. Adrien had a wicked crush on him. I think I did too. It was an old movie but a goody.

Chapter 30

Well, Pinocchio finished. It was fun being on stage but not as much as being behind the scenes. I had six months off not doing anything. Elizabeth was another year older and going to preschool two days a week. Things were pretty good. Musical Comedy Company were starting a new show, 'The Best Little Whore House in Texas'. Karen rang me to see if I would be her assistant again.

"Yes!" I didn't even have to think about it. I so missed everyone and couldn't wait. Auditions were the following Saturday.

"We need at least ten young good-looking guys," Karen told me.

Friday came. I asked Gabriella if she wanted to go out to the club. I arranged a babysitter so that Adrien could go too.

We headed out to our local RSL club. They had live bands on Friday nights, usually with attractive young guys. Adrien disappeared as soon as we got there. Great help he was. Gabriella and I got some drinks and found an empty table. The band hadn't started yet. There were a few people around.

"We need to find some young, good-looking guys that can sing," I said to Gabriella. After a while, my glass was empty. "Want another drink?"

I took our empty glasses to the bar, and then this guy came and stood next to me waiting to be served; he was good-looking and tall with long blonde hair. I couldn't help myself.

"Hi, are you married?"

"No," he replied, a little shocked at my direct question.

"Do you have a girlfriend?" I asked.

"No," he said again.

"Are you gay?" I was hoping he wasn't.

"Is that a problem?" he asked me.

"No, not at all." Just then, his boyfriend came over. "I'm Mel, and this is Glenn." I couldn't believe how brash I was. I was usually quite shy, well, sometimes.

They ended up joining us. We had a few drinks, and before long, we were singing show songs from *South Pacific*. They were such nice guys. I told them about the audition that was happening the next day, and they said they would come. I hoped they would.

It turned out to be a great night. The band had started to play, and we all got up to dance. Mel and Glenn enjoyed themselves as they got to dance with us and nobody questioned that they were gay. It was 1987, and there were a lot of people against gays. I couldn't see anything wrong with it. It didn't hurt me, so it didn't bother me. I knew plenty of gay people, and I lived with one.

I didn't see Adrien all night. I got home at about 1.30 am as I didn't want to stay out too late because we had auditions the next day. Elizabeth was asleep in my bed, so I slept in Adrien's room, which I did most nights. Adrien didn't come home till 5 am. He crawled into bed next to me.

"Your late," I said, barely awake and went back to sleep.

I woke again just after 7 am. I heard Elizabeth up, so I got up and let Adrien sleep. I had to be at the theatre before 10, and I had a load of washing to do. I quickly loaded the washer and put it on. Elizabeth was hungry. I sat her at the table and made her some toast and vegemite. I needed a cup of tea – strong and black. I put some toast on for me and turned the radio on, not too loud, as I didn't want to wake up Adrien. We sat there eating our breakfast, listening to the radio. They started playing *Queen*: *Love of my life*. I began to think about Brett. I looked down at my tattoo on my hand and touched it with my finger. I closed my hand holding on to it. *Oh, Brett, I miss you*. I wondered if his spirit knew where I was.

I drank my tea and cleaned up Elizabeth. She was doing a lot for herself now, but she still made a mess. I chased her up the stairs so she could get dressed.

We were all dressed, and I had packed some food and stuff to keep Elizabeth happy for the day. I sat her in front of the TV so she would stay clean while I hung out the washing. Then I went in to say bye to Adrien.

I gently woke him. "Hi, sweetie, I'm going to the theatre now. You stay in bed, come down later." I kissed him on the cheek.

Elizabeth and I took the car. We got there just as Karen arrived.

"Where's Adrien?" I explained where he was. I also told her about Mel and Glenn, so I hoped they would turn up.

We got everything set up. I put the urn on for the tea and coffee. Some people started to arrive as Gabriella came running in.

"Sorry, I'm late," she said. She was carrying bags of stuff like milk and biscuits so we wouldn't starve.

There were a few new faces but also some familiar ones. Then Mel and Glenn walked in.

"Hi, I'm glad you made it."

Karen was impressed. "They're not bad looking either," she whispered.

It was a busy day. We had our ten guys, and they were all gay.

"That would be right; we'll have a stage of half-naked woman, and none of the guys will care," Karen said with a laugh.

We had a four-piece band for this show, so it should be good.

It was a long day, and we got a full cast for the show. Rehearsals started the following week on Mondays and Wednesdays. Adrien never turned up. I loaded up the car and headed home.

Elizabeth ran inside, glad to be home. It was just after four and no sign of Adrien, his door was still shut. I got Elizabeth a drink and put the telly on for her. Then I went to check on Adrien. On opening his door, I saw he was still in bed, but he was awake.

"Hi, sorry I missed the auditions," he said, sounding so hung over.

"Can I get you anything?" I asked. I could see he had an empty coffee cup beside his bed.

"No, I'm going to get up now, I need a shower," he said, but he wasn't moving. I let him be.

I went to the kitchen to cook some dinner for us. I made spaghetti. I didn't know if Adrien would be hungry or not but Elizabeth and I were. I was just about to dish up when Adrien made an appearance, as he leant over Elizabeth, who was sitting at the table to kiss her and then to me. He put his arms around me while I was trying to dish up dinner.

"Thanks, darling, I'm starving," he said.

"I've only got spaghetti."

"That's okay," he said.

I was slightly puzzled. "You don't eat meat."

"That was last year. This year I do," Adrien said.

I just shook my head. "Sit down, then." I wasn't going to argue.

After dinner, I cleaned up and put Elizabeth to bed. Finally, we sat down in the lounge room with a hot cup of tea. Adrien sat next to me.

"So what happened to you last night?" I finally asked.

"You don't want to know," he said.

He was right. I didn't want to hear about his sexual encounters.

"Oh, why is that?" I said, hoping he wouldn't tell me.

"Because you get all shitty with me every time I mention meeting anyone."

"No, I don't. I met someone last night too, and he came to the auditions today, and now he's in the show. What do you think of that?" I said, quite pleased with myself.

"I bet he's gay."

I said nothing. I just drank my tea.

"He is, isn't he?" Adrien started laughing at me.

"Oh, shut up," I said, throwing a cushion at him.

"You always fall for men that you have no hope of ever getting. They're either gay or married, and if they show an interest in you, you run a mile."

I moved to the end of the sofa, sulking.

"I'm sorry," he said with his puppy dog eyes. "I don't want you to fall for any other gay guy, except me. I'm a jealous guy, you know."

He always knew how to make me smile. That night, I slept in my bed.

Adrien was right; I did always fall for guys I knew I would never get. I suppose it was safer that way. If I never needed anyone, then I could never get hurt again. That night, I went to sleep dreaming of Brett, I so missed him.

Chapter 31

We had such a great cast and crew for 'The Best Little Whore House in Texas'. It was like a great party that kept ongoing. Last four weeks we brought the band in for rehearsals. John on drums, Paul on guitar, Simon on bass guitar and Graham was our musical director on keyboard. They were all in there forties at least, maybe older. They were a lot of fun.

Most of the cast were in their early twenties. We had some good-looking young men in the show. Real eye candy. A pity they were all gay, but at least, they knew how to party.

Tickets for the shows were selling well. We were running for three weeks this time. Set build started at the weekend. Bill, the president, had been involved with the company for over twenty years. He hadn't been in any shows for some time now he was nearly eighty. He was very old school, especially when he made comments like, "I don't think I want any of the show parties at my place this year, not with all those poofs."

I think my mouth dropped open. "Bill, you can't say that," I said, looking around and hoping no one else heard.

Bill and his wife had a lovely home with a pool and outdoor area for entertaining. We'd had a few parties there but not for a while.

"Well, I don't feel comfortable having all of them, in my pool," he said.

"Fair enough." I would keep that conversation to myself. Otherwise, Adrien would get into a massive argument.

However, I told Gabriella what he said. She just laughed.

"He's just old-fashioned," she told me.

"But that's awful." I was still shocked he would say such things. Bill was getting old and grumpy. He would do anything for anyone usually.

"I guess I shouldn't suggest having any get together at Bill's place then," Gabriella said with a laugh.

It was set-build time again, and this time, we had a great turn up of helpers. That was a first, even John from the band turned up. He was hot looking for an old guy, but he was married, I think? I wasn't going down that road again.

This time, we had to extend the stage and build a wing on the right side for the band. We made a lot of progress on the first day, and they had most of the wing built. I went up to have a look, but they had a hole in the stage right in front of where the band would be.

"What is this?" I said, pointing to the hole.

"That's for the prompt to sit in," Mitch said.

"But I'm the prompt!" I said, not knowing anything about this.

Karen explained to me that because we were losing the front row of seats, they didn't want to lose any more places for the prompt, who would typically sit in the front of the stage next to the keyboard.

"So you get a hole to sit in," said Karen.

"Oh." I wasn't sure about that.

Rehearsals were going well. Costumes were coming along. Karen had been to every Op shop in Sydney looking for boots and cowboy shirts for the guys. The girls were wearing underwear, which they mainly bought for themselves. No one wanted second-hand underwear!

The first dress rehearsal was hilarious. We had a stage full of half-naked woman and a bunch of good-looking guys that didn't know what to do with them. Karen was in stitches laughing when she asked one of the young guys to hold on to Cherrie, one of the girls. He didn't know where to put his hands, and he looked so awkward.

Karen got up on the stage, grabbed hold of Cherrie to show him how to do it. Everyone started to laugh. The poor guy was so embarrassed.

Karen said to me later, "It's probably the first near-naked girl he's ever seen or touched." She laughed again.

Everyone was on a high for our final dress rehearsal. The band was in top form, John, Paul and Simon each had a beer nearby. Graham was a true professional, and he only drank water. I climbed down into my hole. Simon gave me a hand. I had everything I needed down there, a script, tiny light, a cushion on my chair, a bottle of water to keep hydrated. A great view of the band and the stage, this was kind of cool. The dress rehearsal was terrible; so many people forgot their lines that I had to prompt all through the show. I was rather glad when we finished.

Everyone came back on the stage so Karen could talk to them.

"Well! You know what they say, terrible dress rehearsal, fantastic opening night. So go home, rest, 'learn your bloody lines', and I'll see you all tomorrow night."

Well, that was pretty mild. Karen would generally say that was shit and do it again, but it was after eleven.

We started packing up. Chris was doing the lights. It had been a long time since we had our night together. It was a little weird, but we just talked as if we were old friends, which we were. Things were back to normal, which was so good. I so preferred this company to the other one.

The opening night was full of excitement. I dressed in my stage crew clothes of black jeans and a black shirt with 'The Best Little Whore House in Texas' on the back and my black boots. Adrien was in the show, so I had to bring Elizabeth with me. I was going to get a sitter for the final night, that was all I could afford. Gabriella was going to keep an eye on Elizabeth backstage, as I would be stuck in my hole.

I had to climb in when the band made their way to the stage. Simon helped me climbed down in the dark. It was quite scary. I couldn't see a thing until the lights came up on the band and I could turn on my little reading light.

The band started up with the overture. I opened my script, which I had to follow very carefully since there had been so many missed lines last night; I was feeling a little nervous. Everyone was on their best behaviour although the band still had their beers in a cooler box behind John, the drummer. Every time there was a break in the music, the box got opened. I stuck with my water. I needed to stay focussed. But as it turned out, I didn't need to prompt anyone. It was the best opening night, with a standing ovation; it was fantastic! Everyone thoroughly enjoyed the show.

After the show, we were so excited we just had to party, and boy, did this cast and crew know how to party! Every guy was up on stage dancing and singing to *Rocky Horror Picture Show*. Then Glenn appeared dressed as 'Frank-N-Furter'. Glenn looked terrific, and everyone was having a ball. I was getting a drum lesson from John, flirting a little. I told him my favourite drummer was Roger Taylor from *Queen*.

"But John, you're a close second."

I didn't want to offend him, flirting again. Sometimes I couldn't help myself. That had always been my downside. I blurt out things without thinking them through. John was showing me how to hit the drums leaning over me with his hands on my hands. He was so lovely.

"I think you better play," I told him. "I need a drink."

After an hour of dance music, most of the cast headed home. We had another show the next night. Then the band had a bit of a jam session. They were excellent. There were only a few of us left: Gabriella, Trace, Mitch, Chris, Adrien and the band, except Graham who always went home straight after the show as he was a bit older than the rest of the group.

They started to play a familiar song, *Don't Stop Me Now* from *Queen*. I jumped to my feet, and I sang along with the band. I didn't have a mic so no one could hear me anyway. I hadn't even had much to drink, but I was having the time of my life, dancing and singing. I knew all the words. It was one of my favourite *Queen* songs ever. I didn't care who saw me, and they were all quite drunk anyway.

I had to drive home. Adrien was drunk, and Elizabeth was asleep. I managed to get them both home and tucked into bed.

I was so fired up and full of this energy, I couldn't sleep. I started thinking about Brett again. I didn't think I would ever get over him. He was my rock. He believed in me. I remember telling him once how I wanted to make movies and be a director like Steven Spielberg. I never thought I would be doing theatre. I wished I could share this with Brett. I wondered if John was married.

The next morning, I was so tired. Elizabeth was awake early as usual. I dragged myself out of bed to get breakfast. Adrien had slept in, so I didn't see him until after eleven when he came out fresh looking after he'd had a good night's sleep. I must have looked a fright. He said he would watch Elizabeth if I wanted a nap before the show. I took him up on his offer, so after lunch, I lay down and slept for two hours.

I came out to find Adrien with Elizabeth and my table covered with play dough. Adrien had made a pile of it. It was all over the kitchen table.

"Well, you two have had fun, I see." Elizabeth was showing me what she had made. I sat down with a cup of tea.

What a great father Adrien would be, I thought. He was like a fabulous uncle who loved playing kids' games. I finished my cuppa.

"We better get cleaned up," I said. "It's getting late, and we have a show to do."

This time, I took my scotch with me to the theatre. I put it down in my hole in the stage so I could have a drink with the band, as they were the only ones who could see me. This group was so great for parties, and I think I could like John; he is so sweet.

Every show had a funny story to be told. On the second night, Tracy couldn't wait to tell us what had happened to Tricia, who was the madam in the show. She was wearing a low-cut dress and had huge breasts. She came up to Tracy backstage a bit panicked saying she had lost her lolly and thought it might be stuck in her hair. "Look for it!" she said.

Trace couldn't stop laughing. "It was sitting right on top of her boob. She picked it up and said, 'shit that was sitting there all through the whole of the first act.' She stuck it in her mouth and went on with the show."

Every night, the after-show party was different. I was so pissed I couldn't get out of my hole. I had emptied my bottle of scotch. Simon tried to give me a hand. I was laughing so much I fell back in. The whole band were laughing at me. It took Simon and John to get me out.

I was flirting with John, just in a fun, harmless way. He was such a lovely guy; the more I got to know him, the more I liked him. He was kind of hot in a fun way. I think I just had a thing for musicians. I didn't know how old he was, but age shouldn't matter.

I did love to dance, and the only guys around here that danced were gay, so I danced with them.

Mel turned out to be a great ballroom dancer. That night, he and I danced around the stage doing the waltz. Mel was so good, zooming me around the stage. We were so great together, and he was a great teacher.

"If only you weren't gay," I said as we danced.

"That's what my mother says," he replied.

I wasn't sure how to take that. Did Mel think I was as old as his mum? Or did he think I reminded him of his mum; if so, he wouldn't give me a second thought? Either way, I needed another drink.

I went and sat with Adrien, as he was sitting in the middle row on his own. I was quite drunk.

"I need a cuddle," I said, leaning on his shoulder.

"Why what's wrong?" he asked.

"Do you think I'm attractive?" I asked, looking so sad.

"Of course, you are, darling. Why?"

"Mel thinks I'm like his mother."

"Maybe his mother is attractive." Adrien always cheered me up. Adrien leant in close to my ear. "Or maybe it's because you don't have a big dick."

I just looked at him and pulled a face.

"Why don't you chase a straight guy? You would have a better chance." Adrien was always blunt. "I hear John's available."

"What do you mean? I thought he was married."

"He's divorced. Has been for over a year."

Why was I the last one to know these things?

We went home that night, and I slept alone. I only had one night left to get John's attention, I thought. I might never see him again after the show finished.

Chapter 32

The final show was here again. Adrien had been trying to hook up with young Chris. I was so wrapped up, flirting with John and Mel that I hadn't noticed. I didn't mind if Adrien had a boyfriend. I just didn't want to know about it all the time. That was very selfish of me, but I didn't want to lose him.

I finally got an opportunity to make a move on John. We had about an hour till the curtain was up, and I needed to go to the bottle shop to pick up some more scotch. John said he would drive me. I got in his car next to him.

"Where's Elizabeth tonight?" John asked.

"I have a babysitter. We left the car at home so Adrien and I can have a few drinks."

We pulled into the drive-through bottle shop and got out of the car. I went to get my scotch, and John went to get his beer. We got back in the car and headed back to the theatre. I was feeling a bit lost for words.

"So where are you staying tonight?" I said. It sounded like it was an invitation. I felt my face heating up.

"I'll probably sleep in my car," he said, as he touched my hand and my heart missed a beat; John had a station wagon. I wasn't sure where John lived, but I knew it was about an hour's drive. I wanted to invite him to my place, but I didn't.

We had a full house again; we had full houses most nights, which was fantastic. The band had a warm-up jam before the audience came in. I just stood there watching them play, totally dream-eyeing John. I think I'm falling for him.

Gabriella came up behind me.

"You like him, don't you?" she walked off, leaving me with a red face of embarrassment. I had to stop doing that, but I couldn't help it.

I didn't need to prompt. The cast hadn't needed me at all. I loved my seat down in the stage where I could sit and watch the band play each night.

I went backstage, not having Elizabeth there tonight, I felt a bit lost. I just sat backstage with the crew. The band joined us while we were waiting for the audience to come in.

Simon sat next to me, making conversation. "Did you get your scotch?"

"Yeah, already down in my hole."

"Oh, really," Simon said with a big smirk on his face.

I shoved him, nearly pushing him off his chair, and he shoved me back.

"Hey, take it easy," John said to Simon. I just smiled at my protector.

With his headset on, Mitch announced, "Okay, are we going to do this?"

The band and I headed out to the stage in the dark. John helped me down into my hole, and he kissed my hand. Now John was flirting with me! I nearly fell in, but he had me by the hand. It was always so dark.

The music started, the lights came up on the band, and I could see John just between the cymbals. He looked so intense when he hit those drums. I probably wouldn't see John after tonight, I suddenly thought. Did I want a one night stand? I wasn't sure. I poured myself a drink. I was feeling a little sad that this was our last show. I had a sip and looked up at John. He raised his beer to say cheers. My sadness was gone, and I had another sip.

The audience sounded fantastic, and they were thoroughly enjoying themselves. I never really saw the audience as the lights came up at the end of the show. The band played a walking out bit of music and as I never got out of my hole until John or Simon helped me, which wasn't until they had finished. Even at the interval, the audience had mostly gone by the time I got out.

We had extra stage crew on that night. As it was the final night, they all wanted to work and stay for the last show party. Simon helped me out at the interval. John was still putting his empty bottles out of the way. We all went backstage for a cuppa and a biscuit. I got my cup of tea off the tray, turned around and found all the seats were gone.

"Oh, not enough seats tonight," I said.

John patted his leg. "You can sit here."

"Okay," I said, as I went over to John and sat on his lap. He put his arm around my waist. Nobody seemed to care but feeling his fingers so gently rubbing my back was lovely.

Act Two of the show was about to start. I didn't want to move, but I had to. John walked me back to my hole in the stage. As I stepped down, he held my hand. I turned and kissed his hand this time. I don't think anyone saw, but our eyes met, and he smiled, I could see his white teeth from the light reflection. I had left my light on in my hole.

I didn't want to get too drunk, so I took it easy for the second half of the show. I wasn't even paying attention to the show; I just kept an eye on John. He was such a good drummer. He had been playing the drums for nearly thirty years. I was hoping he had started at the age of two. I didn't want to know his age, and I didn't care.

Because it was the last show after the finale, everyone did an encore, which was explosive. The audience was screaming. It was so cool. When the curtain had closed, the band kept playing until the audience had mostly left. Some stayed there listening until the band had stopped. John came over to help me out, and he gave me a gentle kiss on the lips. "Congratulations," he said.

"What do you mean?"

"You were the assistant director, weren't you?"

"Oh, yeah, I was." I had almost forgotten. "Thanks," I said.

I went to help Gabriella set up a table in the foyer for the food and drinks for the party. The music was playing over the sound system, as the band needed a break. They would probably play later. Karen brought out six bottles of bubbly for everyone to share. The party had started to the sound of corks popping, as the cast got changed and made their way to the foyer.

Everyone had really enjoyed this show, and it had been such a fun cast and crew. We all got on really well. The band weren't into bubbly thou beer was more their preference. I had a glass of bubbly, only one, as I didn't want to be sick later.

Mel was having a glass of bubbly, but Glenn wasn't anywhere to be seen, so I went over to talk to Mel.

"Hey, Mel, great party, where's Glenn?" I asked.

"I don't know." He shot down his drink.

"Let's dance." He dragged me on to the stage. There were a lot of people up dancing; we could hardly move, so he held me close. I did love dancing with Mel. I noticed John watching me. Mitch was talking to him; I wondered what they are saying. Now they were both looking at me. I was feeling very self-conscious. Mel was holding me so close.

"Are you okay?" I asked. He wasn't. "What's wrong?"

"Glenn's walked out on me."

"Oh, I'm sorry." I held Mel close now, hugging him.

"Let's get a drink," I suggested after the song had ended.

We went out to the foyer. It was very noisy out there, so we went and sat on the front steps with our drinks. "So, what happened?" I asked.

Mel began to tell me about how jealous Glenn had become.

"But who is he jealous of?" I asked, thinking I hadn't seen Mel flirt with anyone.

"He's jealous of you."

"Me?" I was dumbfounded. "But—"

"I know it's ridiculous."

"I'm sorry," I said. I just held onto Mel's arm with my head on his shoulder. Then he changed the subject.

"So what's going on with you and John? He's like twice your age," said Mel.

"No, he isn't," I said, trying to make him seem younger than he was. Why was everyone concerned with John's age?

"I don't know? It's just a bit of flirting," I said, knowing that I really did like him.

"It's more than just flirting. I've seen the way he looks at you," Mel said.

"Really, like how?" I asked, smiling.

"Like he wants you," said Mel in his sexy voice.

Just then, I could hear the band starting to play. "Let's go in," Mel said. He was feeling a bit better.

When we went in, they were having a great time playing some rock 'n' roll.

Mitch handed me a drink. I smelt it. "Scotch! Thanks." We sat down on the seats in front of the band. They were excellent, I thought, looking at John.

Mitch whispered in my ear, "John thinks you're avoiding him."

"But I'm not!" I suddenly had the urge to talk to John. I went up on the stage with a beer for him as the song finished.

"Sorry, I'm not avoiding you, Mel and Glenn had a fight, and he was upset. That's all." He took the beer and kissed me. "This one is for you."

The band started to play *We are the Champions*. Mel got on the mic to sing, and I joined him on the stage. It was so cool, everyone was singing. Then the band played *Don't Stop Me Now*, another *Queen* song. John already knew I could sing that one. Mel only knew the chorus bits, so I sang on my own. Mel joined me for the parts he knew. It was so much fun.

I didn't notice that everyone from the foyer had come in to see who was singing. When we had finished everyone cheered and clapped. It was the best feeling.

Karen came up to me. "I didn't know you could sing."

"I can't," I said, terrified she would put me in a show.

I quickly got down off the stage to get another drink. The band played another rock song, which was great dance music. I got up to dance with everyone. This time I focussed on John, not taking my eyes off him. After a few dances, they put early eighties' music on.

John sat with his beer in the front row of the middle section. I went and sat on his lap. The lights were dimmed low, and it was dark. Mitch had put flashy disco lights on the stage.

John and I just kissed. He was such a good kisser, so sweet and gentle. Adrien was flirting with Mel. I didn't think Mel was his type. He had even told me once that Glenn was more his type. Oh, well, I didn't care. I just hugged into John. He was so lovely, and I was getting so drunk. I felt so safe in John's arms.

By about 3 am, John suggested we go for a walk out the back of the theatre that was where his car was parked. We climbed in the back of his station wagon, as he had a mattress and blankets in there. It was quite comfortable. It was a bit tricky to get my jeans off in the back of the station wagon, but I managed it, as did he. He must have had a lot of practice at that, this wasn't a first for John as he seemed very prepared; he even had a condom, but I was too drunk to care. I just felt comfortable in John's arms. It was so dark that no one would have seen us if they had walked past. I could barely see John. He was so passionate. Once he was inside of me, oh, he was so good. I had wanted him so much. The windows were fogging up from the heat happening between us, and I didn't want it to end. When it did, we just held each other for the longest time. I didn't want to let go.

We must have fallen asleep; I opened my eyes, and it was daylight, though only just, my guess was about 5.30. Someone banged on the window. I couldn't see who it was; I was still naked.

John stirred. "It's too early," he mumbled and went back to sleep.

I had to get home. I started looking for my clothes. It was tough to see getting dressed in the back of the station wagon. I managed to find my clothes. I got dressed feeling twisted and uncomfortable.

As I was putting my boots on, John asked, "Where are you going?"

"I have a daughter, remember? I need to go."

He pulled me towards him. I fell back, lying back next to him, and he kissed me.

"Do you need a lift?" he asked. That wasn't what I was hoping to hear. What about, you were wonderful; I want to see you again; I can't live without you…? No, he just went back to sleep.

"No, I'm fine. I have to go."

I got out of the station wagon, straightened myself up and fixed my jeans so I could do them up. I headed out to the main road to hail a cab. I looked at my watch, and it was only 5 am.

By the time I got home, the sun was coming up. I snuck in expecting to see the sitter asleep on the sofa, but no one was there. Maybe Adrien had sent her home. I opened his door, and he was alone. I crept in and climbed in next to him, and he rolled over to hug me.

"Did you have a good night?" he asked.

"Just hold me," I said, not knowing how I was feeling.

When we finally got up for breakfast, I was very quiet. Elizabeth was doing all the talking. She'd had a great time with Angie, the sitter. I sat at the table with my mummy smile, hiding what I was feeling, so tired and exhausted, with a slight headache and wanting to see John again. Sipping my tea, Elizabeth was going on and on about what they had done. The morning went fast. We had to be back at the theatre by 11 am for the set strike.

We pulled up and parked the car. Adrien drove; I noticed John's car was gone. We went inside. I looked up at the stage where the band had been. It was empty; they must have packed up early and left. My heart sunk, but there was no time to think about that.

All the usual ones turned up to help. Gabriella was always on time, and she had brought food to make sandwiches for lunch. Tracy, Mitch, Chris, Karen even Mel and Glenn turned up. They looked like they had made up, and I was happy for them.

Tracy asked me, "What happened to you last night? You disappeared."

Mitch overheard. "She fell asleep in someone's car, maybe," Mitch said with a smirk.

Tracy was dying to know. "You and John?" she whispered. I said nothing, giving a false smile.

We all went back to pulling the set down. The front of the stage was all pulled apart. My little hole, hidden from the world, where I had sat for three weeks, was all exposed. It was a sad moment. I had so enjoyed this show.

The day was a bit of a blur. I had a terrible headache, but we just kept working. We didn't stop for lunch until two.

I helped Gabriella make sandwiches for everyone and tea and coffee. Everyone was tired, and nobody was talking much. We just sat around a bit deflated after such a great party that had lasted three weeks or three months for some of us. When we got home, life would go back to normal, whatever that might be.

We all said our goodbyes and went our separate ways. I drove home with Adrien and Elizabeth.

Chapter 33

A year passed. Elizabeth had started school; she was in kindergarten, which was great as I could work more days. Adrien was working a lot more too, with longer hours.

Some nights, I just had my own company, which was okay. I would play my records listening to *Queen* after Elizabeth was in bed. One night, I was feeling very down. It was Friday, and I was listening to sad songs. They weren't really that sad, but they made me think of John. I hadn't seen or heard from him at all. Then my thoughts went back to Brett. I got out a notepad and started to write about my lonely, troubled life. I wrote about Brett and how I had loved him and lost him. I'd always loved writing, but I lacked confidence. I don't know if it was the music of *Queen* or my thoughts of Brett, but I just started writing.

About the only thing that kept me going was Elizabeth. I had to for her sake. At least until she no longer needed me. I wrote about my aching heart that couldn't love anyone else. My heart was so damaged; I didn't know why I kept screwing up any relationship I tried to make.

Why was I here? Maybe I was only here to make everyone else happy. Sometimes it felt like no one understood me. Everyone just laughed behind my back. I had such big dreams that only Brett believed could come true. I was the only person on this earth without a voice. The invisible person that was always there, that's me.

I left my notepad on the coffee table and went and climbed into Adrien's bed. He was still out, and I didn't want my bed tonight.

I didn't hear Adrien come home until he climbed into bed next to me. He just held me while we slept. The next morning after breakfast, Elizabeth was out the back playing. "Tell me about Brett." My eyes started to water.

"I can't." He had my notepad in his hand. "I can't."

Adrien took me into the lounge room and sat me on the sofa. "I think you need to." The tears just ran down my face. "I can't," I said.

He just held me. "Maybe later."

The day went like any other Saturday. I did the washing, listened to some music and Elizabeth played with her toys. After dinner, I put her to bed and went to sit on the sofa. Adrien came in with the scotch bottle and two glasses. He poured us a drink each and sat next to me, handing me one and I just started talking.

"Brett was my first love. He was the love of my life." I had a sip. "He believed in me when no one else did. He was the most caring and understanding guy, and he was my best friend. I loved him." The tears started to flow. I emptied my glass and Adrien filled it up again. "Brett and I had one wonderful night together. He was my first. It was almost by accident, but it was meant to be. We came together so easily. He will be in my heart forever."

"Brett had a girlfriend, but she didn't love him as I did. Brett was torn between her and me, but he stayed with her. Brett was still my closest friend. He told me he loved me, and I know he did. Brett was always there for me. He was my soulmate. Nobody knew about our one night together, and we kept it our secret. Even though Brett stayed with her, we had the best friendship. We spent a lot of time together. I would tell him all my dreams, what I wanted to do with my life, and he would listen. Brett never laughed at me. He believed in me. Brett would tell me I could do it all. I just had to believe in myself. Nobody had ever believed in me before, not even my mother."

"Brett was so lost. His girlfriend treated him so bad; she cheated on him with our flatmate. He was so distraught that I think he blamed himself. Then one day, I watched him ride off on his motorbike." Tears started filling my eyes. "I saw a friend of his about a year or so later, and he told me that Brett had been killed; it was a road accident. I just died inside. I lost the love of my life." I had another drink. "My life went to shit after that."

"I was with Shane by then; I thought he was a decent guy, but by the time I realised he wasn't, I was already pregnant with Elizabeth. I had got myself into a deep hole with no way of getting out."

"But you did get out," Adrien said, wiping the tears from my face.

"Do you have anything of Brett's, any photos?" Adrien asked.

"No," I just shook my head. "This is all I have." I held up my hand.

"Your tattoo?" Adrien looked closer.

"It's a star," I said.

"He told me I would be a star one day. He gave it to me on my seventeenth birthday." Adrien laughed. "Sorry, that sounds so corny, sorry." Adrien wiped the tears from my face. "So that's why you give yourself such a hard time! You need to start living, girl, make these dreams come true. Brett wouldn't want you to throw your life away on self-pity. I read your notes, and you're a good writer. Why don't you write about it? Write a play."

Chapter 34

Adrien worked in the city at some government building. I wasn't sure what he did. I did ask, but he would say, "Too boring to talk about." So we never did. Unbeknown to me, Adrien was doing a little investigation work of his own, trying to track down Brett's accident. He knew people who worked in birth, deaths and marriages. He had given them as much as I knew about Brett, which wasn't much, to see what they could find out. Adrien found out a few weeks later that there was no record of Brett dying at all. He kept that to himself. Adrien was hoping he could find out something so that maybe I could visit his grave and say goodbye. Perhaps, he was under a different name, Adrien thought.

In the meantime, I started writing a play. I was getting right into it. It was cumbersome and a little too dark, but I thought it was a good start. However, it needed something else. I thought it would make a great musical. I couldn't write music; I could hum a tune, but that's not writing music.

Before I could think of that, I needed a script first. So I spent a few months trying to work it out, working full time now my time was limited. Every spare moment I would be working on the script, and every now and then, I would read it out to Adrien.

"Crap, but I like the ending. And that bit in the middle, but the rest is crap," he would say.

I just kept writing, and before I knew it, I had a small play written. I let Adrien read it. He went into his room and shut the door. He seemed to be in there for ages.

Finally, he came out. It was very late at night, so I was just about to go to bed. He said nothing. He went over to the table and poured two scotches and handed me one and clinked my glass.

"Congratulations, this is fabulous," he said. "I've never read such a beautiful story. It came from your heart. We should make this into a musical," he said.

I couldn't stop smiling. "You think we can?"

A few weeks had passed. Adrien had set up a play reading to 'air it out', he said. "We need to see how it feels."

We got a few of our theatre friends to meet at the theatre, which wasn't in use at the moment. Adrien had picked up a key. We had only six actors to do a reading. We read through and swapped roles around to see a different sway on things. Adrien and I just took notes about what worked and what didn't. It was a good night, and we came away with a lot of great ideas. We agreed to meet again next week.

Adrien and I talked in the car, both thinking the same thing, we needed Toby. He would be great for the lead.

"I'll call him tomorrow," said Adrien, who had everyone's number.

Toby had been in *Anything Goes* a couple of years ago. We didn't even know what he was doing now, but Adrien would track him down. He had a knack for talking people into anything.

We spent the week rewriting and changing a few scenes. Then we were ready for another play reading.

We were back at the theatre, and yes, Toby was there. Toby was handsome with a back street rough look and beautiful singing voice, which would be great if we had music.

Once again, we had our play reading with Toby. It was magic. Toby was perfect. We had made a few changes from last week, and it seemed to flow well with just a bit of tweaking here and there. I thought it would work. We thanked everyone and told them we would be in touch when we had it ready for a musical reading.

"Now all we need is music."

"We need Graham," Adrien said.

Graham, of course, was our pianist. He was a very talented and very busy man.

Adrien organised for us to meet for lunch, about a week later on my day off. Adrien seemed to get a day off whenever he needed it.

It was a beautiful sunny day, so we met in the park café. I wasn't sure Graham would remember me; he was always very professional during shows, and he never stayed late for the parties.

"Lovely to see you again, Stephanie," he said, kissing me on the cheek.

I was a bit nervous in case he said no. Good thing for me Adrien never shuts up.

We ordered our lunch and Graham ordered a bottle of white wine. I hated white wine, but I smiled and thanked him. Wine goes straight to my head, so I sipped slowly.

"Well, tell me about your play, Stephanie."

My mouth opened, but nothing came out. Finally, I said, "I thought you might like to read it."

"I'm sure I will, but tell me about it," he asked again. I took a rather large sip of my white wine, trying not to make a face. I looked over at Adrien for support, but he just sat there drinking his wine and let me do all the talking. Once I had started, you couldn't stop me. I talked right through our lunch and the second bottle of wine.

Graham was so delightful; he just enjoyed his lunch hardly saying a word, smiling and nodding now and then. When we had finished our lunch, we had coffee. I hated coffee, but I drank it. Graham stood to leave, taking the script.

"I'll take this. I would love to see what music I can come up with and just listening to you talk about it has already given me some ideas. I'll call you in a few weeks."

I couldn't believe it. We sat back down, and I looked at Adrien. "Wow, this might happen."

"I never doubted it," Adrien said as he emptied his glass. I was once again lost for words, trying to take it all in.

Adrien and I staggered home on the bus. It was a good thing we had left the car at home. Oh and the coffee! I was not feeling well. We caught the bus back.

Life was back to normal. I had my work at the coffee shop; Adrien went into the city for his work, and Elizabeth had school. Four weeks had passed, and we still hadn't heard from Graham. I tried not to think about it, but I was so worried that he didn't like my musical idea. Adrien said I had to be patient.

"Graham's a busy man."

Another week had gone. I convinced Adrien to give him a call to check how things were going.

He rang his number, but no one answered. He said he would try later. This time, he got an answering machine.

"Hi, Graham, Adrien here, we hadn't heard from you, just checking everything is okay. Give us a call back when you get a minute. Thanks, talk soon." He hung up.

Two days later, Adrien got a call from Graham's daughter, Beth. Graham has had a heart attack, and he'd had heart surgery. He was in St Vincent's Hospital recovering.

"Oh my God, is he going to be okay?" I asked.

"Yes, he'll be fine, but he needs complete rest for six weeks at least."

"Adrien, we should go visit him."

"Beth said not till the weekend." Adrien was concerned as much as I was. I could tell he was trying to hide it.

Come Saturday, Adrien and I decided to see Graham at St Vincent's. We caught the bus taking Elizabeth with us. I told her she had to be good and quiet as Graham was sick. Adrien told her if she were, we would get Macca's on our way home. Adrien hated Macca's, but it was Elizabeth's favourite. Bribery was our friend that day.

We went up the lift to the heart ward. I didn't know what to expect, but I was hoping he could at least talk to us. I got Adrien to go in first in case Elizabeth couldn't go in. A few minutes later, he came back out.

"It's okay. You can come in…and Elizabeth."

I hated hospitals. I hung onto Elizabeth's hand as if she was nervous, but she was okay. I was the wreck.

There he was sitting up in bed, looking like nothing was wrong. "Finally, some visitors!" he said.

"How are you?" I asked quietly. He pulled his gown open, showing stitches on his chest. I cringed.

"Oh, it's nothing," he said. "It looks worse than it is. I'm going home at the end of the week, and I'll be fine. Sorry, I'm taking so long to get back to you; before this happened, I was making good progress," he said, sounding like he just had a headache, not heart surgery.

"That's okay," I said quickly. "Plenty of time for that when you're well."

"Nonsense! I'll get back to it once I'm home," he said. I wished I believed him.

It took Graham a lot longer to get well than he thought. A couple of months passed, and we went to visit Graham at his house. He lived on his own as his wife had passed away over ten years ago. His daughter was looking after him, and she had moved in as a temporary arrangement. According to Graham, she was driving him crazy. She just cared about her dad. She was so lovely. She had a full-time job as well.

It was mid-August before Graham was back to his old self. Elizabeth was now six and doing well at school. We had another show happening: *South Pacific*. An oldie but great music. I was the assistant director for Karen again. We worked well together. There was most of the same cast as *Whore House* with a few new faces. We needed two little kids, so Elizabeth got to be in the show this time. She was so excited.

I had cut back on my drinking, as I think I overdid it last time. Elizabeth was getting older, and what would she think?

Adrien had a part too. He was Lieutenant Cable. He was quite tall and good-looking, and he made a great lieutenant. Rehearsals were going well. We had quite a large cast. We had plenty of men to play the army and navy blokes, and all the girls were nurses. We had a new member; Linda played Bloody Mary. She was only 21, but she had a voice that was so powerful, perfect for Bloody Mary. Her boyfriend Craig was in the show too. He had a small part; he was also a good singer as well.

Opening night was tonight, and everyone was a little tired as usual. We had been up late, working on the set. Chris had broken up with his wife. He had always said he wasn't happy. He had a new girlfriend, Laura, and she was lovely. She even helped out with set building.

Because Elizabeth was in the show, I helped out backstage. She only had one costume and wasn't on stage much. The other kid was Peggy's grandson Blake. Peggy was in charge of costumes, so she looked after the kids until it was time for them to go on stage.

I was a very proud mum watching Elizabeth up there. She had three lines and a little song with Blake. He was only five, and they were so cute together on stage.

Opening night was running well. We had a full house, but the rest of the shows weren't doing so good. We had to do a giveaway on the radio for some free publicity. Hopefully, tickets sales would pick up.

Well, a standing ovation is always good; it was a great show. I went out to the foyer. Chris told me he had seen Graham in the audience. I had to say hello. He had a crowd around him, everyone asking how he was. I had to wait my turn. Then he spotted me. "Stephanie, fabulous show, darling!" He was very extravagant. I couldn't imagine him with a wife. If I hadn't known any better, I would swear he was gay. Adrian thought so too. He gave me a big hug.

"Glad you enjoyed it! How are you?"

"I've never felt better! I was going to come and see you after all the shows had finished. We have a lot of work to do."

He left me feeling somewhat overwhelmed. Maybe my dream might just come true.

The shows did fill up. Most of the seats were sold, by word of mouth and in this business that went a long way. Our last show closed the first week of September, and we had our usual end-of-show party. I had a few drinks, but I didn't feel the need to drink as I used to. I felt pleased with my life. It was almost a scary feeling, something I hadn't felt before.

Adrien partied on, and he was enjoying himself too. I sat down, sipping my champagne and watching everyone dancing.

Chris came and sat down beside me. "You look happy," he said.

"I am. I think things are finally starting to happen for me."

"I heard you'd written a musical," he said.

"Yes, I have. We still have a way to go, but it's coming along."

"I'm so pleased for you." Then he went off to be with Laura.

I suddenly realised I'm all alone again. A sadness washed over me as I thought of Brett. But I knew Brett would be pleased for me.

Elizabeth was fast asleep across the seats next to me. Adrian was still up dancing. I was on my own, but I didn't mind. I smiled to myself. Life was good.

Chapter 35

A few weeks later, I was over at Graham's house, listening to some of the music ideas he had put together. He played this beautiful melody, a love song. He sang it to me. He was no great singer, but it was beautiful, and the words touched my heart.

"That was beautiful. The lyrics were perfect," I said with a tear in my eye.

"They're your words. They come from your story," Graham said.

I was overwhelmed. Graham played two more love songs he had written. They were every bit as beautiful and took my breath away.

Just then, the doorbell rang. "Ah, now my next idea," Graham said, walking towards the door.

I sipped on my tea, but I could hear a familiar voice coming down the hall. My heart missed a beat. It was Paul, Simon and John, from the band. I hadn't seen John since that night in the station wagon.

John kissed me on the cheek. "Good to see you," he said.

It had been nearly two years. Paul had his guitar with him, so did Simon.

"What's going on?" I asked.

"Well," Graham stated, "this is my other part of the music. I think we should make it into a rock musical, so we need drums and guitars for starters."

We didn't waste time getting into it. Graham already had drums set up, as he always had jam sessions in his house. John and Paul had been working on a few ideas already. I listened to what they had done so far. It was so loud. I tried to follow along, but I couldn't read music that well. Graham was on the piano while John and Paul sang the lyrics. It sounded pretty good, very catchy. It went on like this for most of the afternoon. I suddenly remembered Elizabeth.

"Shit, I have to go; Elizabeth's at school. I have to pick her up."

"Bring her back with you," Graham suggested.

"Okay, I'll be back." I ran out the door.

It would take me at least 20 minutes to get there, and I was going to be late. Green lights, trying not to speed, couldn't afford a ticket, looking at my watch, shit the bell would be ringing now. I was only five minutes late, but to a six-year-old, that's a lifetime. I had to bribe Elizabeth with Macca's. She didn't want to go to Graham's so I detoured home, hoping Adrien would be there.

I opened the front door and heard music playing. Great.

Adrien was baking; this was his latest thing. It smelt like biscuits. Elizabeth was in her glory. I quickly filled Adrien in on my day's events, and he was happy to keep an eye on Elizabeth. So I took off, heading back to Graham's.

It was unusually quiet as I walked up the path to the door. Graham had a glass in one hand. It must be happy hour. They were having a break, waiting for me, they said.

"We have finished one of the songs. The opening song actually," John said.

"But you have to sing it," added Graham.

"I'll give it a go." I looked at the music. I could hardly read the lyrics. "What's this line?" I showed John.

"I can't go on without you," he said. I think I just blushed. I grabbed my glass to take a sip; I never did like singing in public.

"Just tell me when to start."

They started to play, and John gave me the nod to come in. After about the third go, I relaxed and began to get into it. It was terrific. It had a fantastic beat to it, rock 'n' roll. Everyone agreed that the song was a keeper.

That night, we finished two and a half songs. We had too much to drink, and the writing was getting sloppy, so we decided to call it a night. We were going to get together on Friday night again. Paul decided to drive me home as I had had too much to drink. John had his van out the front.

"Where's the station wagon?" I asked with a smile.

"This is more comfortable." He kissed me on the cheek with a sweet smile. "Goodnight."

Paul drove me home, as he only lived around the corner from me.

"John's still single," he said.

"That's a shame," I replied, very un-affected by that comment. I was over John. That was nearly two years ago. Though he still looked pretty good.

We had a few more sessions together, but then we had to stop for a few months as Paul, Simon and John were in a band of their own and they had to work. They had three months of work set up doing gigs. So once again, we had to set it aside for a while.

Adrien and I decided to do a show together. Adrien had always wanted to do *Jesus Christ Superstar*. So this time, I was going to direct it myself, only because Adrian wanted to play Jesus. He was perfect for the role. We had open auditions on Saturday and Sunday, and it was well received. We had such a significant turnout that we had to run over two days. Adrien was on the casting committee, and I had Graham for the musical director. We were hoping John, Paul and Simon could play for us. It was going to be on in February, so we checked with them, and they were available. Fantastic, I thought.

The auditions were tough. There were so many talented people out there. I knew what I wanted. Lauren has been in a few of our shows, and I thought she could do the part of Mary. However, her audition wasn't what I was looking for, so when we had a break, I went over to talk to her. I told her it was a rock musical, and I wanted some soul and depth to her singing. After the break, Lauren had another go. She had taken everything I said on board, and she was brilliant. I had my Mary.

Judas wasn't what I was expecting. This guy called Tim turned up dressed in ripped black jeans and a black T-shirt. He looked like he was off the streets. A long-haired homeless guy maybe. He got up to sing *Heaven on their minds*. Everyone was blown away. Tim was brilliant. I was feeling thrilled with the cast that was coming together.

By Sunday afternoon, we had fully cast the show. This show was going to be one great musical. My first musical, directed by me.

Chapter 36

Rehearsals were going great. We were in our third week, and we were only rehearsing with piano at this stage, as the band were busy. They would only be there for the last three weeks, which was making some of us a bit nervous. I found out in the second week that Tim could play the piano, which was great because Graham had a family wedding in the third week and had to fly to Melbourne. So Tim took over playing for that week, and he was fantastic.

He was a lovely guy, about 30 from Perth. He had moved over only a few months ago. He said he did some theatre over in Perth, mainly at the university where he had done an arts degree in music. He was staying in Sydney for a while; he then wanted to go to England to see if he could get in any shows over there. He was so talented; I was sure he would make it.

The show was coming together well. Graham came back, and things were on schedule. Gabriella was my assistant, and she was so well organised; she made my job so easy, and I didn't have to worry about too much.

We had to swap one rehearsal around as Tim got a cold and had a night off. Gabriella just rang around and changed the rehearsal time. The chorus came in early that night, so no wasted rehearsal time; everything ran smoothly.

Our high priests sounded unbelievable, and their harmonies were just brilliant. Everyone was at their best. The next week finally our band would be joining us. I was looking forward to seeing John in particular.

I got off work a little early so that I could open the theatre for the band. They wanted to start an hour early to practise before everyone else arrived. I opened the theatre, but no one was there yet. Adrian had dropped me off and taken Elizabeth home for a few hours so she could do her homework and eat something before they came back for Adrien's rehearsal.

I was so excited; this was going to be a great show. I stood for a minute, just taking in my thoughts. How different my life would be if I ever got my musical going.

I walked into the theatre; it was so eerie being in an empty theatre. I turned the lights on. Suddenly, I saw a shadow move across the stage. Shit, what was that? Everyone was always saying that the theatre was haunted. I just froze for a second, and I could feel the hairs on the back of my neck stand up. Then I heard the band arriving.

They came in to set everything up, so we moved some of the front rows back from the stage so they could fit all their gear. We couldn't start the set build until the weekend, and Mitch was working on the plans. Graham turned up a little later. They started playing. I got goosebumps; the band's music sounded so fantastic. They were still playing when Adrien and Elizabeth arrived.

As people started to arrive, everyone came in to sit and listen; nobody spoke. Everyone was moved by how good it sounded.

I let the band have a quick break before we started the rehearsals. Tonight, we were doing the first act. We started with *Heaven on their minds*. The band started up, and Tim sang; he was so near perfect. It was like the role was written just for him; he sang it so well. It was going to be indeed a fantastic show.

The next number was *What's the Buzz*. Adrien started okay but kept stopping. He said the band was too loud and he couldn't hear himself. The group turned it down some. I was getting frustrated with Adrien; he was never usually this difficult.

"What's the problem?" I asked.

"I can't fuckin hear," he said, very stressed.

"Okay, everyone, have a break," I told the cast.

Everyone headed out to the foyer for a coffee break. "Adrien, do you want to have another go with just the piano?" I asked.

"No, I've got a sore throat; I should be at home resting. As a matter of fact. I'll see you at home."

Shit, what was going on with him? Gabriella came in with a cup of tea for me.

"Did Adrien just leave?" she asked.

"Yep, don't worry. We can go on without him," I said, slightly stressed.

It was going to be a long night. We carried on with the rehearsal, but it was so hard without Adrien. I was mad at him.

By the end of the night, I had a rotten headache. Then I realised Adrien had taken the car. Great, nearly everyone had gone. John was loading his van.

"I'll give you a lift home," he said.

"Thanks." Elizabeth was still awake. She had school tomorrow. It was going to be hard to get her up in the morning. John drove us home, dropping us off, and he left. He must have realised I was not in a chatty mood.

I went in. Adrian was in bed. I got Elizabeth to bed then made myself a drink and sat in the lounge room. Adrien came in and sat near me.

"Sorry," he said. I sat there in silence, drinking my scotch.

"My friend Jim died last night," he said. "He overdosed."

"Oh God," I said under my breath. Jim was Adrien's friend. He had been dating him on and off for five years. "I'm so sorry." I moved closer to Adrien and hugged him. Adrien just sobbed like a baby. I knew there wasn't anything I could say. After some time, I walked Adrien to bed and lay down with him till we fell asleep.

It was after eight when I woke up, and I was still dressed from last night. I kissed Adrien as he woke.

"Stay there. I've just got to get Elizabeth to school, and I'll be back."

Elizabeth was late again. I rushed her into school then hurried home. I took the day off work. I didn't want to leave Adrien alone today.

We spent the day lounging around, just talking about friends we had lost. We both had our crying moments. Adrien had lost his mother when he was only nineteen. I hadn't realised that. He had also lost one of his brothers in a car accident a year later. He made me think my life wasn't so bad. Then I remembered my mother and my sister and their horrible experiences with their life. At least Adrien knew his family loved him.

We decided to have a game of Scrabble to cheer us up. Adrien set the game up, and I went to get drinks. I made tea.

"Fuck that, I need a real drink," Adrien said, reaching for the vodka.

"I can't drink; I have to pick up Elizabeth at three," I said, but that didn't stop Adrien.

We played scrabble right up to lunchtime. Adrien was getting very drunk. I made him eat a sandwich and have a coffee. We had music playing. Adrien had put one of my favourite records on, *A night at the Opera*, so we took our lunch to the lounge to eat.

We were enjoying the music. Adrien was trying to sing the words with no hope as he didn't know them, but he did make me laugh.

"I'm in love with my car," he started mocking.

"Hey, don't make fun of Roger; he's my favourite. I love that song, no mocking allowed." I made this very clear.

"So if I played the drums, I might have a chance with you? You seem to have a thing for drummers," Adrien joked as he tried to dance with me. He was so drunk, hanging on to me as we fell over the pillows that were on the floor. I landed on top of him, and I couldn't stop laughing.

"You're my best friend; I love you," he said so sincerely.

"I love you too."

He hugged me, and I tried to get up, but he pulled me back to kiss me.

"What are you doing," I asked, laughing and pushing him away. *You're my best friend* started playing on the stereo. "How perfectly timed; it's our song!" I said.

I got up and sat down on the sofa. Adrien sat on his knees in front of me. "Why don't we get married?" he said. I nearly laughed, but he wasn't joking.

"Because you're gay," I said.

"Yeah, but we're so well suited. We're perfect together," he said.

We sat there listening to the music; I took the glass from Adrien and had a sip.

"No, you're right," Adrien finally said. I laughed and leant on his shoulder.

"You know, we'll always be friends; you know everything about me," I said. He picked up the bottle, and I clinked my glass against it.

"I'll drink to that, to always being friends," we both said and had a drink.

Sometimes, you need a day off. Adrien didn't go to Jim's funeral; it was going to be in Melbourne, that was where his family were from. We both went back to work the next day.

"On Saturday, we're starting our set build. Mitch and Tracy are coming over tonight," I reminded Adrien.

We both looked around the lounge room. "What a mess!"

"I'll clean up," said Adrien, "and you better go pick up Lizzy. Hey, Steph, thank you!" I smiled, grabbed my bag and ran out the door.

Mitch wanted to show me his plans tonight. He always had a great vision. I told him what I wanted, and he just made it work. We had an early dinner so I could clean up before they arrived. I was trying to hurry Elizabeth in the shower when Adrian yelled, "They're here!"

It couldn't be eight already, I thought. I got Elizabeth out, told her to get her PJs on and get into bed. "Only one book tonight, you've had too many late nights recently."

Heading down the stairs, I could hear Tracy laughing. "So what's so funny? What did I miss?"

They were sitting around the table.

"Nothing much, Trace, and I will head into the lounge room so you and Mitch can talk shop." They walked off.

Mitch had his plans on his computer. He had them all printed out to show me. I didn't know what I was looking at, no idea.

"So what's that?"

He started to explain each set change, but they all looked very similar to me. We must have talked for an hour at least.

"I think they all look great and the budget looks fine. How about a drink?"

Mitch packed up all his plans. I grabbed two more glasses, and we headed into the lounge room. Adrien and Trace were playing Scrabble.

"Adrien cheats," Tracy announced.

"I do not! That is such a word," Adrien protested.

"Where's the scotch?" I asked. It was on the coffee table half empty. I poured Mitch and myself a glass.

The Scrabble went everywhere. "I think I've had enough of Scrabble," Tracy said.

"That's just because I was winning," Adrien stated.

"Okay, that's enough, kids," I said, making fun of them. "Why don't you put another record on?" I asked Adrien as the last one had just finished. We just sat back to relax, and Adrien disappeared to the toilet.

"I heard Adrien stormed out of rehearsal last night," Tracy asked. "Everything okay now?"

"Yeah," I explained quickly about Jim before Adrien came back.

We didn't have a late night; Mitch only had one drink before they left. We all knew what was ahead of us.

Chapter 37

We made it to our set build. It was a cold day, which was unusual for February. The rain was miserable. The set was taking shape. We had to create a wing on the front right side of the stage. This time we had two levels so that the drums could be slightly higher. John was happy with that. John turned up to help. The musicians never usually helped with the set building.

Gabriella whispered in my ear, "Wonder who he's trying to impress?"

I quickly got on with the painting I was doing, but now I couldn't stop thinking about John. Don't be stupid, I told myself; he's not interested in me. He's already had me. I suddenly thought, maybe he was so drunk he didn't remember that night. My smile was gone.

We all stopped for lunch. Gabriella had bread rolls and homemade soup, which was so yummy. Everyone was enjoying their lunch, and the soup was warming us up. It was still raining outside. Adrien finally turned up. He had to go to work for a few hours since he'd had a day off. He said he had to catch up. Adrien was not known for his handyman skills; costumes were more his thing. John sat down next to me with his lunch.

"How have you been?" John asked.

"Busy, tired," I said, trying to sound casual.

"It's going to be a great show," John said, trying to make conversation.

"Yes, I think it will be." I got up to take my plate to the kitchen.

I kept myself busy for the rest of the day. Adrien was getting bored with it, and by three, he had had enough and wanted to go home; he used Elizabeth as an excuse to go. I didn't mind. He said he would cook dinner.

"I'll find a lift home, if you could keep me some dinner and I'll heat it when I get home," I told him.

Most of the cast were heading home. Gabriella said she had to go. Her husband was away, and she had her daughter at home. John was still there, just hanging around and looking a bit nervous. I picked up some empty coffee cups and took them to the kitchen to wash them. John followed me out. He looked like he wanted to go home, but he was trying to tell me something. I was trying not to notice.

"Are you heading off?" I asked, trying to sound like I didn't care.

"Yeah, I was wondering, would you like to go out for dinner, sometime?" I had never seen John so nervous.

"Why would you want to go out with me?" I didn't mean to say that; it just came out. I kept washing the cups.

"I just thought it would be nice to go out some time," he said a little shy and awkward. He was about to leave.

"Yes, that would be nice."

"I'll see you tomorrow, then." He smiled and left. He had a lovely smile.

I hadn't been on a date since before Elizabeth was born; now I suddenly felt nervous.

Tracy, Mitch and I were the last ones left. Trace and I sat on the seats in front of the stage, exhausted. It was only nine but felt later. We had finished for the day. Mitch was fiddling with microphones as we had a rehearsal the next night, and we wanted them working.

"John asked me out," I suddenly told Tracy.

"Oh, my God?" I just nodded. "That's so great, I knew he liked you; he's a lovely guy."

What had I got myself into, I thought. I didn't know if I wanted to start anything right now.

Trace and Mitch drove me home. I checked on Elizabeth, who was in bed fast asleep. Adrien heated me some leftover pasta he had cooked hours before, and we sat on the sofa watching some music video show that was on.

"What do you think of John?" I asked.

"He's all right, quite hot for an older guy. Why?"

"He asked me out," I said, eating my pasta.

A long pause. Adrien finally spoke, "I don't remember you ever having a date. When is this date?"

"I don't know."

"Lucky you." It was quiet for a while, then Adrien broke the silence. "Haven't you already had sex with him?"

I just smiled at him, not saying a word.

The next day, we went to finish off the set build. It was a pretty basic set. We had black steps going up the centre of the stage with lights all around the front of them. They were only on for 'King Herod's song' and the end of the show when Jesus died. It was going to look fantastic. On both sides of the stage and right at the back, we had scaffolding that the cast could climb on. We had even purchased some new lights that were going to look amazing.

We had a rehearsal starting at 6 pm, so I was trying to clean up the mess, which was all over the floor on the stage. We needed to clean up because the band had to set up as well. The band didn't like moving their gear once it's in place. So I quickly pushed the broom over the stage.

It was already five. Adrien, Elizabeth and I had been there all day, so had Mitch and Chris. They wanted to get the lights going so that tonight's rehearsal could focus on sound and lights.

I was going to sit up with Chris in the lighting box, so I could tell him what lights I wanted. Chris was very efficient. He had his script full of his notes. We had already gone over them, but just in case I wanted extra lights, Chris could add notes so he could program the lighting board later.

The costumes were looking fantastic; Adrien had been helping with most of them. Tim arrived. Oh my God, he had dreadlocks and wow! They looked really good. Tim had such a great voice that he was going to steal the show. Adrien would hate me if I said that out loud, but I'm sure deep down he knew that too.

John was setting up his drums, and Graham was getting help with his keyboard. Mitch was helping them both with their amplifiers. All the cast had arrived.

The band was ready, and they were doing sound checks. Paul and Simon on the guitars and everything were taking shape. It was five past six. I wanted to get started.

"Hey, Mitch, just about ready?" I looked at him, hopeful. He indicated with his hand, five minutes.

Ten minutes later, we were ready to start. I made my way to the lighting box. Chris had a headset on so he could communicate with Mitch, who was the stage manager. They didn't have a spare for me, but that was okay. I could concentrate on the stage lights. Chris was so good at his job; I didn't have to tell him too much. Lighter downstage, more colour, blackout here, spotlight there. Chris had an old recruit, young Ben, who was very keen to do the spotlight. By the end of the rehearsal, Chris had written all over his script.

We have dress and tech rehearsal on Monday night, Tuesday night is the final full dress rehearsal, and we opened on Wednesday night.

All the posters and signs were up on the front of the theatre. I went out to have a look.

It looked amazing. I must have had the biggest smile on my face. Mitch yelled out the door at me. "Great feeling, isn't it?"

Sure is, I thought.

John came out and stood next to me. "The show is fantastic, well done."

"Thanks," I said, feeling on top of the world.

"How about an early dinner on Wednesday before we open?" John asked.

"That would be nice, but I don't know if I can. I still have a lot to do before we open." I saw the look of disappointment on his face. "Friday night might be easier?" I said.

I still wasn't sure if I wanted to pursue this, but I didn't want to hurt his feelings. "Wednesday it is then," I said.

He leant over to kiss me, and it was a very gentle kiss. "See you tomorrow."

He still took my breath away, and I think I wanted more.

Chapter 38

John took me to a lovely Italian restaurant not far from the theatre. I didn't usually drink before a show, but I was so nervous I had a glass of red wine and John had a beer. After a while, I realised John was even more nervous than I was, which helped me relax.

We ordered pasta. Our conversation was all about the show. We talked about Tim, Adrien and Lauren, who were playing Mary Magdalene. We were laughing at Tim's jokes. For someone who seemed reserved, Tim had become the life of the party. Before we knew it, time had flown. We had to be getting to the theatre as the show was starting in forty minutes. John paid the bill. I felt uncomfortable about that. I wasn't used to all this generosity from a guy. It made me feel like I owed him something.

We got back in his van. John leant over to kiss me, and he was such a sweet kisser.

"I had a nice time," he said.

"So did I, thanks," I added. We hardly talked in the car. It seemed to take forever to get to the theatre.

I headed into the theatre, anxious to check everything was ready to go.

"You're late," Tracy said, as I walked backstage. "Adrien told me you had a date, so how did it go?"

I suddenly heard the drums, which made me tingle inside, John doing his warm ups with the band. "I'll tell you later," I told Tracey. I didn't want to talk about it right now.

I headed down to the green room where all the cast were doing their vocal warm ups with Tim. He took on the role since he could play the piano, doing scales.

Elizabeth was there with Adrien doing her warm ups after South Pacific. Elizabeth wanted to be in every show. The theatre was like her second home.

She spotted me and ran over for a hug.

"Adrien made pizza for dinner," she couldn't wait to tell me.

"Do you want to stay back here or watch the show with Chris?" I asked.

"Can't I sit in the audience?" Elizabeth asked.

"No, it's a full house, but you can watch it from the lighting box. Chris and Ben will be up there."

"Okay, I'll sit with Chris," Elizabeth decided.

"Break a leg, everybody. You're all fantastic. You've worked so hard. Have a great show! Enjoy yourselves."

The doors were about to open. The band was backstage waiting, so were Chris and Ben; they were about to head up to the lighting box. Chris said he would love to have Elizabeth up there, so off they went.

I was so excited and nervous. My first show! I couldn't believe how far I had come since moving to Sydney. I was quite proud of myself.

John kissed me. "You did well," he said.

I decided to stay backstage, as there wasn't much to do, only moving a table and a few props. But it was all hands on deck for the second half – the crucifixion – we were using red water paint that looked like blood. It made a hell of a mess, and everyone seemed to get it on themselves. Mitch was also taking care of the sound and microphones. He had to wire all the principals, as they were all using head microphones. We hadn't used them before, but they worked great in rehearsals.

I sat backstage, keeping out of the way and hoping it would all go well tonight. I was so nervous for everybody. I was feeling a little sick, so I went downstairs to the bathroom to wash my face. I think the excitement just got the better of me. Everyone was upstairs about to go on stage. I could hear the music. I closed the lid on the toilet and sat down, and I wasn't feeling well.

I must have passed out. The next thing I knew Gabriella was standing over me.

"Give her some air! Are you okay, Steph?"

I was feeling like crap.

"We called an ambulance; they'll be here soon."

Someone put a jacket under my head. I don't know what happened, and I couldn't move. My stomach hurt. The paramedics came, and they decided to take me to the hospital. They got me up onto the gurney, which was outside the back door.

"What about Elizabeth?" I said.

"Don't worry. I'll talk to Adrien. He'll look after her," Gabriella said, quite worried for me.

I went off to the hospital. I didn't realise how sick I was. They took blood and more blood. I had two IVs hooked up. I must have looked a sight. Adrien was suddenly there. "What are you doing here? You should be on stage!" I said a little out of it.

"The show finished forty minutes ago, darling." I couldn't take it in, as I was so out of it. Adrien was anxious, holding my hand. Nurses were fussing about, checking IVs; they hooked up a bag of blood to my IV.

"What's wrong with her?" Adrien asked.

"You'll have to talk to the doctor," the nurse said.

Adrien went out to find the doctor. The doctor said I had a bleed somewhere; he wasn't sure where. They had to do some tests. My blood count was dangerously low, so they had to give me blood, three bags I was told later.

"Will she be okay?" Adrien asked.

"She's still critical, but she should improve once we get the blood into her. Then we can do tests to find out the cause of the bleed."

Adrien got Gabriella to mind Elizabeth for the night, as he didn't leave my side. The next morning, I woke still feeling like crap. Adrien was asleep in the chair next to my bed, still holding my hand.

The nurse came in. "How are you feeling?" she asked me.

"Like shit. What time is it?" I asked.

"Three o'clock in the afternoon," she said.

Adrien woke up. "How are you?" he asked.

"I feel like shit." I started to get all teary.

"It's okay. You're going to be fine. You had a bleed in your stomach. There's an ulcer, but you're on the mend now. Everything will be okay." It sounded like Adrien was trying to convince himself.

"Is Elizabeth okay?" I asked, still all teary.

"She is having a great time at Gabriella's. I was going to bring her in, but I thought I'd wait till tomorrow."

"How did the show go?" I asked.

"Standing ovation, they loved me." Adrien could always make me smile. "John's been asking about you. He wants to come and see you, but I told him you were too sick. Can I tell him he can see you tomorrow?"

"Maybe, I must look like shit," I said, looking at my hospital gown.

"I'll bring your things tomorrow and fix you up for a visit. I'd better go, as I have a show to do! Bye sweetie." He kissed me goodbye.

The next day, Adrien turned up with some makeup, hairbrush and my lovely soft blanket to cover the ugly gown. Just as he finished making me look a bit more presentable, Gabriella came in with Elizabeth. It was so good to see her. She climbed up on the bed. I only had one IV in now, and Elizabeth was full of questions.

"Why did you leave me at the theatre? Are you better yet? When are you coming home?"

They didn't stay too long. Then John turned up with a bunch of flowers and a caring, concerned face. He was so sweet. Adrien took that moment to say goodbye and took Elizabeth home. Gabriella left with them.

"How are you feeling?" John asked.

"Been better." He handed me the flowers. "They're beautiful." I sat them on the tray table.

"I wanted to come sooner, but Adrien said you weren't up to visitors."

"Yeah, today was my first visit from Elizabeth too. How's the show going?"

"The show is fantastic! You have yourself a hit, so you better get well so you can make it to some of the shows." John was still trying to make a positive conversation. "And I'd like to take you out for a second date. I hear they're better than the first dates."

"That would be nice," I replied with a smile. John didn't stay too long, and he gave me a sweet kiss. Goodbye.

After he left, I started to realise how much I did care for John. But I couldn't, could I? I was always arguing with myself.

I was in the hospital for five days. When I finally went home, I was put on medication for my stomach and was told I had to rest at home for another week. I had an appointment with my doctor in a week.

John called over every day to check on me. I did what I was told and stayed home to rest. Adrien was fabulous. He took Elizabeth to school and picked her up. I think John was a little jealous of Adrien. He kept offering to do things for me, but Adrien kept saying it was taken care of and not to worry. It was sort of funny between the two of them.

The end of the show was coming up, and I wanted to go. Adrien fussed over me like a mother hen, but he agreed to let me go to the final show.

I wasn't allowed to drink for a few months. My doctor said my drinking was what caused the ulcer, but I wanted to see my show. The first show I had directed and I hadn't even seen it yet.

The night came. I was feeling so much better, not ready for a party, but I wasn't telling Adrien that. I got dressed up and wore the new blacktop and a pantsuit that I had bought weeks ago. I so wanted to look good.

Adrien left early with Elizabeth. He didn't want me to wear myself out before the show. John was coming to pick me up, and they had reserved a seat for me in the theatre. I was feeling a bit emotional. I had missed my entire show, and this was the last night.

The show was to start at eight so John came to pick me up at seven. He was dressed in his black costume shirt with gold embroidery over the shoulders. He looked perfect, so handsome, but I didn't notice the look he was giving me.

"You look so lovely," he said, giving me a sweet, gentle kiss, with his eyes smiling. He had such pretty eyes, I thought.

He took me by the arm and opened the car door for me, a real gentleman. At the theatre, I told him I wanted to see the cast. John walked me down to the green room. We walked in, and everyone gave me a round of applause. It moved me so much that my eyes filled with tears, such emotion. Everyone was so pleased to see me. Adrien came over in his Jesus costume to hug me. "You look gorgeous!" he whispered in my ear.

John had to get upstairs. I told him I would be okay, so he went to get ready. I said hello to Tracy and Mitch backstage, and then I went to find my seat Adrien had saved for me. It was right in the front row. Chris walked me on his way to the lighting box.

The band started. John looked so wonderful up there. He really was a great drummer. The show began. I was glad I had tissues, as my eyes didn't stop overflowing through the whole show. At the interval, Chris came running down to see me. He brought me a cup of tea, and everyone was fussing over me; I was a little embarrassed.

I had thought I was alone and had no one, but that night, I realised all these people were my friends. They cared about me, and they were like my family. They were my family.

The final song had finished. I stood along with the entire audience absorbing the applause. Then instead of a blackout, the whole cast came forward and stood at the front of the stage. Adrien spoke, and we all retook our seats.

"Tonight is our last show. We are so blessed to have our wonderful director Stephanie here. She became ill on our opening night, and tonight she got to see her show for the first time. We want to say thank you to Stephanie!"

Tim came to the front of the stage with the biggest bunch of flowers I'd ever seen. I was speechless, and the tears just ran down my face. I stood, and Tim jumped off the stage to give the flowers to me with a kiss and hug. Everybody applauded. I couldn't talk. I just mouthed 'Thank you'. and sat back down. I couldn't move, trying to pull myself together. The audience all left. The band finished playing, and John was at my side.

"Can I get you a drink?" I smiled at John. He was so caring.

I only stayed a little while for the party, as I was feeling tired. Everyone was having a great time. Adrien wanted to drive me home, but I didn't want to drag him away from the party. I stayed for an hour, but then I had to go, as I was exhausted. Gabriella offered to drive Elizabeth and me home, and I took her up on her offer. John was enjoying himself having a jam with the band. He saw me packing up my things and came running down.

"Are you going?" he asked.

"Yeah, I'm exhausted. I'm fine, you stay and enjoy yourself."

He gave me the biggest hug in front of everyone. Well, it was no secret anymore. I was falling for John.

Chapter 39

A month had passed since *Jesus Christ Superstar* closed. I was back at work in the coffee shop. John was away working as his band travelled a lot. Elizabeth was doing well at school. Adrien had a new boyfriend, Tony. I liked Tony, and he was a lot of fun. He was also a massive fan of *Queen*, so when he came over, he always played my records, and it drove Adrien nuts. Tony and I would sing along, just to annoy Adrien.

Tony seldom stayed over, and when he did, he left before I got up. Adrien told me once he didn't want to confuse Elizabeth.

"She's already confused," I said to him. "She tells people Adrien is Mum's boyfriend." She had asked me once if Adrien minded me kissing John. She told me she didn't want me to marry John because she didn't want to leave Adrien.

Adrien was flattered. "I wouldn't worry," he said. "You're not planning to marry John, are you?"

"No," I quickly said. "I'm never marrying again, I did that once, not doing that again, besides I'm still married!" Adrien gave me a face.

"What's that look for?" I asked.

"Well, John might be a bit old-fashioned about that. What if he asked you?" Adrien's words were putting fear into me.

"Nope, I told him ages ago I was never getting married again, and I was still married to Shane."

Now thanks to Adrien, that's all I kept thinking about, John would be home on Monday. He said he would come over after he had unpacked. He had three weeks at home then he would be off again. I needed to back off a bit and let John know I wasn't ready to settle down. I have a musical to finish. I needed to focus on that. I'm sure he knew that anyway. He'd been away for two weeks. He'd probably be the one who would want to back off. He could have anyone, so why would he want to settle for me? I needed to concentrate on my musical. It was taking forever. I should talk to Graham and get things moving again.

Monday came around. I had to work in the morning, but I was finished by two. John turned up at work to pick me up. I felt the pressure. John was assuming I would be happy to get picked up, what if I'd had things to do? I felt annoyed, was he controlling me? I didn't like it, and it made me feel uncomfortable.

"Is everything okay?" he asked.

"Yeah, I'm just tired. I was hoping for an early night," I lied.

"That's okay. We could stay home," John suggested. "I had a message from Graham last night. He wanted to know when we could get together to work on the musical," said John. "I'd like to get back on track with that, as it seems to be taking forever."

I needed to tell him, but I didn't know how I didn't want to hurt John.

"I need some space. I feel like I'm leading you on…into something, I'm not ready for, I need to get control of my life again, and I can't have any distractions."

I could see the tension on John's face as he pulled up outside my place, probably wondering what he did wrong.

"I'm sorry; I've always been a bad bet for relationships." I went to get out of the car and John raced around to my door.

"What did I do? You can't just leave it like that," John said, looking very much thrown.

"I just need space," I said, getting angry.

John grabbed me by the arm. "Please talk to me! What's happened?"

"Don't grab me!" I screamed at him and headed to the door, closing it behind me. John just stood there, but I didn't look back.

I heard his car drive off. I started to shake. I didn't want to hurt him as I slid to the floor, crying.

After a while, I got up and went to the bathroom to wash my face. I looked in the mirror, and my face was all red and blotchy. I started to cry again.

"What's wrong with me?" I shouted. I put some music on and went and laid on Adrien's bed. That's where I could hide from the world. Adrien was picking Elizabeth up today. She won't come into his room. I just wanted to be by myself.

I heard them come home. Elizabeth went running up the stairs to her room. Adrien locked the door, and my music was still playing. He went through the house looking for me. It wasn't long before he came to his room.

"Who are you hiding from?" he asked, trying to joke. The room was dark, and when he walked closer and saw my face and his tone changed.

"What's happened?" he asked, concerned. He shut the door and lay down next to me with his arms around me.

"I broke up with John," I cried. "What's wrong with me?"

Adrien just lay there holding me for a while. "You have to stop punishing yourself. You're a good person, and you're allowed to be happy." He sounded a little mad at me. "You need to put your past behind you and start liking yourself, so then you can love someone else. John's a good guy."

Just then, Elizabeth knocked on the door. She knew never to enter Adrien's room unless asked.

"You stay here, and I'll get some dinner happening." He told Elizabeth that I was tired and needed a nap and that they needed to cook dinner. They headed out to the kitchen.

"Is Mum sick again?" Elizabeth asked.

"No, she's fine. What are we going to cook for dinner?" Adrien was very good at distracting Elizabeth.

"Pizza!" Elizabeth said with excitement.

"What about pasta?"

After dinner, he put Elizabeth to bed. "As soon as you're asleep, your mum will come up to kiss you goodnight," he told her.

"Adrien?" Elizabeth asked from her bed. He stopped at her door to look back. "Can you be my dad?"

Adrien paused. "I'll have to ask your mother that one. Now go to sleep." He turned off the light, smiling to himself.

He cleaned up the kitchen and made a plate up for me.

"Elizabeth in bed?" I asked. "Yep, she's waiting for her goodnight kiss. I made you some dinner," he said, holding up a plate.

"I'll just say goodnight to Elizabeth first."

Elizabeth was almost asleep. "Are you okay, Mum?" She asked.

"Yes, darling, I'm fine, I'm just a bit tired that's all, good night." I kissed her and headed downstairs.

Adrien had turned the kitchen light off. He was sitting in the lounge room. With two drinks already poured and a plate of pasta was sitting on the coffee table. It was always pasta every time Adrien cooked; I smiled.

Now, this was nice, I thought, as I sat down. I ate my pasta and drank my drink, non-alcoholic these days. Adrien poured another for us.

"So what happened?" he asked. I had another sip of my drink.

"I don't know, I started to care for John, and it freaked me out."

"So you dumped him because you were falling in love with him?" Adrien knew me so well.

"Maybe," I said. Hearing it out loud made me sound like an idiot.

"Are you scared of being happy?" he asked.

"No, I'm happier on my own. I can't be dependent on anyone. That's how you get hurt, and I've done better on my own." I finished my drink. "It's too hard to pick up the pieces when it all goes wrong."

"Sometimes, it works out, you know," said Adrien. "Elizabeth asked me if I could be her dad." He drank his drink. I just looked at Adrien and smiled. He already was.

On Friday, John rang Adrien and asked to meet up while I was working. Adrien agreed, and they met at the local pub for a drink. John wanted to know why. Adrien knew what John was asking.

"Steph will never let anyone get close to her. She got hurt so bad once, and she's still running from it; I don't think she will ever trust anyone again."

John was frustrated. "But I love her."

"That's your problem. Steph knows you love her, so she'll run a mile. Steph will keep pushing you away until you give up. She's falling for you, but she got hurt terribly a long time ago, and it scares the shit out of her. If you love her, you have to be patient, let her go, if she comes back, she's yours, if she doesn't, she never was."

John drank his beer. "Then I won't give up."

John kept his distance, giving me some space.

I knew he was going away. I started to be my old self again.

I felt like having a party.

"Let's invite Tracy, Mitch and Gabriella around on Saturday night," I suggested to Adrien. But Adrien was going out with Tony. I didn't want to stay home alone again. So I phoned around, but everyone was busy.

I ended up watching the video *Grease* again. I think I've viewed it a hundred times and drank myself to sleep.

Then the next day, I was woken by the phone ringing. I jumped up to answer it. It was Graham. He wondered if I was free to come over and work on the musical.

"Yes, that will be great." Finally. Now I could get out of this rut.

I had a slight headache from my drinking binge, so I took some Panadol with my breakfast. Adrien just arrived home.

"You late or early?" I said as he went straight for the coffee.

"Shit, I had a great night," he said, sitting down to drink his coffee.

"Did you stay at Tony's?" I asked.

"Nope, I spent the night at Terry's, you know from work. He had an awesome party, and Tony didn't want to go."

"Oh," I said, must be trouble in paradise, I thought.

"Well, I'm going out to Graham's to do some work so can I take the car?" I asked.

"Yeah, sure, Elizabeth can stay here if she wants; I'm not going anywhere."

"Yes, can I stay?" she begged.

"You're not too tired?" I asked Adrien.

"No, I slept fine." He winked at me. I didn't want to know.

I arrived at Graham's place, and Paul was there.

"I thought you were all away this week?" Paul said he wasn't leaving until next week.

No mucking around, we went straight to work. Paul played a new song he had been working on called, 'I can't go back'. This was a heavy rock song, and it had a great rhythm. A compelling song about leaving and having the courage to keep going. I loved it. He played it again, and this time, I sang along. It was for the female lead to sing. Graham played the piano, and we sang it a couple of times. We changed a few words that fit better. We had spent nearly all morning on that song. We were all pleased with it. Paul told me I had a great rock 'n' roll voice.

"Really?" I said, enjoying the compliment.

Then we had a short break, and Paul wanted to start on the other song he had been working on called, *Let Me Die, Don't Leave Me Here Alone.* A very dark song. It made the hairs on the back of my neck stand up. The song was about not wanting to go on as she had lost the love of her life, and she wanted to die with him. It brought tears to my eyes when Paul sang, and Graham played on the piano. The saddest song but so beautiful and exactly the way I felt when Brett died.

"I don't think we need to do anything with that. It's perfect," I told Paul and Graham, wiping the tears from my eyes.

Graham had been working on three other songs, and he wanted Paul to add in the guitar chords. I just sat back listening to them work it out. I was smiling to myself, and things were back on track. We had eight songs, so far all worked out. We still needed at least four more. Then we could workshop them again.

Paul was going away for two weeks, so we made time to have another workshop when he got back. Graham was going to work on two songs and Paul would do two as well. I was so pleased; it was all starting to come together. They talked about having a happy and powerful ending for the musical. "Everyone should leave feeling good after a show, not sad," Graham said.

Two weeks came around pretty fast, and this time, we had the whole band, including John. But he was fine. He said hello, kissed me on the cheek and asked how I was. We did the small chat thing and then got to work. I did a lot of sitting around. They needed to work out the drums and bass to fit in with the music. Simon came up with a fantastic riff on his bass. I just made the coffee and later handed out the beer to Simon and Paul. John only had one beer as he said he had to drive.

We kept going well into the night. I rang up and ordered pizza, so we stopped for a quick break.

Graham said, "I think we've got it all sorted now. We should sing them after we've eaten. Paul and Steph, can you sing the lyrics so we can see how it sounds?"

"No worries," I agreed, I was getting used to singing with the band.

We now had ten songs. We might need one more, maybe? We would have to see after we work-shopped it. We had a great run-through. Some of the song's lyrics were so moving that I had to wipe away a tear or two, which I tried to hide. The songs had such depth it was like they had read my mind, and they knew exactly what I wanted to say, but nobody knew about Brett; they all thought I had made him up, although it was never talked about, no one but Adrien knew the truth.

"Steph, I'm sure you should have been a rock 'n' roll singer; you're quite good you know," Paul said, and Graham and John agreed.

I knew they were just being nice; I would die on stage as a lead.

We were all really pleased, as it sounded so great. It was well after two when we called it a night.

Chapter 40

Another few weeks went by before we organised a reading and singing rehearsal to see how it worked. We booked the theatre for three days, hoping we could get all the bugs out of the show by then.

Graham helped ring around to get some good singers. He knew a lot more people in the business than I did.

It was hard to organise as everyone gets so busy, but Graham managed it. He got five females and five males that could sing and that we're willing to work for a free lunch. Adrien looked after Elizabeth so I could concentrate without disruptions. I didn't know what I would do without Adrien. I didn't want Adrien to see the show until I was utterly thrilled with it. He was very judgemental, and I wasn't ready for the critics.

The first day everyone turned up, which was a great start. I handed out the music. We just worked on the songs. Tina and Tim sang the leads, and they were such a good fit together. If I were putting this show on tomorrow, I would cast them in a second. I was lucky they were available as they were both about to start a new show across town.

We also had Amy, Lisa and Helen. Fiona was our high soprano. Their harmonies were so beautiful. Graham worked with the girls and Paul worked with the guys. We had Ross, Luke, Stephen and Matt. Stephen had a beautiful bass voice so he could hit all those low notes. They all worked so well together. By lunchtime, we were concentrating on four of the songs. Graham and Paul had to change a few of the notes around that were better in a different key or something like that. Anyway, it sounded better with Tina's voice. She had such a beautiful range so she could hit all those high notes as well as that rough rock 'n' roll style we were trying to produce. I didn't want the high soprano singing in the show, but there was one song, 'My heart is breaking', which had a lot of high notes that Tina and Fiona could hit. The two of them made it seem easy.

We had a fantastic day and got a lot of work done. Everybody seemed to enjoy themselves. Then I looked up to see John waiting for me at the car, and I suddenly got nervous.

"John, everything okay?" I asked. Everyone else had gone.

"I was wondering" – John hesitated – "if you would like to get a bite to eat?" I think he saw the worried look on my face. He continued, "Not a date, just two friends having a bite to eat."

"I can't tonight; I've got to get home. Adrien's going out," I lied. "Some other time, maybe," I said, trying not to hurt his feelings, yet again.

"Okay, see you tomorrow," he said as he headed to his van.

I got in my car, feeling a bit guilty for lying, but I didn't want to say no. We were getting on so well as good friends should, and I didn't want to spoil it.

When I got home, Adrien and Elizabeth had a surprise for me. I had to close my eyes and Elizabeth held my hand and led me to the kitchen where I was told by my excited daughter to sit down.

"Now open your eyes!" Elizabeth yelled.

There, sitting on the table was this beautifully decorated birthday cake.

"Happy birthday, Mum!" Elizabeth yelled with delight. I was so surprised. "You thought we had forgotten, didn't you?"

The truth was, I had forgotten about my birthday.

Adrien, Elizabeth and I were a family. I never had much of a family growing up. I had never had many birthdays that I wanted to remember, so I didn't give it a second thought. Elizabeth was more excited than I was about giving presents.

I played along. "I wonder what this is…on the shape of a record?" I opened it. Wow, the new *Queen* album, *A Kind of Magic*. It had been out for a while, but I just hadn't gotten around to buying it yet. Fantastic! Just what I wanted.

Elizabeth ran to put it on. Adrien gave me a much smaller present. "Happy birthday!" he said.

I opened it up. It was a stunning necklace with three gold hearts joined together. "It's beautiful."

"Let me put it on. Our three hearts together forever." Adrien put it around my neck. I stood up and hugged him.

"Thank you."

Suddenly, the screaming sound of *Queen* was coming from the lounge room.

"A bit loud!" Adrien ran in to turn it down a bit. We had such a lovely night of pasta, cake and dancing to *Queen*. It was the best birthday, with the two people I loved the most. I was twenty-six now, wow.

The next two days were inspiring. We had made such progress, so we were ready to do a run-through of the whole show. Adrien and Elizabeth came down to watch. I was a bit nervous, as Adrien hadn't heard the music yet.

We had the whole band there, John, Paul, Simon and Graham on keyboard. Mitch came to help. He set up equipment to record the music so we could listen to it later.

Everyone turned up on time and got on the stage, ready to sing, following along with the sheet music and improvising. Some had three or four characters as we didn't have a full cast. I thought it sounded brilliant, but I was wondering what Adrien was thinking. He could be brutal when he wanted to be.

We ran through the show, stopping briefly in between songs but pretty much kept going. When we had finished, I was waiting for Adrien to say something. He and Elizabeth had sat up the back for the whole rehearsal.

"Well done!" I thanked everyone for their help. They all said they would love to be in the show when it was up and running.

"You will be my first choice, that's for sure. You're all wonderful. Thanks so much."

Everyone was leaving. The band were packing up all their equipment. Elizabeth was dancing around on the stage even though there was no music playing.

I turned around to see Adrien still sitting there quiet, which made me nervous. I walked up the aisle and sat next to him.

I was almost afraid to ask. "Well, what did you think?" I asked, dying to know and hoping he was going to be kind.

He shook his head. "I think you're going to have a hit show on your hands. It's fuckin brilliant!" I couldn't stop smiling.

"Really?" I said. I had never felt so happy.

"You still haven't given it a name?" Adrien asked.

"I know I hadn't wanted to until it was all finished."

"Well, it's finished," Adrien said, waiting to hear me say it.

"I'm calling it, 'Brett, the Love of My Life'."

Chapter 41

Adrien and I continued to be involved with the theatre company doing at least one show a year. I started writing a book to fill in my spare time. John and I still saw each other as good friends getting closer all the time. I did love him I just couldn't tell him that; I think I'm too afraid it would ruin it. Our friendship was working out quite well. Elizabeth was happy with John being in our lives. I explained to her Adrien would always be in our lives and so would John.

One November morning, Elizabeth had gone to school, and I was putting the breakfast dishes in the sink when I heard the news on the radio that 'Freddie Mercury had died'.

"Oh, my God!" I sat down in the kitchen, unable to move.

Adrien was heading to work when he heard the news on his radio. He knew I would be upset, so he came straight home. He came in, and we just hugged each other; it was so sad.

"I didn't even know he was sick," said Adrien.

"Neither did I." I guess that was the first time I realised AIDS was actually real.

We had a *Queen* party to celebrate Freddie's life. We played non-stop *Queen* records all day. I told Adrien how I fell in love with *Queen* and Brett at the same time. It was one of the saddest days, but we made it a memorable one in honour of Freddie.

Four years had gone so fast. Elizabeth was eleven now. Adrien had broken up with another boyfriend, and I had managed to stay friends with John. We were good friends. We saw each other a few times a week, and he stayed over occasionally. We were friends with benefits but no pressure, just how I liked it. No demands for living together or any thought of getting married…and no chance of getting hurt. I was happy.

We had finally got a company to do my show. It had taken so long. The original cast had all moved on. Some were doing other shows, and Tina and Tim had moved overseas.

We got approval to do 28 shows, and if sales went well, a possible 28 more dates. I wanted to direct it, but they said that I didn't have enough experience. What a load of shit! I put my foot down, and they agreed to a co-director with this guy called Phillip. I wasn't so sure about that, but I decided to agree; I felt like I had no choice.

We had a terrible relationship, and we were always fighting. We finally agreed on the cast. When rehearsals started, our fights got worse. We couldn't agree on anything. After the first week, Phillip quit. The producers were going to pull out, but they came to a rehearsal and decided to let me continue. They argued that they had already invested money and needed to get some back. Ticket sales were going well, but they wouldn't admit that I was right.

We only had a six-week rehearsal, so we rehearsed at night while the set was getting built during the day. Adrien came down every night to see how it was going. I think he and Elizabeth were my biggest fans. Elizabeth was so excited about the show. She wanted to be in it; however, I had to explain she was too young and that there were no children in this show. I told her next time I would write a show that had a role for her in it.

We had an excellent musical director, Peter Young. We had a great band: a drummer, two guitarists, a bass guitar and a keyboard player. Peter was brilliant, and he had everything flowing beautifully. John couldn't play in the show, mainly because he had gigs with his band already booked for the next six months, but he was at some of the rehearsals being very supportive. I was starting to feel safe and in control of my life. John and I had an understanding, and he didn't crowd me. He knew when to give me space.

Peter was in charge of the musical side of the show, and Graham was okay about it. I think I had worn him out. He was having a break from shows. He was nearly eighty, so he was slowing down a little. Just for a while, he said. He was coming to opening night as my date; he told me, Adrien and John could get in line. He made me laugh. I could never have got this show going without Graham. I owed him so much. He was like a father to me, the one I never had.

Adrien had dragged me out shopping. I was never one for shopping much, mainly because I'd never had any money to spend. So this was all new to me, spending money. I was thirty years old, and I needed to find an outfit that would make me feel and look 'spectacular'. Adrien's words, not mine.

Because of him, I was shopping for a new outfit for my opening night. I was so excited, but it was all a bit surreal.

Adrien knew where all the excellent fashion shops were, which was strange since he didn't wear dresses, but he said he knew this lady who owned this fashion shop and he'd known her for years. Through the theatre, Adrien knew so many people. He'd been involved in amateur theatre since he was very young. His mum got him involved. She was a great singer and actress, he told me, but she passed away years ago.

We seemed to walk for ages through the streets of Sydney.

"Where is this place?" I asked, getting sick of walking.

"We're here," he said. We stopped in front of a boutique. It didn't look like much, but we went in. I was a bit surprised as I scanned the shop. There weren't many clothes.

A lady came in from out the back.

"Ah, hello, Adrien!" she said, with an accent, that I couldn't place. Perhaps it was European. She was walking toward us.

"Hello, darling," Adrien replied in his flamboyant gay way. "This is Stephanie."

"Lovely to meet you," she said.

This was all a bit much! I thought.

"My name is Ruby. I have some lovely gowns for you to try, follow me." She led us to the backroom, which was more impressive than the little shop. There were a few chairs and a small table with two glasses and an opened bottle of champagne.

Adrien followed us, and he took a glass of champagne from the table.

"Is this for us?"

"Yes, darling. Help yourselves," she replied.

We sat down, and Adrien passed me a glass. It was only ten in the morning. Who drank at this hour? I raised my eyebrows and tried not to laugh.

Ruby brought over a lovely sparkly long golden dress.

I looked at Adrien. She had to be kidding.

Adrien loved it, but he looked at me and knew what I was thinking.

"Maybe something not so sparkly?" he said. I had another drink. I was starting to realise why you needed champagne when you shopped here.

The next dress was bright blue with a naked back. I had another drink starting to doubt I would find what I was looking for in this shop. Adrien had another chat to Ruby. "Maybe something a little less…wow-look-at-me and more…I'm-a-lady-of-style?"

She nodded her head and disappeared behind a curtain door. I think Adrien was starting to worry that we wouldn't find a suitable dress. He poured himself another drink.

Then Ruby reappeared carrying this three-quarter-length black fitted dress with a flowing skirt, long sleeves of lace, which flowed over the whole dress and a lace-up crisscross tie at the back.

I liked it. I looked at Adrien and nodded.

He stood up. "I think you should try this on," he said.

I went into the dressing room behind the curtain.

Ruby helped lace me up. "You need heels, what size?"

"Seven."

Ruby came back with slip-on black high heels. I stepped into them.

I turned around to look in the mirror. Wow! I hardly recognised myself. I walked out to Adrien, and he was stunned, speechless.

"Perfect," he whispered, walking around me. "You look beautiful."

I couldn't stop smiling. "Who could have known you would look this good in a dress?" Adrien said with a little sarcasm, as he had been telling me for years to wear a dress. I never wore dresses, as a rule, I was a jeans girl or long pants. I was amazed myself. I had to have this dress.

Adrien beat me to it. "We'll take this one," he told Ruby.

"Excellent choice," she said.

I couldn't believe the cost, but Adrien said, "You can afford it."

Yes, I could. For the first time in my life, I could. My show was finally putting money in my bank.

I was still uneasy spending so much on one dress, not that long ago, I couldn't afford anything new. Op shops were my shopping sprees.

We walked out of Ruby's with not much change out of five hundred dollars. I was feeling a little light-headed from the champagne, but I still had to buy shoes.

"I need something to eat," I told Adrien. As we walked up the street, I spotted a McDonald's.

"Macca's will do," I said.

"You've just bought a five-hundred-dollar-dress and you want Macca's?" Adrien said, horrified. We headed in to order.

"Can I have a cheese-burger, fries and a coke? What do you want, Adrien?"

He had the same. We sat there, eating our cheeseburgers.

"I remember when you were a vegetarian," I said, smiling at Adrien as he took another bite of his cheeseburger.

"We need to get you some shoes." He was still horrified we were eating Macca's.

After we ate, we found this little shoe shop that had a 30% sale.

"Let's look in here," I suggested. I headed towards the high heels. I found a lovely black pair of heels, and they weren't too high, so I tried them on.

"What do you think?" I asked Adrien while putting the second shoe on. He turned his nose up at my choice. He had a high-heeled pair of shoes that were way too high for me.

"I would fall over," I told him.

"But you're so short; you need height."

"No, I like these." I stood and walked to the mirror. Adrien thought they were too dull. Annoyed at me, he walked off to look again.

I kept looking then Adrien came over to me. "Try these," he said, holding a lovely black sparkle high heel. "Not too high," he added. I tried them on, and they felt good. I walked to the mirror.

"Yes, I like these," I said, looking down at my feet. "Well, that will do me."

"You're such a bore when it comes to shopping. In, out, let's go home. That's you. If you could shop from home, you would," he said.

"Maybe one day we'll shop from home, how great would that be?" said Steph, Adrien just rolled his eyes.

Chapter 42

One night, we were sitting on the sofa having a quiet drink and watching the telly, Adrien said, "You're going to lose John."

I looked at him, wondering where that was coming from. "What are you talking about?"

"After this show opens, you're never going to look back. You're going to be famous."

We went quiet for a while. I thought about what Adrien had just said. "I'm not going to change," I said, trying to picture being famous. "I'm the writer and director, nobody will remember me," I said, laughing it off. "Besides, John isn't mine anyway. We're just friends…good friends." I smiled at Adrien.

"He's happy the way things are; we both are," I said, feeling confident. "The only thing that has changed is I'm no longer broke, and I can live with that."

The show was getting close to opening night, and I was so busy. Thank goodness, Elizabeth was at school. She had some lovely friends and stayed over for sleepovers. It made life a lot easier when I had so many late nights; it took the pressure off me feeling guilty.

A few weeks later, it was Thursday afternoon, and Adrien had a surprise for me. He dragged me out on this raining miserable day with a bag full of something he wouldn't tell me what was inside. We jumped on the bus that took us downtown towards the theatre.

"What's going on? Rehearsal isn't till four," I asked.

"It's a surprise. You will find out soon enough," he said.

We got off the bus and walked around the corner and were across the street from the theatre. I looked up at the billboard above the theatre, and there was my name up in lights.

"Oh, wow," I said. It was amazing! I had finally done it. It read 'BRETT, Love of My Life' Musical by Stephanie Zinone. I just stood there looking up at the billboard.

Adrien stopped and opened his bag. He had two glasses and a bottle of champagne; he popped the cork and poured us a drink.

"Here's a toast to you, Steph, congratulations! You did it!" We clinked our glasses and drank, standing in the rain. I didn't even notice I was getting wet. How had I got here? I was getting teary.

Adrien held me as we danced in the rain with our champagne. People walked past looking at us, but we didn't care. It was wonderful.

Brett was the love of my life. He hadn't been in my life for some time now, but he will always be in my heart till the day I die.

The first four weeks sold out, and Peter had a press interview a few days before opening night. I got there early so I could watch. The press had already arrived when I walked in. Some of the cast came in as well so we could get a few photos in the paper.

I just walked casually past the reporters who were in the foyer. They had no idea who I was, which was how I liked it. Peter was a bit nervous, but he was used to it.

I whispered to him, "Just picture them naked!" He was always saying that to me to calm me down.

"Why don't you talk to them?" Peter said.

"No way!" I laughed.

I sat down in the theatre away from them, looking over my notes of things I needed to check on or do. I was a very private person. I never did speeches or spoke in public; it wasn't my thing, and it terrified me.

There were only about five reporters and some photographers. They took a couple of photos of the cast in costume and asked Peter some questions.

"Do you think the show will be a hit?"

"Is it true the writer is an Australian, and this is her first show?"

"Will it be travelling to Broadway or London's West End?"

So many questions. Peter had a prepared note to read out. "Stephanie Zinone is the writer and director, and Graham Logan is the composer of this fantastic new musical. It's been a pleasure working with Stephanie to get this show-up and running. I believe she has a promising career ahead of her as a writer and a director. I'm pleased to introduce Stephanie to you."

Oh my God, how could you? I thought as he walked towards me.

Suddenly, my mouth was dry. Now all the questions were directed to me. Peter took me by the hand to get me on my feet. I could have died.

"Is the story based on a true story?" asked one reporter.

They were waiting for me to answer. "Yes," I finally said. "It's the story of a dear friend of mine that I lost a long time ago."

I couldn't believe I had said that; nobody but Adrien knew that.

I don't remember what else I said, but suddenly, it was all over the entertainment pages in the paper.

"Stephanie Zinone, an unknown, has written about the lost love of her life, Brett. The new musical opens tomorrow night." I couldn't believe it.

Adrien was reading the article out of the paper over breakfast. "You're famous, my dear," he said, thinking it was a joke.

I was horrified. "I don't want everyone to know my business!"

I sat to drink my tea. "Don't worry; your photo is so small no one will notice it."

I grabbed the paper. "Show me! They didn't take my photo!"

He was teasing me.

"Stop it. I'm already so stressed about this." As I read it to myself later, I was a little flattered. Wow, my fifteen minutes of fame. I couldn't believe they printed that Brett was still the love of my life. What would John think of that? Maybe he wouldn't read it. I took it out of the paper and put it in my bedroom as a keepsake.

Elizabeth was staying at her friend's place. It was the school holidays. Adrien said it might be a bit of a circus. I'm glad I agreed not to bring Elizabeth after last night. I wanted to protect Elizabeth from the crazy media.

Opening night was finally here, and it was almost time to go. We were picking up Graham on the way. John, Paul and Simon were all coming as well, and they were all listed as the music composers for 'Brett'. I couldn't have done this without them, and they were always going to be in my heart forever.

Just before we were to leave, the phone rang and Adrien answered it. I was still in the bedroom checking my makeup and dress, as I walked down the stairs feeling and looking like a million bucks. Adrien came into the hall and looked worried.

"What's wrong?" I asked.

"It's Graham."

Suddenly, fear flowed through me as I made my way down the stairs. "What is it?" I asked again, scared of what I might hear.

Adrien held my hands. "He's had a heart attack. He died an hour ago." I suddenly couldn't breathe, Adrien held me.

"Oh, God, no!"

Adrien helped me to the kitchen chair to sit down. I couldn't believe it; I had become so close to Graham. Adrien poured us both a scotch. We sat there trying to take it in. The tears were welling up in my eyes. I drank the scotch down and got some tissues and wiped my face.

"We're going to be late," I said, standing up and straightening myself as if nothing had happened. Adrien was a bit taken aback, trying to work out what must be going on in my head.

I looked in the mirror that hung on the wall. "Shit, my makeup is a mess. Adrien, can you help me?" I pleaded.

"Come here, let me fix it." He wiped off the mascara that had made its way down my face and freshened me up with some new makeup. "Good as new."

"Are we doing this?" Adrien asked. Adrien had ordered a limo to take us to the theatre. There was a knock at the door. "Sounds like our car is here," he said. "We can do this."

He escorted me out the door to the limo. I had never been in a limousine before. Adrien held my hand.

"Are you sure you'll be okay?" he asked.

"Yep. Graham would want me to go. I have to for him," I said, trying to keep it together.

"By the way, you look beautiful," Adrien said, squeezing my hand.

As we drove up to the front of the theatre, I suddenly panicked. There was quite a crowd.

"Don't stop!" I yelled at the driver. "I can't walk past all those people." So Adrien asked the driver to go around the back.

"We'll go in the stage door," Adrien said. I started to calm down.

"I don't want to talk to anyone," I told Adrien.

"Okay, we can just go to our seats," he said, trying to get me in the back door. There was a security guard on the door, and we had to show our IDs to get in. Adrien tried to explain, but the guard didn't know who we were. Adrien was annoyed.

"It's okay," I said.

"But you wrote the bloody show." He made me laugh. He was still trying to argue even after the guard let us in.

Peter was already inside and came over to us as we walked in.

"My dear, you look beautiful," he said, kissing me hello. "We just heard about Graham. I'm so sorry."

I had to keep it together. "How is everyone? Ready to go?" I asked.

"Yes, do you want to wish them well? They're in the green room," Peter said gently. Everyone was dressed in their costumes, looking fabulous.

"Break a leg, everyone! You're all fantastic! Have a great show!" I didn't realise I was crying. Adrien was behind me when he took me by the arm and led me up to my seat. We had a box seat with all the boys; John, Paul and Simon were there waiting. I felt like a ragdoll going weak at the knees. Adrien held on to me and walked me to my seat while everyone was fussing.

"Sorry. I'm okay." I was annoyed at myself. Everyone sat down. Adrien had a pocket flask full of scotch, as he thought I might need some. He poured some into a paper cup, and I shot it down.

"I'll be fine unless the shows a flop." Adrien smiled. John sat on the other side of me and held my hand.

"You look beautiful," he whispered.

The lights were dimming. "It's nearly time," Adrien said. He was so excited for me.

The band started…The show ran brilliantly, and the audience seemed to be enjoying it. It ended with thundering applause. I was so thrilled. Everyone stood, and the praise kept going. Adrien gave me a huge hug. "Congratulations!"

"Congratulations!" said John with a loving kiss, followed by a hug.

Everyone applauded once again. Then everyone sat down, and the band started up for the finale. The cast sang their hearts out; they were fabulous. It was the most overwhelming experience.

My show: 'Brett'. I looked at the tattoo on my hand. Thank you, Brett, wherever you are. Adrien put his arms around me. We had a party set up for the cast, crew and guests in the building next door, which had a large function room. Adrien said we could go home if I wanted to. But I knew Graham would want us to celebrate, at least for a little while. John took my hand and walked me out of the theatre. I felt like a million bucks. Who would have ever thought this could happen to me? I hung on to John, who looked so handsome in his tux, as we walked into the function room. Adrien followed close behind.

Everyone was having a lovely time at the party; Gabriella, Mitch, Tracy, Chris and Laura were all there to help me celebrate. I then realised I had left my coat in the theatre. Adrien offered to run back and get it for me. There was champagne popping, music playing, appetisers getting handed around and a great atmosphere. Everybody was congratulating me. It was so fabulous!

Everyone was having a wonderful time, so I didn't notice how long Adrien was taking to get my coat. It was a truly magical night…my dreams had come true.

I looked at John. "I love you," I told him.

He held me. "I know, I love you too," he said. He handed me a glass of champagne. I finally felt safe and happy. I had found a new love in my life, John.

At the theatre, the staff were cleaning and locking up. There were a few people still standing around the front doors talking. Adrien was looking very handsome wearing the tux he had hired for the occasion. He found my coat and headed back through the theatre. When he came back out the front door, a man was waiting to talk to him.

"Excuse me," the man said, "can you help me? I'm looking for someone."

Adrien stopped and looked at this good-looking but somewhat rough man, about thirty or so, wearing a leather jacket like a biker.

"Who are you looking for?" Adrien asked.

"Stephanie Zinone."

Adrien suddenly felt a little alarmed. "And who are you?" he asked.

"I'm Brett."

Part 2: 'Brett'

Chapter 43

Being a single mum in the seventies was extremely hard. What made it even harder was trying to raise two boys when their dad was in prison. Carol lived in the city; she had a job working in a café, and the boys were all she had.

Brett was only six and his brother Rodney was four when their dad was sent to prison. Carol had to fend for herself. Nobody wanted to know, and times were tough. Brett was going to school, and he was in first class. He was getting bullied by the other boys, and Brett was having a tough time fitting in. He was small for his age, so he had to grow up fast.

He had two choices, get bullied or fight back. So Brett became a fighter. If anyone bullied him, he would punch them and make their nose bleed. When the kids saw blood, they got scared and left Brett alone. He only had to fight twice at school. The first time was because the kids found out his dad was in prison, and they teased him about it. So his mum got called to the school that day; the principal told Carol if it happened again, Brett would be getting suspended. A week later, the same kid called him a sissy, so he punched him to the ground. This time, Brett got suspended.

Brett had to try a new school. His mum thought a Christian school might be a better option. Carol couldn't afford the school fees but offered to work one day a week in the office in exchange for a reduction in the costs. That worked fine for a little while until the day Brett came home with black and blue bruises all over his legs; that's how the brothers dealt with bad behaviour. So Carol quit working at that school and took Brett out of there and sent him back to the public school. She told the principal nobody was going to harm her boys, and she made Brett promise not to fight.

By the time Rodney was starting school, Brett had got in more trouble stealing lunch money from some kids in his class. He told his mother he wanted to buy her a present for her birthday.

"But you shouldn't steal." She was very tough on her boys. She always worried about her boys ending up like their father.

Carol worked as a waitress in the city; she had been working there for two years now. It was so expensive, living in Sydney. Carol often thought about moving out to where rents were cheaper. Then she wouldn't have to work so much, and she could spend more time with her boys.

At work, there was a polite gentleman who was a regular and had taken a liking to Carol. He was very charming. He would leave a generous tip for Carol, trying to impress her.

He was very tall, almost six-foot, good-looking and very sure of himself. Carol was flattered by the attention. It wasn't long before they were dating. He was great with her boys. He would play cricket with them out in the street. They called him Uncle Paul.

After about four months of dating, Paul had asked Carol to marry him, but Carol was still married to the boy's father, Rick. She tried to explain to Paul that she was going to get a divorce, but it cost so much, and she didn't have the money. Paul didn't come over so much after that.

Carol worked so hard, so Brett had to look after his brother. He would walk him to school and home again. Brett had a key to let themselves in. Carol wouldn't get home until nearly six each night. Brett would make a sandwich for Rodney and himself for an after school snack. He put the TV on, and they would watch the afternoon shows. It was only a small black and white TV, but it kept them entertained until their mum came home.

By the time Brett was eight years old, he was looking after his mum and brother. He had learnt how to cook, well, he knew how to open a can and heat it on the stove, so he would have dinner ready for when his mother came home. He loved his mum and brother so much that he would do anything to protect them. His mum came home early one day. Rodney was so excited as she worked so much.

Brett was concerned, as his mum never came home early. She was putting on a brave face, trying not to alarm her boys. Carol had lost her job. Brett knew something was wrong. Carol used to say Brett had an old soul, as she couldn't hide anything from him.

Every day, Carol went out looking for work. She had to lie about her husband, saying he was dead. Every place that Carol went to they asked why her husband didn't look after her. Well, she couldn't tell them the truth that he was in prison for theft. Even though she had no part of her husband's criminal doings, they tarred her with the same brush.

It had been three weeks with no income. Money was running out, and she couldn't pay the rent. The landlord turned up on the doorstep one night and told her to pay up by the end of the week, or he would throw her out on the street.

She was so desperate. She finally got a job washing dishes for a restaurant, but they didn't pay enough to pay expenses and the rent.

A week later, Carol had to pack everything she could into two suitcases; they were homeless.

She went to a homeless shelter in the city, but they were full. It was getting dark, and she had to find somewhere for them to sleep. She found a church. Carol thought they could sleep there, but it was locked up. There was an undercover side entrance, which looked like it might be all right. She got the boys their clothes from the suitcase and put extra layers on them to keep them warm. It was only March, but it was already getting cold at night. They had a packet of biscuits for dinner that night, which she shared with her boys. She said she wasn't hungry, but Brett refused to eat unless his mother ate as well. He was a smart kid. No one could outsmart Brett, his mother thought.

At the age of eight, Brett had to grow up so fast. They huddled together to keep warm as they spent their first night living on the streets. Carol could hear noises through the night, and she didn't sleep much. It was quite scary in the dark, the sound of rats scurrying about and the odd drunk making his way home. They were all hidden from the road, but Carol still didn't feel safe. She stayed awake most of the night until she finally fell asleep.

The next morning, Carol woke to find Brett missing. Frantic, she packed up their meagre belongings while yelling out for Brett. Rodney was not quite old enough or strong enough to carry the heavy suitcase.

"Stay there and don't move," she said to Rodney.

She had only got one block when she saw Brett running towards her.

"Where have you been? Don't ever run off like that. What if I lose you?" She was angry and upset.

"It's okay, Mum. I got us some food," Brett announced with a big proud smile on his face while he opened his coat. He had bread, a jar of peanut butter and a bottle of milk; Carol didn't ask where he had got it; she was just glad to have her boy back. They had a good breakfast that day.

Carol made sure she got to the homeless shelter early the next night, so they all got a warm bed. They had ten days living on the streets, making it to the shelter each night.

Carol met a social worker at the shelter who offered to help her. She found her a room to rent at a boarding house. It was only one room, but at least, they were off the streets and safe. Carol managed to find another job in a restaurant, so things were a little better. Paul started to visit again. He had moved to the country, but he came to the city to see Carol.

The boys had to change schools again as the old school was too far to walk to, so they started at a small public school only around the corner from the boarding house. Things were okay for a little while. The new school was going well for Brett and his brother.

Brett would walk his brother home after school every day. They had to sneak in and be very quiet. The landlady had told their mother if there were any noise, they would have to leave. Brett didn't want to sleep on the street again, so he had to make sure his brother kept quiet. They would lie under the bed and Brett would tell his brother stories of adventures in wonderful places far away. Rodney loved Brett's stories. He would act them out with their toy soldiers.

They stayed in the boarding house for three weeks until their mum came home with great news. Their mum's friend uncle Paul had a house in the country, and they were all moving there. Their mum was able to marry Uncle Paul now and things were going to be better. They were going to be a family.

Chapter 44

Brett and Rodney were so excited. Paul turned up with a car to pick everyone up and take them to the country. It was a long drive. It took ten hours to get there. They had to stop a few times. Rodney got car-sick and threw up all over himself. Paul was very nice about it. They pulled off the highway, and Carol cleaned up Rodney while Paul walked up and down the road having a smoke. Brett tried to help his mother. He was worried Paul might change his mind and think two boys were too much trouble.

When they finally got to their new house, they were all so tired. It was late at night; Rodney was asleep, so Paul carried him into the house. The house was so big! It had two bedrooms. Paul took Rodney to the boy's room and put him into bed. There were two single beds with warm blankets, and the bathroom was just off the hall next to Paul and his mum's room.

The next morning, Brett woke up at first light. Their mum had told them before they left Sydney that they had to be on their best behaviour so Brett looked over at his brother. He was still sleeping. Brett quietly opened his door and went out to the lounge room to have a look around. There was a large TV, and there were orange lounge chairs with a large sofa and coffee table.

Brett jumped when he heard a noise coming from the bedroom. He quickly headed back to his room.

It wasn't long before their mother came and opened their door.

"You boys awake?" she said with a big smile on her face. Brett hadn't seen his mum smile for some time. "Are you two hungry?"

Brett was starving but not game to say.

They all sat down at the table in the kitchen to have breakfast, which was something they had never done before. Paul had plenty of food. There were Weet-Bix, cornflakes, toast, butter and jam, Brett and Rodney hadn't seen so much food in a long time. They were a family. His mum was happy, and Brett and his brother had a home.

Brett's mum had enrolled the boys in the local public school. Brett was in year two and Rodney was in kindergarten. They fitted in well. It was a small country school, and things were going great.

Carol got herself a part-time job at the RSL club in the bistro. Paul had told her she didn't have to work, but she wanted to contribute to the household. Paul had a good job, as he was a mechanic. Paul was always working on someone's car in the back yard for extra money. Brett was keen to help, and they were all settling in well.

Brett made friends with some local kids. There were a lot of kids in the neighbourhood, so plenty of friends.

Paul got some pushbikes for the boys. They were second-hand, but they worked on them and fixed them up like new; the boys loved their bikes. After school, they would rush home, get changed and take off on their bikes.

All the neighbourhood kids would be out playing until dark. There were parks nearby and a small creek with bush tracks for riding bikes. For a while, things were just perfect. The boys would play outside until dinnertime. Life seemed to be great for Brett and his family. Nothing much changed for the next five years.

Brett started high school. He was having a little trouble with bullies again; the town was growing, a lot of new families moving in. Brett was now 13 when he came home from school with a black eye. Uncle Paul wasn't happy, and Brett was sent to his room with no dinner that night with a warning if he were ever fighting again, he would cop a belting. Carol had a chat with Brett in his room. He told his mother this kid at school had tried to shove him in the toilet, so he had to fight back. Carol was understanding but told Brett to try to keep out of trouble.

A few weeks later, Brett came home with a ripped shirt. Uncle Paul went right off, giving Brett a hell of a beating and leaving bruises all over his legs. Rodney was scared of Uncle Paul after that; he was so tall, like a giant compared to the small boys. They both started to hate their stepfather. They were hardly ever home, always out on their bikes with the neighbourhood kids.

For Brett's 15th birthday, Carol bought him a guitar. She thought music might be a way for Brett to stay out of trouble. Brett was a natural. Every spare moment Brett would be strumming his guitar. Uncle Paul loved playing music on his record player. He had a few records: *The Beatles, Jimmy Hendrix, The Who* and *Deep Purple* were just some of the collection he had. Brett liked playing them as well, but he wasn't allowed to touch them without permission. Brett would try and play along with the records on his guitar. He never had lessons, so he taught himself.

Brett was not doing great at school, so Carol let him leave, he was almost 16, and he had got an apprenticeship with Uncle Paul. Brett enjoyed working on engines. One of the other guys he worked with had a motorbike, and this sparked Brett's interest so he couldn't wait until he was old enough to get his licence and his own, motorcycle.

Brett worked hard at his job, and this pleased Paul, but Paul always pushed him hard. Brett had to pay some money to Paul for his board and lodgings now that he was working. But he still managed to save a little, and by the time Brett was old enough to get his licence, he bought a second-hand motorbike. Brett fixed it up and worked on it every chance he could.

Just before Brett's 16th birthday, Paul had an unfortunate car accident. He was in the hospital for a few weeks. Paul had injured his back. When he came home, things had changed for the worse. Paul was unable to work, and he was on some pretty powerful drugs for pain. Carol was the only one earning any money. They were doing okay, but Paul was miserable and more depressed. Not being the primary income provider was hard for Paul to live with.

Brett was working and not home as much these days. He had his motorbike licence now and had made some new friends with other guys that had motorbikes. When Brett was home, he didn't notice how unhappy things were. Carol was working all the time, and Paul was drinking more and more. Rodney was in year nine at high school and kept talking about joining the army; that's all he ever wanted to do. Brett didn't realise Rodney's eagerness to join the army was to get out of the hell his home life had become.

Brett became good friends with Keith. Keith was a truck mechanic and was a little older than Brett, but they both loved motorbikes. Every weekend, they packed up their bikes for a long ride out of town. Brett was keen on Keith's sister Sally. She was sixteen, almost the same age as Brett. Keith was very protective of his sister and told Brett if he ever touched her, he would flatten him. Brett kept his distance, and he became more like her other brother. Brett spent a lot of time at Keith's place. His mum and dad were both lovely people and often invited Brett for dinner. He spent more time at Keith's these days than he did at home, which was probably the reason it took Brett a while to notice the trouble brewing.

By the time Brett was eighteen, things had gotten quite bad at home. He came home on his mum's birthday to find Carol and Paul having a huge fight. As Brett opened the door, Paul punched his mum to the ground. Brett rushed over with fists of rage throwing punches at Paul, but even though Paul was injured, he was much bigger than Brett and managed to bash him rather severely. Carol managed to get up to stop Paul from killing Brett.

She screamed at Brett, "Get out; I'll handle it!"

Brett didn't want to leave. He had a bad cut to his eyebrow, probably from Paul's ring, and blood was dripping down his face. So Brett got on his bike and took off. He ended up at Keith's place where Keith's mum patched him up.

Brett didn't tell Keith's mum what had really happened. She just thought he had got in a fight at the pub, but Keith knew. Brett and Keith were like brothers; they looked out for each other. Keith would do anything for Brett and vice versa; they were friends for life.

Keith asked Brett to move out with him if he wanted to get out of that madhouse, but Brett said he couldn't. Not while his mum and brother were there. He needed to make sure they were okay. He wished his mum would leave Paul, but she told Brett she couldn't. She felt like she owed him for taking care of her and her boys. Before she had met Paul, they were homeless she reminded him.

Things were not so bad for a while. Paul and Brett hardly spoke after the fight. Carol took on extra hours at work. Paul worked on his old car in the backyard but only a for a short time each day as his lousy back would start to give him pain, and he would have to lie down again. Rodney was doing well at school and still keen to join the army. It was all he talked about, and he couldn't wait till he was old enough.

By the time Brett was nineteen, he had finished his apprenticeship, and Rodney was finally old enough. Brett said goodbye to his brother. He was very proud of him. Brett watched him leave for the airport; he was heading to Melbourne to join the army.

Brett got on his bike and headed over to Keith's place like he did most days after work. As he walked into Keith's house, he knew something was wrong.

"What's going on?" Brett asked. Keith's mum and dad were looking very stressed and worried.

"It's Sally. She didn't come home last night," Keith said.

"Where the hell is she?" Brett asked, showing his concern. Sally was like a sister.

"She told mum she was staying at her friend Sue's place, but Sue said she hadn't seen her since Saturday."

It was now Monday.

"Well, let's go find her," Brett said, wondering why everyone was sitting around. "I've been out all day looking; she's nowhere," Keith said with frustration.

"Have you called the police?" Brett asked.

"Yes, of course, we have. We made a report, and the police said that was all they could do for now."

"Then we just keep looking," Brett said, putting his helmet back on. Keith grabbed his helmet and followed Brett out.

They rode around most of the night, stopping to talk to people along the way asking everyone they knew and people they didn't know. Keith had a picture of Sally in his wallet, showing everyone, but nobody had seen her. It's like she just vanished. They finally headed home hoping she was there, but she wasn't.

They all sat around the table, going over Sally's movements and trying to trace her steps. Nobody got any sleep that night. Keith got a map out, and they all worked out what areas they could search tomorrow. Keith's mum and dad were so distraught. Brett finally fell asleep on the sofa in the wee hours of the morning.

It was six in the morning when they were all woken to a knock at the door. Keith opened the door. It was two police officers, a female officer and an older man in uniform.

"Have you found her?" Keith asked.

"Can we come in?"

Everyone sat in the lounge room. "We're sorry to inform you, we've found a body that we believe is you daughter Sally," said the officer.

Keith's mum let out a terrible howling scream. "No!" Everybody just sat there in shock.

"Are you sure?" Keith asked.

They needed someone to come down to the hospital morgue to identify the body. Keith couldn't let his parents do that so he decided he would go and Brett went with him.

They took Keith and Brett in the back of the police car down to the hospital. They were both taken down in the lift to the morgue. Before they went into the room, they told Keith his sister had a few facial injuries. They were trying to prepare them for what they were about to see. They walked in, and there on a table was a body covered with a white sheet. They stood next to each other, trying to prepare themselves. A man in a white coat lifted the sheet back to show a young woman with cuts on the sides of her face, pale blue looking.

"Oh my god, Sal!" Keith said.

Rage was flaring up in Brett. "Who did this?"

Keith and Brett hugged each other. Keith whispered in Brett's ear, "We'll kill who did this. We'll kill them."

Chapter 45

The funeral was a week later. The police had no idea about how Sally ended up murdered. The cops found Sally on the side of the highway dumped like rubbish. Keith's mum and dad were in such pain they could barely function, and they never left the house. Keith was learning to deal with the loss of his sister, but Brett was so full of anger; he was like a time bomb ready to explode.

A few months had passed, and the police were still no closer to solving Sally's murder. Keith and Brett were sure the police had just stuck the file in a drawer and forgotten about her.

It was a Saturday afternoon. Keith and Brett went down to the local pub for a beer. They were sitting there quietly enjoying a moment of peace. There were four young guys playing pool, and they sounded like they had been drinking for a while. They were laughing and having fun then Brett overheard one of them say, "Remember that bend on the highway where that dead bitch was found?"

Brett flew out of his chair, diving on to the guy, crashing him to the floor and punching his head to the ground. The other guys started bashing Brett. Keith had to rescue Brett, but it was four to two. Brett was so full of rage he wouldn't stop until the police turned up to break it up. Brett and Keith were both arrested and taken down to the police station.

They were sitting in a holding cell for three hours waiting. Keith's dad came down to bail them out. He didn't ask what happened; he just dropped them off back at the pub so they could pick up their bikes. They both got on their bikes and headed home.

Brett came into his house with the sounds of Paul and his mum yelling at each other. Paul had been drinking all day. He said it was because of the pain. Brett wasn't buying that anymore; Paul was just a useless drunk. As Brett walked in, he noticed his mum picking up broken dishes off the floor and what was left of tonight's dinner. Brett just went to his room, shut the door, turned on his music and played his guitar.

Brett hated living at home with Paul, but he stayed for his mum. He still loved his mum and thought the world of her. The next day, Brett sat at the kitchen bench drinking a coffee that his mum had made. Paul was still in bed.

"Why don't you leave him, Mum?" Brett asked.

"I owe a lot to Paul. He was always there for me. And things will get better," she said, sounding like she was trying to convince herself. Brett grabbed his jacket and helmet, kissed his mum goodbye and headed out the door.

It had been four months since Sally had been killed. Keith had learnt to live with it, but he had never stopped thinking about Sally. His mum had never gotten over Sally's death. She still never left the house. Keith's dad did everything for his wife, the shopping, the cooking and the cleaning. His mum just watched TV. No matter how hard they tried to get her to go out, even just for a drive, she refused.

Brett was still having nightmares about Sally. He would wake up in a sweat trying to reach out for her, but he couldn't save her. Brett would have the same nightmare over and over. He stopped going over to Keith's place so much. Seeing his parents weren't helping Brett with his nightmares.

Brett would often go for a long bike ride up the coast, stopping to sit on the headland and looking out to sea, trying to find peace. Keith always knew where to find Brett when things were troubling him. They were as close as brothers.

Brett still had his job working as a mechanic, but he wasn't happy there. He would prefer to work on motorbikes. But he stayed working to help his mum out with paying bills as Paul was still unable to work and spent most of his mum's hard-earned money on grog.

It was a Friday afternoon. As usual, Brett had just finished a beer down at the local pub. He usually went home first, but today, he was feeling good, so he went to the pub with a few workmates. His mates were planning to stay for a while, but Brett decided to head home after one beer.

"See you all." He got on his bike and headed off down the road.

Just as he headed around the corner, Keith rode into the pub. He jumped off his bike and ran inside and noticed Brett's workmates. "Hey guys, have you seen Brett?" Keith asked.

"You just missed him, he just left. He's heading home," they said.

With a panicked look on his face, Keith ran back outside, jumped on his bike and took off in the same direction as Brett.

Brett got home. There were police cars out the front of his house. Paul and his mum must have been fighting again. He got off his bike and took his helmet off. Two policemen stopped Brett from going inside.

"I live here. What's going on? Where's my mum?" Brett said, getting angry that he couldn't go in his own house.

"Sorry, you can't go inside at the moment. This is a crime scene," said one of the officers.

"Where the fuck's my mother? Is she all right?" Brett screamed, still pushing against the police officers.

"If you don't calm down, we will have to restrain you." Brett was still fighting to get inside. The police officers pushed Brett to the ground and handcuffed him.

Just then, another motorbike pulled into the drive. It was Keith. Two more officers come out of the house, warning Keith to stay back. Keith dropped his helmet with his hands in the air.

"I'm a family friend. I'm here to help."

Keith looked at Brett, laying on the ground. "Brett, you okay?" he asked.

"They won't fuckin tell me what's going on!" Brett said with his face pushed into the front lawn and the two officers still on top of him.

"We need you to calm down," the officer said. They got Brett into a sitting position still handcuffed.

"Your mum has been badly beaten," the officer said. "She didn't survive. I'm sorry."

Brett screamed with so much pain. Keith got down on the ground hanging on to Brett. The two of them crying in pain.

After a while, the coroner's van arrived to collect Carol's body. Brett was un-cuffed now and just sitting on the front lawn with Keith having a smoke. The coroner's van left with his mum. Brett was destroyed; he had so much anger inside; it was tearing him apart.

"I want to kill him," Brett said in a whisper.

"Yeah, I know, mate," Keith answered, knowing exactly how Brett was feeling. Paul was nowhere to be seen. He had already been arrested and taken away.

After the police left, Brett and Keith were still sitting on the front lawn, not talking, just smoking. It was well after ten by now.

"How about we go inside?" Keith said. They both stood up, put their cigarettes out on the grass and walked in the opened door. Brett took one step inside and stopped. He looked around. He could see the empty bottles of beer on the kitchen bench and the bottles on the coffee table in the lounge room. There was broken glass all over the floor, and a small amount of blood was on the floor near the hall. That must have been where his mum had died. Brett went down on his knees, sobbing. Keith put his arms around Brett, letting him know he was there for him.

Keith spent the next week with Brett. Rodney came home; he was only given two days off from the army to go to his mum's funeral. Brett stayed sober all week. He wanted to make sure his mum got the best send-off that she deserved.

He was so proud of his brother who looked so handsome wearing his army uniform. He took him to the airport so that he could return to Melbourne. "I'm going away for a while. I need to get away," Brett told his brother. Rodney understood. He gave his brother one last hug.

"Keep in touch," Rodney said before heading to his plane.

Brett spent the next day emptying his mum's house. He packed one box of things to keep. He sealed it up and dropped it off at Keith's place. Keith put it in the garage up on a shelf.

"So where are you heading?" Keith asked.

Brett got on his bike and shrugged his shoulders. "Queensland? Don't know yet."

"Come home when you're ready; you always have a home here, mate," Keith said, not knowing how long it would be before he saw his best mate again. Brett just gave the nod as he rode off.

Chapter 46

The highways were long and lonely for Brett. He had his guitar and a change of clothes on the back of his bike. Brett just kept riding. He would stop at truck stops to have a bite to eat. Brett would sleep in bus sheds when it was raining or next to his bike if the stars were out. When he needed some money, he would pull up in the main street and play his guitar. People were generous and would throw him a few dollars that would keep him going. He didn't need much. Just enough for food and petrol for his bike.

Months had passed while Brett was on the road and winter had started. Brett was between towns when his bike started mucking up, so he pulled over to see what was going on with it. It conked out. He tried to start it again, but it refused to start. He sat down next to his bike and lit a smoke. A few cars went past before a Ute pulled over. The driver had his window down.

"You okay, mate?" the man yelled.

"Bike troubles," Brett said back.

His name was Wayne. He gave Brett and his bike a lift into town, and he offered Brett a place to stay till his bike was back on the road. Brett told Wayne he could fix his bike, but he just needed some parts. Wayne lived close to town on a five-acre block. He had a timber house and a rather large shed. Brett said he was used to camping out and would be fine in the shed.

"You can camp on the back veranda if you want; it looks like rain coming," Wayne said, looking up at the night sky.

Wayne was about forty. He had a wife, Katie, and they had three teenage kids. Brett didn't want to intrude, but Katie talked him into staying. Katie set another place at the table. "Where are you from?" she asked Brett.

"Nowhere really, been travelling for a while," Brett said. He was a bit out of practice with talking to people.

"Brett's just passing through, he needs some parts for his bike," Wayne said, passing Brett a cold beer from the fridge.

They all sat down to eat. Brett just ate in silence, watching the family eating and talking. He was amazed at how happy they all seemed. After they had finished, Brett thanked Katie for dinner. The kids helped their mum with the dishes while Wayne and Brett headed outside with another beer to sit on the veranda.

Wayne was doing most of the talking. He worked as a plumber with his own business. Katie had a job in town working four days a week for a dry cleaner, and the kids all went to school. This was what a typical family was like, Brett thought. He was starting to relax a little. These were decent people.

Brett made a bed on the veranda. Katie gave him an extra blanket. "It gets cold in the mornings. Goodnight," she said, heading back inside.

The next morning, Brett was invited in for breakfast. The kids were rushing down their cornflakes, not wanting to miss their bus for school. Katie had made their lunches, which she gave them as they headed out the door. Wayne made coffee, and they sat down to enjoy the quiet now the kids had gone to school. Katie finished her coffee and kissed her husband goodbye.

"Brett, you're welcome to use the bathroom if you like. Wayne will get you a clean towel. I'll see you tonight," she said, before heading out the door.

Brett had a shower. He hadn't had one for some time, and he also washed out his clothes under the tap in the shower and hung them outside to dry. Wayne gave Brett a razor so he could shave; by the time Brett had finished, he was looking half-decent again.

Wayne worked for himself; he said he had a quiet day – only one job on today. So he took Brett for a ride into town so he could get some parts for his bike. The only problem was that Brett was a little low on money, so Wayne paid for the parts. He told Brett he could tune up his Ute as payment. Brett was happy to do that. Wayne needed his truck for work, so Brett worked on his bike during the day and Wayne's Ute at night. Wayne had a big shed, so he hooked up some lights. Brett found himself smiling. He was actually enjoying himself.

Peter, Wayne's son, was watching Brett work on the truck. He was asking Brett all kinds of questions about engines. He wanted to be a mechanic when he left school.

"He still has two more years of school before that will happen," Wayne said.

Brett stayed with Wayne and Katie for almost two weeks. His bike was all fixed; everyone's cars were tuned up, including Katie's, and it was time to move on. Brett said his goodbyes and headed off back down the highway.

Brett rode for another week before stopping in a small beach town. It seemed friendly enough; Brett thought as he had a steak and chips at the local pub. There were a couple of bikers sitting nearby, and they started chatting with Brett. They told him about a caravan park down the south side of the main beach if he wanted cheap accommodation. Brett thought he might stay for a week or so. The guys seemed decent enough. They invited Brett to come and have a beer with them anytime as they were always at the pub after work most days. He shook hands with them and headed off to find the caravan park.

The park was a little out of the way and hidden, but he found it. He stopped at the office and parked his bike. There was an old bloke behind the counter watching a small TV.

"What can I do for you?" the man said.

"I want to rent a van," Brett said.

"You got any trouble with the law?" the man asked.

Brett wasn't sure why he would ask such a question. Then Brett saw a glimpse of his reflection in the mirror; maybe he looked like a guy on the run, who needed another shower.

"Nope."

"Well, that's okay then. I'm Patrick, call me Pat." He put his hand out to shake Brett's hand.

Brett got a history talk about the park and the area. Pat had lived there all his life. Pat walked outside, pointing down the back of the park.

"That's yours, number six," he said and gave Brett a key.

Brett got on his bike and rode up to his van. It was a little stuffy, he thought, as he opened the door and walked in to have a look. There was a bed in the end, a sink and a table near the door and a small fridge. It was the first home Brett had had in three years. He thought it looked pretty good.

He unpacked his stuff. He didn't have much, a blanket, some clothes, his guitar, a bottle of water and some tools for his bike. He put everything inside then got on his bike and went for a short ride into town to buy a few things he might need. It was a tiny town. Only one convenience store, a post office, which was also the bank and a chemist.

By the time he got back to the caravan park, there were a few cars parked nearby. When he got off his bike, a sweet voice from behind him said, "Hi!"

Brett turned around. There was a pretty young woman just standing there looking at him. She looked about mid-twenties with long light brown hair. "I'm Sky," she said.

"Hi, I'm Brett."

"You just moved in?" she asked.

"Yeah, that's right."

It didn't take long for Sky and Brett to become friends. Sky had been living there for seven months. She had a husband, but he shot through, so she told Brett. Sky was working at the local pub. She worked on Saturdays and Sundays as a barmaid. Brett thought it was nice to have someone to talk to.

There was only one garage in town, and the owner was Ted. Brett asked if there was any work going. He offered Brett two days a week. Things were slow, he said. Brett was happy with that. This place was only a small town so he knew there wouldn't be much work. On his day off, Brett went for a ride to the next town. It was a lot larger and only an hour's drive. He had a look around. There were plenty of shops there, but he liked the quietness of his small town near the caravan park.

Sky looked just like a hippie who had stepped straight out of the seventies. She was also a vegetarian and had her own little garden, in boxes outside her van. She had a lot of different veggies growing. She had come from a place called Byron Bay in New South Wales. Brett had heard of it but had never been there. Sky said she wanted to go back someday but not yet. Sky flirted at Brett with a smile. She was older than Brett, but he didn't mind; he liked her. He loved her free spirit.

It wasn't long before she had flirted her way into Brett's bed. She was very free about her feelings and sex.

"A girl has needs, more than a man does," she said, totally high on pot.

She grew her own marijuana and sold a bit on the side. She kept her pots inside up near the window, "They need sun. It's natural. You grow it, so it must be good for you." That was her motto.

It wasn't long before it became their afternoon routine. They would smoke pot then make out. Brett wasn't in love with Sky, but she was a bad habit he was becoming addicted too. He liked her, and she made him feel good.

Brett had made a few friends. They would meet at the pub after work and have a few beers. Steve and Pete, they were the bikers Brett met the first day he rode into town. They noticed how close Brett was to Sky.

"You know Sky's like the town bike, don't you?" Steve told Brett one afternoon.

"What do you mean?" Brett said, thinking Sky was the sweetest person he knew.

"Everyone in town has ridden her!" Pete said, laughing. Brett didn't like hearing that piece of information, so he finished his beer and headed home to his van.

When Brett got back to his van, he lit a smoke and picked up his guitar, strumming out a tune of *Stairway to Heaven*, trying to take his mind off what he just heard down at the pub. Maybe it was time to head home, Brett thought. Brett had become quite fond of Sky. Perhaps she would come along with him.

Chapter 47

The next morning, Brett woke up with Sky asleep next to him. She must have slipped in after she had finished work. Brett reached over to grab his smokes. Sky kept sleeping as Brett took a drag, got up and opened the door to take a piss behind the van. It was pretty quiet; Sundays were always quiet around here. He was just wearing his jocks. He reached over to the chair where his jeans were lying and pulled them on with his smoke still hanging from his mouth. He went back inside and put the kettle on to make himself a coffee.

By the time Sky got up, Brett was sitting outside finishing his coffee. He had the radio playing with laid-back seventies music on, which Sky loved. She walked out with her coffee and sat next to Brett.

"I'm thinking of heading out of here," Brett said, lighting another smoke.

Sky was alarmed. "What do you mean?" she asked.

"You know, moving on. Maybe heading back down the coast," Brett said, very casual.

"You going to leave me?" Sky said, slightly flirty.

"Well, I thought you might come with me," he said with a smile.

Sky sat there drinking her coffee, thinking for a moment. "Maybe I could," she said.

The next day, Brett was packing up his stuff. He could only take what would fit on his bike, which wasn't much. Sky was in her van, sorting out her things. She found a box full of photos, and there were pictures of babies and family shots.

"Shit," she said. She put the photos back and went outside to talk to Brett.

Brett was tying his stuff on the back of his bike when Sky sat down on the chair next to him. "I can't go," she said.

Brett turned around to face her. "Why not?" he said.

"I have kids." It was the first Brett had heard about it.

"What are you talking about?" He had no idea who this person was; he thought he knew Sky.

"I never told you. I didn't want you to know what a bad mother I was. I only get to see them once a month because I'm an unfit mother, so the courts say." Sky took a drag of her smoke before putting it out in an old can on the table. "If I go away, I'll never see them."

Brett was a little confused and shocked by this news. He lit a smoke and sat down on the other chair, trying to work out what he should do. "Then I'll stay," he finally said.

They ended up moving into one van. Things were going well for a few weeks. Sky had her visit with her kids coming up. Her ex-husband had remarried, and they lived in the next town an hour away. Brett dropped Sky off for her visit and planned to come back in an hour to pick her up. Brett was just about to ride off after his smoke when Sky came running back from the house all upset.

"They're not here." She was holding a note. "They've gone away for a holiday. I can't see them for another month." Sky just put her helmet back on. "Let's get out of here."

They rode home to the caravan park. By the time they got back, Sky had said she was fine, but Brett thought she seemed to be in a crazy happy mood. "Let's get some takeaway for dinner," she said with enthusiasm.

"Are you sure you're okay?" Brett asked, a bit confused with her mood swings.

"Yes, I feel great. I'll have a shower while you go get some takeaway."

So Brett got on his bike and headed off to the pub for some takeaway. He had a quick beer while he was waiting.

Brett picked up the takeaway and headed back home. It was just getting dark, as he needed his headlight on travelling back to the van. Brett parked his bike, no sign of Sky. He opened the door, but she wasn't there. He put the takeaway on the table. She must still be in the shower, he thought. He opened a beer and sat down to wait. After ten minutes, Brett was becoming concerned, so he headed over to the shower block.

He could hear the shower going, so he yelled out. "Sky, hurry up! Your dinner is getting cold."

There was no answer; Brett had an uneasy feeling and started to worry. He walked into the ladies shower room. "Sky, you in here?" he yelled again. Still no answer. He couldn't see anyone as he looked around, but there was only one shower going. He crouched down to look under the door. Sky was lying on the ground, unconscious. Brett climbed under the door and turned the water off.

"Sky!" He tried to wake her, but she was unresponsive. He ran outside to yell. "Call an ambulance!" He ran back in and put a towel over Sky's naked body. He sat there holding her lifeless body, "Oh, Sky, what have you done?"

The ambulance came, but they couldn't save her.

She died that day. Brett found an empty bottle of pills in the van later that night. The next day, Brett had packed up and was back on the road heading down the coast.

Chapter 48

Brett decided to go back to New South Wales. A few weeks later, he found himself in Byron Bay. He decided to look up Sky's family; she had mentioned she had a sister that worked at some health retreat, so he decided to look her up. Brett asked at the local garage when he was filling up his bike, as everybody knew everyone in small towns. He followed the directions from the guy at the garage.

He rode up on his bike, parked and walked in. There was a café that only sold healthy stuff, no burgers or fries. Not really Brett's thing but he asked if Karen was there. They were very accommodating. It was Karen's day off, but as Brett was a friend of her sister, they told him where to find her. She had a house in the bush not far from the retreat, so he headed off to look for her.

He followed the directions they told him. He was riding along a winding dirt road thinking he must have missed the turnoff, then finally there was the house with a bright yellow letterbox. He turned in and rode up to the house. It was very isolated and surrounded by bush.

A woman came outside to see who was there. "Are you lost?" she said.

"I'm looking for Karen," he said, knowing he had found her; she looked just like Sky.

"Well, you found her," she said, curious to know who this rugged good-looking fellow was.

Brett told her he was friends with Sky, and he had promised her he would look up her sister on his way through. Karen was very welcoming and made a pot of tea for Brett with fresh banana bread that she had baked that morning. They sat outside to enjoy the sunshine. "So how do you know my sister?" Karen asked. Brett wasn't quite sure how to tell her the news.

"We were living next to each other in a caravan park up in Queensland."

Then he told Karen about how Sky had died. Karen didn't seem to be that shocked; she was upset but not surprised. Karen talked about what Sky was like growing up.

"She had a lot of dreams. Sky was going to move to the city and become a singer or movie star. She was quite talented, and she could sing; she had a voice like an angel." Karen spoke with such love. "Then she got knocked up by her high school sweetheart and married him. A big mistake that was."

Karen just sat there for a moment thinking about her sister almost forgetting that Brett was there. They had been talking for a few hours; time just flew.

"Have you got somewhere to sleep tonight?" she asked Brett.

"No, not yet, I was going to find a caravan park to stay at."

"I have a spare room. You can stay here," Karen said, getting up to take the teacups inside, not waiting for Brett's reply.

Just then, a car came in the drive. It was Karen's partner Harry. He was a tattooist just getting home from work. He was very welcoming as well to Brett, offering him a beer. They didn't have a TV. They didn't believe in watching rubbish, Karen said. Harry was covered in tattoos – not what Brett was picturing for Karen's partner. Harry was such a great bloke. He and Brett got on well.

He offered to do a tattoo for Brett, so the next day, Brett followed Harry into town to his tattoo parlour. It was amazing. There were so many pictures of such different tattoos. Brett decided to get a tattoo on his arm of some wings with Sky, Carol and Sally written underneath the wings. Someone had to remember them all. Brett was starting to think that every woman close to him ended in tragedy. He told Harry about his mum and Sally. It was the first time Brett had spoken about them since he left home. They were both smoking some good weed at the time. Brett needed someone to talk to, and Harry was a good listener, even if they were stoned.

"Don't mention the weed to Karen; she thinks I quit," Harry said. "I only smoke at work, so that doesn't count," he said with a grin.

Brett ended up staying in Byron Bay for about six weeks. He got a few lessons in tattooing from Harry and by the time Brett was on the road again, he had tattoos across his fingers. 'Love' on one hand, 'Hate' on the other, which was what life was.

"You can't have one without the other," he said a little stoned.

Harry just looked at Brett. "You're pretty fucked up, aren't you?" Harry took another drag of his weed. Brett needed to go home.

The next day, Brett said his goodbyes to Harry and Karen. Karen gave Brett a farewell present. It was a record: *Queen,* their first album.

"This was Sky's favourite. She would have wanted you to have it."

Brett took it with a hug from Karen, packed it in his guitar case and loaded it on the back of his bike. He hit the road for the last of his journey home.

Chapter 49

A few weeks later, Brett was riding down the main street back home.

It was bizarre driving into town. Brett drove to his old house. He stopped out the front for a moment to find a different family was living there now. It hadn't changed much. It had been three years since Brett had left. Brett drove off, heading to Keith's place. He hadn't spoken to Keith since he had left. It was just getting dark as Brett pulled into the driveway. Keith's motorbike was parked in the front, as it was when Brett had left, and the light was on in the house. Brett parked his motorcycle next to Keith's, and he turned the motor off and looked up to see Keith at the door.

"Holy shit, is it you!" Keith said, opening the screen door. "It is you! You bastard, why didn't you tell me you were coming back?"

Keith walked over and hugged Brett. They were both so glad to see each other.

Brett and Keith went inside and sat down at the table for a beer. Keith talked and talked while Brett listened intently, trying to take in everything.

"Where's your mum and dad?" Brett finally asked.

Keith's expression changed. "Mum's gone. She passed away two years ago. I wanted to tell you, but I didn't know where to find you."

"And your dad?"

"He's fine. He's down at the club. He's discovered the pokies since Mum's gone. He's always down there. He'll be thrilled you're back."

Brett wasn't quite sure what he was going to do. He needed some money. The next day, Brett went for an early ride. He visited the cemetery to see his mum and Sally and to put flowers on their graves. Then he headed back to the garage where he used to work to see if he could get his old job back.

His old boss Jack was glad to see Brett and shook his hand. "Things are a bit quiet, and I've got full staff at the moment. Sorry, Brett, I haven't got anything for you, but it's good to see you."

Brett rode around to another garage. It was the same thing, no work. Brett went down to the local pub and sat with a quiet beer. It was nearly four and all the locals would be in for a beer soon as well as Keith. It wasn't long before a sizeable hairy biker walked in; it was Bubbles, Keith's mate. Bubbles knew everyone in town. If there were work going anywhere, he would know about it.

"I'm looking for work," Brett told Bubbles.

"Well, we'll have to find you some, won't we?" said Bubbles, emptying his glass. Brett went and got two more beers.

It wasn't long before the pub filled up. All the tradies were knocking off from work. A bloke with a long ponytail down his back walked in.

"Hey, Robbie!" Bubbles yelled out. Robbie turned and spotted Bubbles and gave the nod, grabbed a beer and joined them. Bubbles introduced Brett to Robbie.

"Brett's the best motorbike mechanic around, and he's looking for work," said Bubbles.

"Well, you'd better work for me then." Robbie owned the only motorbike shop in town. "When can you start?"

"Tomorrow," Brett said. He barely had enough money left to shout the next round.

Keith noticed how broke Brett was and gave him fifty bucks till payday. Brett loved working on motorbikes, and he also got to work on some beautiful bikes. Brett was envious; he always wanted to get himself a better bike. Brett worked hard. He was a good mechanic, and people liked him. He was working on a Triumph. It was so beautiful. Brett was polishing it up for the owner who was due to pick it up at any moment. The owner walked in behind him, watching Brett buffing over the tank with a soft cloth.

"She's a beauty, isn't she?" the owner said.

Brett obviously, loving his bike. Brett turned around with a big smile on his face. "She sure is."

"I'm Neal," he said, putting his hand out to shake Brett's hand. Neal had long brown hair, very skinny with tattoos all over his arms and looking a little like he just escaped from somewhere. Brett shook his hand.

"She's all ready for you," Brett said, a little sad to see her go.

"You new around here?" Neal asked.

"Yeah, sort of. I used to live here. I've been travelling for a few years."

"Might see you around then." Neal started up his bike and rode out of there.

Brett had been living with Keith for about a month. Keith's dad was very depressed. He was drinking a lot, and this made Brett feel uncomfortable. Brett would go down to the local pub after work, where he had made a few friends. Bubbles was always down there, and Neal started turning up for a drink on Wednesdays. They were all sitting around talking about the Darkwood Rally. It was a weekend for bikers to talk bikes, drink and look at other bikes, listen to bands and have a fabulous time. It sounded like something he shouldn't miss.

The weekend came, and Keith, Bubbles, Neal and Brett all headed off to the Darkwood rally. The bike shop closed early that day, so they could have a head start on Friday afternoon and get there before dark. It was a two-and-a-half-hour ride to get to Darkwood. The rally was on a large property with tents set up everywhere; Brett hadn't seen so many bikes. He was in heaven. They had to have tickets to get in, but it was well worth it. There was live entertainment with bands playing all weekend.

They rode into the property and set up camp. They all had tents. Keith had a spare that he lent to Brett. By the time they had set up, it was almost dark. They were all feeling pretty hungry, so they headed over to the barbeque area. There was a massive fire burning in the centre of the camp where people were drinking and talking and meeting new people from all over the place. Keith and Brett were chatting to this guy Steve. He was from Bundaberg in Queensland. He and his brother had come down just for the weekend. They were hoeing into their sausage sandwiches. The food was all included with the entry ticket.

A band was just about to start playing, so Brett and Keith filled up their beer mugs at the keg and headed over to check out the group. There were a few chicks up dancing in front of the stage. They already looked pissed. Brett didn't dance, but he was having fun watching the girls and enjoying the music. The band played till midnight. Everyone was pretty drunk and exhausted by then. Some had already hit the sack, and some looked like they were going to go all night. Brett and Keith decided to get some sleep as they had a whole weekend to enjoy full of activities and bikes to check out.

The next morning, dribs and drabs of people started to head over for some breakfast. They had plenty of food. Brett and Keith piled their plates up with sausages and beans, and there was plenty of hot coffee.

The morning was a little slow, but by ten o'clock, things were happening. Everyone was heading over to the front of the stage.

"What's happening?" Keith asked the passer-by.

"Wet T-Shirt competition!" one yelled back. Brett and Keith looked at each other and followed the crowd. There were so many people; they could barely see. The girls got up on the front of the stage. There were at least twenty girls – all shapes and sizes. Some of the women had the biggest boobs and some with not much at all. The buckets of water had to be thrown over the girls while the crowd was yelling out with excitement. It was down to four girls in the final. Then one of the girls pulled her shirt right off. Everyone just went wild so no doubt she was the winner.

After all that excitement, they all got into teams for a tug-o-war. The ground was all muddy after the wet T-Shirt competition, which made for a lot of mud sliding around. Brett and Keith fell in the mud. It was a good thing that they brought a spare set of clothes. There was mud everywhere.

It was the best fun Brett had ever had. After lunch, another band was starting up, all the bands sounded great. The whole weekend was fully packed with entertainment, food and so many bikes to look at, and all the people were so into their bikes. Everyone had the same interest, never short for conversation.

"It was totally awesome," Brett said to Keith on Sunday after breakfast. Some people were packing up and heading home for their long ride. The weekend officially finished at two o'clock.

They were filthy, dirty and exhausted but so happy. Brett and Keith had the best time.

When they got home, they cleaned their bikes, hosed all the mud and dirt off and then unpacked their dirty clothes. Brett's jeans were so muddy he threw them over the clothesline and hosed them off before they went in the washing machine. Keith's dad wasn't home yet. He was probably down at the club.

Keith and Brett had both had their showers, sitting on the sofa having a beer and watching TV when Keith's dad came in. He was so drunk Brett wondered how he had managed to drive home. He sat down in the lounge room.

"Where's my beer?" he said.

"Haven't you had enough?" Keith replied. They started to have a huge argument. Brett got up and headed out the front to get away from it.

The fights were happening a lot lately. Brett couldn't cope with the fighting. It reminded him of what his mum had gone through. He decided to look for his own place.

Chapter 50

Brett told Keith that he felt like he had intruded on his home for long enough.

"But you're family!" Keith said.

The next day at work during smoke'o time, Brett looked through the local paper to see what was around. He had saved a little, but he didn't want anything too expensive. There were a few two-bedroom flats for rent. He circled two of them and thought he would check them out on Saturday.

Saturday came, and Brett put on a clean shirt and a jacket he had borrowed from Keith's dad to hide his tatts. Nobody wanted to rent to bikers.

"God, I hardly recognise you!" Keith laughed.

Keith borrowed his dad's car to drive Brett to the flat. They drove down towards the jetty area of town where there were a lot of units. They both walked in to look at the first flat. Brett liked it straight away, and there was an old Triumph motorbike parked outside one of the neighbouring units.

"Ah, look at that!" Brett said, checking it out and almost drooling over the bike.

Brett didn't have to look any further. "This is it," he said to Keith. He signed the lease and moved in the next day.

Brett had nothing really except the one box Keith had kept for him and his record collection. All he had left in the world from his past. He loaded up the car for Keith to drive, and Brett rode his bike to the new place. They unloaded the car and dumped everything in the middle of the floor of the very empty flat. Brett was pleased with his new home. He looked around.

"I need some beer," he said to Keith.

"You need more than that, mate," Keith said with a big grin. "I'll be back later. I've got a few things to do."

Brett headed out as well. A while later, he came back with a few of life's essentials including, some food and a kettle. Brett was putting some of his shopping away when Keith came back with a trailer loaded up on the back of his dad's car. He had a second-hand fridge and an old sofa. Brett helped Keith carry them inside.

"Fantastic!" Brett said as he sat on the couch. Keith also had a carton of beer on the back seat. They both sat on the old sofa and drank a beer.

"You need a telly," Keith added. "I'll be back."

Brett stacked the beer in the fridge, which was working as it was starting to cool. He put his clothes in the bedroom where there were a built-in wardrobe and a table with a mirror and drawers next to it. He didn't have a bed yet, but he had a pillow and a blanket. He could sleep on the floor or the sofa, but he thought the floor looked cleaner.

He picked up his guitar. He hadn't played since he had left Byron Bay. He laid it on the floor and opened the case up. There sitting on top of his guitar was the *Queen* album that had belonged to Sky. He picked it up and had a look at it; it had been well loved once. Then he heard Keith pull up outside.

Keith walked in, carrying a record player. "It's not a telly, but at least you can listen to some music."

Brett helped carry the rest of the stuff in, speakers and a box of old dishes. Keith said they were spare things they didn't need from home, great! Brett unpacked them on the kitchen bench. Keith was trying to get the stereo up and running by connecting the speakers. Brett opened the box from his past. It was nearly three years since he had packed this box and he had forgotten what was in there. The first thing he saw was a picture of his mum. Brett paused for a moment then went and put the photograph in his room on the table next to Sky's *Queen* record. He then went back to the box. All his old albums were in there, *Led Zeppelin, Deep Purple* and a few other heavy metal bands he had forgotten he had. Keith walked over and grabbed the *Led Zeppelin* album off Brett.

"I'll have that." Keith went to put the record on the stereo to see if it still worked. It hadn't been used for a while; it was Sally's, but Keith knew she would have wanted Brett to have it.

He lifted the needle on to the record, and it crackled a little and sounded very mediocre. Brett turned the volume up. "That's better." Brett smiled.

"One way to meet the neighbours," Keith said.

It wasn't long before the owner of the bike at number one came up to say hi. His name was Levi, Brett had heard about Levi. He was well respected, amongst the bikers. Brett and Levi hit it off straight away, talking bikes. Levi was moving out next week as he had just bought a property out of town. He invited Brett and Keith to his house warming party the following week.

During the week, Brett bought himself a bed for his flat. It was looking more liveable now.

Brett and Keith were going over to Levi's place for his house warming party. Brett had his clean black Tee Shirt, jeans and a leather jacket. A bottle of Bourbon that was tied on to the back of his bike, and they were ready to go.

It was about a thirty-minute ride out to Levi's place, and by the time they got there, there were bikes and cars everywhere. Music was playing; there was a bonfire burning outside. Brett saw a lot of people he had met through work. Brett was a good mechanic at the only bike shop in town, so the word was spreading. Everyone who had a bike wanted to be friends with Brett with the hope of cheap repairs for their bikes.

There were quite a few people he recognised from the Darkwood Rally. Keith was talking to Neal. Neal had just lit up his smoke when a heavily pregnant, blonde woman came over and took it from him.

"I need a fuckin smoke," she said as she walked off.

"That's my old lady," Neal said to Keith. Neal took another smoke out. Neal was very tall and skinny and his missus looked like she could and would easily knock him to the ground.

Neal was talking about getting away next weekend for a road trip. Brett was keen, but Keith had plans. His mate Robert said his girlfriend Stacey was having her eighteenth birthday party next weekend, and he had told Rob he would go.

Jonesy was Levi's brother. Jonesy was a lot younger than Keith. He was only eighteen, and Keith was a good ten years older. Neal at twenty-two was the same age as Brett. They made their plans for the weekend.

Chapter 51

The party was pretty amazing! Levi had a large property of about fifty acres in the valley. It was very green with plenty of bush and a large timber house. Neal had just bought a property up the road from Levi's. It was only five acres, and they were moving in two weeks. That's why Neal wanted to get away; he said the missus was driving him crazy.

"She's letting you go away?" Brett questioned.

"Shit, no, don't tell her. I'll just go. She'll probably beat the crap out of me when I get back," Neal said, laughing.

Brett just drank his Bourbon. This guy was a nutcase, but he made Brett laugh. He was scared shitless of his woman.

A week later, Brett, Levi, Neal and Jonesy all headed off down the coast for a road trip. It was only to be an overnighter. Neal said there was a great pub they could stay at about a two-hour drive away. When they got there, the pub was empty. Brett had his doubts, but it was only 11 am. They all went in and had a beer and a game of pool when some locals started to arrive for lunch. The barman said they had a band playing later. They booked into their rooms, so they at least had a bed for the night.

There was a swimming hole not too far away, so after lunch, they all went for a ride down to have a look. There were people everywhere, a popular spot; however, there was one girl that caught Brett's attention. She had long brown hair and was beautiful. She was there with some girlfriends. The boys all sat down on a log that was near the river and had a smoke, but Brett couldn't take his eyes off the girl.

"Watch out for that one, Brett. She's a rich bitch. She'll break your heart," said Levi.

Brett just gave a weak smile as he dragged on his smoke.

The girls came out of the water and walked right past the boys. Brett just followed her with his eyes.

"Hey, ladies! Looking good," said Neal.

The girl looked straight at Brett, and he smiled and walked over to her. "Hi, do you want to go to the local pub tonight? There's a good band playing."

The girl smiled at Brett, enjoying the attention. "We're already going, so I guess I'll see you there." She then continued walking to her friend's car.

Brett yelled out, "What's your name?"

She looked back. "Sharon."

Brett walked back to the boys as she drove off.

"She'll break your fuckin heart," Levi said, but nothing could take the smile off Brett's face.

They got back to the pub, and Brett put on a clean shirt. They all went downstairs to have some dinner before the band started. There was quite a crowd for dinner, and the tables were filling up fast. They all ordered steak and chips, which they were hoeing into. Brett kept looking around for Sharon and her friends but still no sign of them. Brett was on his third beer when he spotted them walking to the bar.

He jumped up and headed over to her. "Can I buy you a drink?"

"I've just ordered," said Sharon.

He pulled out some money to pay the barman. "Allow me," he said.

"What's your name?" she asked.

"It's Brett."

"Nice to meet you, Brett. Thanks for the drink."

The band was starting to play. They played so loud it was hard to talk. Brett just stood there, enjoying the music. Sharon and her friends wanted to dance, so Brett looked after the drinks. Neal was on the dance floor flirting with the girls. He was trying to grope one of them as she pushed him away.

"Come on, you know you want it," he said to her. Neal walked back to Brett. "Those bitches are just cock teasers."

Brett was falling for Sharon; she was different from the girls he had known. She was nicely dressed. She didn't smoke or drink much. Sharon had manners; she was perfect. At the end of the night, Sharon told Brett she had had a good time. Brett wanted to see her again, so she gave Brett her phone number. He went to kiss her good night, but she moved her head, and all he got was a cheek.

He tried calling her, but her mother said she was out. The next day, he tried again, the same thing, she was out. He told Keith about her at the pub after work.

"Let's go to the drive-in on Saturday night," Keith suggested to Brett. "We need to find you another girl."

Brett and Keith went to the drive-in and parked their bikes near the front of the shop. Bubbles followed them in on his motorcycle. They went into the canteen to buy some drinks and hot chips. Walking back to their bikes, they noticed two young girls walking towards them.

"Hey, Keith, Bubbles, how you doing?"

Her name was Steph, and Brett had seen her around and thought she was quite cute.

"Hey, Steph, this is Brett," said Keith.

Brett and Steph talked all night sitting on the wall next to his bike. She told Brett about her new job she had just started. At the interval, Brett bought her a coke. Keith made an appearance to get drinks, and he said they were having a private party in the back row. Brett said he was fine where he was talking to Steph.

After the drive-in, Brett said bye to Steph and said he would come and see her at work sometime soon. She seemed to like that idea. Keith went back to Brett's place to play some music and drink some beer.

"How do you know, Steph?" Brett asked.

"I've known her family for a few years. Her sister was dating Robert, my mate from work," he told Brett. "She's a good kid; she's only sixteen."

"She's nice," Brett said. He liked her.

Chapter 52

Brett had bought a new electric guitar and amplifier. He loved playing along with his records, and it was *Led Zeppelin* when Neal and Bubbles turned up. Neal was on the back of Bubbles' bike and was off his face stoned. They came in with more grog and some weed to smoke. Neal had been fighting with the missus again, and she kicked him out. They had a baby now, and Neal said he couldn't do anything right. They partied on into the early hours. Everyone fell asleep wherever they could, and Brett went to bed.

A few days later, Neal called in to see Keith. He had made up with the missus, and they were having a big party on the weekend. "Tell Brett to come; he can bring whoever he wants."

On Friday, Brett and Keith decided to invite Steph. They headed over to the service station where she worked. Brett was falling for her, Keith thought. Steph was so happy to see them but trying not to show it. Brett asked Steph if she wanted to go to the party, and she said she would. So he organised to pick her up.

Brett and Keith rode off, stopping at Brett's work on the way home, as he had some spare parts he had to pick up. When he walked in, his boss told him he had a message from a Sharon. She was working at the Pizza Hut tonight, and he could meet her after work.

"Oh, wow!" Brett was happy for a second. "Shit."

"What's up?" Keith asked.

"Sharon rang; she wants to meet up tonight." Brett tried to think about what he could do. They headed back to Brett's place to get ready. "I don't have to pick Sharon up till 10.30," he said. "I can still take Steph to the party and duck out and pick up Sharon."

Keith wasn't happy. "You can't do that to Steph."

"I like Steph, but Sharon is so beautiful and—"

Keith butted in, "Fuckin rich. She's trouble. She's never going to fit in with us. She probably wants to chase you just to piss her family off."

Brett got annoyed. "Everyone I have cared about in my life has died. I can't deal with any more shit. I want someone normal who comes from a happy family without all the shit that goes with fucked up families. I want some normal in my life."

They got ready to go pick up Steph. Brett had a car he had been working on for his brother, who was coming to visit next week. Keith thought Steph's mum wouldn't let her go out on a motorbike, so they took the car.

Brett was amazed to see Steph had made an effort; she looked so hot. He didn't know how he was going to tell her he had another date. By the time they got to the party, Brett still hadn't told Steph about Sharon.

Brett got Steph a beer and started to mingle with everyone. Levi was there, and Jonesy got talking with Steph. Brett was relieved but kept an eye on her from a distance. She seemed to be drinking too much. When Steph went to the bathroom, Brett had a quick word with Jonesy.

"Could you look after Steph? I have to pick up my girlfriend, Sharon, at 10.30. If I don't get back, could you drop Steph home?" Brett asked.

Jonesy was a little confused. "I thought you were with Steph?"

"No, she's just a friend. Can I trust you to make sure she gets home safe?" Brett had a quick word with Keith and told him he wouldn't be too long. He took off in the car to pick up Sharon.

Brett arrived at the Pizza Hut five minutes late, just as Sharon was coming out the door. There was a pub within walking distance, so they headed there for a drink. Sharon wasn't keen on going to a biker's party, so Brett didn't push the idea. They found a quiet corner in the bar and Brett went to get their drinks. Sharon talked about her new job at Pizza Hut. Her father wanted her to go to university after year 12, but she had just turned 18 and wanted to live a little.

"Where's your family?" Sharon finally asked.

"My dad died when I was very young, and my mum died three years ago. It's just my brother and me now. He lives in Melbourne." Brett hoped she didn't want details. She didn't.

They had a lovely time at the pub. Sharon had to say goodnight. It was getting late, and she had told her mum she would be home by midnight, and it was an hour's drive. Brett walked her back to her car. They kissed goodnight, this time on the lips. They made plans to meet up the next week after work again.

The next day, Brett was having his morning coffee when Keith arrived. Keith walked in and made himself a coffee.

"How was your night?" Keith asked.

"Great," Brett said with a smile.

"That's good," Keith said.

"Did Steph get home okay?" Brett asked.

"I wondered if you were going to ask," Keith said a little annoyed. "Yeah, Jonesy drove her home. She got drunk when she found out you dumped her to go get your girlfriend."

Brett was now annoyed. "Who told her that?" he asked.

"Jonesy said that's what you told him."

Brett calmed down a bit. "I told Jonesy to make sure she got home safe, or he would have me to deal with."

The next weekend came, and Brett met up with Sharon again. This time, she told her parents she was staying at a friend's place and went back to Brett's flat for the night. Brett was a little shocked. He thought she was different from all the other girls, but she was very passionate, and it wasn't long before they were making love in the bedroom. She was on the pill she told him. The next morning, Keith turned up when Brett was still in bed. He got up and opened the door to let Keith in.

"You still in bed? You lazy bum." Just then, the bedroom door opened and Sharon came out.

"Well, hello," Keith said, a little shocked.

"This is Sharon," Brett said. "This is my best mate Keith."

"Nice to meet you, but I need to use the bathroom." Sharon headed into the bathroom and closed the door. Keith looked at Brett and shook his head, and then he sat down on the sofa to drink his coffee. Sharon came back out and started to pack up her stuff to go home. It was her dad's birthday, and her family were having a party. It was catered for so she couldn't invite Brett at such a late stage, she said. She gave Brett a slow sweet kiss, said goodbye and headed out the door. She had her own car, a flashy new one.

"You need to apologise to Steph. She's upset with you," Keith told Brett.

"I'm going to pick her up tomorrow and bring her over here," Keith added.

Brett looked at Keith. "Okay." He liked Steph, but she had so many problems and was as damaged as he was.

The next day, Brett cleaned up his flat a little. Sharon was coming over on Wednesday to spend the night, and Keith was bringing Steph over this afternoon. After he cleaned up, he decided to play Sky's *Queen* album, and this was the first time he played it. Brett put it on and listened to it. Wow, he thought, it was not what he expected to hear, so he played it again. This time, he tried to play along with his guitar.

It was such great music and lyrics. There must be other albums out there by this band. Brett decided to go for a ride down to the record store to have a look.

"Can I help you with something?" the guy in the store asked.

Brett told him he had an old seventies' record from a band called *Queen* and was wondering if they had any more.

The guy pointed to a poster on the wall. "That's them." Brett looked up at the poster. Oh, yeah, he did know them. He had seen them on *Countdown*; they looked so cool.

"Yeah, they have quite a few albums out." He showed Brett where to look. Brett had a flick through and decided to buy two albums, *Sheer Heart Attack* and *A Night at the Opera*. The guy in the shop gave Brett a poster for free. Brett gladly took it and headed home.

He couldn't wait to play his new records, so he put one on as soon as he got home. Brett then put his poster up on the bare wall. He stood back to have a look, Freddie Mercury, Brian May, John Deacon and Roger Taylor. They looked so cool up on the wall. He sat back to listen, taking it all in. Brett had always wanted to play in a band. He picked up his guitar without turning it on so he could hear the music as he played along.

Time flew, and it was nearly two o'clock.

"Shit!" Brett had almost forgotten he had to pick his brother up at the airport.

There was Rodney, leaning against the pole outside the airport. Brett hardly recognised him. He was well dressed and not in uniform, with a short, neat haircut. Brett got out of the car. He hadn't seen his brother since their mother's funeral. They shook hands and Brett opened the boot of the vehicle for Rod's bag.

"You can drive if you want, this is your car." Rod had written to Brett asking him to find a good, cheap and reliable car that he could drive back to Melbourne. Rod liked what he saw, so he got in to drive.

"How long are you staying?" Brett asked.

"About two weeks," Rod replied. Brett gave directions, stopping at the bottle shop for supplies of Bourbon and coke.

"I've got a few friends coming over. You remember Keith?" Rod was very quiet and just nodded.

By the time they got back to the flat, they had hardly said two words. Brett had put two single beds in his spare room. A mate was throwing them out. Rod had a look around the flat while Brett got two glasses out of the cupboard. They sat on the sofa and Rod looked at Brett's record collection.

"Didn't think you would be a *Queen* fan," Rod said, picking up the *Queen* album. "I've got *Queen II* back home. I'll send it to you if you like. I haven't heard the first one."

Brett went to put it on. "A friend gave it to me. It's pretty good."

"So, you got a girlfriend?" Brett asked.

"No, have you?" Rod asked back. Brett told him about Sharon.

"Keith is bringing Steph over soon. She's a nice girl. I kind of need to talk to her. I took her to a party and left her there."

"No worries, maybe Keith and I could go get some pizzas or something." Rod was starting to feel hungry.

Brett just nodded wondering what he was going to say to Steph.

"Just curious, if Sharon is your girlfriend, what were you doing on a date with Steph?" Rod asked.

"I like Steph. She's a great girl, but Sharon is different. Steph has too many family issues. We've seen what that does to families. I don't want that," said Brett. Rod just nodded he understood.

Brett got up and went out the front with a cloth to clean his bike. Rod followed.

"You still got the same bike, I see. I thought you would have upgraded by now," said Rod.

Just then, the sound of Keith's bike riding in caught their attention. They both stood up as Keith and Steph got off the bike. Keith shook hands with Rod.

"Good to see you again! How have you been?" Keith asked.

"Hi, Steph, this is Rod, my brother," said Brett, very proud. "My good friend Steph," he said, hoping Steph was still his friend, then they headed inside. "Want a beer, Steph?" Brett asked. The music was still playing. Steph took a beer and went to look at the records.

Brett looked a little awkward. Rod noticed and said, "Anyone for pizza? I'm hungry. Keith, do you want to come with me? We'll go get some pizza for dinner."

Keith took the hint. "Yeah, I'll come with you." They both left in Rod's car.

Brett was sitting on the sofa, playing his guitar quietly to the music, trying to put his words together.

"I'm sorry about last week. I didn't know Sharon needed me to pick her up until that night. We only just started going out." Brett was hoping Steph would say something. She just sat there quiet. "I hope we can still be friends," he said, looking at her for a sign that she forgave him.

Steph looked at Brett and smiled. "Of course, we can still be friends."

Brett leaned over and kissed Steph gently on the lips. He already liked Steph more than he thought he did.

They were listening to the *Queen* song *Great King Rat*.

"This song could be about my stepdad," Steph said with a half-laugh, trying to lighten the mood. Brett started to listen to the lyrics. Just then, Rod and Keith returned.

Chapter 53

Sharon moved in a week later, and Rod went back to Melbourne. Brett was so happy since Sharon had moved in, but she had lied to her family. They thought Brett was just a flatmate. If they ever came to visit, Brett had to move his stuff into the other room. Brett was talking to Keith about it one afternoon. Keith had never really liked Sharon. He thought she was stuck up. However, Brett was so in love with Sharon; Keith was worried he was going down a path with her that wasn't going to end well; love stuffs up your brain. Nobody could convince him any different.

Keith had become everyone's big brother. He was hoping Brett and Steph would get it together. Brett knew Steph was crazy about him, and Keith thought they were a perfect match. Deep down, he was sure Brett was crazy about Steph too, but his infatuation with Sharon blinded him. After Sharon moved in with Brett, Keith kept his distance a little. He was hoping Brett would wake up and realise Sharon was just a stuck up bitch, and she would eventually go back home.

Then one day, Keith called in to get some fuel from Steph at work. She was telling Keith she was moving in with Brett and Sharon. Keith was stunned. Steph said she couldn't stay at home any longer and that her mum was just as bad as her stepdad. Keith understood; he wasn't told anything but had a fair idea what Steph and her sister had been dealing with, and there were rumours. He knew Steph's sister was doing drugs now and was on a very destructive path.

Keith was trying to look out for Steph since he had lost his little sister. He had a soft spot for Steph, as a big brother should. He didn't know how Steph was going to cope living with Brett and Sharon, knowing how Steph was crazy about Brett. She never admitted it, but Keith could tell by the way she looked at him.

Steph moved into the spare room and settled in quite well. The fact she hardly saw Sharon was a good thing. Steph worked during the day and Sharon worked at night, so Brett was delighted with the way things were.

Every weekend was a party. Neal and Jonesy came over a lot, and there were always people sleeping over. But during the week, it was so lovely Brett and Steph spent a lot of time together on their own. They would talk a lot, and Steph opened up to Brett about her home life; he was a good listener. Steph had all these dreams of being a famous actress and Brett was always encouraging her to follow her dreams and never give up. Brett told Steph how he would have loved to be in a band, and she said to him he shouldn't give up on his dreams either.

They were becoming very close, and their friendship was something special. Most nights, they would play Brett's records, and Steph would sing along while Brett played his guitar. They enjoyed each other's company immensely. Brett likes the fact Sharon worked nights; Keith seemed to be the only one who noticed how close Brett and Steph had become.

One night, Jacko, one of Neal's mates, was having a lot of drinks, and Jacko started flirting and grabbing at Steph trying to kiss her. She tried to push him away, but Jacko was too strong. Brett walked in from the bathroom and saw what was happening. His anger just exploded. He grabbed Jacko and pulled him off Steph throwing him out of his flat. The look on Brett's face was scary like he could have killed Jacko, even Steph was a bit shocked.

Neal was very drunk and said, "What the fuck, Brett? She's not your girlfriend." Brett told Neal he could piss off too. They all decided to leave so Brett could cool off.

Steph sat down on the sofa. Brett put another record on and sat down next to Steph. "I'm sorry," Brett said. Steph was so in love with Brett. No one had ever protected her like that before.

"Thank you," she said. She leaned in and cuddled Brett. He put his arms around Steph, and he kissed her; there was a real passion behind that kiss. Brett was falling in love with Steph, but he couldn't; he stopped himself. He got up to get another drink and poured Steph a scotch and coke.

Nothing happened that night. Brett finished his drink and went to bed before Sharon came home. Steph didn't tell anyone. She loved Brett so much.

Brett gave Steph a ride to work every day. He enjoyed having her on the back of his bike, her arms wrapped around him. When they went on weekend rides, Sharon was always on the back of Brett's bike, and Steph usually went with Keith. Brett would ride behind Keith so he could keep an eye on Steph. Once Brett slipped up in conversation, he said he could feel Steph falling asleep behind him when Keith corrected him.

"Don't you mean Sharon?"

"Yeah, I mean Sharon."

Later, Keith got Brett alone. "What the hell is going on?"

"What do you mean?" said Brett; he knew exactly what he was talking about.

"Steph. Something is going on with you two," Keith said, worrying about what might be brewing.

"I don't know," Brett finally said it out loud. "I think I love her." He looked at Keith for answers. "She's incredible. She has so many dreams. If she stayed here with me, none of them would come true, and I can't do that to her." Keith just nodded. "I'm no good for her. Everyone close to me has fucked up their lives. I care for Steph way too much to do that to her."

"That wasn't your fault," Keith said, thinking of the night Brett's mum was killed and his sister Sally was murdered. "You said yourself, Sky was a drug addict. None of their deaths was your fault," said Keith.

"I couldn't stop them. I couldn't protect them," Brett said with anger, his eyes filling with rage. The two of them just sat there, not knowing what Brett should do.

"I think you should go with your heart," Keith said, hoping he would break it off with Sharon.

The next day, it was taken care of, Sharon and Steph had decided they should all move to a house with more room. They had found one they wanted to look at, and the three of them went over that morning. It was in Hood Street, which sounded appropriate. The rent was more expensive, but if they got a fourth person, it worked out the same. So they decided to take the house. Keith knew a guy called Yowie, who was looking for a home to share.

That night, Yowie came over with Keith to say hi. He seemed lovely. He wasn't a biker, and he had a bright green Datsun car. Yowie ended up staying for the usual Saturday night party. Neal came over, as he hadn't seen Brett since the night that Jacko groped Steph. He came in bearing gifts; he had a bottle of Jim Beam as a peace offering and said he was sorry to Brett and Steph. Brett shook hands, and Steph said, "As long as Jacko stays away." They had a great party. Yowie fitted in well. He was like an overgrown teddy bear, a gentle giant.

Chapter 54

Just after Brett got home that Friday, Keith dropped Steph home. Steph came and sat on the sofa next to Brett but didn't seem like her happy self.

"Everything all right?" Brett asked.

"My aunty came to see me at work today. My sister's dead," Steph said.

"Shit, I'm sorry, Steph," he said. They just listened to some music. Brett was playing *Led Zeppelin, Stairway to Heaven*.

"Maybe that's where she is," Steph said with a blank face and not a single tear.

A few days later, Keith said to Brett, "Steph's sister's funeral is tomorrow. She should go."

"She won't talk about it. It's like if she doesn't talk about it, it didn't happen." Brett was quite worried about Steph. The next day, Steph had a day off work and went down to the beach for a walk. Brett went for a ride to look for her. It took him a while to find her sitting on the pier, dangling her legs over the edge. Brett sat down next to her.

"Been looking for you. Catch any fish yet?" Brett said, trying to get a smile. "Come on. You need to say goodbye to your sister."

They rode out to the cemetery after everyone had gone home. Steph looked down at her grave.

"You're free now," she said. She broke into tears as she opened up to Brett, telling him about the hell both she and her sister had to live with and what their stepfather had done to them. "He took away our innocence; she died years ago." Brett just held Steph, both sitting in silent thought.

The evening was approaching when they got back on the bike, and Brett decided to take Steph to the headland at the beach where they sat for ages and talked. They talked about Brett's mum, Keith's sister and Sky. They were the best of friends who were there for each other.

Brett knew he had met his soulmate. He leant over and kissed her. He loved her, and that's why he had to let her be free.

A week later, they were moving into their new home on Hood Street. It was handy having Yowie's car to move stuff. They had Sharon's car as well. Keith borrowed his old man's car and trailer, which was great for the fridge and beds. They were all exhausted at the end of the day when Sharon had to go to work.

Yowie had a drum set he put in the back room, which was like a built-in veranda. Brett set up his guitar and amplifier out there as well. They all thought Yowie played the drums, but Yowie was hopeless. He said they were a debt payment from a mate.

The first night, they ordered pizza from down the road. Yowie went to pick them up, and Brett bought a bottle of scotch, he knew Steph liked scotch.

It didn't take long for people to find out they had a house. Bikers from all over turned up to the party. By the time Sharon came home from work, she could hardly park her car in the drive. The music was blasting, and everyone was having a great time. Jonesy turned up, and Brett kept an eye on him, he had a feeling he had a thing for Steph. But Steph didn't seem interested, and she kept her distance. Levi turned up for a while but left early. He had a wife and kids now. Keith said he was henpecked but not to his face. Nobody would ever say that to his face.

Living in the house was pretty good. Everyone got along well. They had the best parties and went out to the drive-in movies or would go to this nightclub called Night Moves. The girls loved it. It wasn't Brett's thing; he called it the Gay Club. The manager was gay, and the girls thought he was so hot. Steph had become good friends with Gary, the manager of Night Moves. He would buy her drinks and dance with her. Brett would watch.

One night, Brett was drinking a lot, and he was getting very jealous. It looked like he was going to start a fight with Gary, just because he was dancing with Steph. Keith noticed Brett's jealousy flaring up and calmed the situation.

"Don't even think about it," Keith said, hanging on to Brett's arm. Brett realised he had to calm down. "He's a fuckin faggot, Brett."

Yowie came back from the loo, wondering what was going on.

"Watch the girls, Yowie. Brett and I need some air." Keith dragged Brett out of his chair and went outside.

"Brett, you have to stop torturing yourself. If you love her, tell her," said Keith, who was so getting sick of keeping Brett from fighting.

"I can't hurt Sharon; I love her," said Brett, not sounding very convincing.

Keith was getting frustrated with Brett. "I thought you loved Steph?"

"I do love Steph, that's why I can't tell her. I'm no good for her. I've told you that." Keith didn't know what more he could say. They had a smoke.

"Don't you think Steph should have a say about what she wants? She is a great girl and she's crazy about you."

No one was going to convince Brett. He wanted the world for Steph, and he didn't want to be the reason she didn't get it.

A few weeks later, they had an awesome party. Neal had a bong set up in the lounge room and was getting stoned. Brett had a barbeque happening out the front and could see out of the corner of his eye Jonesy sitting next to Steph on the front steps. Brett wasn't worried. Steph had told him she didn't like him as a boyfriend, but Jonesy seemed to be trying hard to get Steph's attention. The next time Brett looked up, Steph had left. Brett just smiled to himself.

After the barbeque, Brett took all the cooking equipment inside to the kitchen.

"Hey, Brett, you think you could do that tat for me now?" Keith asked. Brett had told Keith he would give him a tattoo of a knife down his arm.

Keith was clearly in pain, so Sharon gave him a shot of Jim Beam. Brett had a very steady hand, and he was a rather good tattooist.

"You should open a tattoo parlour," Keith said. He was indicating to Sharon for another shot.

Neal put his head in the kitchen. "What are you bastards doing?" Neal had a joint and offered Keith a drag. Keith held it up to Brett's mouth, and he took a hit. Brett hadn't had any pot in a while. Just then, Steph stuck her head in the kitchen.

"Can I have a drag?" she asked Keith as he had another hit. Neal handed it over to Steph; she had never had pot before.

Brett had just finished. Keith was pleased with his tattoo but ran to the bathroom; he said he had to take a piss. The kitchen had emptied except for Brett and Steph.

She sat down opposite Brett and asked, "Can you give me a tattoo?"

How could he refuse those adoring eyes? He thought. "What would you like?" Steph just smiled at Brett.

"It's my birthday. Surprise me!" Brett had no idea it was Steph's birthday. She held up her hand. "You can do something on my palm."

She was stoned, he thought. Brett hoped she wouldn't regret it in the morning. What could he do? A star for his little star. She didn't even flinch.

"How much have you had to drink?" he asked.

Steph just smiled. "A bit," she said, staring in his beautiful eyes. Brett was concentrating, wanting to do a good job and not hurt Steph with the needle.

When he had finished, Steph looked at the star. Perhaps it wasn't what she was expecting.

"One day, you will be a star." He kissed Steph on the hand. "Happy birthday."

Steph smiled. "I love it."

Brett locked the doors. Everyone had gone home except the ones who were asleep on the sofa. He needed to go to the toilet when he had finished; he opened the toilet door and ran into Steph who came out of the bathroom at the same time. She was wearing only a towel and seemed upset. She ran straight into Brett's arms.

"What's wrong?" he asked. Steve had tried to jump in the shower with her. Brett wanted to kill him. It all happened so fast. Before he knew it, he was in Steph's bedroom, and he was kissing her.

"Oh, Steph!" He had wanted Steph for so long he couldn't stop himself. They made passionate love that night.

Brett suddenly thought about what had happened. He got up, leaving Steph on the bed and went to his room and he climbed into bed, but he couldn't sleep. He was thinking about Steph and how much he loved her.

Oh God, Brett thought as he laid there looking at Sharon who was fast asleep. He wanted to go back to Steph's room. Brett's head was spinning. *What the fuck do I do?* Brett couldn't sleep at all that night. The last thing he wanted to do was hurt Steph or Sharon. When morning had woken Sharon, Brett closed his eyes. He couldn't face her. Sharon got up thinking Brett was hung over and let him sleep.

Brett stayed in bed all day. Sharon had gone to work when Brett finally came out of his room. He headed out the door past Yowie and Steph who was watching TV on the sofa. "See you later, I'm going out," he said and left.

Brett headed over to Keith's place. Keith wasn't doing too much, just watching the telly. Keith was starting to wonder what was going on when Brett was so quiet.

"Everything all right?" Keith asked.

Brett had a drink from his beer. "Not really."

Keith just sat there waiting for Brett to tell him. He finally got the words out, "Steph and I…" He stopped there.

"You didn't." Brett just nodded. "Shit," Keith said. They had another beer, not saying much for a while. "What are you going to do about Sharon?"

Brett said nothing. He had no idea what he was going to do.

Brett just kept out of Steph's way. He loved her and didn't want to hurt her. He also loved Sharon, but he knew Steph's love was unique. She was the love of his life.

He sat on the headland where he had kissed away her tears. He had to leave both of them. He couldn't stay with Sharon now he had cheated on her. He couldn't live with that, and he couldn't stay with Steph because he loved her too much. She deserved the best. She had so much ambition; he needed to set her free for her dreams to come true.

When Brett got home that night, Sharon and Yowie were sitting in the kitchen. He noticed Steph's bedroom door was closed. He went to the fridge for a beer, suddenly feeling awkward and guilty. Perhaps they knew.

"Brett, I have to tell you something," said Sharon. "I need a break from us. I think I have feelings for Yowie. It just happened. We didn't mean for it to happen, but it did."

Brett was stunned, trying to comprehend what he was hearing; it took him a minute for it to sink in.

"Sorry, mate," Yowie said. Suddenly, Brett's temper was flying. Before they knew it, Brett and Yowie were bashing into each other. Brett pushed Yowie's head into the wall making a large hole.

"Stop it!" Sharon was crying. Things went flying off the table. Then they were in the hall smashing another hole in the wall. Yowie was larger than Brett and could have easily knocked him senseless, but he held back because Brett was so angry. He was out of control, and Yowie finally shoved him to the ground. Brett sat there for a moment, looking at the mess. He calmed himself for a second, got himself up and headed out the door.

Brett drove for most of the night up the highway, trying to calm down. He made his way back to town. Then he went to the cemetery to visit his mum's grave. It was late, and the gates were locked. So he parked his bike outside the gate and climbed over. There was a full moon, which guided his way to her grave, and he sat down and started to cry. Brett had never gotten over his mother's death. He laid down there on the grass next to his mum's grave and fell asleep like a helpless child.

The next morning, he was woken by the sound of lawnmowers. He sat up, brushed himself off and headed back to the gate to get his bike. He decided to head to Neal's place.

Brett didn't go to work at all for the next week. He was sleeping on Neal's sofa and smoking some serious shit, spending his time stoned off his face. Keith finally found out what had happened. He guessed Brett must be at Neal's. When Keith found him, Brett was wasted and feeling sorry for himself. Keith told Brett he had to come home.

"I haven't got a fuckin home," he screamed at Keith.

"My home is always your home, you stupid bastard." Keith knew he couldn't ride in this condition so he let him sleep it off, waiting there so he wouldn't drink or smoke anymore. The next day, Keith got him home.

Keith went with him back to the house so Brett could get his stuff. Yowie was there, but Brett was quite calm now knowing he was better off that this relationship with Sharon was over. Brett told Yowie he wouldn't be back.

When they got back to Keith's place, Brett had all his stuff packed in a box again. "Do you want a beer?" Keith asked.

"No, I'll have a coffee; I need to keep a clear head."

Keith was impressed, so he had a coffee as well. Brett had been thinking about what he needed to do.

"I want you to tell Steph that I had to go away for a while. Tell her I've moved up to Queensland. I want her to get on with her life. She has always wanted to move to the city, and this will set her free." He felt confident he was doing the right thing.

Brett wrote a letter of goodbye to Steph, telling her he loved her, but he had to leave. He put it in the *Queen* album she loved so much and asked Keith to take it to her.

Brett asked Keith to look after Steph. Check on her now and then. I'll give you a ring in a few weeks when I land somewhere. Once again, he packed up his bike and rode out of town.

Chapter 55

A few weeks had passed. Brett found himself back in Queensland in a one-horse town living in a caravan park. He went to a phone box to give Keith a call.

"How're things?" Brett asked.

"Not bad, just working too much, not much else happening," Keith answered.

"How's Steph? Have you seen her?" Brett asked.

Keith didn't want to tell Brett the truth. She had been so depressed and miserable since he left, but he was sick of the craziness of Brett's choices. So he lied. "She's doing great. She's made some new friends at work and has been going out a lot. I've hardly seen her."

Brett was glad she was doing okay. "I'll ring you in a month or so." Brett hung up the phone; however, he felt Keith wasn't telling him everything. He missed Steph more then he thought he would, but it was for the best. If he had stayed, he would have brought her down.

Brett got a job at the local garage. He only worked two days a week and spent the rest of his time playing his guitar and busking in the main street. He enjoyed playing his guitar as it gave him a sense of peace.

It wasn't long before he made some new friends, Jimmy, Nathen and J.J., her real name was Janelle Jenkins, but everyone called her J.J. She was Nathen's girlfriend, and they were great together. She was like a hippie from the sixties who didn't realise it was the eighties, and she reminded him of Sky but more together. Brett liked her. She was so easy to talk to. They all lived in an old shack of a house near the beach and Brett ended up moving in with them. They were all vegetarians. Brett wasn't, but that didn't bother him. He didn't eat meat anymore, well, not around them anyway. Brett was enjoying life in Queensland. He started to relax and make a life for himself.

After a few months, J.J sat down with Brett to have a chat. "Brett, who are you running from?" she asked.

Brett was a little surprised. "No one," he said, not very convincingly.

J.J completely ignored his response. "What's her name?" she asked.

There was something about J.J. Brett found himself telling her everything. He couldn't stop himself. He told her all about his mum, Sky and Steph and how much he truly loved her and why he had left.

"Why did you do a dumb thing like that for?" J.J. was always very direct.

"Because she deserves better than me," he said, feeling a little down. He missed her so much. He missed their chats. Brett didn't realise how much until he started talking to J.J.

"You need to go home and tell her you're sorry for leaving and tell her how much you love her." Brett sat there thinking; it had been a year already. The last time he had spoken to Keith, he'd said she was happy and had gotten her life together. He didn't want to spoil that.

J.J. was never going to let up until she had convinced Brett to change his mind. About a month later, Brett decided to head home. He went straight to Keith's place. Keith was thrilled to see Brett, so they headed down to the local pub for a drink and caught up on all the happenings. Keith's father had passed away two months ago. Brett was sorry; he hadn't known as he would have liked to have been there for Keith, but he hadn't rung Keith for some time.

"Have you seen Steph lately?" Brett asked.

Keith took a deep breath. "She's married, mate."

Brett sat back, taking it in. He finally spoke. "That's great then, she's happy." He was guttered on the inside. Keith sat there drinking his beer, knowing that Steph wasn't happy at all. He had heard from one of Neal's mates that her husband was very abusive. Keith couldn't tell Brett that. It wasn't Brett's problem, so best he didn't know.

A few weeks later, Brett decided to see Steph. He found her working at a coffee shop at the Plaza. Keith didn't think he should see Steph at all. But Brett just had to see her.

He walked past the food court and looked in. He could see her making coffee and smiling. She did look happy, he thought, as he watched from a distance. After a while, he walked towards her. He stood right out the front, looking over the counter straight at her. She finally spotted him. She looked like she wanted to cry.

"Brett!" she said. She asked for a break and came out to see him. Brett gave Steph a loving hug. He had missed her so much. He bought some coffees, and they sat down at a table.

"You look good," he said, smiling.

"Thanks, so do you. Queensland weather must be agreeing with you."

"I heard you got married. Congratulations! I'm so pleased for you," Brett said, trying to look pleased. Steph just nodded. "I knew you would find happiness," he said, still smiling.

Steph just smiled, hiding her true feelings.

He told Steph about his new home and all about J.J, Nathen and Jimmy. Steph hardly spoke, letting Brett do all the talking.

It was time for her to go back to work. "Will I see you again?"

Brett told her he was going back to Queensland the next day. She kept her disappointment hidden. They both stood and gave each other another hug.

"I'm so glad you're happy," Brett whispered in her ear before they parted ways. Brett walked off, not game to look back.

It was too late, Brett thought. He had lost Steph forever.

When he got back to Keith's, Brett told him he was going back to Queensland. He couldn't stay here. It was too painful.

Chapter 56

Time had gone by so fast, and Brett was still living with J.J and Nathen. Jimmy had got himself a girlfriend, Tash. They had moved into a place not too far away. Brett wasn't interested in finding a girlfriend. He told J.J., "Girls were too much trouble."

J.J asked about the girl who had stolen his heart; she knew he still loved her. "Why did she break your heart?"

"No, it wasn't her; it was me," Brett said. "I had a chance and blew it. She's married to some other guy now. I thought she would—" Brett stopped talking.

"Thought she would, what?" J.J asked.

"I gave her up so she could follow her dreams. I didn't think she would still be stuck in that town and married," Brett said with regret.

Brett just lived his life day to day, playing his guitar and working when he needed money. He made a few friends, and they formed a band, 'Hot Sticks'. There was Dickie on the drums, Mark on the keyboard, Brett played lead guitar, and Dom played the bass and sang. They were pretty good, and they got a gig once a month at the local Bowling Club. They all had other jobs to pay the bills; the band was just for fun. Life ran pretty steadily for a few years.

Brett still rang Keith and popped down for a quick visit a few times a year. On one of his visits, Keith wasn't going to tell Brett about Steph, but he decided to let him know.

"Steph's not happy, mate. Her husband is a real bastard. He treats her terrible. I don't know why she stays with him."

Brett started to get angry. "Why didn't you tell me?"

"I only just found out," he lied. "Steph's friend that she works with, Melissa's her name, she's Jacko's missus, she told me." Keith paused for a moment. "She has a kid, a daughter."

Brett calmed down. All these thoughts were going through his head. What could he do?

"Why doesn't she leave him?" Brett asked.

"He's violent, a real arsehole. If Steph leaves him, she would have to leave town to get away from him," Keith said.

"Maybe I need to take care of him," Brett said, so angry that anyone could hurt Steph. "That's why I wasn't going to tell you."

"Why doesn't she leave, what's stopping her?" Brett said, trying to make sense of it.

"She's still hoping you're coming back. She still loves you, mate."

Brett just sat there taking it in. He couldn't take another man's wife.

Brett went for a ride down to the beach. He sat on the headland, trying to work out what he could do to help Steph.

After a while, it all seemed very clear what Brett should do.

"I want you to tell Steph that I've been killed, in an accident," Brett said with confidence.

Keith was in shock. "You can't do that to her."

"Now listen. If Steph thinks I'm dead, then she'll leave him and get out of this town. It's the only way."

"Why don't you just go with her?"

"I can't do that," he said. "I can't take another man's wife."

Keith couldn't believe what he was about to do. A week later, Keith went to see Steph at work, where she was just knocking off. He hadn't spoken to her in some time. Steph was pleased to see him. They hugged each other and sat down for a coffee in the food court. Keith didn't know where to start. As soon as the words came out of his mouth, he regretted it.

"Brett was killed in an accident." Keith was never good at lying. He was so angry with Brett for asking him to lie to Steph. Keith saw the hurt and pain in Steph's eyes. He just hugged her for the longest time. "He would want you to take care of yourself and do what's best for you and your daughter," Keith told her, hoping she would.

When Keith got back home, he couldn't look at Brett. He got a beer and sat down. "How did it go?" Brett asked.

Keith had a drink of his beer. "That was the worst thing you could have ever done to her." He was so angry.

Brett shook his head. Now Steph could leave and start a new life. A few weeks later, he heard Steph had left her husband and left town. It didn't take Shane long before he had another woman in his life. He threw out all Stephanie and Elizabeth's things. He told everyone he kicked them out. Brett was pleased Steph was finally free of Shane. He hoped that she had moved to Sydney and was living her dream.

Brett never let anyone get close to him. J.J tried setting him up with a few different girls but ended up giving up. Brett was a loner. He seemed happy just playing his guitar. He still thought about Steph but never really talked about her.

Ten years flew by and still nothing much had changed. J.J and Nathen had three kids now. They were nine, seven and six. Brett still lived out the back of their house in a shed they had built. He loved their kids. Brett was finally happy. He enjoyed playing with the kids, giving them a ride on his bike around the backyard. These were good times for Brett.

Brett hadn't been back to see Keith since he told Steph he had died. Brett sent him a card at Christmas to say hi, and he rang him on his birthday. He felt terrible about making Keith lie to Steph. Things were never the same between them after that.

It was a Sunday morning. They were all having breakfast when Nathen dropped the Sunday newspaper on the table before grabbing a coffee. J.J couldn't wait to read the entertainment section; Nathen only liked the sports section and Brett never bothered with the news. He just wasn't interested.

"Hey, look at this, Brett; there's a new musical named after you: 'Brett, the Love of My Life'," J.J said with a laugh.

Brett froze for a second. "Show me."

"The writer said she wrote about the love of her life, Brett. She had lost him a long time ago, but she still loved him." Brett took the paper. There was her name, 'Stephanie Zinone.' It jumped out at him like a slap in the face. Brett had the biggest smile on his face.

"Goddam, she did it!" he said.

J.J noticed the massive smile on Brett's face. "Is that her?" she asked.

Brett just kept reading, then his smile faded. He looked at J.J. "She still loves me."

Brett was so happy for her but also confused. She thought he was dead.

J.J reread the paper. "It opens tomorrow night in Sydney."

"You have to go to her," she said.

Brett was trying to think, but a thousand thoughts were racing through his head.

"You're the love of her life." J.J was so excited. "You'll have to fly. It's a four-day drive to Sydney, and you'd never make it."

Brett was still sitting there, trying to take it all in. J.J was looking for the phone number to book a flight. Brett pushed the book closed.

"She thinks I'm dead. I can't go down there," Brett said, starting to panic. "I can't." He went outside, got on his bike and rode down towards the beach. He always felt closer to Steph sitting on the headland.

He sat on the grass looking out to the sea. He could still see Steph's face. God, he thought he was 35 now and Steph must be 30. She was probably married or at least had found someone else by now. Maybe he could see her, to make sure she was happy. She would have moved on. It had been too long. But he had to make sure she's okay.

Brett rode home. He walked into the kitchen. "Looks like I'm going to Sydney."

J.J. clapped her hands, excited for Brett. "I already booked you a ticket. It leaves five tomorrow night. It was the earliest I could get."

Chapter 57

Brett had never been on a plane before, but he didn't think about that until he was walking up the steps to board the flight. He tried to relax. The older man sitting next to him noticed how tense Brett was.

"Is this your first time flying?" he asked.

Brett tightened his grip hanging on to the arms on the seat. "How can you tell?" he said, trying a smile. The plane's engines got louder, ready for take-off.

Brett relaxed a little once they were up in the air.

"Where are you headed?" the man asked.

"Sydney, to see an old friend," he said with a smile.

"Must be a girl," the man said.

"Why do you say that?" Brett asked.

"Only a girl could get you on a plane, I'm guessing. She must be some girl," the man said as he put his seat back and closed his eyes.

She sure was. Brett sat there for the rest of the trip, wondering what he was going to say to Steph. The plane finally landed safely. Brett only had a small bag, which he stored in the overhead above his seat, which he grabbed and headed down the aisle.

The old man called out, "Good luck with the girl!"

Brett made his way through the airport to the taxi line, and it wasn't too long before he was in a cab heading towards the city centre. J.J had booked him into a pub a block away from the theatre. Brett hadn't been to Sydney since he was a kid, and it was peak hour, and the traffic was a little overwhelming. By the time Brett got to the pub, it was 7.30. The show was starting at 8. He put his bag in his room and got directions to the theatre from the front desk and headed out.

As Brett approached the theatre, he could see the crowd of people standing outside the theatre talking while waiting to go in. Brett's hands were sweaty. He made his way through the crowd of people to the box office where there were people lined up.

Finally, Brett made his way to the window.

"Can I get one ticket, thanks?"

The lady looked at him. "What show would you like?"

Brett was confused. "Tonight's show." What else would he want, he thought.

"Tonight's show is sold out. We're sold out until next month, sir," she said apologetically.

Brett walked away from the window. What an idiot; of course, they would be sold out. Brett went to the street at the front of the theatre and lit a smoke. His name and Steph's were on the billboard. What the fuck was he doing here? He thought. What was he going to do now?

People were starting to move in. He looked at the crowd, thinking he might see Steph, but his hopes faded when the last of the masses went through the doors.

She must be in there, he thought. Maybe he could send her a message. He went back to the ticket window again.

"Any chance I could get a message to Stephanie Zinone?" Brett asked.

The lady smiled kindly. "Yes, of course, you can. You could leave a note. She might not get it until tomorrow though. Are you a friend of hers?" She was probably wondering what this biker guy would want with Stephanie.

"Yeah, an old friend. Do you have a bit of paper and a pen?"

The lady gave him what he needed, and he leant on the counter to write.

Hi, Steph, I'm an old friend of yours. It's Brett. I was hoping to see you and catch up. He screwed that note up. Shit. What the hell could he say? He looked at the lady again.

"What time does the show finish?" Brett asked.

"About 10.30, but there's a private party afterwards," she said.

He started writing again.

Hi Steph, I'm an old friend of Keith's. I would love to see you. I'm staying at the pub on the corner of Clarence Street.

Brett suspected if he put his own name, she would think it was a joke and not come. He signed it Room 7.

The lady gave Brett an envelope. He sealed it and wrote Stephanie Zinone on the front and handed it back to her.

"Please make sure she gets it," Brett said, feeling a bit down.

"I'll personally make sure she does," she said. Brett nodded with thanks and walked off.

Brett was feeling a little hungry, so he headed back to the pub to have some dinner. The pub was bustling with people; however, he found an empty table in the back where he sat to eat his dinner and have a cold beer.

After Brett had his dinner, he went up to his room and lay on his bed with the TV on, but there was nothing that interested him. It was almost ten o'clock. Maybe he could go back to the theatre and try to spot Steph coming out. Brett went to the bathroom. He checked himself in the mirror, put his leather jacket back on and headed back to the theatre.

He stood across the road where he might have a better chance to spot her. Three smoke's later, the people were coming out. Everyone looked the same. Men in suits, ladies dressed up. Brett decided to walk back over and get a closer look. Cars and taxis were picking up people everywhere; it was a bit chaotic. This was a waste of time, Brett thought.

He stood near the doorway, watching everyone leave. He knew he must look out of place. He thought he should go, about to give up.

The lady from the ticket box was walking out when she noticed Brett standing there.

"You still waiting?" she said.

"Yeah, I thought I might see her coming out."

Just then, the lady spotted Adrien rushing into the theatre. "See that guy?" She pointed to Adrien. "Catch him when he comes back; he's a good friend of Stephanie's."

Brett anxiously waited for the bloke to come back out. It seemed to take forever before Adrian reappeared.

"Excuse me," he said, "can you help me? I'm looking for someone."

Adrien stopped and looked at this good-looking but somewhat rough man, about thirty or so, wearing a leather jacket, like a biker.

"Who are you looking for?" Adrien asked.

"Stephanie Zinone."

Adrien suddenly felt a little alarmed. "And who are you?" he asked.

"I'm Brett."

Part 3: Brett's Alive

Chapter 58

"Brett?" Adrien said in disbelief. "She thinks you're dead." Adrien knew it was Brett. He had those beautiful eyes Steph had talked about so often.

"Steph's at a private party," Adrien told him. "You're not exactly dressed for the occasion. Where are you staying? It might be better to meet up tomorrow for lunch."

Brett agreed, and Adrien made his way back to the party. When he walked in, he could see Steph and John dancing holding each other close. He thought they looked so in love. He couldn't tell her yet; she'd had enough shocks that day. She needed to enjoy this moment.

The next morning, Adrien got up early. He hadn't slept much. He was worried about what he should do.

He made himself a coffee. He could hear someone coming down the stairs. It was John; he had stayed over last night.

"Morning, Adrien!"

"Morning, John," said Adrien, not as excited.

John made himself a coffee and sat down, smiling.

"Why are you so happy? You're smiling like a Cheshire cat," said Adrien, a little hung over.

"Steph told me she loved me last night," John said, so over the moon.

"Well, everyone knows that," said Adrien.

John continued, "But she had never said it before. I think she's ready."

Adrien looked at John puzzled. "For what?"

"I'm going to ask her to marry me." It was clear John was sure she would say yes. Adrien didn't know what to say, but just then, Steph was making her way down the stairs. "Don't say anything," he whispered to Adrien.

After breakfast, John said he had some things to do, so he headed off. Steph was cleaning up the table from breakfast.

"Can we talk?" Adrien asked.

"Sure, what's up?"

"Can we sit down?" Adrien said. Steph realised Adrien was looking very serious.

"Sure." Steph wiped her hands and sat down next to Adrien.

Adrien didn't know where to start. "You're happy, aren't you?" he said.

"Yeah," Steph replied, starting to worry. "What's going on?"

"You always told me that Brett was the love of your life," Adrien said.

Steph just nodded. "Yeah."

"But you love John now and you're really, happy, aren't you?" Adrien said, taking a breath.

"Yeah," said Steph, trying to work out where Adrien was going with this.

"What if Brett wasn't dead?" Adrien finally said.

"What do you mean? But he is dead," Steph said, full of unpleasant feelings of emotion.

"What if he's not?" Adrien said, seeing Steph's eyes beginning to water. "I saw him last night. He's in town, and he wants to see you."

Adrien felt some of the pain he could see in Steph's eyes.

"He is? He can't be," Steph said with tears running down her face. She finally spoke, "I need to see him. Where is he?"

Adrien convinced Steph not to go to the pub. He was going to go pick up Brett and bring him back for lunch. It would be better for them to meet uninterrupted as Elizabeth was still at her friend's house for another night. Steph went for a shower, her mind was spinning and full of so many questions.

After her shower, Steph got dressed and headed downstairs. She went straight to the lounge room and found her *Queen* album, the one Brett had given her all those years ago. She put the record on and turned up the volume. Steph sat there on the sofa with tears running down her face; Steph had so many mixed feelings of joy and sadness, followed by confusion. Did she still love Brett? But she loved John, but she never stopped loving Brett. Now her heart was getting torn apart with all these emotions.

Adrien headed over to the pub to pick Brett up. He was looking very nervous. He stood up as Adrien walked towards him.

"Hi, Brett." They shook hands.

Brett was looking behind Adrien. "Where's Steph?" he asked.

"She's at home. We thought it might be better to go there for lunch." Adrien saw the relieved look on Brett's face. He must have thought she didn't want to see him.

They headed out to the car. Before they drove off, Adrien said, "You know Steph was very unhappy for a long time, and she means a lot to me."

"I'm not here to make trouble," said Brett. "I'm glad she's happy. You seem like a nice guy. How long have you two been married?" Brett asked.

Adrien smiled. "Steph's my best friend, but we're not together. John's her partner. He's a great bloke. She's happy with him; they've known each other for quite a few years now." Adrien thought he had better leave it there.

"I would never hurt Steph," Brett said, with real love in his voice.

Adrien just nodded, hoping he was right. He started the car.

Opening the front door, they walked in. Adrien could hear *Queen* playing from the lounge room; he led the way. Steph was standing at the window, and he indicated for Brett to go in. Adrien left them to talk.

"Steph!" said Brett. She turned around with tears running down her face. She ran over to hug him, and they hugged for the longest time. Steph finally stepped back from Brett and looked at him.

"It's really, you! You look so great. Where the hell have you been?" They sat down on the sofa next to each other, holding each other's hands. Steph was so overwhelmed she couldn't believe her eyes. Brett was alive. The tears still filling her eyes.

She wiped her face. "It's so good to see you." She was full of questions; she didn't know where to start. "I got told that you were killed in an accident; Keith told me."

Adrien came in with two cups of tea. "I hope you take milk," Adrien said, but he was sure neither one of them heard him. He sat the cups on the coffee table and left.

Brett told Steph he knew about Shane. "I never wanted to hurt you, Steph; I didn't know how else to help you. I didn't want you waiting for me, and you needed to leave Shane."

Steph was angry at first. "How could you lie to me; I died inside when I heard you were killed. It almost destroyed me."

"I'm so sorry," Brett said, realising how much he had hurt Steph.

She understood why Brett had lied, but she was so confused about her feelings; she was pleased to have Brett back in her life.

They talked and talked. Adrien made them sandwiches for lunch, and they kept talking. It was like they had a lifetime to catch up on. The time had flown, and it was almost three o'clock. Adrien was concerned that John would be back soon, and that could be awkward. Maybe he should interrupt them and let them know what time it was. Just then, Adrien heard John coming in the front door. He came straight to the kitchen.

"Hi, where's Steph?" he asked, putting some wine in the fridge for later.

"Steph's got a visitor," Adrien said.

"Oh, yeah, who?" John asked, looking at Adrien, wondering why he was acting weird.

"Ah, Brett," Adrien said, thinking this should alarm John, but John wasn't that quick.

"Brett who?" he asked.

"Brett from her past," Adrien said bluntly.

It finally clicked. John looked at Adrien, confused. "The Brett who is supposed to be dead?"

Adrien nodded. "Yep, the one and only."

John looked around. "Where are they?"

John headed to the lounge room. Brett and Steph were laughing happily with each other talking about old times. John suddenly felt like the outsider walking in. Steph noticed John standing there.

"John, you're back. I want you to meet an old friend of mine, Brett. And Brett, this is John." John shook hands with Brett.

"Nice to meet you," John said. It went to a very awkward silence.

Just then, Adrien walked in. "How about we all go out for dinner tonight?"

Now, Steph looked awkward. "Actually, if you don't mind, Brett and I have so much to catch up on, and we don't want to bore you. We already have plans."

Steph looked for a sign of approval.

Adrien broke the awkwardness. "Sure, that's fine. John, you're welcome to stay here for dinner if you want. We could have a guy's night."

John finally spoke. "No, that's fine. I've actually got something I need to do. So another time, thanks Adrien. Nice to meet you, Brett. I'll see you later."

John headed out the door. Steph ran out after him, "John, are you mad at me?"

John stopped near his car to turn around. "Why would I be mad at you? Your ex-boyfriend has turned up out of the blue, and you're going on a date with him."

Steph was horrified. "It's not a date. I haven't seen Brett for years, and we have a lot of catching up to do, that's all."

"Well, have a good time." John got in his car and drove off without a goodbye kiss.

Steph was cross with herself for letting him make her feel guilty. She tried to push those thoughts out of her mind, but she was so happy to have Brett back in her life that she wasn't going to let John spoil it for her.

Adrien was making small talk with Brett, waiting for Steph to come back in. Finally, she did. "All okay?" Adrien asked.

"Yeah, of course, it is." Steph wanted to change the subject. "Well, I should get ready; I'm taking Brett to see my show tonight," Steph said with excitement.

Adrien looked a little confused. "Why didn't you just tell John that?" It might have been more acceptable.

"He left before I had time to explain," Steph said, thinking she shouldn't have to explain.

Brett was feeling very awkward. "I tried to get tickets last night, but they said they had sold out for weeks."

"Just as well you know the director," said Steph, making light of the conversation.

Brett sat down in the lounge room listening to the music that was playing, *Queen*, of course. Steph went upstairs to get changed, and Adrien followed her.

"What the fuck are you doing?" Adrien asked.

"I'm getting ready, what's your problem?" Steph said.

"You know what I mean. John loves you, and you've tossed him aside."

"I have not. Well, I didn't mean to. John will be fine. He'll be back tomorrow, you'll see." Steph sounded more sure of herself.

Adrien calmed down a little. "You're taking Brett to see a show that you wrote about him." Adrien was trying to make Steph realise what she was doing was wrong. "You're falling for him all over again and people are going to get hurt." Adrien left the room, so Steph could think about what she was doing.

Steph tried not to let Adrien's comments get to her. She finished getting ready.

Steph called a cab to take them to the theatre, and they were going to grab a bite to eat before the show. She paid, as she didn't think Brett would have much money left after flying down and paying for a motel. She was happy to pay and just so excited to have Brett back.

Steph had box seats for whenever she wanted. Brett was feeling a little uncomfortable now. Steph had changed. She had money now; she had made it. He was starting to have doubts about what he was doing there with Steph. He was pleased for her, but she was different, more confident. Perhaps he shouldn't have come.

They sat in their seats, waiting for the show to start. Steph sensed that Brett was uncomfortable, so she grabbed his hand and held it tight. She was smiling at him as the show began.

After the show had finished, she wanted to take Brett backstage to meet the cast. But Brett didn't want to go. He said he was embarrassed as the show was about him.

"Didn't you like the show?" Steph asked a little worried.

"The show was brilliant. You're so talented; you're amazing. You did it, and I always said you could do it. My little star," Brett said, looking into Steph's eyes. He was so proud of her.

"I might have to change the ending, now," Steph said so happy that Brett was here alive.

After watching the show, Brett felt very uncomfortable with himself, as he now realised how much he had hurt Steph. He still cared for her deeply, but he never meant to hurt her.

As they walked out of the theatre, Brett said he was a little tired. He told Steph he would have an early night. Steph didn't want the night to end, as she was so happy hanging onto Brett's arm as they walked to the cab. The next day, they planned to go out on the harbour; Steph wanted to share Sydney with Brett.

As the cab pulled up outside the pub, Brett gave Steph a kiss goodnight. It was only going to be a quick kiss, but Steph's heart missed a beat as she looked into Brett's eyes, and they kissed again with all the passion they had once shared. Brett got out of the cab and forced himself to go. He so wanted to take Steph with him, but he couldn't.

"See you tomorrow," he said without looking back.

Steph had only got two blocks when she realised she wanted to go back. "Turn around! Take me back," Steph said to the driver.

When she got back to the pub, Brett had gone to his room. She paid the driver and ran inside, heading up the stairs to number 7. When she got to the door, she hesitated for a moment, and her heart was still racing when she knocked.

Brett opened the door. There he stood. He had already taken his shirt off. Steph flew into his arms. Brett pushed the door closed, and they passionately kissed, not wanting to let go. Brett stopped for a moment and looked at Steph.

"Are you sure you want to do this?" he asked. He so wanted Steph.

"I have loved you my whole life," she said. "I lost you once. I don't want to lose you ever again."

That was all Brett wanted to hear. He lifted Steph, kissing her with so much love he had kept only for her.

Brett and Steph made love with such passion he had been saving just for her. Suddenly, Steph woke up. She was in her own bed. It was just a dream. Every ounce of her body ached for the love that Steph had always wanted her whole life. The man she had fallen in love with back when she was a teenager.

Chapter 59

It was the early hours of the morning. Steph laid there still awake.

"Why did he leave me that night?" Steph asked herself.

She went downstairs into Adrien's room. He was alone, so she crawled into bed next to him.

"You're late," he mumbled. "Oh god, I hope you know what you're doing?" Adrien whispered as he rolled over and hugged Steph, and they both went to sleep.

Steph had arranged to meet up with Brett at eleven o'clock at Circular Quay. She wanted to take Brett out on the harbour and show him this beautiful city she loved.

Adrien got up to make coffee. He thought Steph would sleep in, but the water had just finished boiling when she made an appearance.

"Coffee?" Adrien asked.

"No, I'll have tea thanks," Steph said, obviously tired. Adrien sat a cup of tea in front of her with a teabag still in the cup. Steph jiggled the teabag a few times, and Adrien held out a small plate for her to put the tea bag on. Then sat down at the table with Steph.

They sipped their drinks, looking at each other. Finally, Steph spoke. "I love them both. What am I going to do? Shit," she said, shaking her head.

"You've dug yourself into a big pile of it, haven't you?" Adrien said, still sipping his coffee.

"Last night was amazing; I was 17 again." Steph smiled. "I never wanted to hurt John."

Finally, Adrien spoke. "John thinks you are finally committed to him. He thinks you want to marry him. You need to sort this shit out. Elizabeth is coming home today, isn't she?" Steph just nodded, drinking her tea.

Adrien seemed upset with Steph. "I'm sorry," she said, almost a whisper. Adrien was quick to respond. "I'm not the one you need to apologise to."

"Adrien! Please don't be mad with me. I need you," Steph said pleading with him.

"I'm always here for you to help you pick up the pieces. You're the love of my life, you little shit," he said with a smile.

Steph finished her cup of tea and smiled. "I need a shower," she said and hugged Adrien.

"You sure do," Adrien said, screwing his nose up. Steph playfully punched him in the arm and headed up the stairs.

While in the shower Steph thought about the night before. It had been just so wonderful. She closed her eyes, remembering her dream. She opened her eyes, and her heart was racing. Steph was so confused with her feelings.

After she dressed, she was drying her hair when Elizabeth came home. She was full of energy, telling her mum about the movie she had watched with her friend Kelly. Finally, Steph had a chance to talk. "I'm taking a friend out today on the harbour to show him around Sydney. Do you want to come?" Steph asked, hoping she would say no.

"I've got a ton of homework to do, which is kinda due tomorrow," Elizabeth said, hoping her mum wouldn't yell at her. She didn't, which made Elizabeth wonder why. "Who is this friend you're going out with?"

Steph tried to brush it off. "He's just an old friend who's in town for a few days."

"Is John going too?"

Elizabeth was asking too many questions. "No, John's busy. You'd better go and start on that homework," Steph said, pushing her out of her room and closing the door so she could finish getting ready in peace. She didn't like lying to Elizabeth, but she didn't want to say too much either until she knew what she was doing.

She looked in on Elizabeth before heading out. She was lying on her bed with her homework books open.

"You'll be okay. Adrien said he was staying home, so make sure you get that homework done!" She kissed her goodbye and headed downstairs.

Adrien was in the kitchen, getting ready to do some baking.

"I'm going now. Elizabeth will be doing homework most of the day," Steph said, noticing how quiet Adrien was.

"I'm cooking dinner for you tonight. I want you to invite Brett." He said it like it was an order, not a question.

Steph felt she couldn't argue. "Okay, I'll see you tonight."

Steph walked around the corner to catch the bus that headed to the quay. When she got there, she looked around for Brett. She couldn't see him at first, but as Steph walked towards the edge of the water, the crowds parted, and there he was. He was standing next to the railing on the pier. He looked so good wearing his jeans and a black T-Shirt, smoke in his mouth; he could be from a Marlboro ad.

He was still so hot looking she thought as she walked towards him.

"Well, hello there!" she said, a little flirty. She leant in to kiss Brett. He threw his cigarette butt on the ground and stubbed it with his boot before holding Steph in close. They kissed for a moment.

"So, are you going to show me around the city?" Brett said with his sexy smile. He hadn't changed. His eyes were so beautiful, and they still made her heart miss a beat.

They bought tickets to take the ferry across the harbour to Manly. It was a perfect day. The sun was out and not a cloud in the sky. They got seats towards the front of the ferry on the right side. They had a perfect view of the opera house as they cruised past.

"Steph had gone there with Adrien to see an opera once. It was amazing, she said. We should go there one night." Steph wanted to show Brett everything she loved, but Brett was a little on the quiet side. "Everything okay?" Steph asked.

"Yeah, I'm having a great time." Steph wasn't convinced. She was pointing out all the sights and Brett was smiling and nodding like he was enjoying himself. Steph just kept talking, which was what she did when she was nervous. It was evident to Brett that Steph was at home in the city. He thought he had never seen her so happy.

By the time they got back to the quay, they were hungry. Steph wanted to eat in a restaurant, but Brett just wanted a hotdog. She tried to convince him saying it was her shout, but he didn't want to. So they ate their hotdogs and walked around to the botanical gardens. They found a lovely spot under a tree and sat down on the grass for a rest. They lay back on the grass looking up at the sky.

Steph remembered the last time they had done this. It was just after her sister had died. It was Steph's turn to be quiet.

"You're thinking about the last time we did this," Brett said.

Steph smiled. They could still read each other's mind, even after all this time.

"A lot has happened since then," Steph said, a little sad.

"I'm so proud of you. You turned your life right around. Let's face it; we had a shit life growing up." Brett was holding Steph's hand, looking at her tattoo and remembering the day he gave it to her. "But you did it. You've made a success of your life, despite your past. I'm so happy for you!" Brett was smiling with that beautiful smile of his. Steph looked back at the sky.

"It's too much for you, isn't it?" Steph said, knowing what Brett must have been feeling all day, overwhelmed.

"I love you, Steph, and I always will. But your life is so different now from my life, which is a good thing." Steph could feel the tears filling in her eyes. Brett gently turned Steph's face towards his. "You're the best thing that has ever happened to me, and you make me so happy. I feel like a little part of me helped you to get where you are, but you did it all on your own, Steph."

"You're going to leave again, aren't you?" she said.

"I don't belong here. And you don't belong where I live. But that's okay." Brett wiped the tears from her face. "You've got so much to look forward to. Your life is just beginning." Brett rolled over, holding Steph in his arms as he kissed her forehead. Steph knew Brett was right, and they were so different now. Part of her wanted things to go back to the way they were when she was 17. But Steph was in a different place now, a happier, more confident place.

It was only a few days ago she had told John she loved him. It was a different love. Brett was the love of her life once. He had taught Steph how to love, when there was so much pain in her life. She had needed Brett, and he saved her. But she no longer needed his love, just his friendship. John's was a love of choice; she didn't need John, but she loved him anyway and wanted him.

They held each other's hands as they walked back towards the bus stop.

"I almost forgot; Adrien invited you for dinner tonight. You will come, won't you?"

"I would love to. And I would love to get to know John as well. He's a lucky guy." Steph still holding Brett's hand. She hoped she hadn't lost John.

They caught the bus back to Steph's place. Adrien had been cooking most of the day. On opening the door, they could smell the aroma of something delicious in the house. Elizabeth came running down the stairs.

"Elizabeth, I want you to meet my friend Brett," Steph said, feeling a lot more at ease with her thoughts.

"Nice to meet you, Elizabeth, you looked just like your mother when she was young."

"Did you know my mum when she was young?" Elizabeth asked, intrigued. She had never met anyone who knew her mum when she was young before.

"Why don't you and Brett pick out some music to put on? I'll be back in a minute."

Steph went to the kitchen to talk to Adrien. "Hi, dinner smells great. Have you heard from John?"

"No, I haven't seen him," Adrien said, noticing the disappointed look on Steph's face. "There's plenty to eat if you want to invite him."

"I won't be long. Brett's in the lounge room with Elizabeth," Steph said, grabbing the car keys. As she passed the lounge room, she could hear the music playing. It was *Queen*. She stopped in the doorway to see Elizabeth showing Brett all her *Queen* records and telling him how much her mum loved *Queen*.

"I gave your mum her first *Queen* record when she was 17," Brett said to a very excited Elizabeth.

Steph was pleased they were getting along; she smiled. "I won't be long, Adrien's in the kitchen. He'll fix you a drink."

"Don't worry, Mum. I'll look after Brett," Elizabeth said, yelling after her mother.

Chapter 60

Steph drove over to John's place. His light was on as she knocked on the door. John was surprised to see Steph but pleased. They went into the lounge room, and John sat down. Steph could see John had been having a beer.

"Do you want a drink?" John asked.

"No, I'm fine," Steph wondered where to start. "I'm sorry. I shouldn't have pushed you aside like that. I was so shocked to see Brett alive; for years, I thought he was dead. I thought…I don't know what I thought…I thought I still loved him. And I do, but it's in the past. It took me a little time to realise that. Brett is always a part of my life; he saved me from some of the worst times in my life. I wouldn't be here today if it weren't for Brett. But John, I love you. I want to be with you. Will you please forgive me?"

John hadn't said a word. He looked up at Steph, who was still standing.

"I told myself, I didn't own you, and I had to let you be free to make your own choices—"

Steph interrupted, "But I don't want to be free!"

"Let me finish," John said very calmly. "I knew that if you came back on your own, then that means you love me and were meant to be together." John got down on one knee, pulled out a ring box and opened it. Steph started to cry tears of happiness. "Steph, I love you. Will you put me out of my misery and marry me?"

Steph ran into his arms. "Yes, yes!" They hugged each other. Then John looked into her eyes and placed the ring on her finger and kissed her with so much love.

"It's beautiful!" Steph said, looking at the ring on her hand. "I love you so much, and I'm so sorry for what I've put you through," Steph said.

"I know you are," said John holding her close and kissing her again.

"Get ready, you're coming to my place for dinner. Adrien has been cooking all day, and I want you to get to know Brett, and I want him to get to know you. They're waiting for us."

John was a little nervous about seeing Brett again, but he knew Steph loved him and was going to marry him, and he trusted her.

By the time they got there, Adrien was ready to dish up.

"Can we please eat?" Adrien said, glad to see Steph and John finally here.

The music was blasting from the lounge room, and it was still *Queen*. Elizabeth had fallen in love with *Queen* too.

They all sat down to share a meal, the four people who Steph loved the most in the world. Her daughter, who she was so proud of; Elizabeth was so smart, much smarter than she ever was, and she was going to do great things. Brett, who was her past but without him Steph knew she would have never of survived; he saved her and Brett will always be in her heart forever. Adrien was her present; he has always been there for Steph and Elizabeth, and he was always going to be her best friend. And John, who was her future. For the first time in her life, Steph was not afraid; she could hold her head up and feel confident and sure of her life. Steph knew who she was and knew her heart and liked who she had become. Steph knew this was her family, and she loved them all.

Everyone raised their glasses as Steph toasted to her three best friends. Brett, Adrien and John.

Elizabeth had gone to bed. Brett was sleeping on the sofa for the night, so Steph threw a blanket over him. Adrien had gone to bed. Steph went in to say goodnight; he was still awake, so she lay down next to him, smiling.

"I have never seen you as happy as you are right now," Adrien said with a big smile.

"I feel like I'm there; the happiest, without a doubt. Everything is perfect. However I might need your help to figure out how to get a divorce." Adrien laughed.

"No worries, I can do that. I am a lawyer."

Steph gave Adrien a kiss goodnight and headed up the stairs with her fiancé John.

The End